KITTY QUEST

WITHDRAWN

MONSTER HUNTERS

ASK ABOUT OUR SPECIAL OFFERS

WRITTEN & ILLUSTRATED BY PHIL CORBETT

RAZORBILL

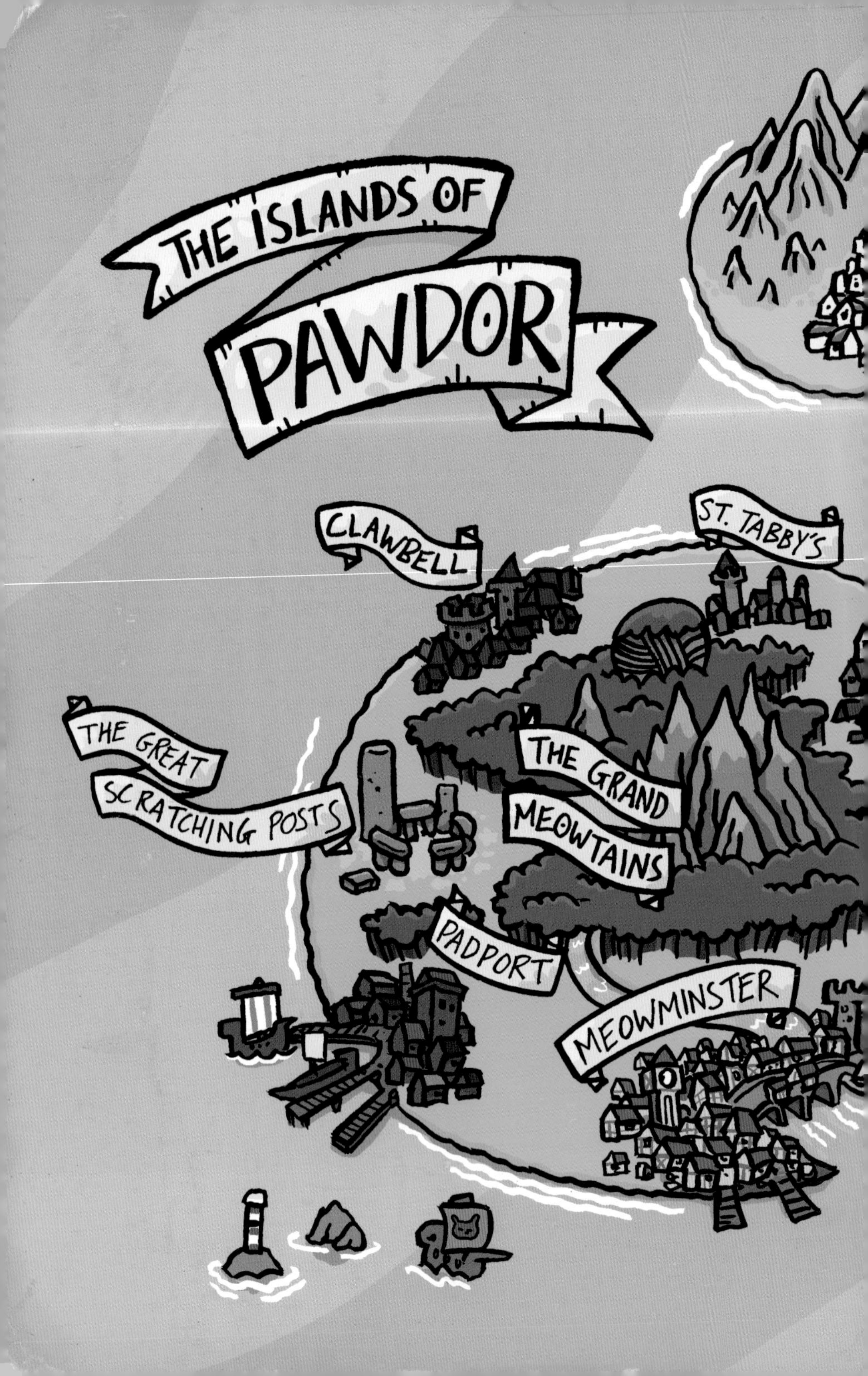
THE ISLANDS OF
PAWDOR
CLAWBELL
ST. TABBY'S
THE GREAT
SCRATCHING POSTS
THE GRAND
MEOWTAINS
PADPORT
MEOWMINSTER

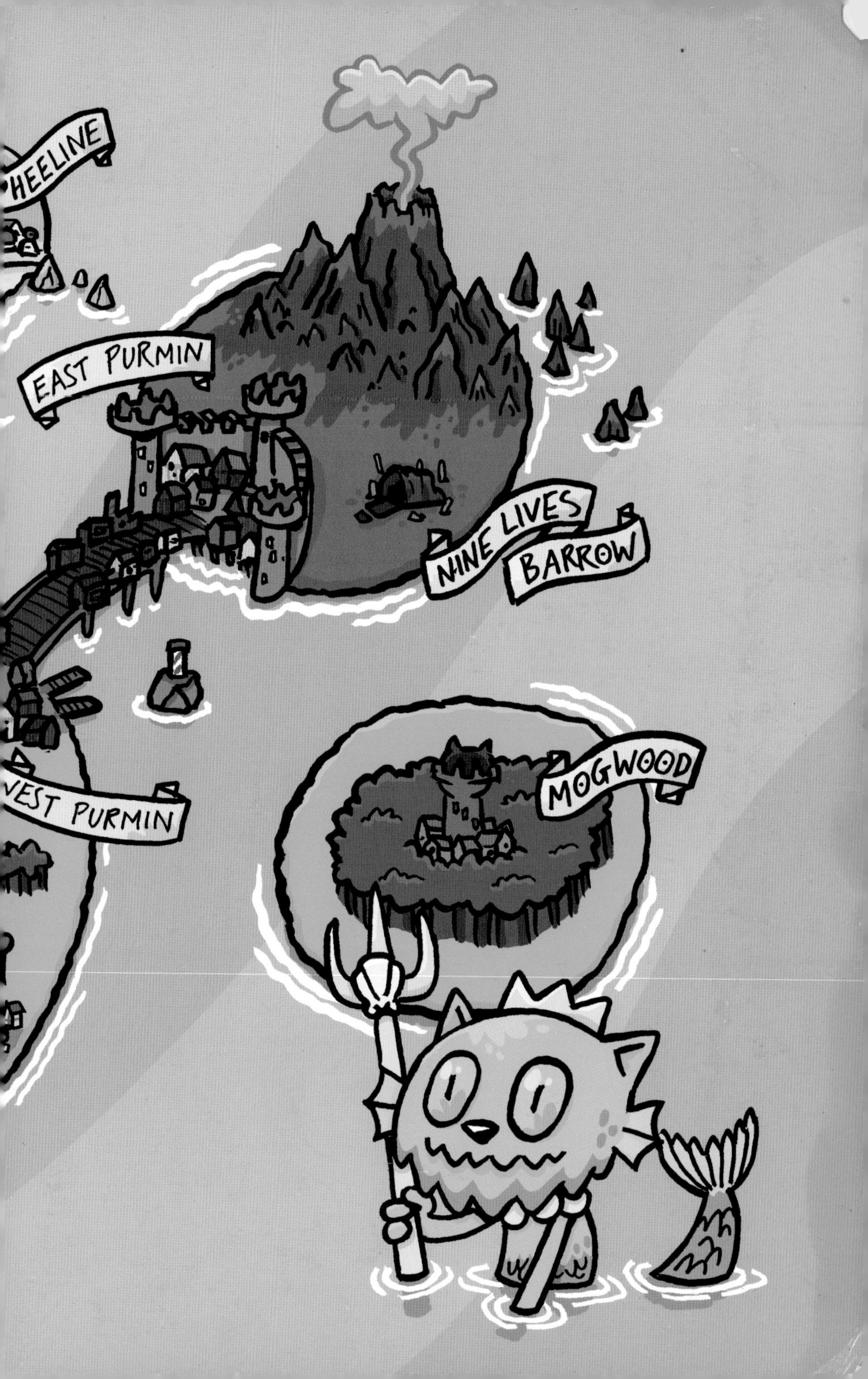

HEELINE
EAST PURMIN
NINE LIVES BARROW
MOGWOOD
VEST PURMIN

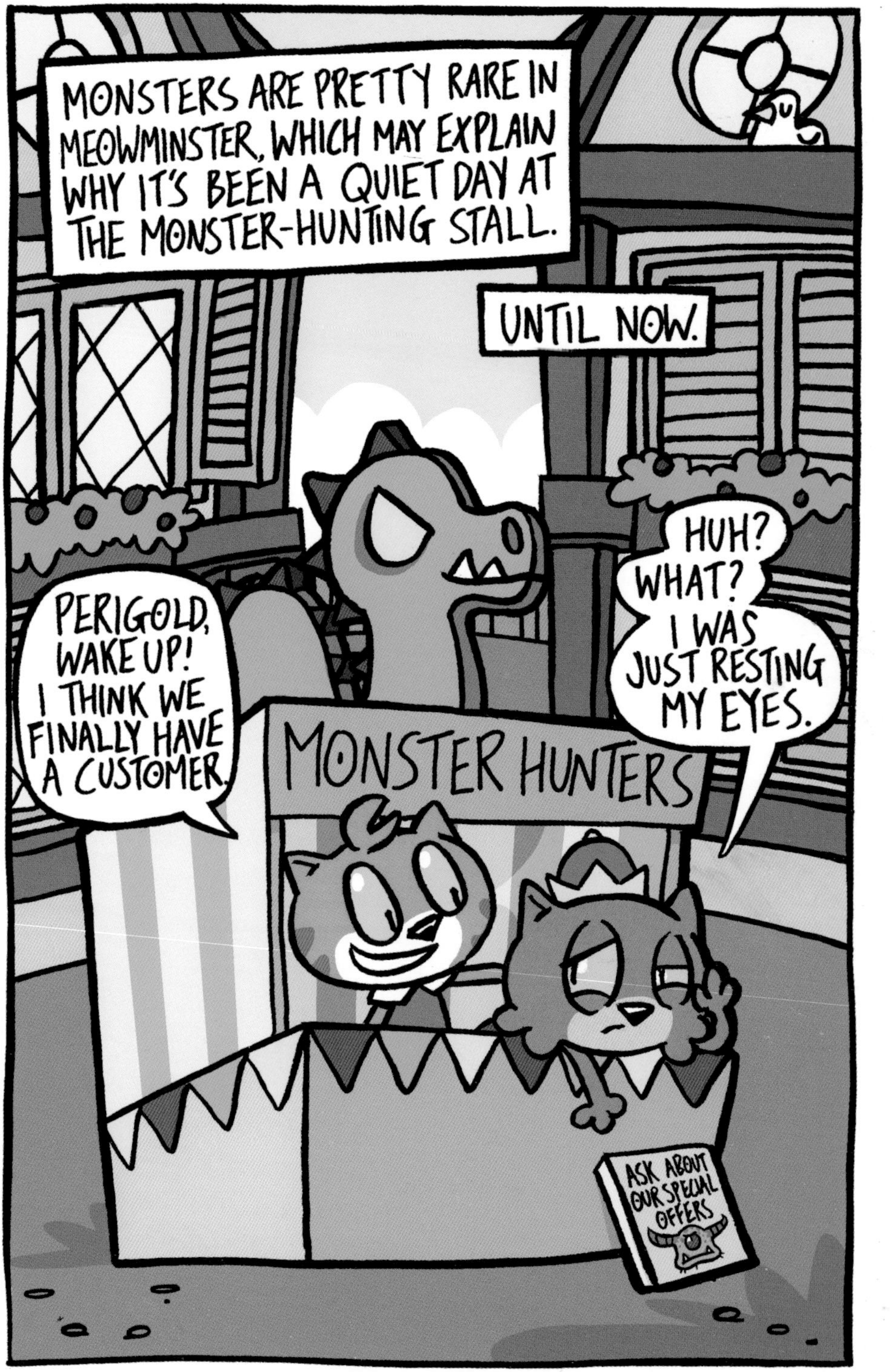
MONSTERS ARE PRETTY RARE IN MEOWMINSTER, WHICH MAY EXPLAIN WHY IT'S BEEN A QUIET DAY AT THE MONSTER-HUNTING STALL.
UNTIL NOW.
PERIGOLD, WAKE UP! I THINK WE FINALLY HAVE A CUSTOMER.
HUH? WHAT? I WAS JUST RESTING MY EYES.
MONSTER HUNTERS
ASK ABOUT OUR SPECIAL OFFERS

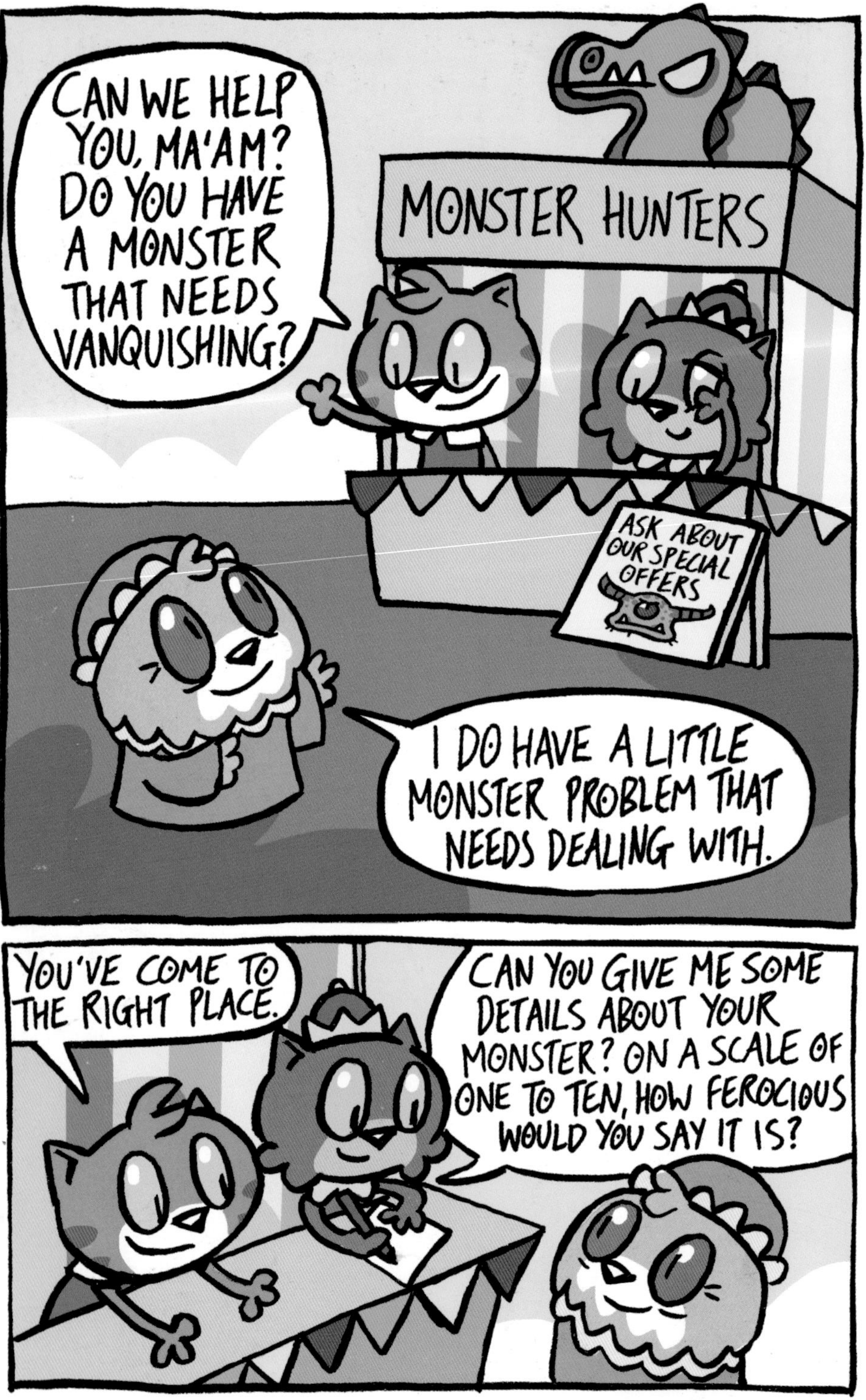
CAN WE HELP YOU, MA'AM? DO YOU HAVE A MONSTER THAT NEEDS VANQUISHING?
MONSTER HUNTERS
ASK ABOUT OUR SPECIAL OFFERS
I DO HAVE A LITTLE MONSTER PROBLEM THAT NEEDS DEALING WITH.
YOU'VE COME TO THE RIGHT PLACE.
CAN YOU GIVE ME SOME DETAILS ABOUT YOUR MONSTER? ON A SCALE OF ONE TO TEN, HOW FEROCIOUS WOULD YOU SAY IT IS?

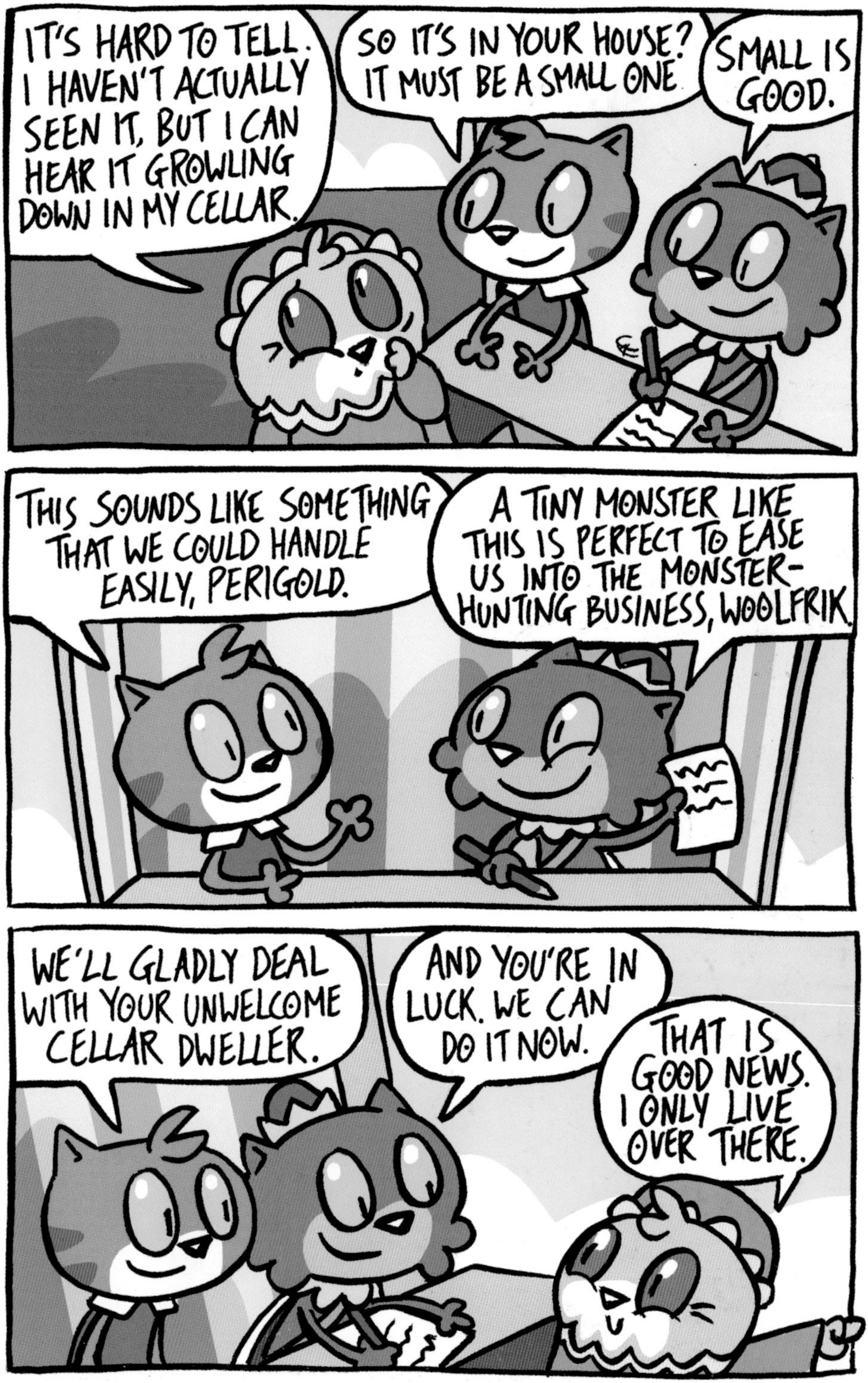

IT'S HARD TO TELL. I HAVEN'T ACTUALLY SEEN IT, BUT I CAN HEAR IT GROWLING DOWN IN MY CELLAR.
SO IT'S IN YOUR HOUSE? IT MUST BE A SMALL ONE.
SMALL IS GOOD.
THIS SOUNDS LIKE SOMETHING THAT WE COULD HANDLE EASILY, PERIGOLD.
A TINY MONSTER LIKE THIS IS PERFECT TO EASE US INTO THE MONSTER-HUNTING BUSINESS, WOOLFRIK.
WE'LL GLADLY DEAL WITH YOUR UNWELCOME CELLAR DWELLER.
AND YOU'RE IN LUCK. WE CAN DO IT NOW.
THAT IS GOOD NEWS. I ONLY LIVE OVER THERE.

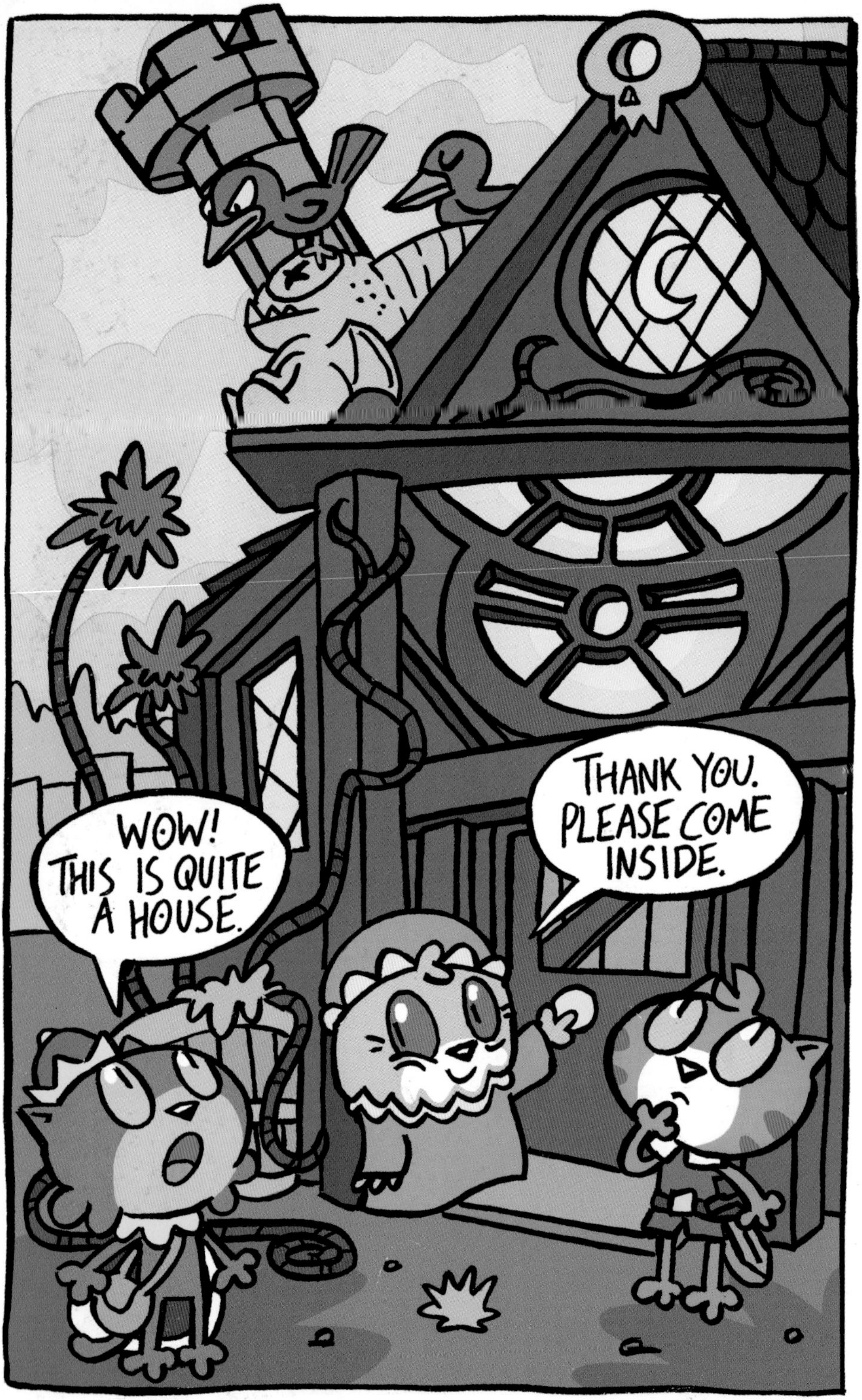
WOW! THIS IS QUITE A HOUSE.
THANK YOU. PLEASE COME INSIDE.

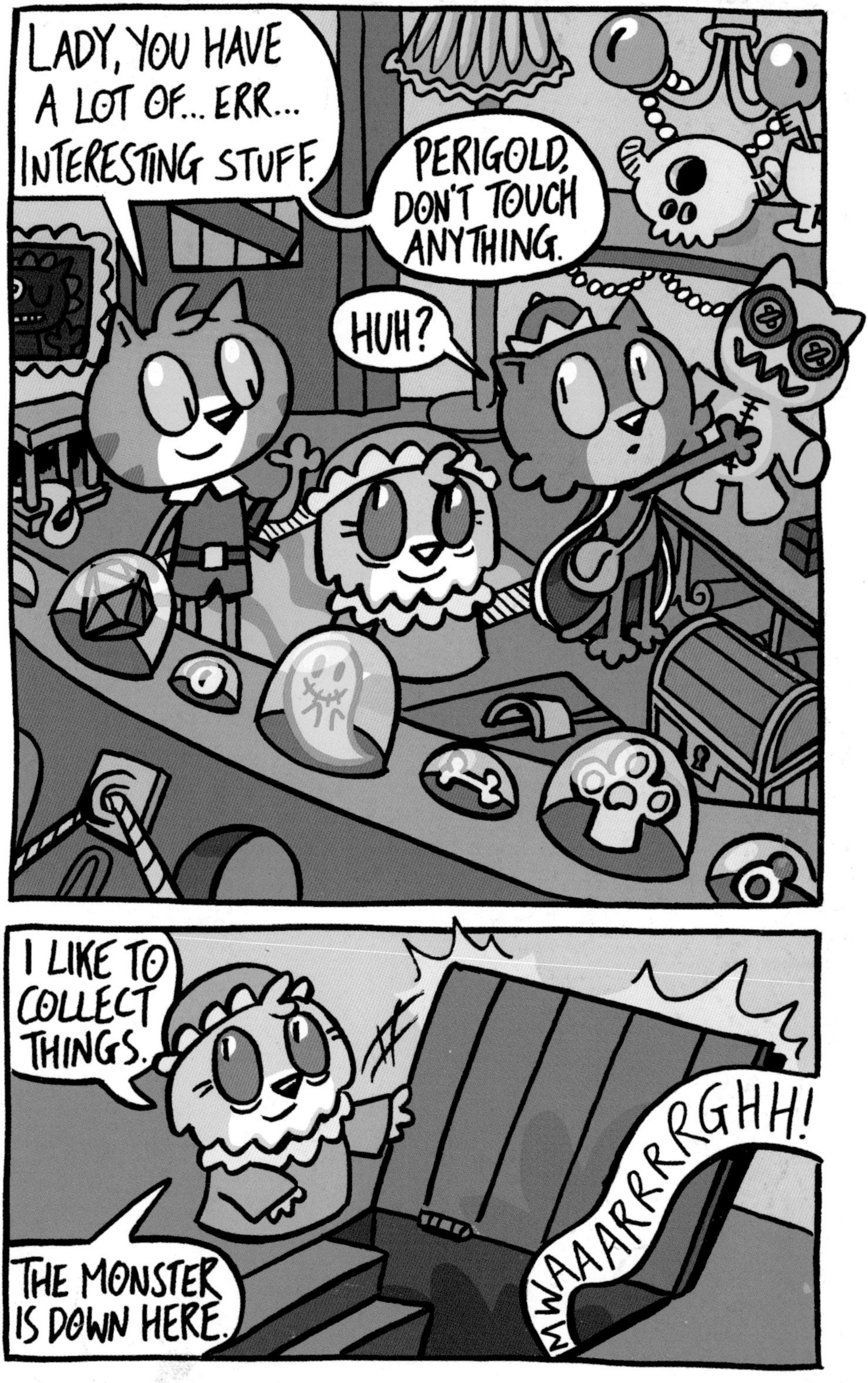
LADY, YOU HAVE A LOT OF... ERR... INTERESTING STUFF.
PERIGOLD, DON'T TOUCH ANYTHING.
HUH?
I LIKE TO COLLECT THINGS.
THE MONSTER IS DOWN HERE.
MWAAARRRRGHH!

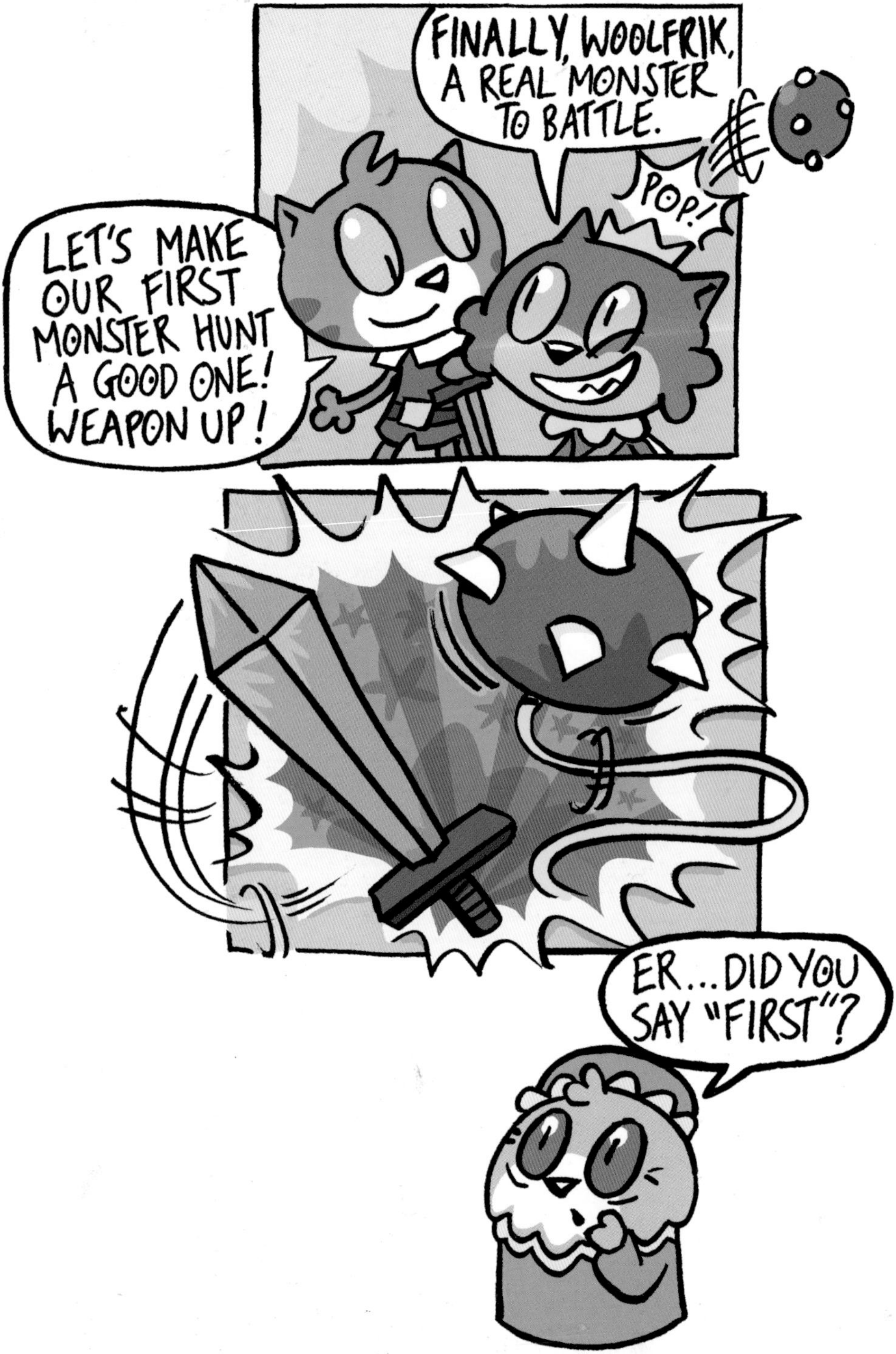
FINALLY, WOOLFRIK, A REAL MONSTER TO BATTLE.
POP!
LET'S MAKE OUR FIRST MONSTER HUNT A GOOD ONE! WEAPON UP!
ER...DID YOU SAY "FIRST"?

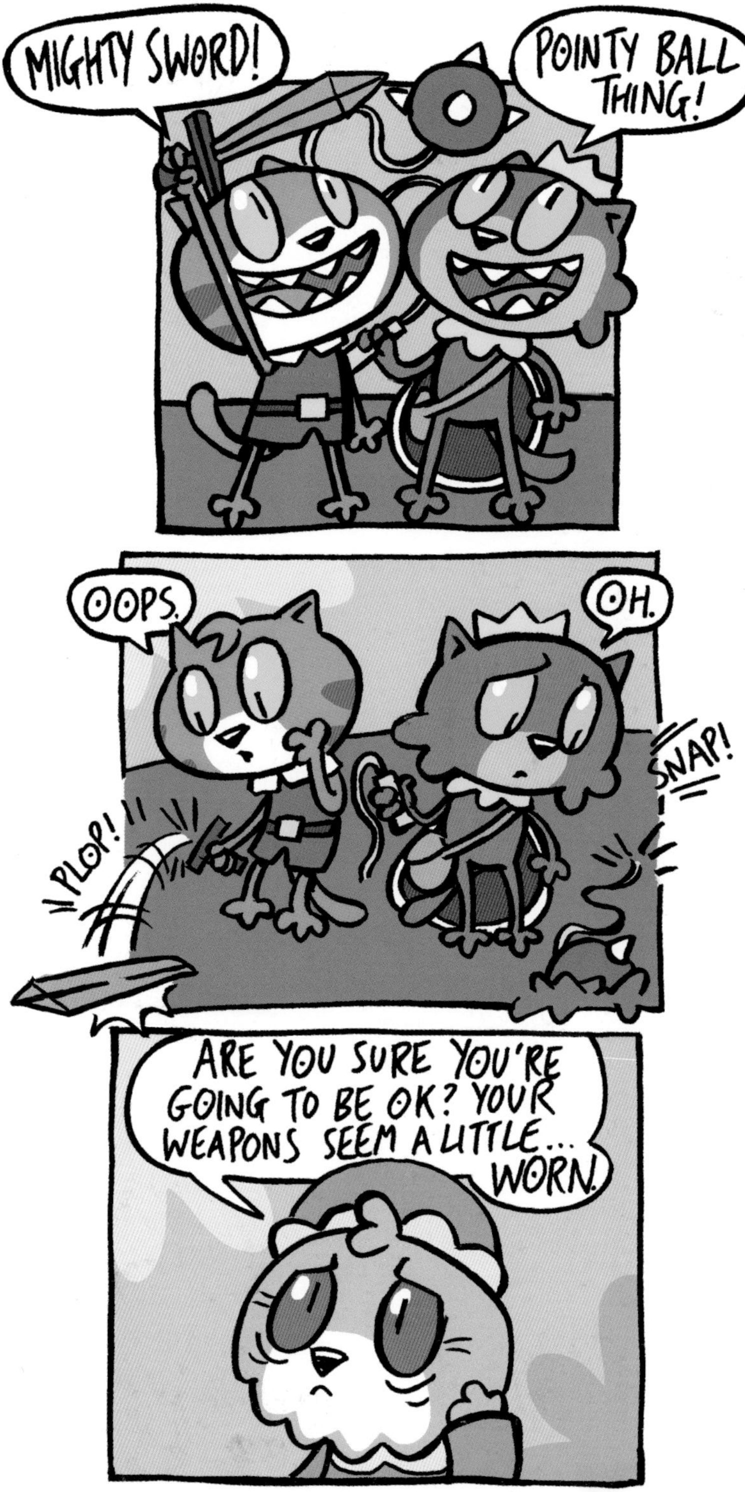
MIGHTY SWORD!
POINTY BALL THING!
OOPS.
OH.
PLOP!
SNAP!
ARE YOU SURE YOU'RE GOING TO BE OK? YOUR WEAPONS SEEM A LITTLE... WORN.

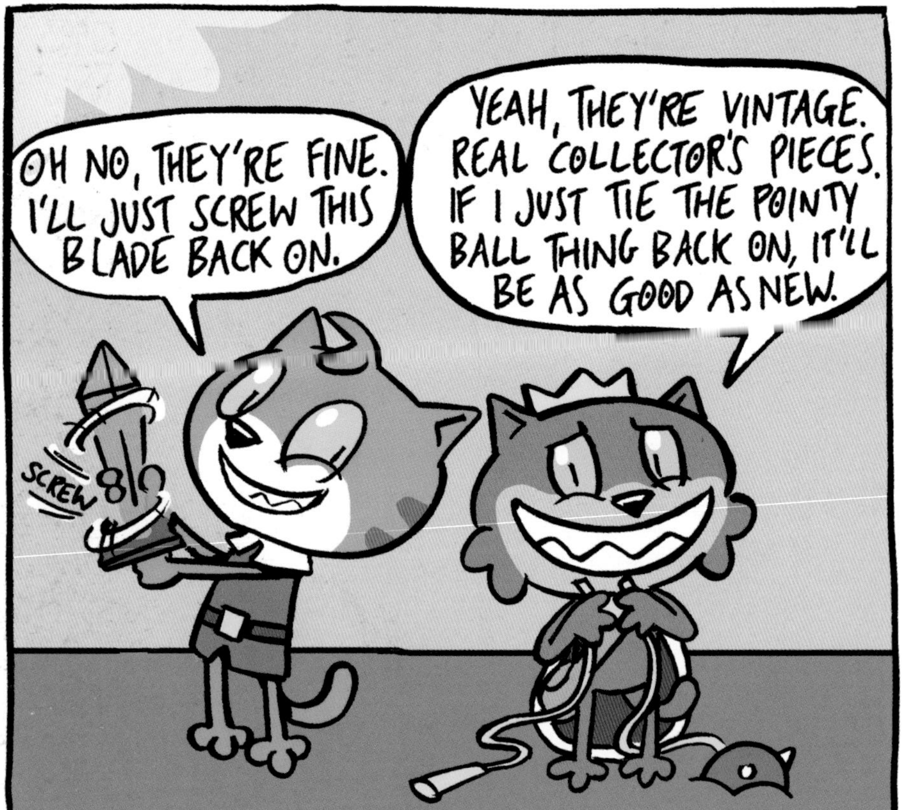
OH NO, THEY'RE FINE. I'LL JUST SCREW THIS BLADE BACK ON.
SCREW
YEAH, THEY'RE VINTAGE. REAL COLLECTOR'S PIECES. IF I JUST TIE THE POINTY BALL THING BACK ON, IT'LL BE AS GOOD AS NEW.

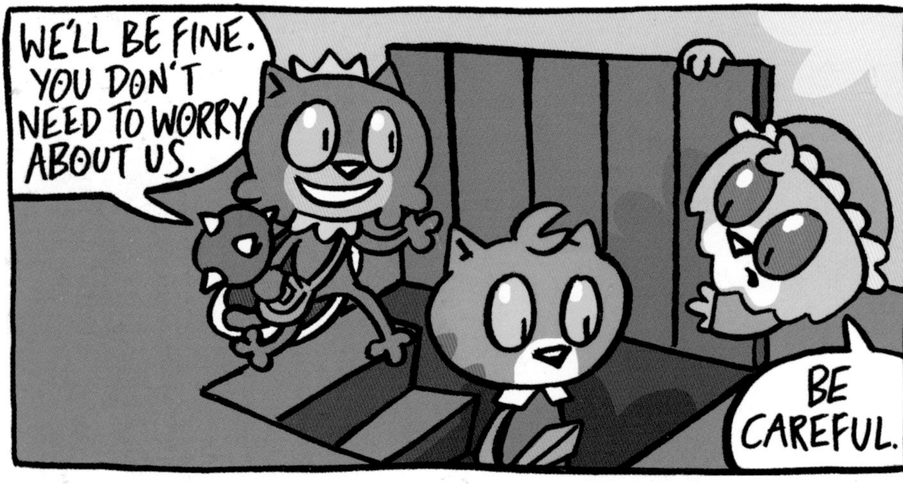
WE'LL BE FINE. YOU DON'T NEED TO WORRY ABOUT US.
BE CAREFUL.

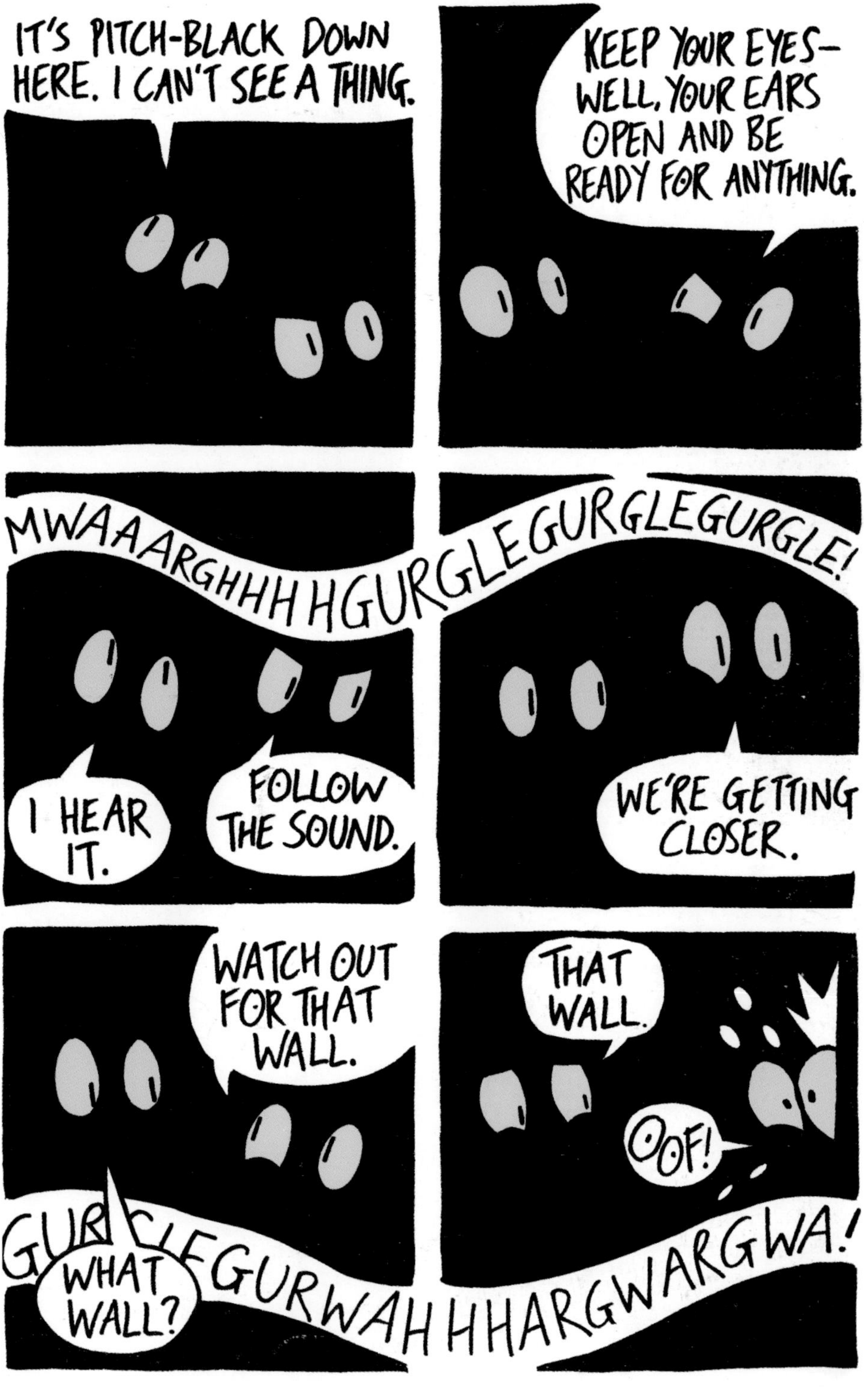
IT'S PITCH-BLACK DOWN HERE. I CAN'T SEE A THING.
KEEP YOUR EYES— WELL, YOUR EARS OPEN AND BE READY FOR ANYTHING.
MWAAAARGHHHHGURGLEGURGLEGURGLE!
I HEAR IT.
FOLLOW THE SOUND.
WE'RE GETTING CLOSER.
WATCH OUT FOR THAT WALL.
WHAT WALL?
THAT WALL.
OOF!
GURGLEGURWAHHHARGWARGWA!

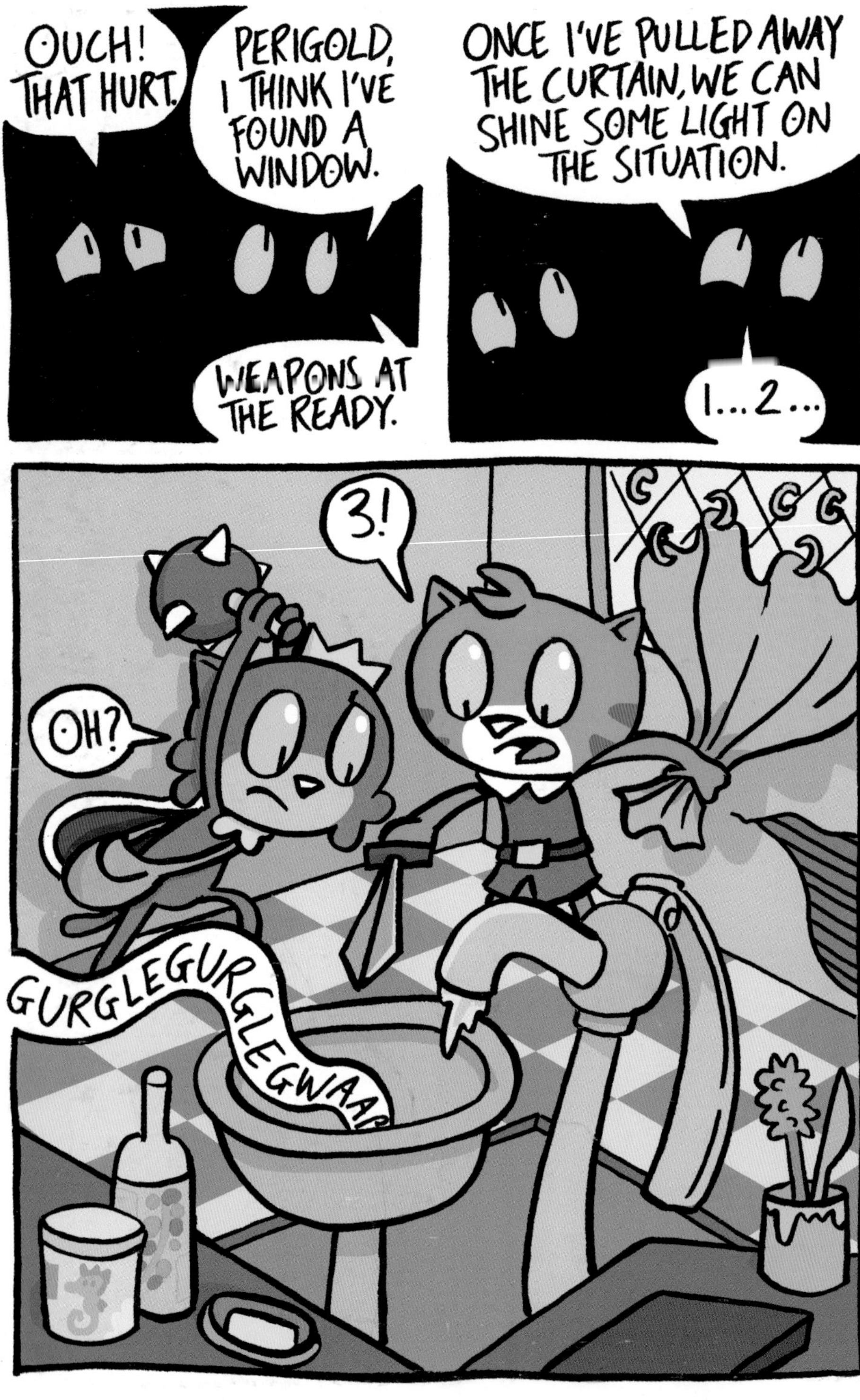
OUCH! THAT HURT.
PERIGOLD, I THINK I'VE FOUND A WINDOW.
WEAPONS AT THE READY.
ONCE I'VE PULLED AWAY THE CURTAIN, WE CAN SHINE SOME LIGHT ON THE SITUATION.
1... 2...
3!
OH?
GURGLEGURGLEGWAA

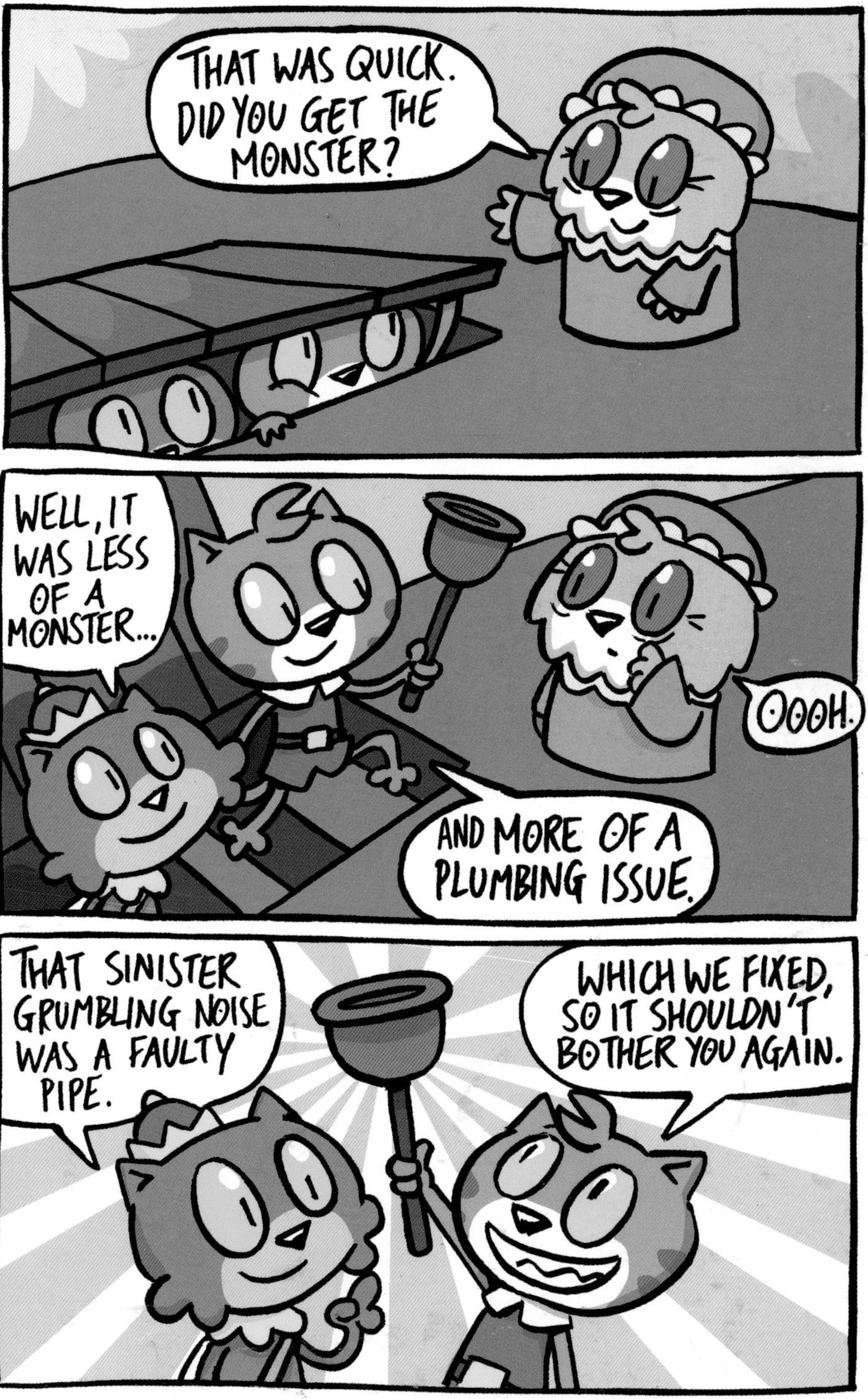
THAT WAS QUICK. DID YOU GET THE MONSTER?
WELL, IT WAS LESS OF A MONSTER...
OOOH.
AND MORE OF A PLUMBING ISSUE.
THAT SINISTER GRUMBLING NOISE WAS A FAULTY PIPE.
WHICH WE FIXED, SO IT SHOULDN'T BOTHER YOU AGAIN.

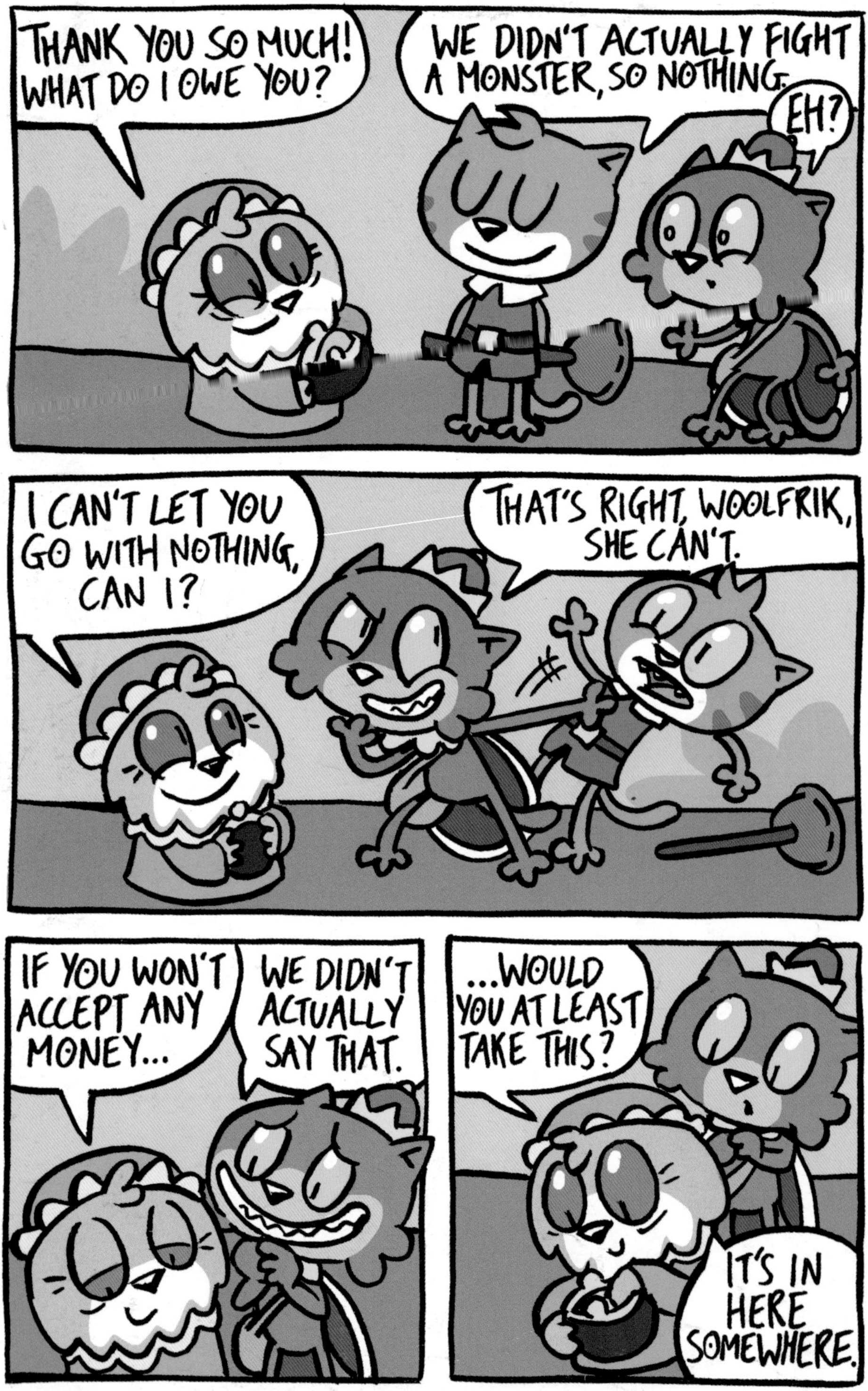
THANK YOU SO MUCH! WHAT DO I OWE YOU?
WE DIDN'T ACTUALLY FIGHT A MONSTER, SO NOTHING.
EH?
I CAN'T LET YOU GO WITH NOTHING, CAN I?
THAT'S RIGHT, WOOLFRIK, SHE CAN'T.
IF YOU WON'T ACCEPT ANY MONEY...
WE DIDN'T ACTUALLY SAY THAT.
...WOULD YOU AT LEAST TAKE THIS?
IT'S IN HERE SOMEWHERE.

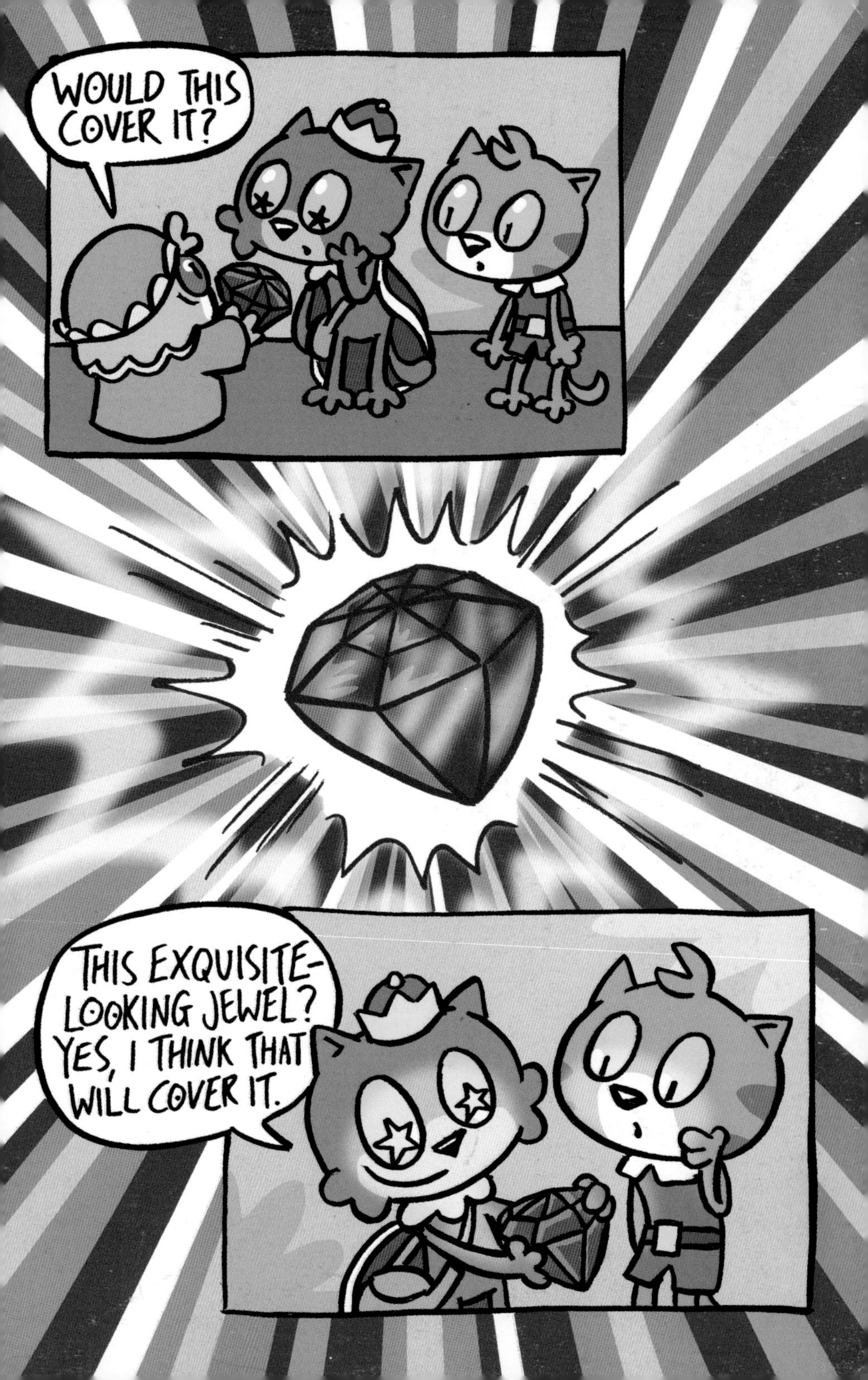
WOULD THIS COVER IT?
THIS EXQUISITE-LOOKING JEWEL? YES, I THINK THAT WILL COVER IT.

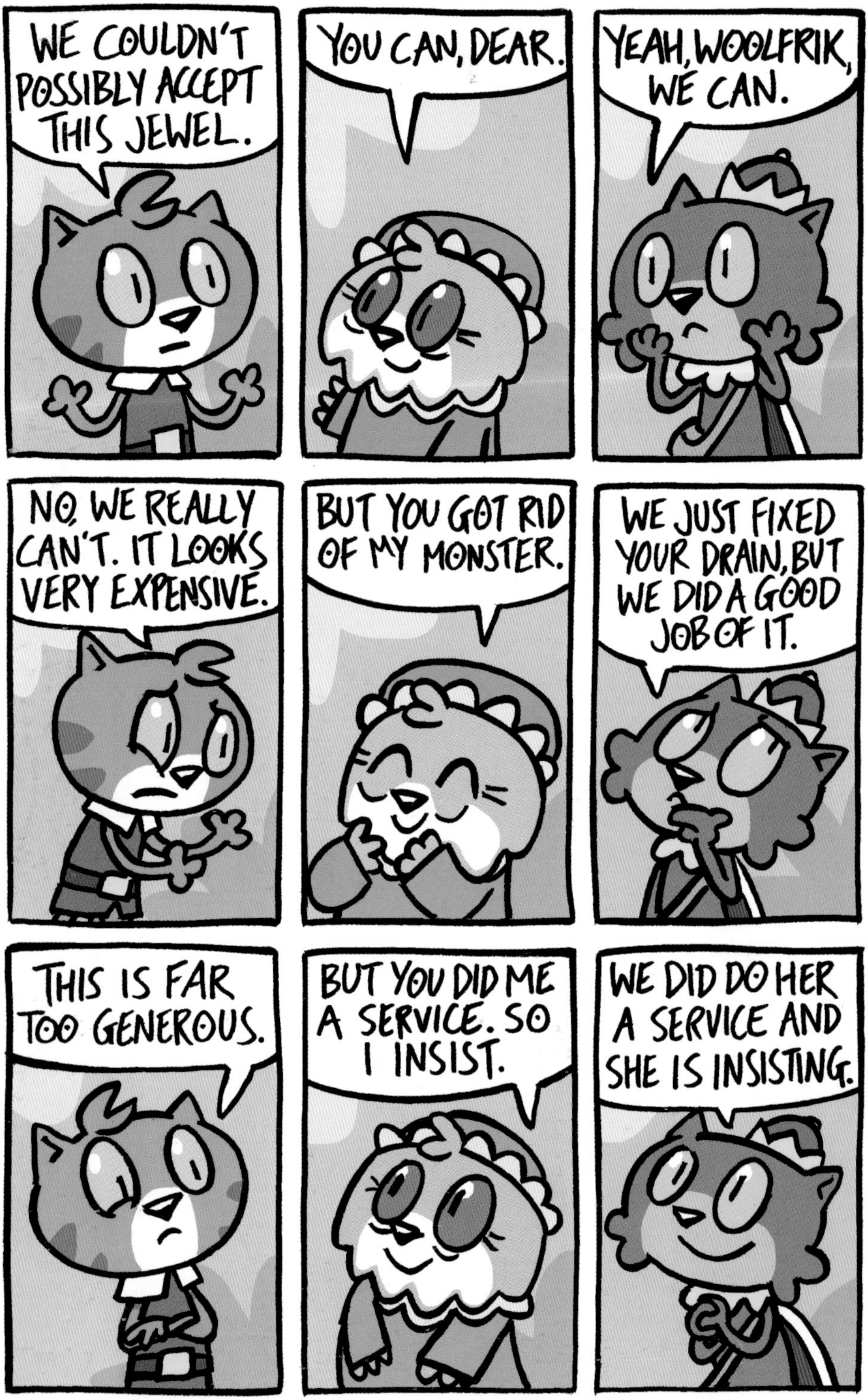
WE COULDN'T POSSIBLY ACCEPT THIS JEWEL.
YOU CAN, DEAR.
YEAH, WOOLFRIK, WE CAN.
NO, WE REALLY CAN'T. IT LOOKS VERY EXPENSIVE.
BUT YOU GOT RID OF MY MONSTER.
WE JUST FIXED YOUR DRAIN, BUT WE DID A GOOD JOB OF IT.
THIS IS FAR TOO GENEROUS.
BUT YOU DID ME A SERVICE. SO I INSIST.
WE DID DO HER A SERVICE AND SHE IS INSISTING.

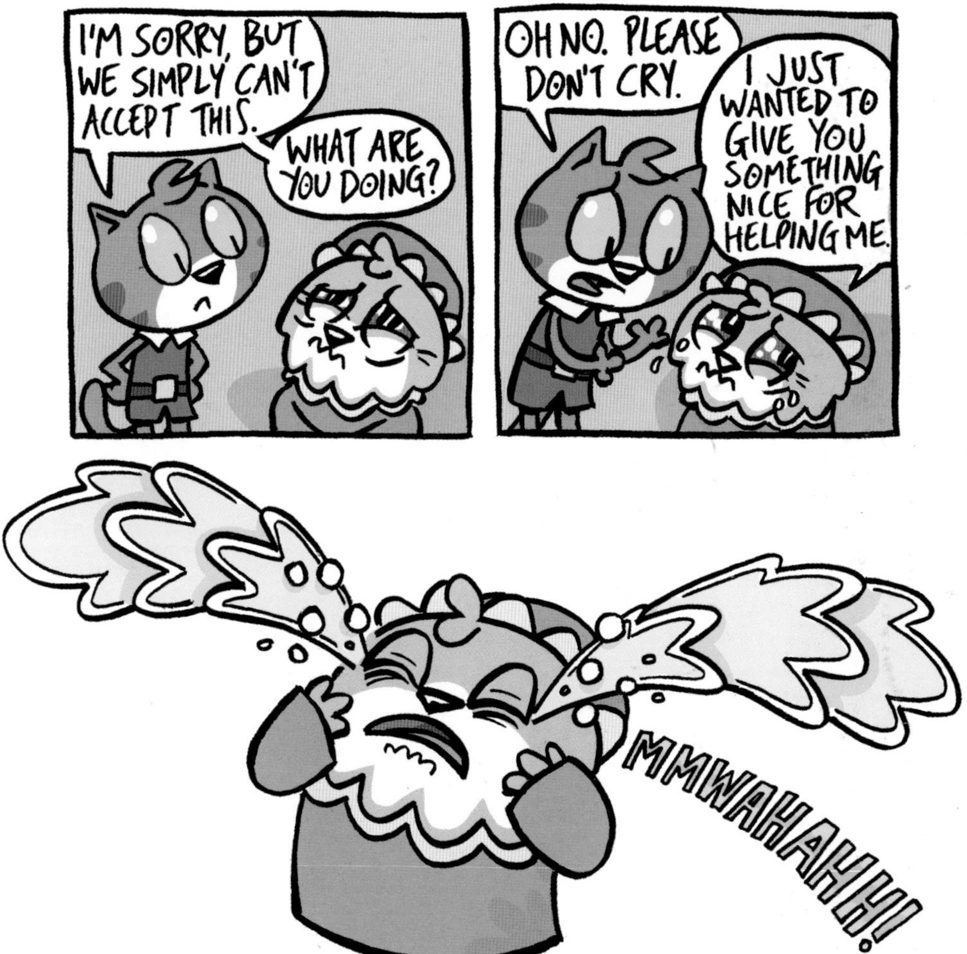

I'M SORRY, BUT WE SIMPLY CAN'T ACCEPT THIS.
WHAT ARE YOU DOING?
OH NO. PLEASE DON'T CRY.
I JUST WANTED TO GIVE YOU SOMETHING NICE FOR HELPING ME.
MMWAHAHAHH!

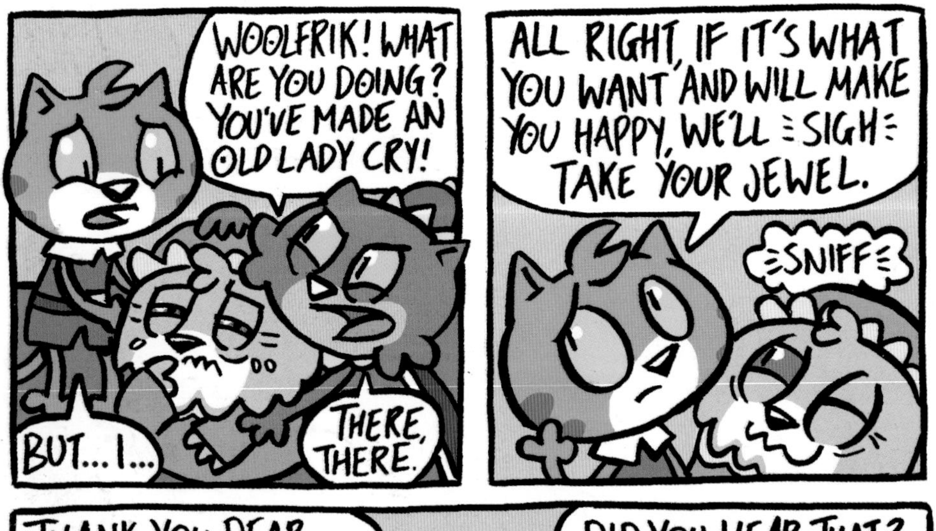
WOOLFRIK! WHAT ARE YOU DOING? YOU'VE MADE AN OLD LADY CRY!
BUT... I...
THERE, THERE.
ALL RIGHT, IF IT'S WHAT YOU WANT AND WILL MAKE YOU HAPPY, WE'LL SIGH TAKE YOUR JEWEL.
SNIFF
THANK YOU, DEAR. YOU'VE MADE AN OLD LADY VERY HAPPY.
DID YOU HEAR THAT? AND ALL IT TOOK WAS ACCEPTING THIS INCREDIBLY EXPENSIVE-LOOKING JEWEL.

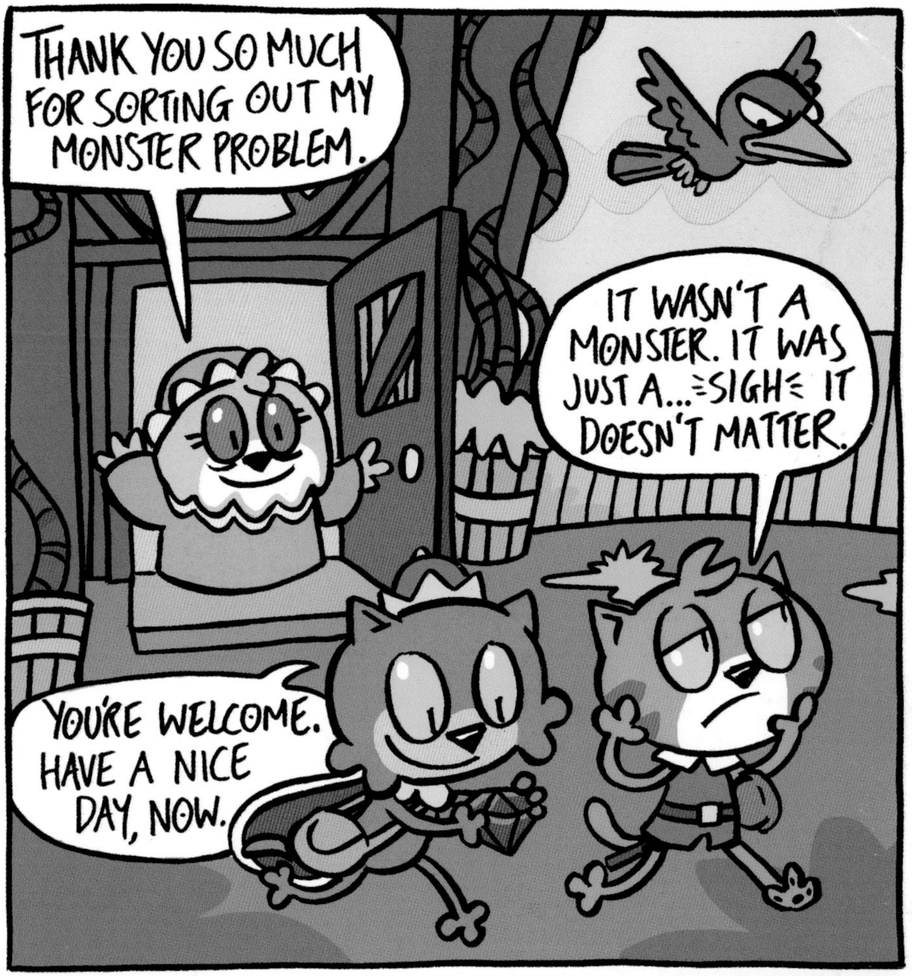
THANK YOU SO MUCH FOR SORTING OUT MY MONSTER PROBLEM.
IT WASN'T A MONSTER. IT WAS JUST A... SIGH IT DOESN'T MATTER.
YOU'RE WELCOME. HAVE A NICE DAY, NOW.

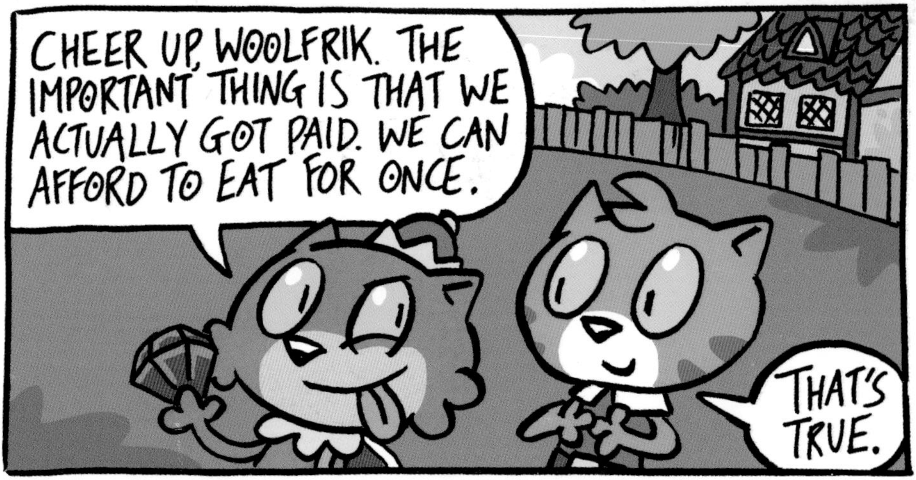
CHEER UP, WOOLFRIK. THE IMPORTANT THING IS THAT WE ACTUALLY GOT PAID. WE CAN AFFORD TO EAT FOR ONCE.
THAT'S TRUE.

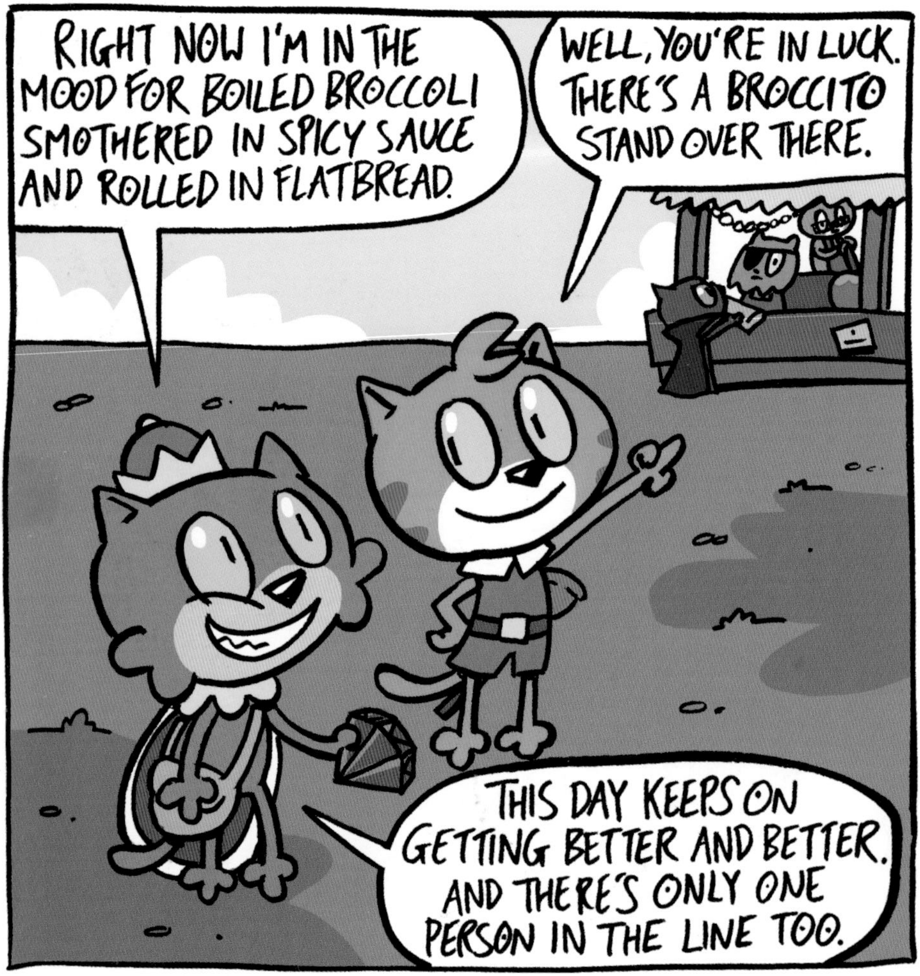
RIGHT NOW I'M IN THE MOOD FOR BOILED BROCCOLI SMOTHERED IN SPICY SAUCE AND ROLLED IN FLATBREAD.
WELL, YOU'RE IN LUCK. THERE'S A BROCCITO STAND OVER THERE.
THIS DAY KEEPS ON GETTING BETTER AND BETTER. AND THERE'S ONLY ONE PERSON IN THE LINE TOO.

HOT BROCCITOS
YOU CALL THIS SPICY? I'VE HAD HOTTER ICE CREAM SUNDAES.
ASK ABOUT OUR SPECIALS

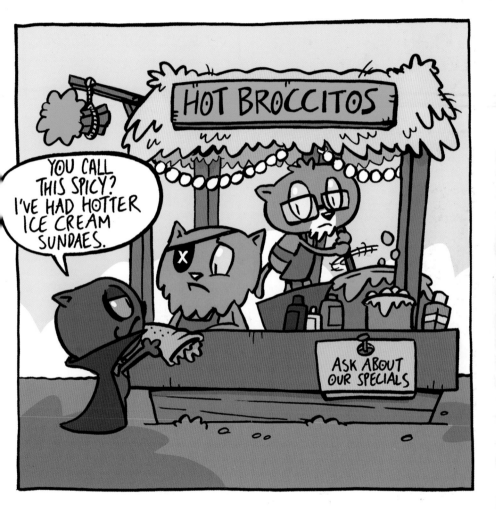

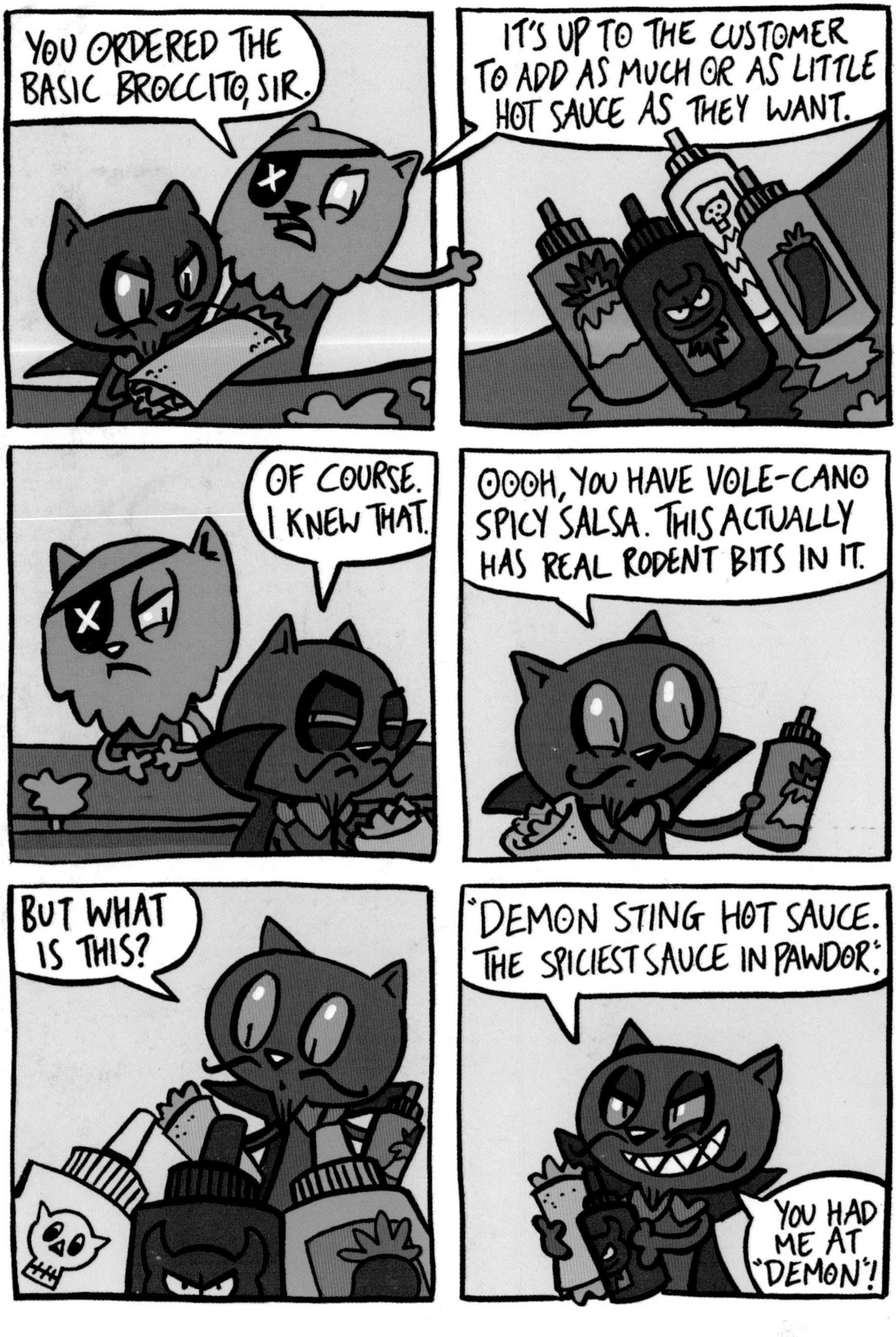
YOU ORDERED THE BASIC BROCCITO, SIR.
IT'S UP TO THE CUSTOMER TO ADD AS MUCH OR AS LITTLE HOT SAUCE AS THEY WANT.
OF COURSE. I KNEW THAT.
OOOH, YOU HAVE VOLE-CANO SPICY SALSA. THIS ACTUALLY HAS REAL RODENT BITS IN IT.
BUT WHAT IS THIS?
"DEMON STING HOT SAUCE. THE SPICIEST SAUCE IN PAWDOR."
YOU HAD ME AT "DEMON"!

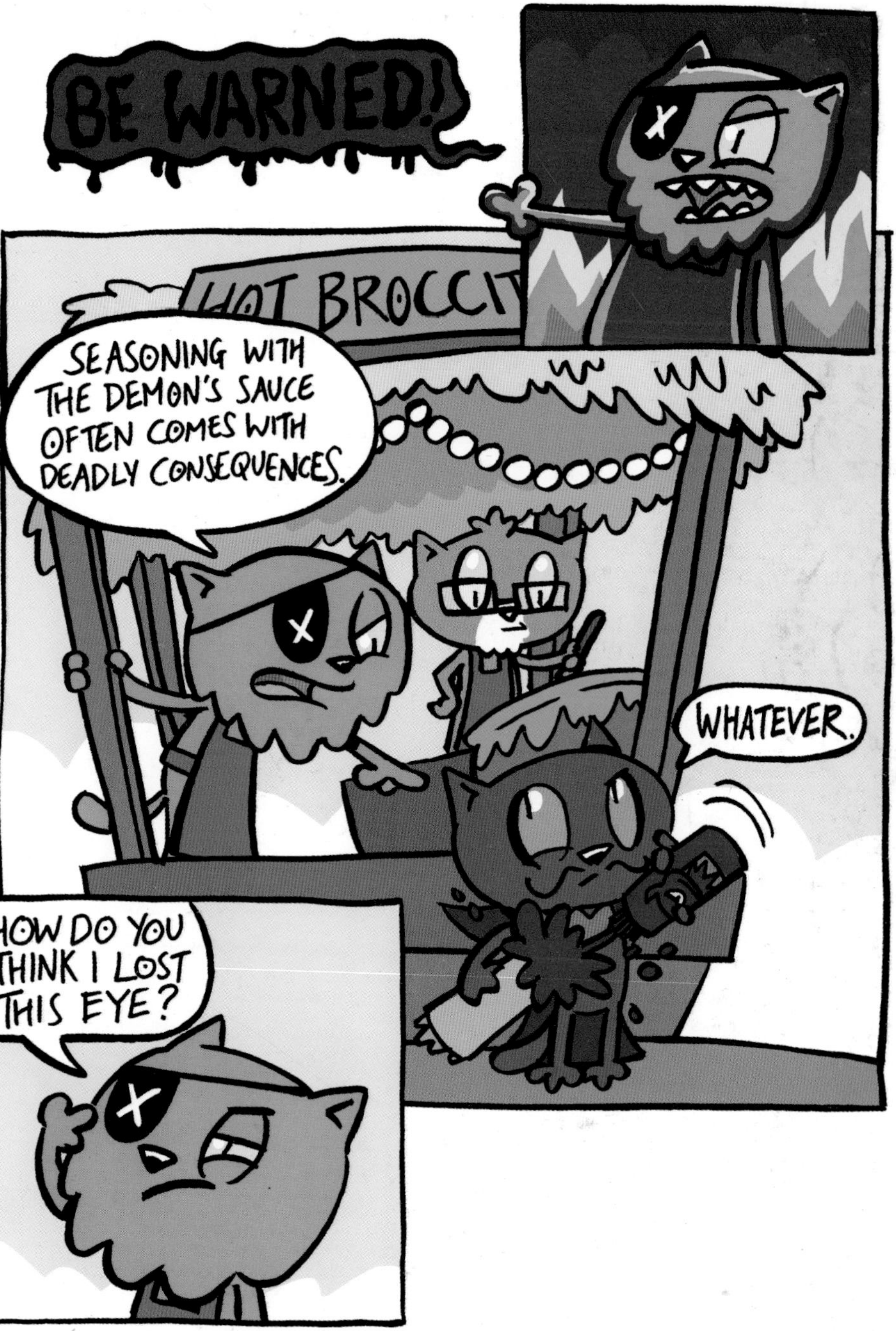
BE WARNED!
HOT BROCCLI
SEASONING WITH THE DEMON'S SAUCE OFTEN COMES WITH DEADLY CONSEQUENCES.
WHATEVER.
HOW DO YOU THINK I LOST THIS EYE?

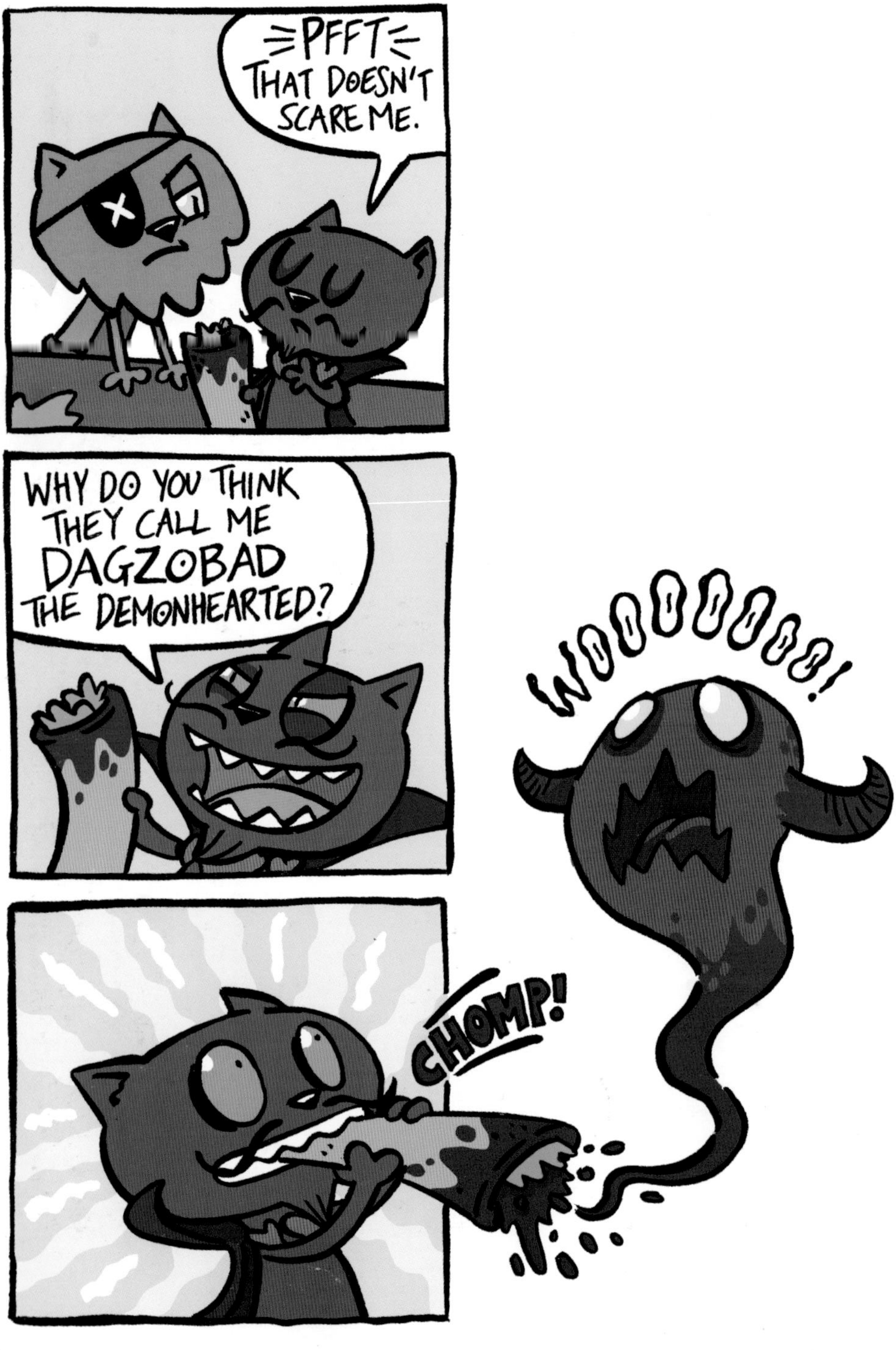
PFFT
THAT DOESN'T SCARE ME.
WHY DO YOU THINK THEY CALL ME DAGZOBAD THE DEMONHEARTED?
WOOOOOOOO!
CHOMP!

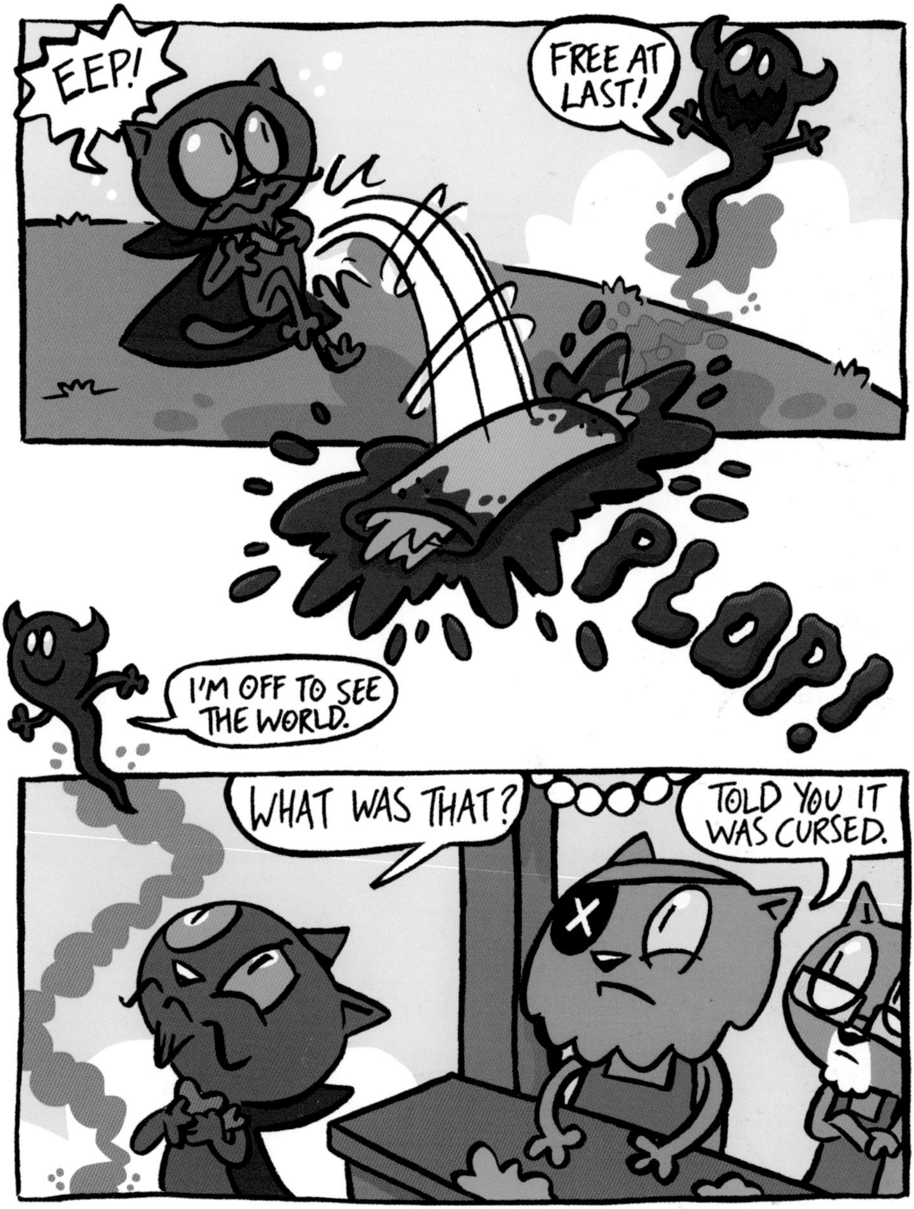
EEP!
FREE AT LAST!
PLOP!
I'M OFF TO SEE THE WORLD.
WHAT WAS THAT?
TOLD YOU IT WAS CURSED.

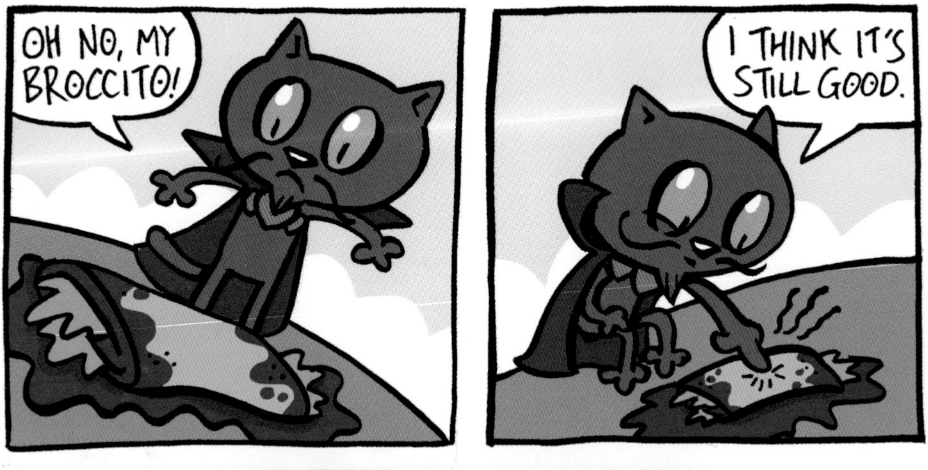
OH NO, MY BROCCITO!
I THINK IT'S STILL GOOD.
SPLAT!

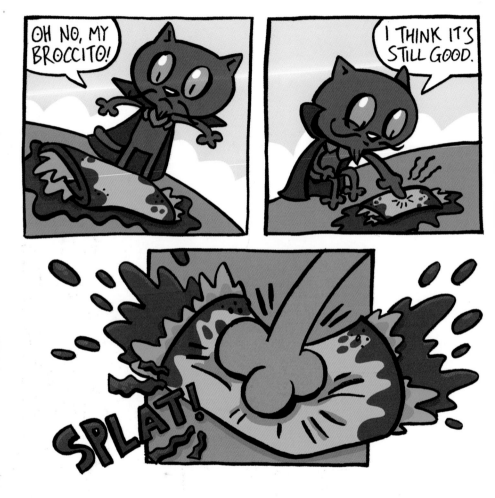

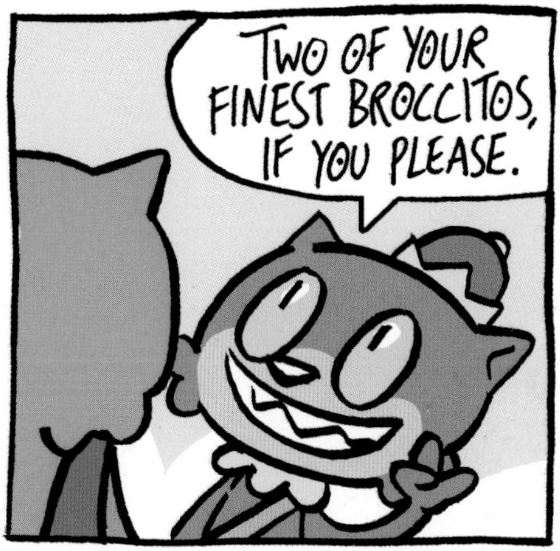
TWO OF YOUR FINEST BROCCITOS, IF YOU PLEASE.

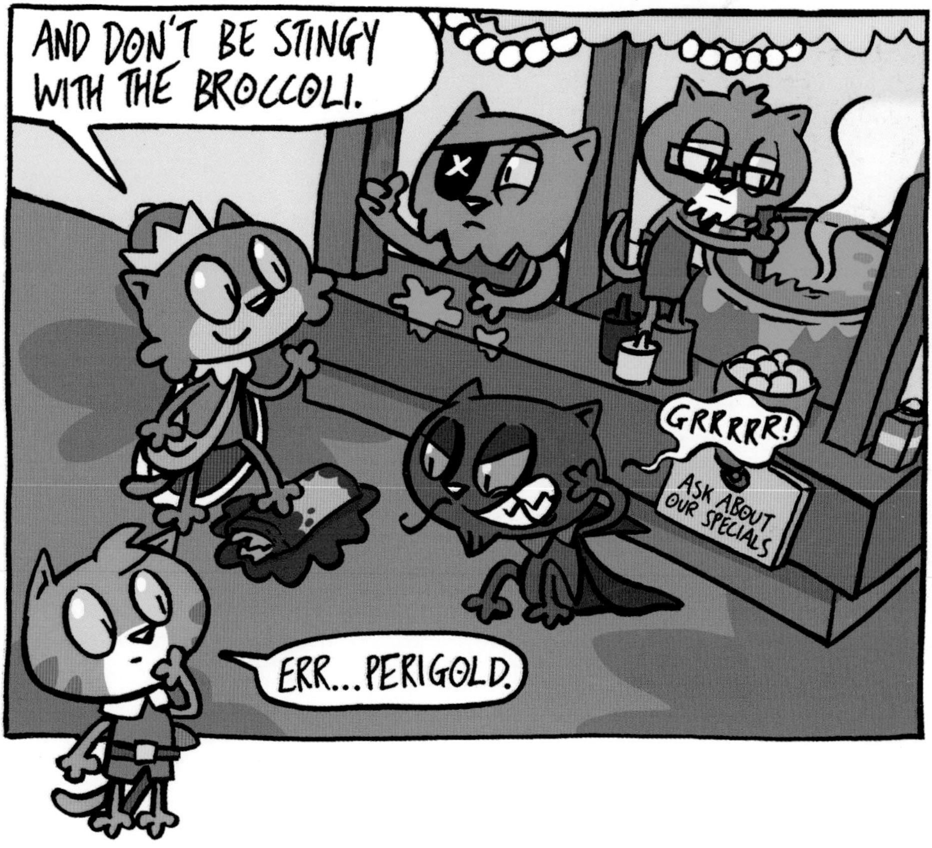
AND DON'T BE STINGY WITH THE BROCCOLI.
GRRRRR!
ASK ABOUT OUR SPECIALS
ERR...PERIGOLD.

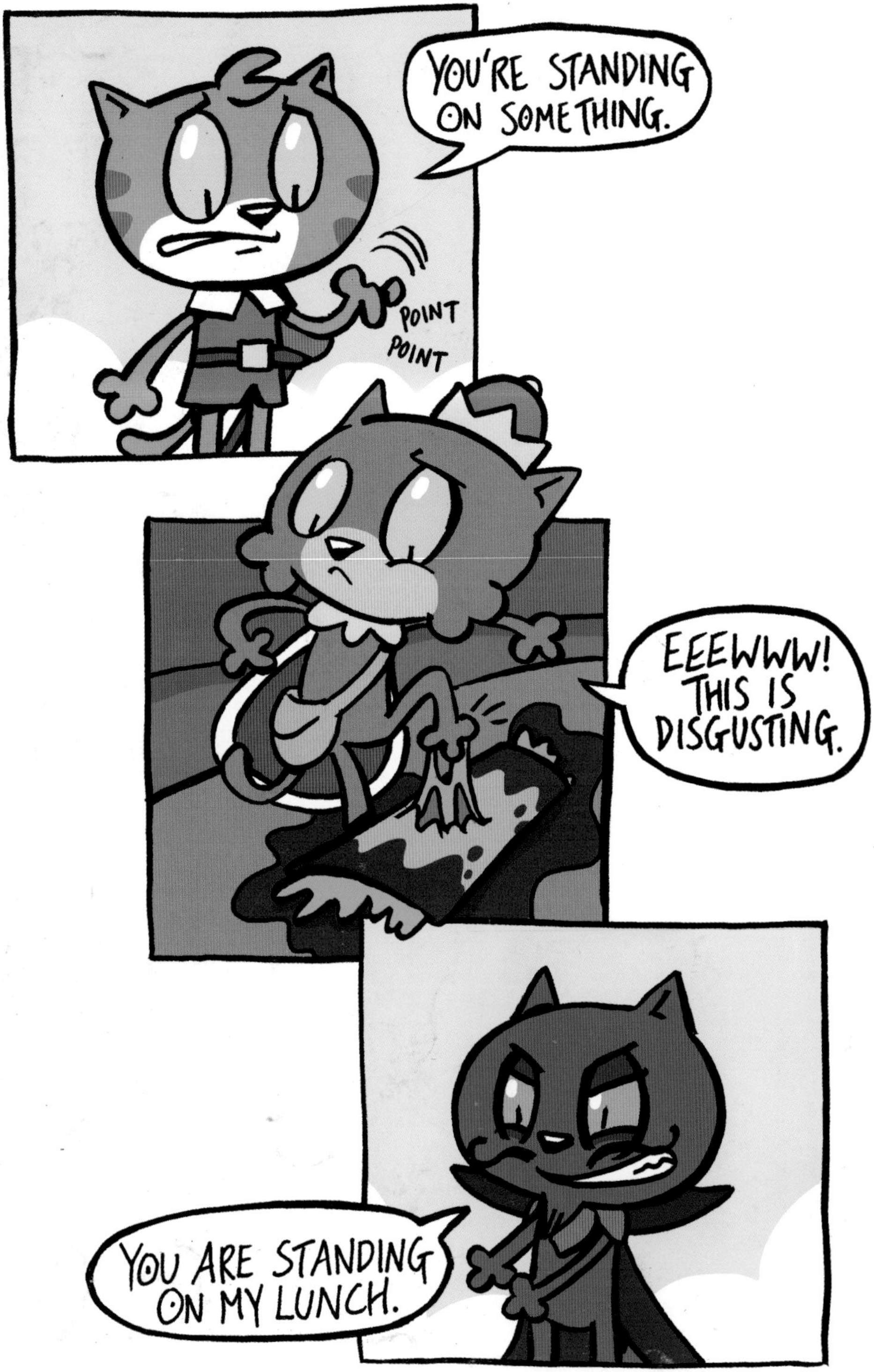

YOU'RE STANDING ON SOMETHING.
POINT POINT
EEEWWW! THIS IS DISGUSTING.
YOU ARE STANDING ON MY LUNCH.

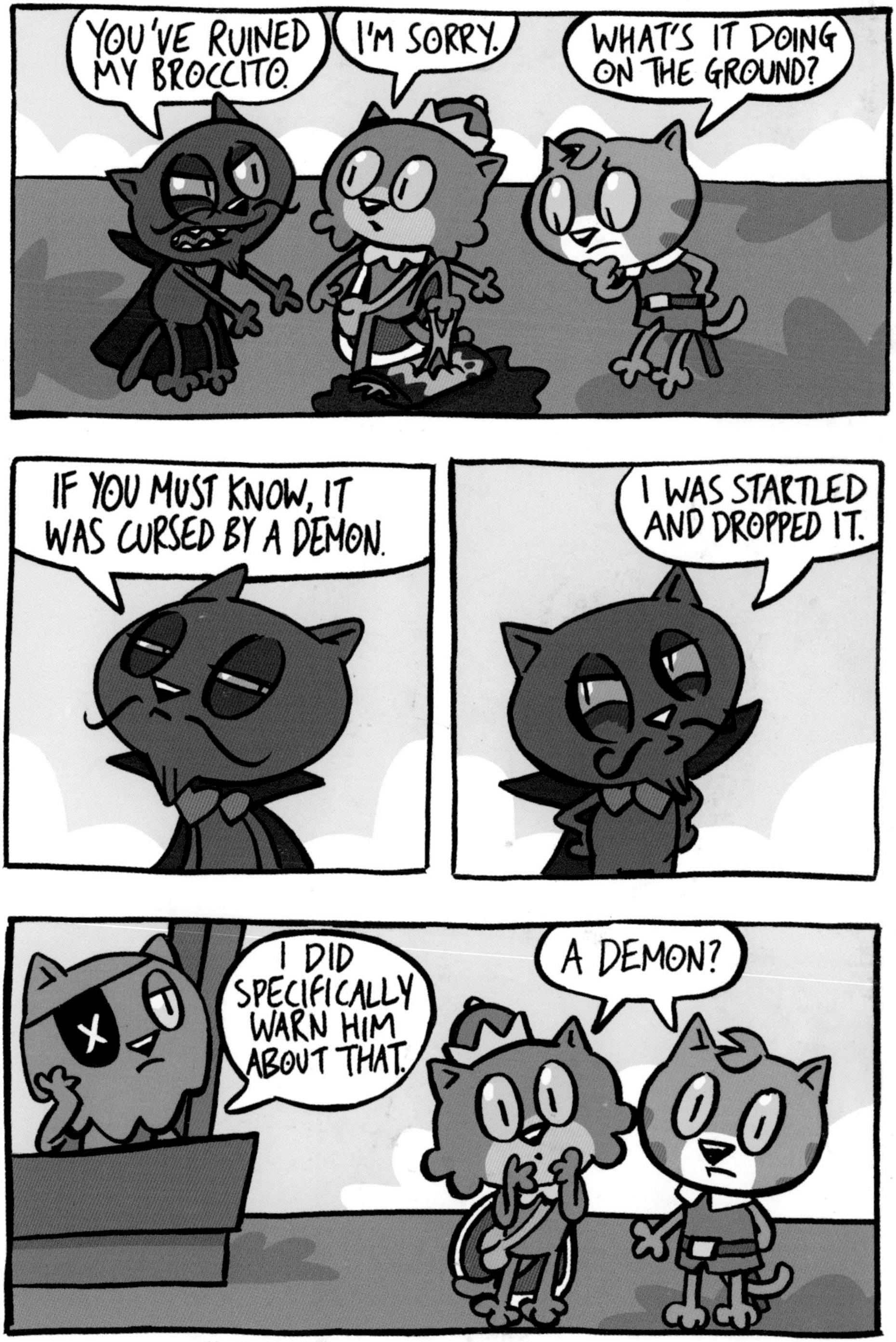
YOU'VE RUINED MY BROCCITO.
I'M SORRY.
WHAT'S IT DOING ON THE GROUND?
IF YOU MUST KNOW, IT WAS CURSED BY A DEMON.
I WAS STARTLED AND DROPPED IT.
I DID SPECIFICALLY WARN HIM ABOUT THAT.
A DEMON?

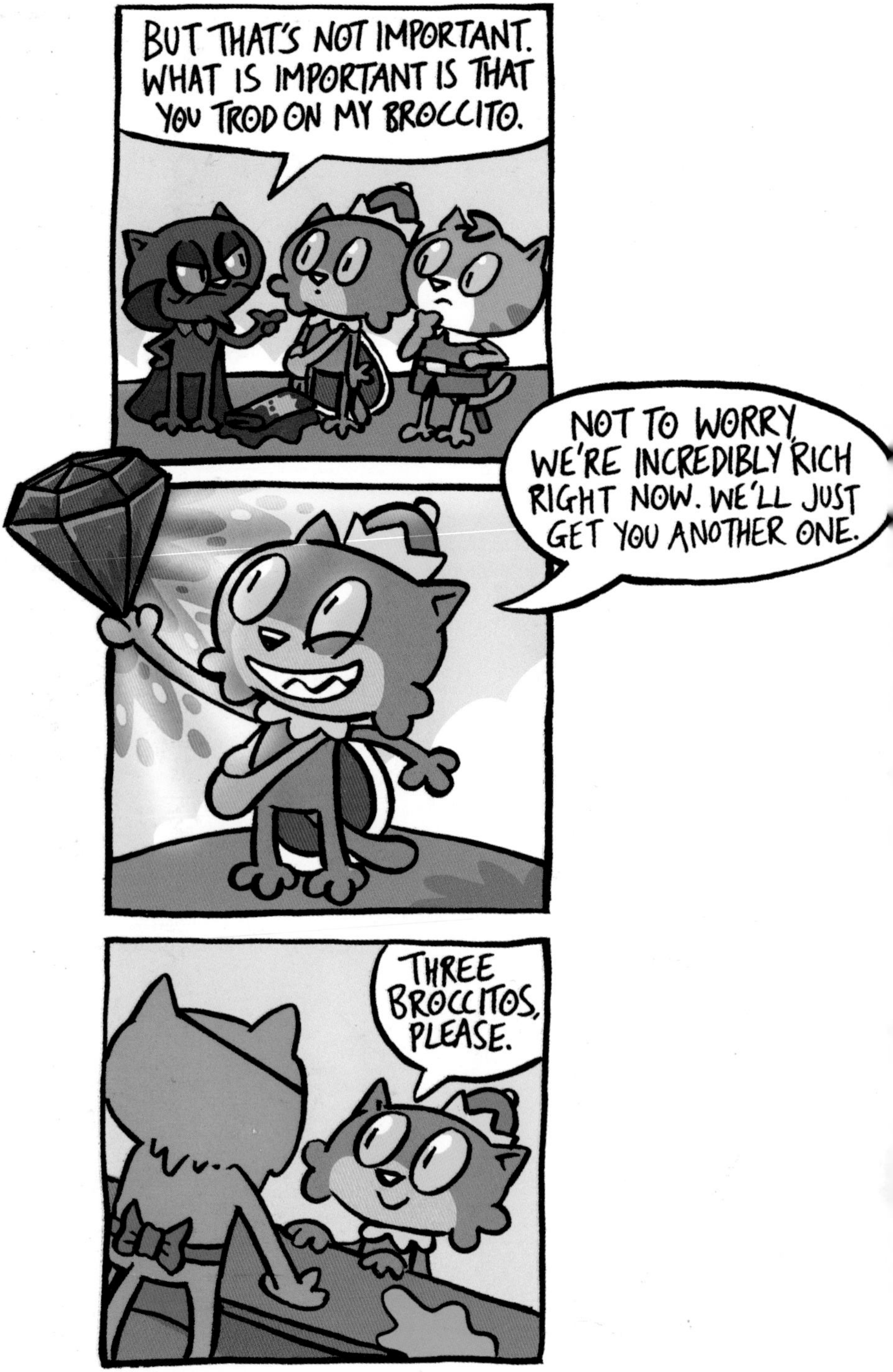

BUT THAT'S NOT IMPORTANT. WHAT IS IMPORTANT IS THAT YOU TROD ON MY BROCCITO.
NOT TO WORRY, WE'RE INCREDIBLY RICH RIGHT NOW. WE'LL JUST GET YOU ANOTHER ONE.
THREE BROCCITOS, PLEASE.

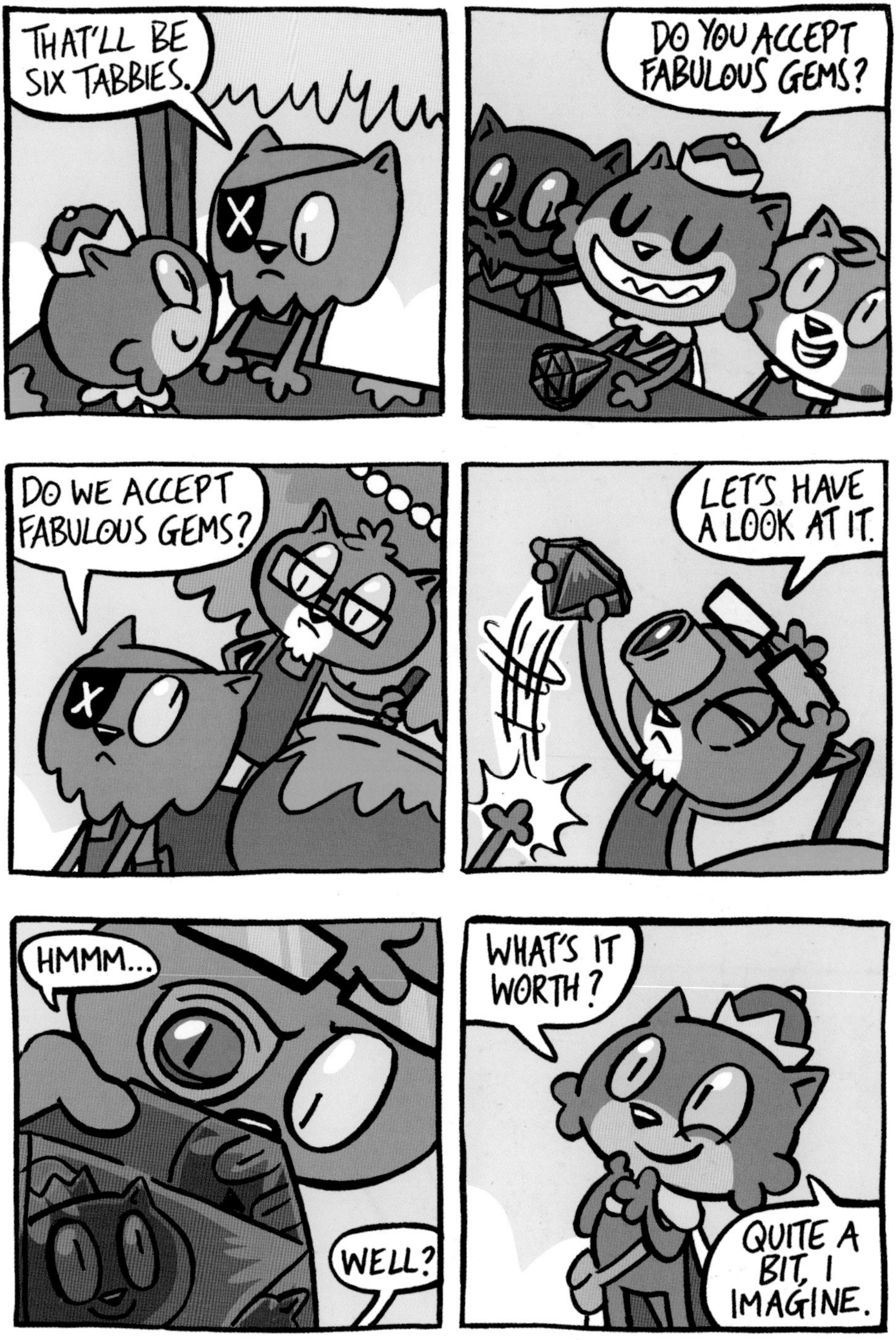
THAT'LL BE SIX TABBIES.
DO YOU ACCEPT FABULOUS GEMS?
DO WE ACCEPT FABULOUS GEMS?
LET'S HAVE A LOOK AT IT.
HMMM...
WELL?
WHAT'S IT WORTH?
QUITE A BIT, I IMAGINE.

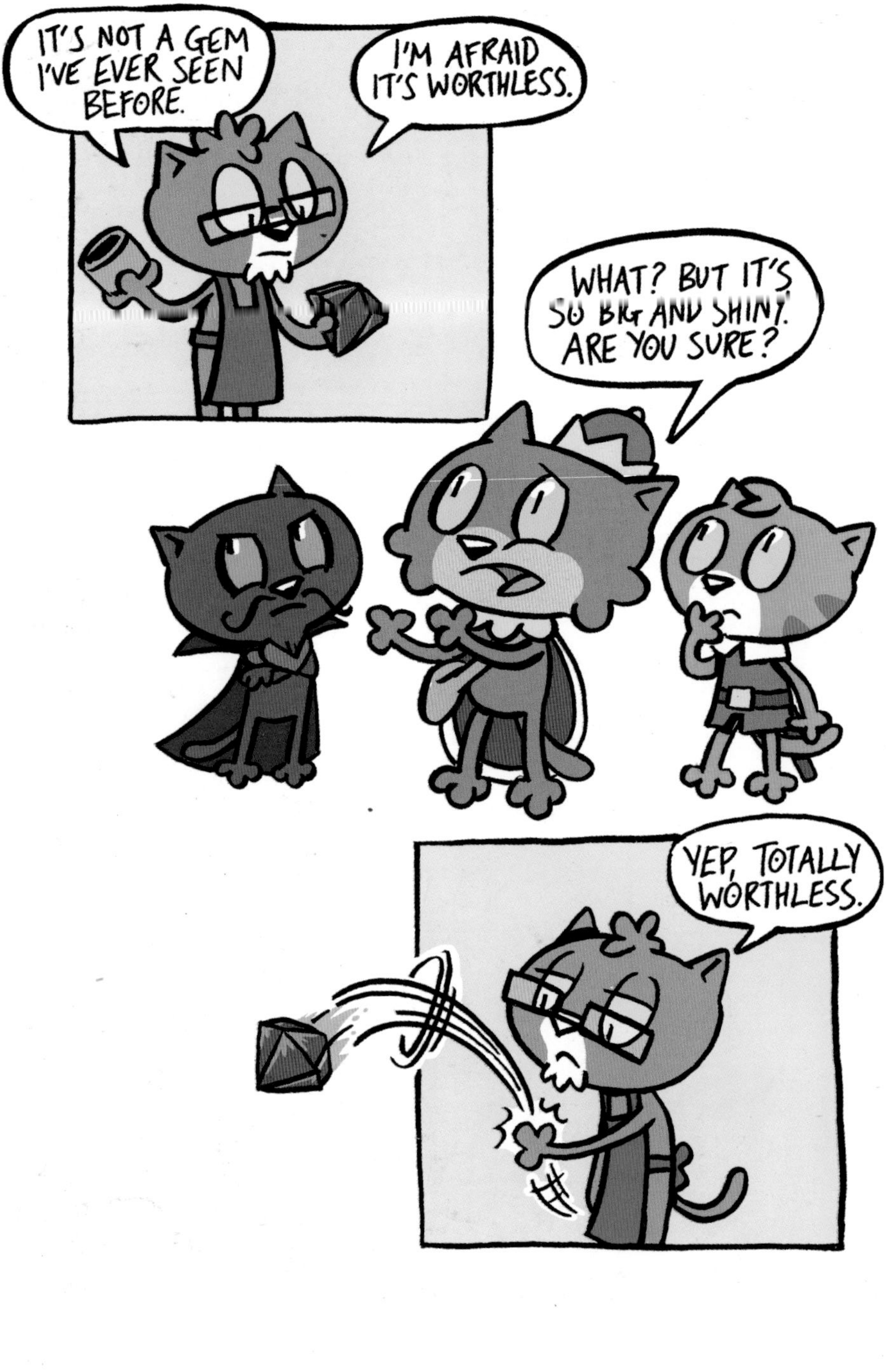
IT'S NOT A GEM I'VE EVER SEEN BEFORE.
I'M AFRAID IT'S WORTHLESS.
WHAT? BUT IT'S SO BIG AND SHINY. ARE YOU SURE?
YEP, TOTALLY WORTHLESS.

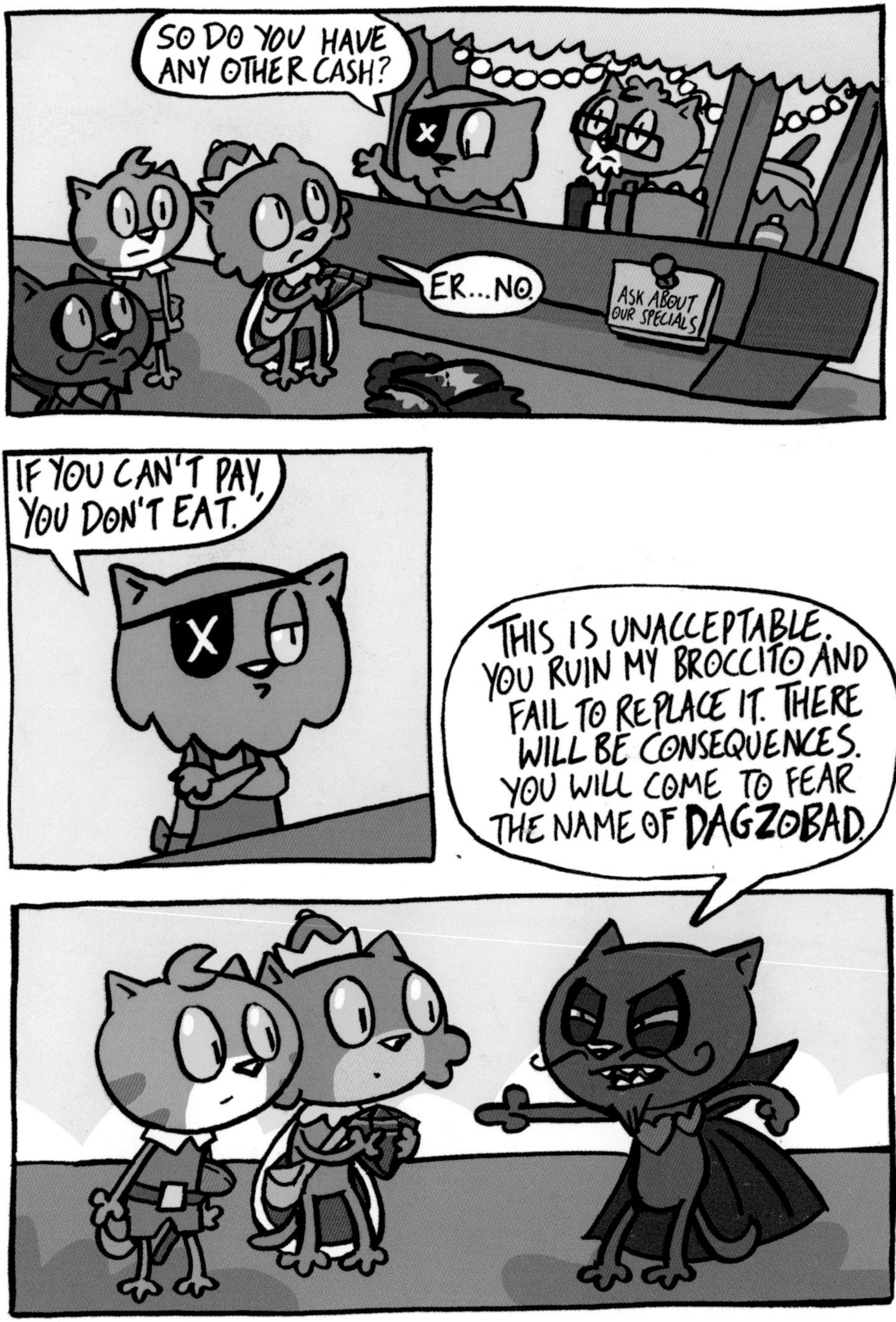
SO DO YOU HAVE ANY OTHER CASH?
ER...NO.
ASK ABOUT OUR SPECIALS
IF YOU CAN'T PAY, YOU DON'T EAT.
THIS IS UNACCEPTABLE. YOU RUIN MY BROCCITO AND FAIL TO REPLACE IT. THERE WILL BE CONSEQUENCES. YOU WILL COME TO FEAR THE NAME OF DAGZOBAD.

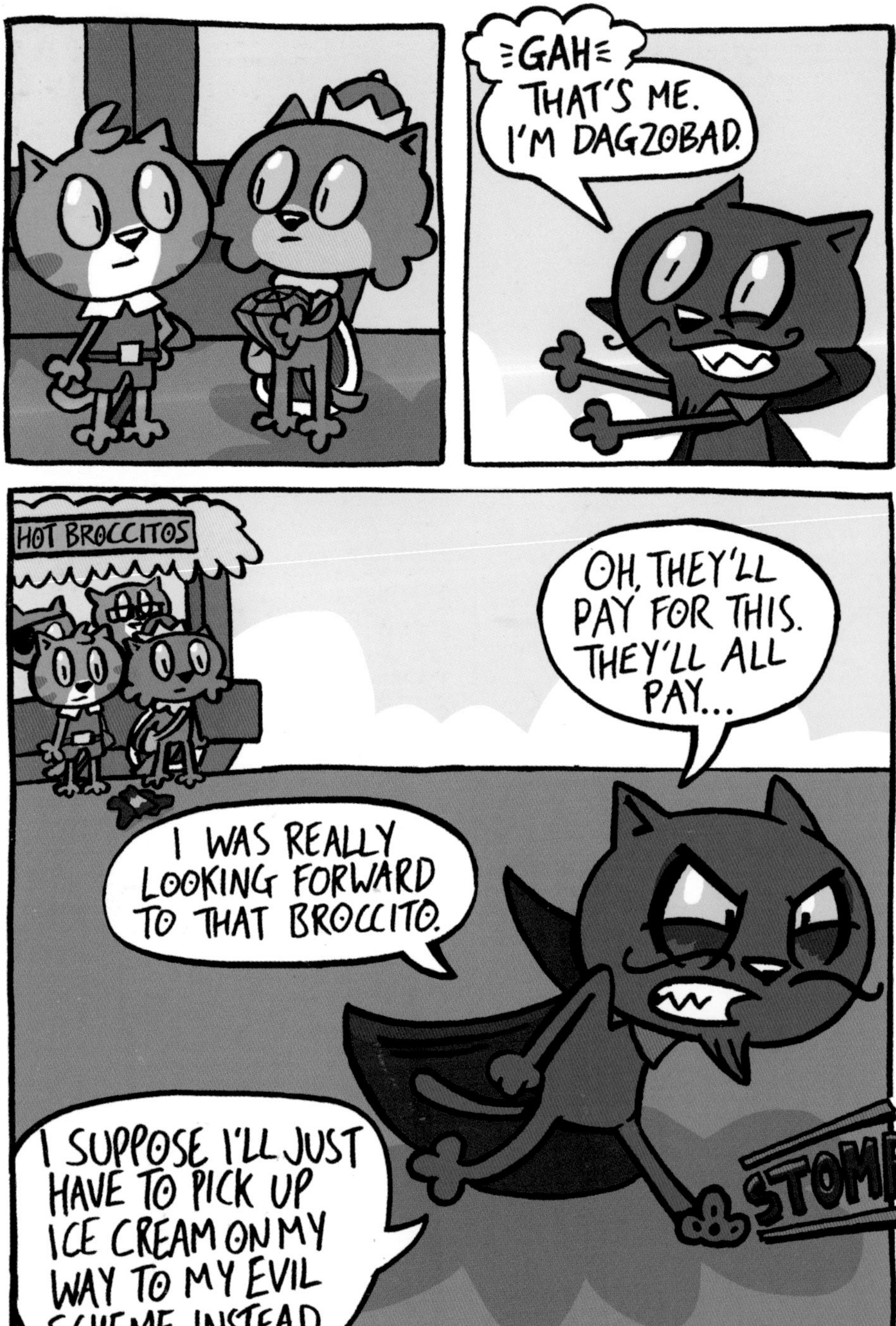

GAH
THAT'S ME. I'M DAGZOBAD.
HOT BROCCITOS
OH, THEY'LL PAY FOR THIS. THEY'LL ALL PAY...
I WAS REALLY LOOKING FORWARD TO THAT BROCCITO.
I SUPPOSE I'LL JUST HAVE TO PICK UP ICE CREAM ON MY WAY TO MY EVIL SCHEME INSTEAD.
STOMP

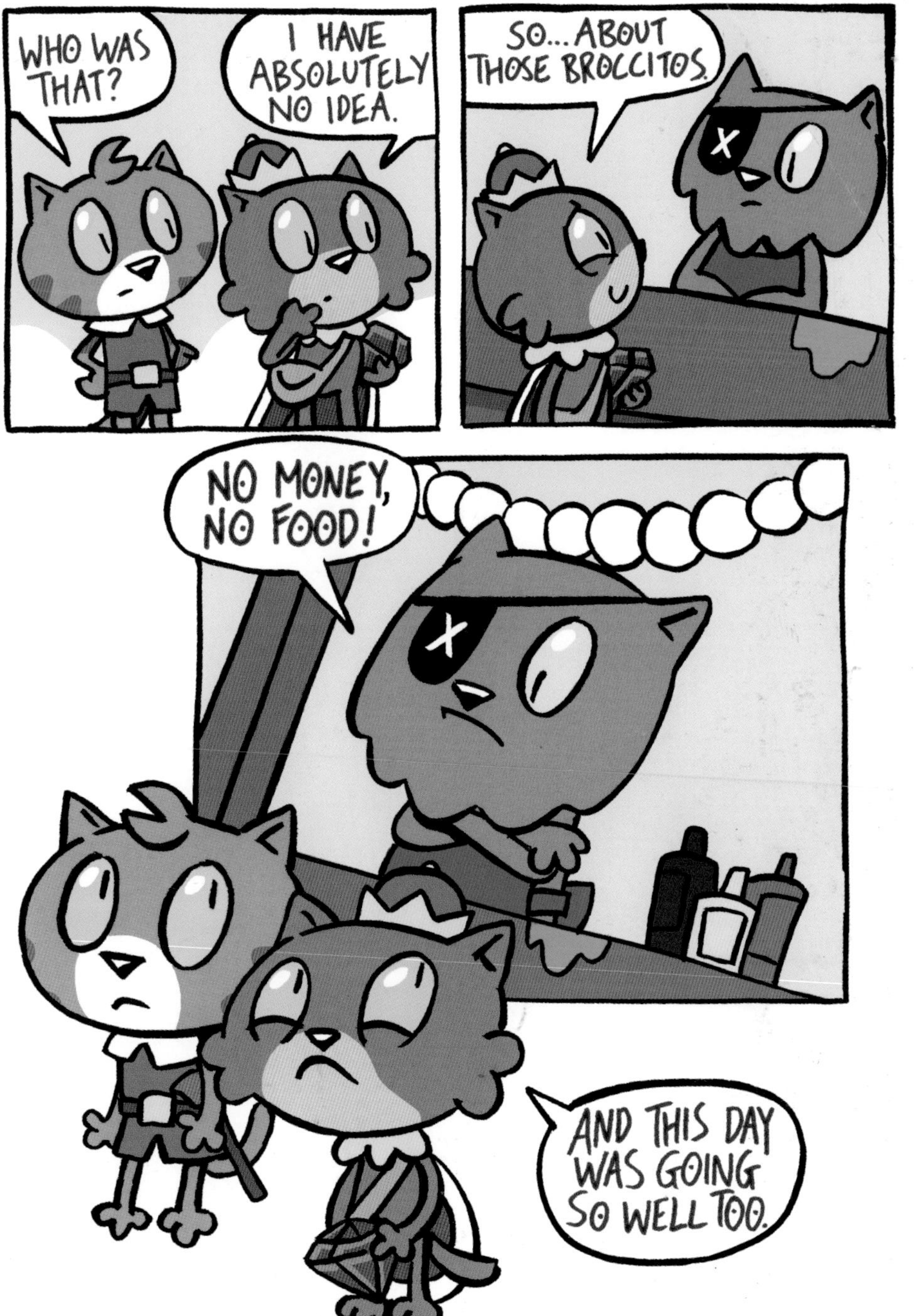
WHO WAS THAT?
I HAVE ABSOLUTELY NO IDEA.
SO... ABOUT THOSE BROCCITOS.
NO MONEY, NO FOOD!
AND THIS DAY WAS GOING SO WELL TOO.

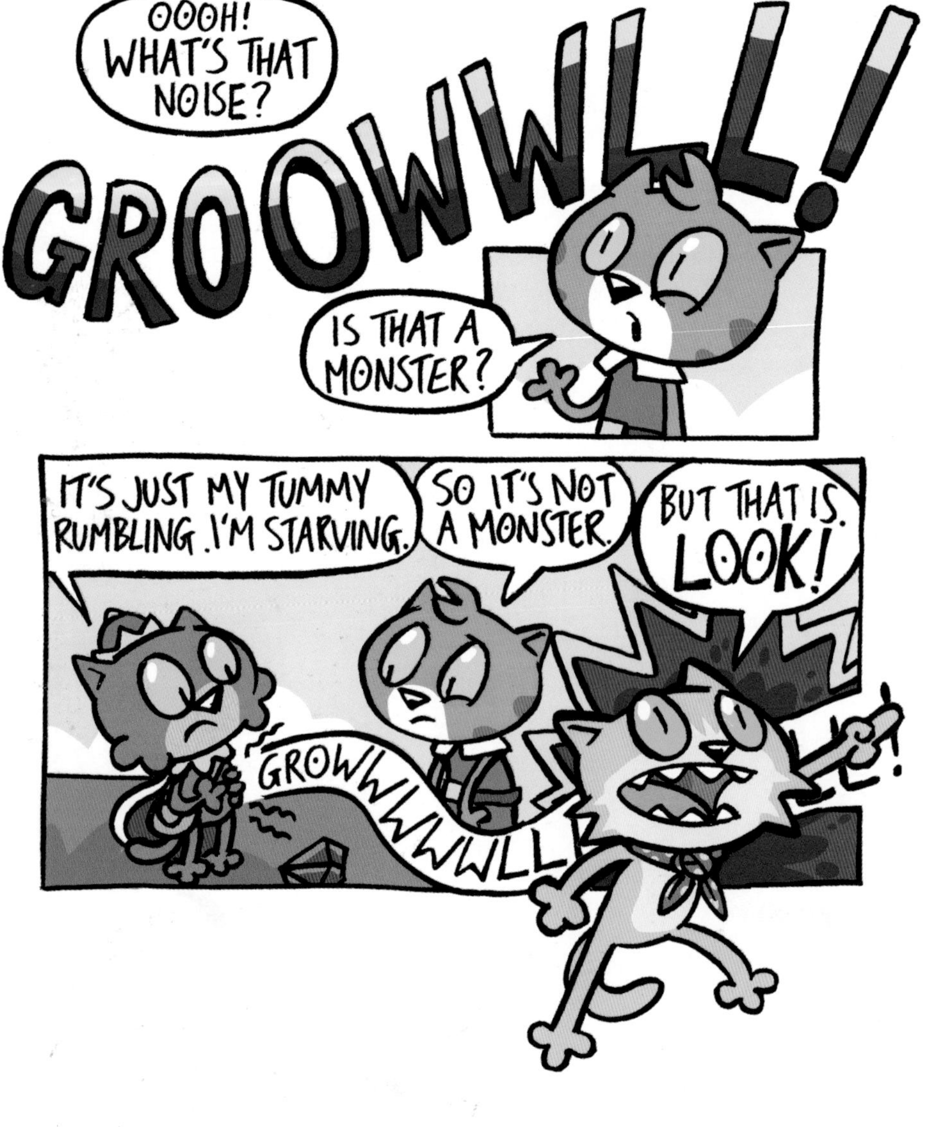
OOOH! WHAT'S THAT NOISE?
GROOWWLLL!
IS THAT A MONSTER?
IT'S JUST MY TUMMY RUMBLING. I'M STARVING.
GROWWWWWWLLL
SO IT'S NOT A MONSTER.
BUT THAT IS. LOOK!

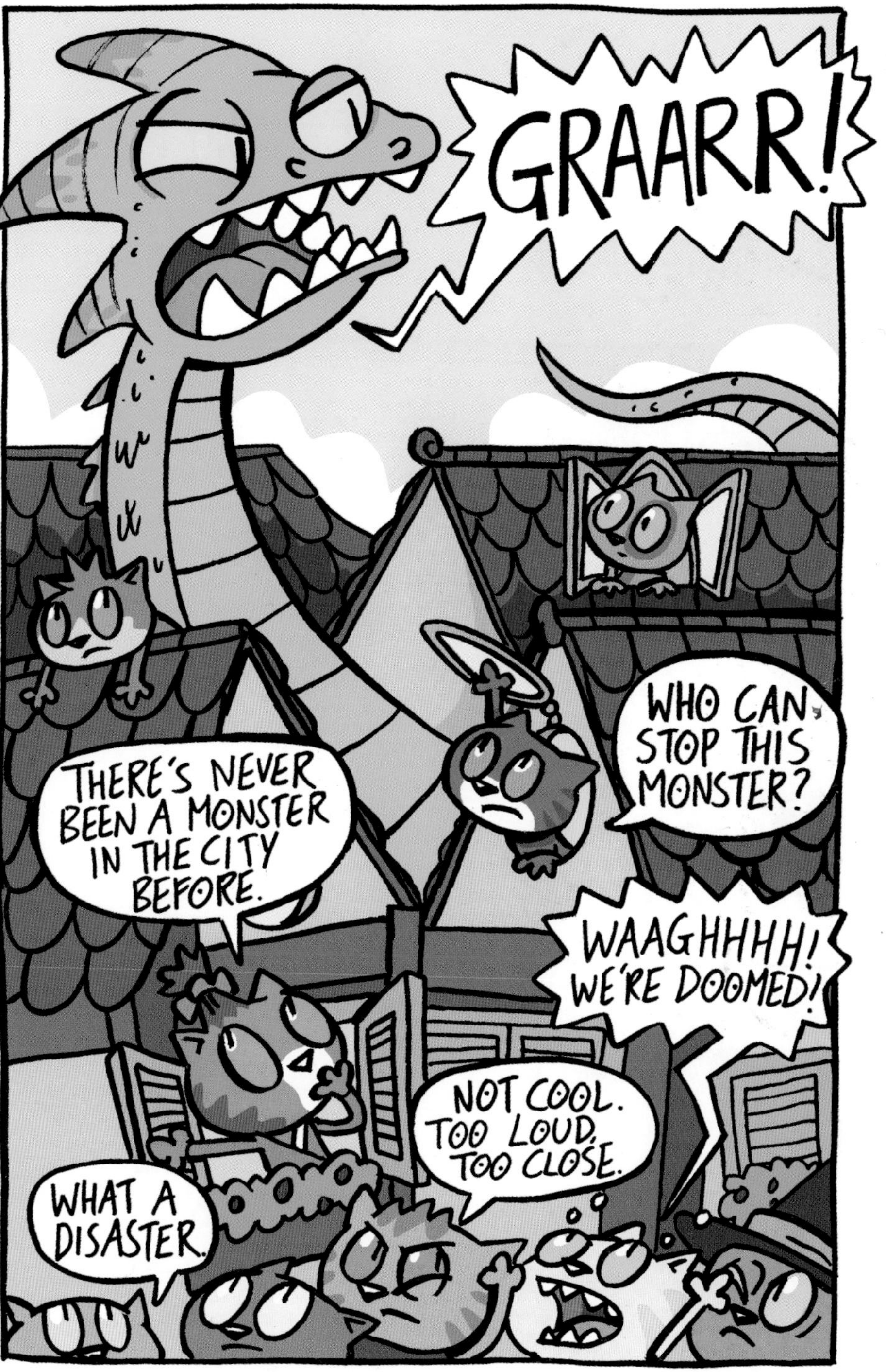
GRAARR!
WHO CAN STOP THIS MONSTER?
THERE'S NEVER BEEN A MONSTER IN THE CITY BEFORE.
WAAGHHHH! WE'RE DOOMED!
NOT COOL. TOO LOUD, TOO CLOSE.
WHAT A DISASTER.

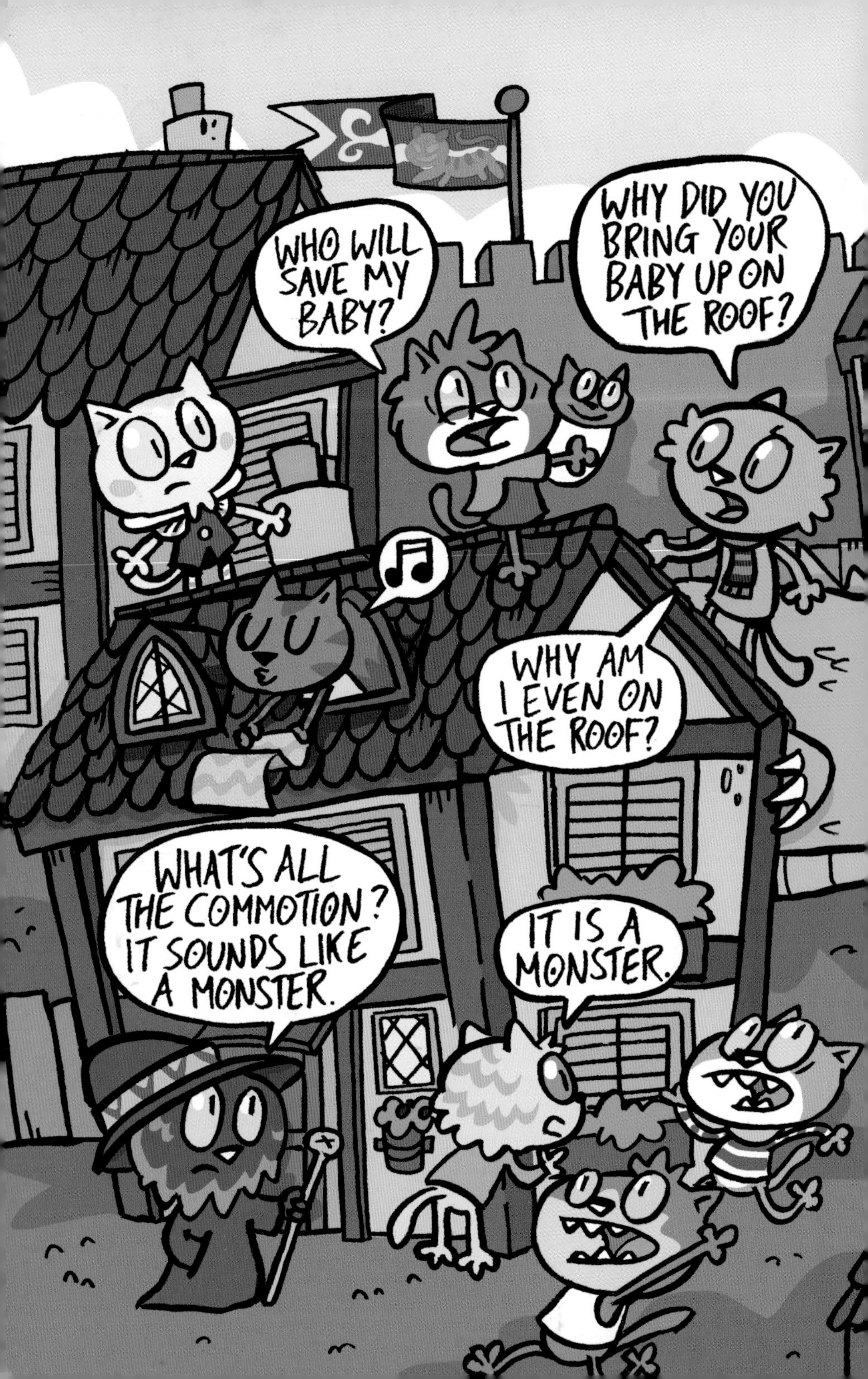
WHO WILL SAVE MY BABY?
WHY DID YOU BRING YOUR BABY UP ON THE ROOF?
WHY AM I EVEN ON THE ROOF?
WHAT'S ALL THE COMMOTION? IT SOUNDS LIKE A MONSTER.
IT IS A MONSTER.

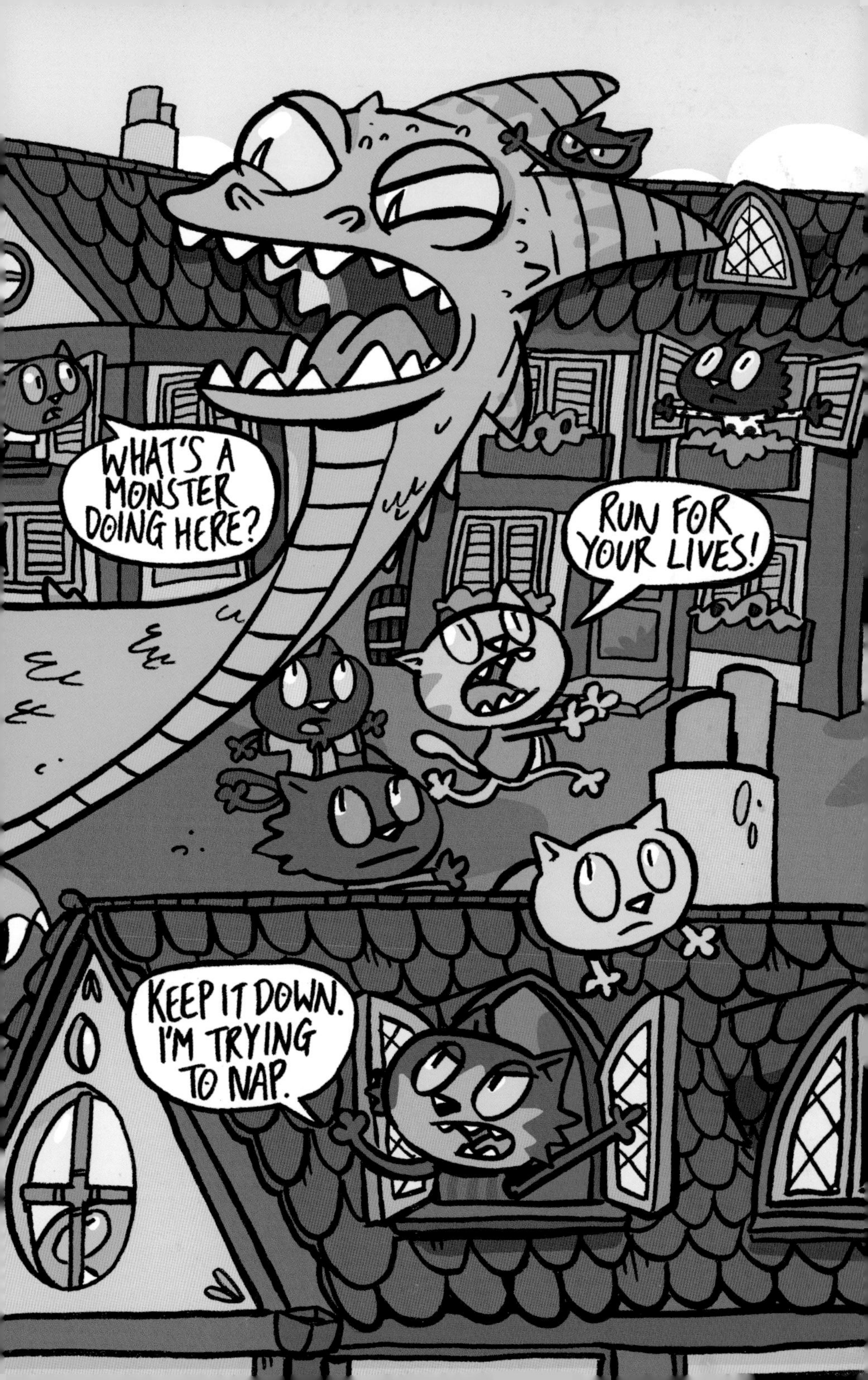
WHAT'S A MONSTER DOING HERE?
RUN FOR YOUR LIVES!
KEEP IT DOWN. I'M TRYING TO NAP.

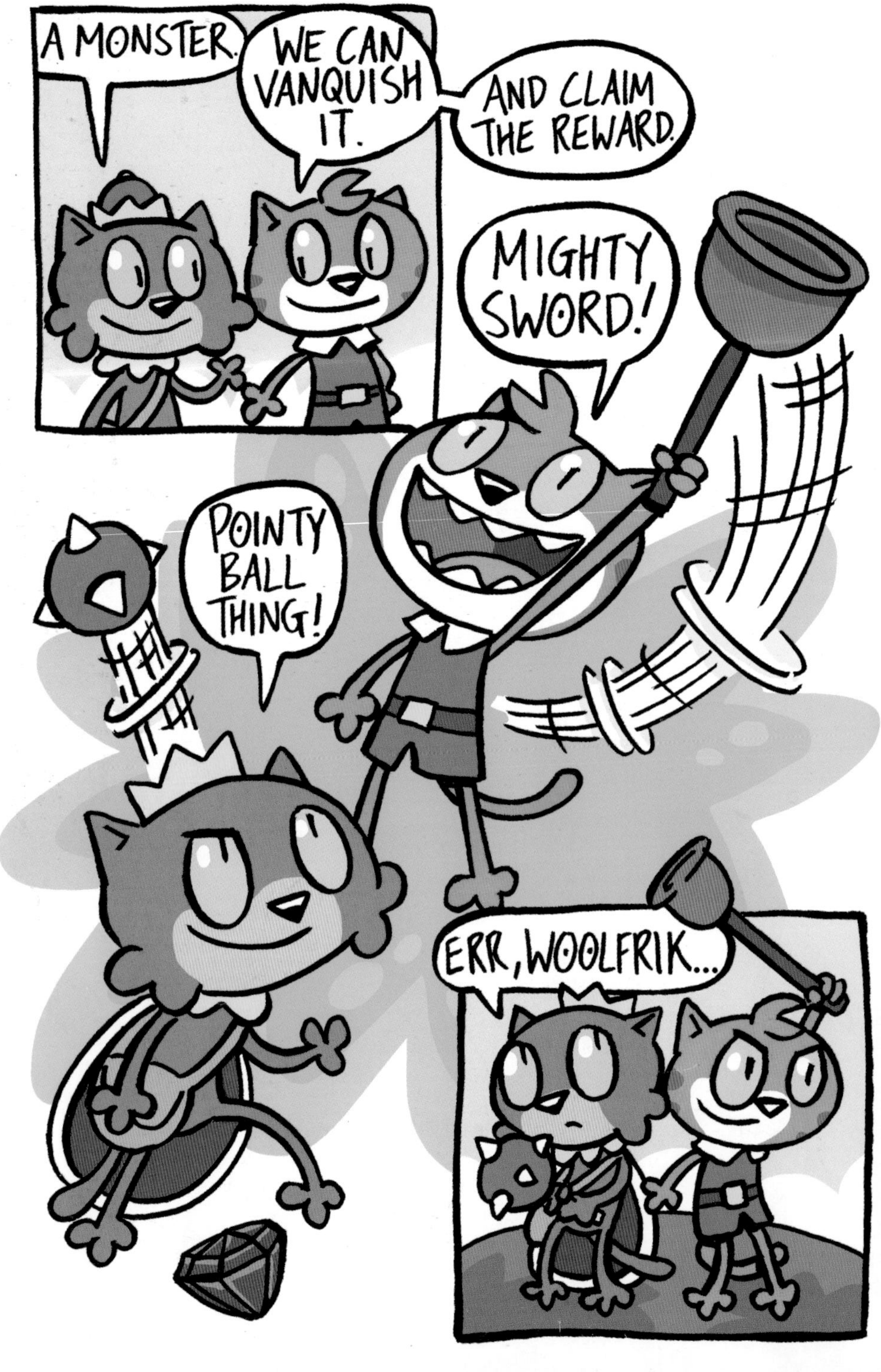
A MONSTER.
WE CAN VANQUISH IT.
AND CLAIM THE REWARD.
MIGHTY SWORD!
POINTY BALL THING!
ERR, WOOLFRIK...

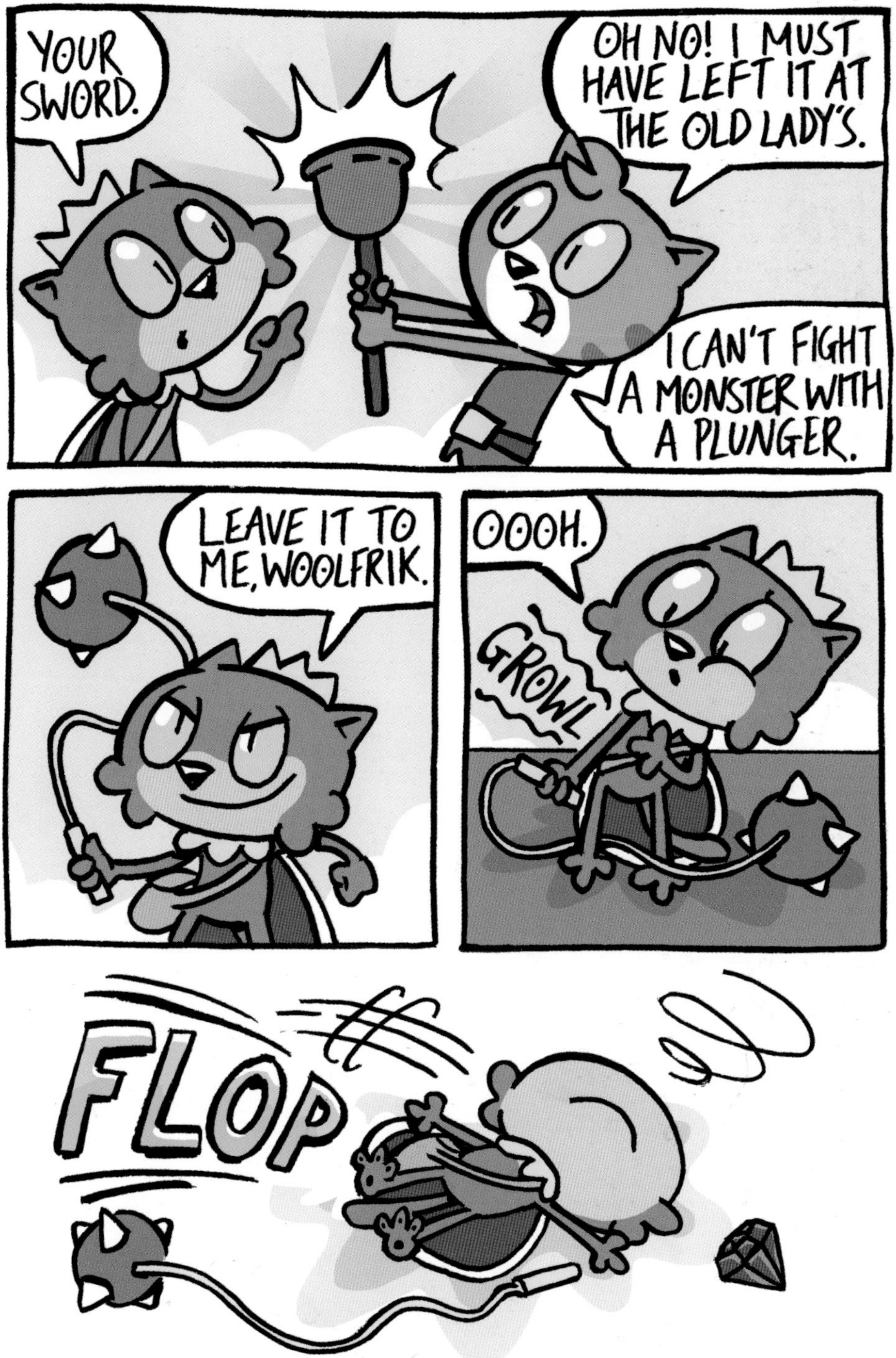
YOUR SWORD.
OH NO! I MUST HAVE LEFT IT AT THE OLD LADY'S.
I CAN'T FIGHT A MONSTER WITH A PLUNGER.
LEAVE IT TO ME, WOOLFRIK.
OOOH.
GROWL
FLOP

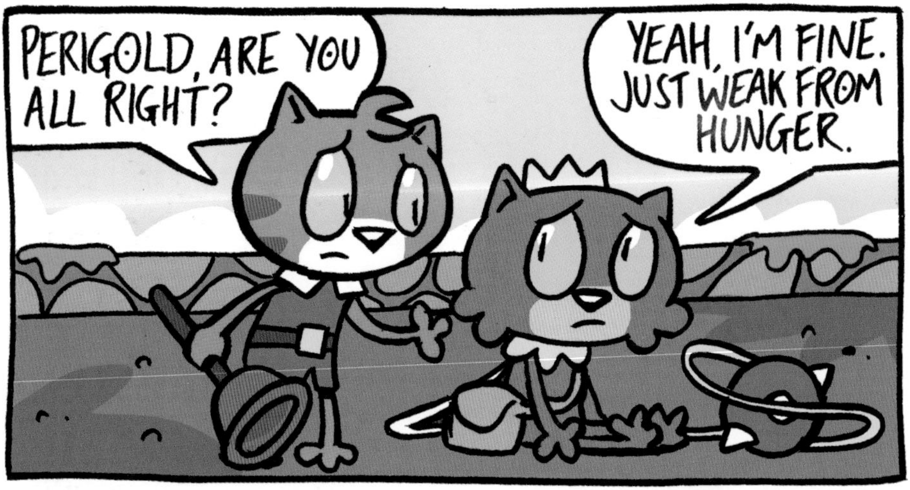
PERIGOLD, ARE YOU ALL RIGHT?
YEAH, I'M FINE. JUST WEAK FROM HUNGER.

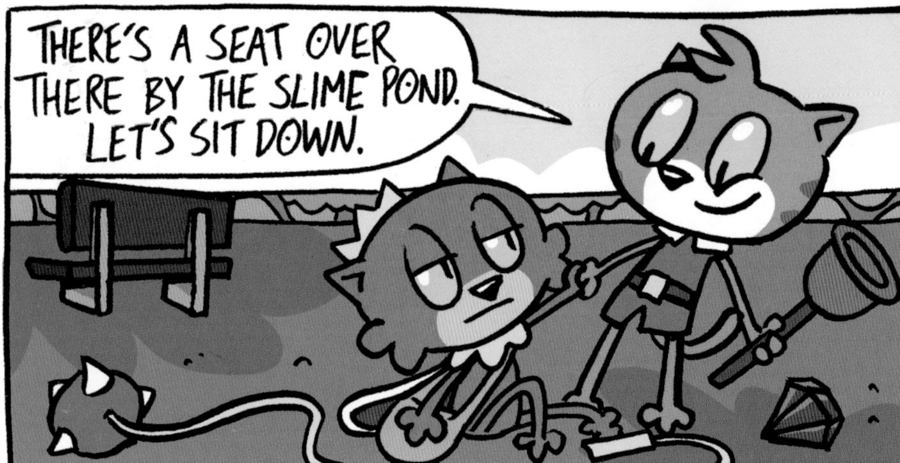
THERE'S A SEAT OVER THERE BY THE SLIME POND. LET'S SIT DOWN.

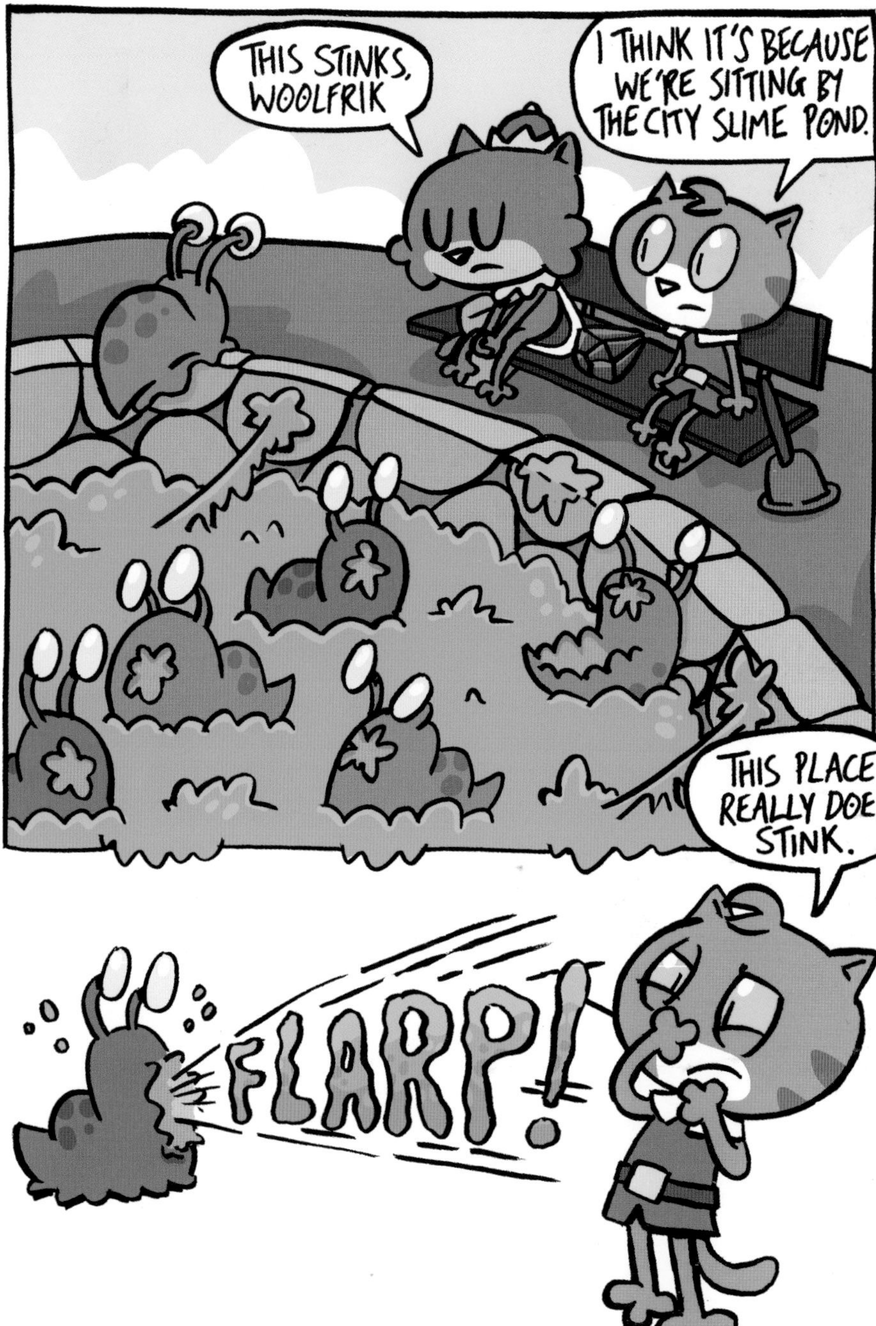
THIS STINKS, WOOLFRIK
I THINK IT'S BECAUSE WE'RE SITTING BY THE CITY SLIME POND.
THIS PLACE REALLY DOES STINK.
FLARP!

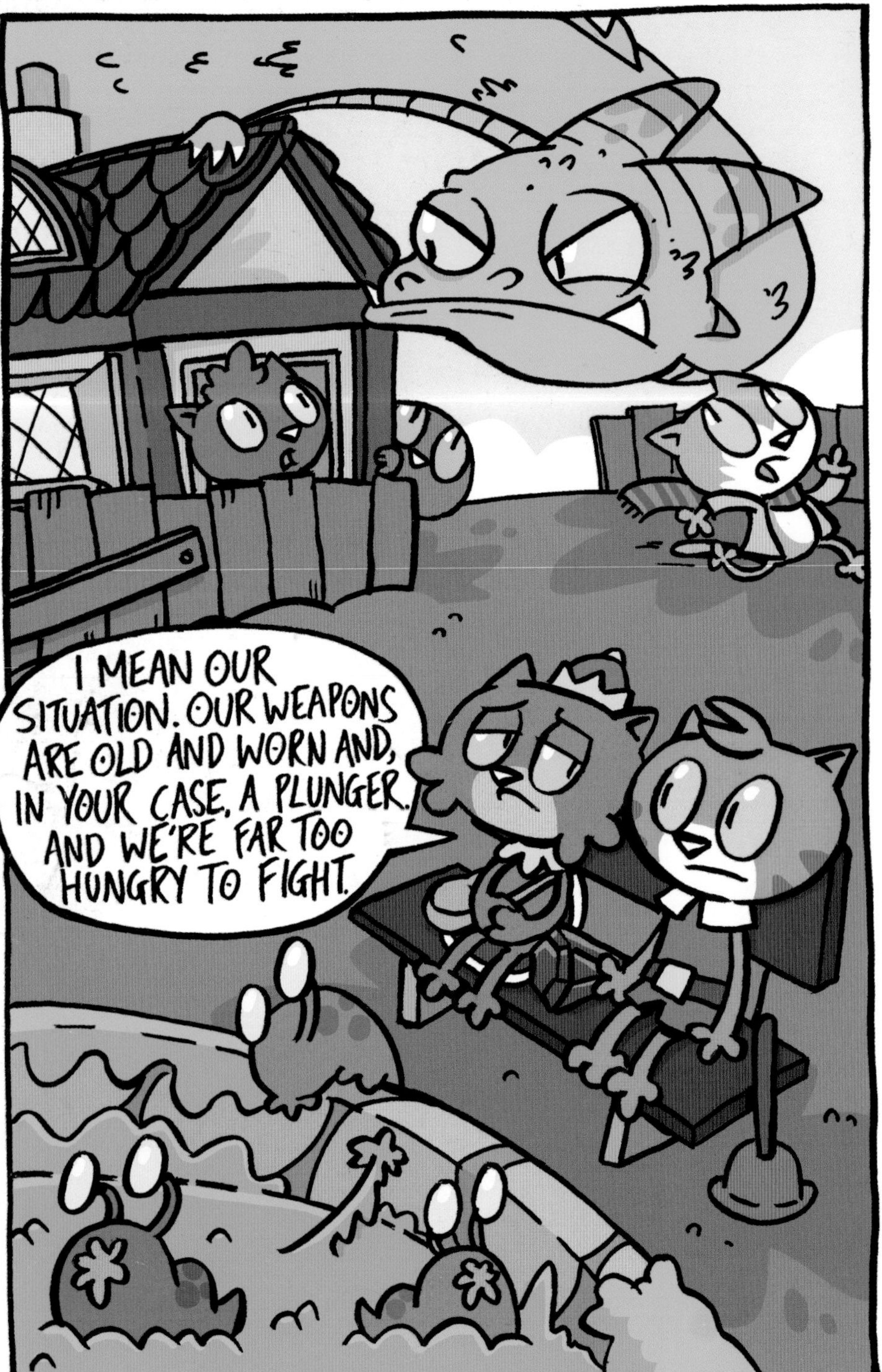
I MEAN OUR SITUATION. OUR WEAPONS ARE OLD AND WORN AND, IN YOUR CASE, A PLUNGER. AND WE'RE FAR TOO HUNGRY TO FIGHT.

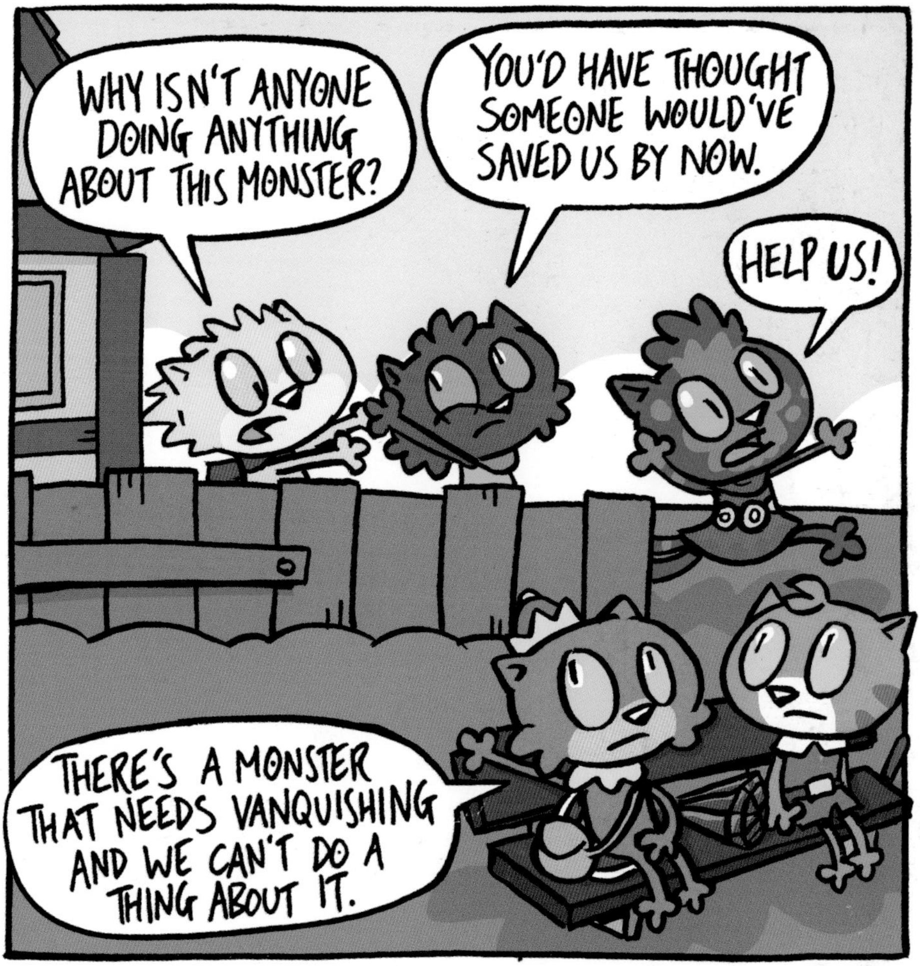
WHY ISN'T ANYONE DOING ANYTHING ABOUT THIS MONSTER?
YOU'D HAVE THOUGHT SOMEONE WOULD'VE SAVED US BY NOW.
HELP US!
THERE'S A MONSTER THAT NEEDS VANQUISHING AND WE CAN'T DO A THING ABOUT IT.

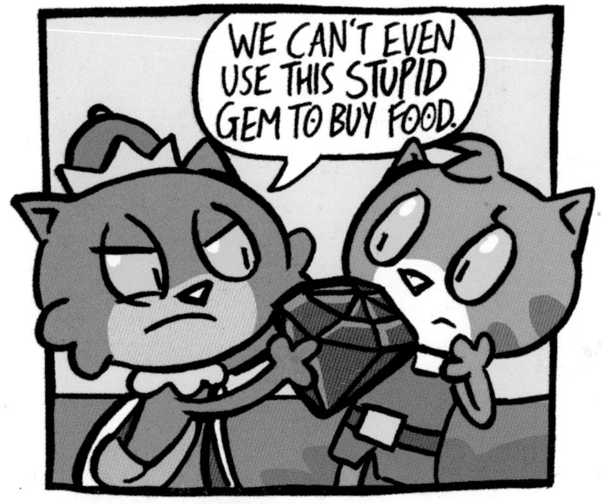
WE CAN'T EVEN USE THIS STUPID GEM TO BUY FOOD.

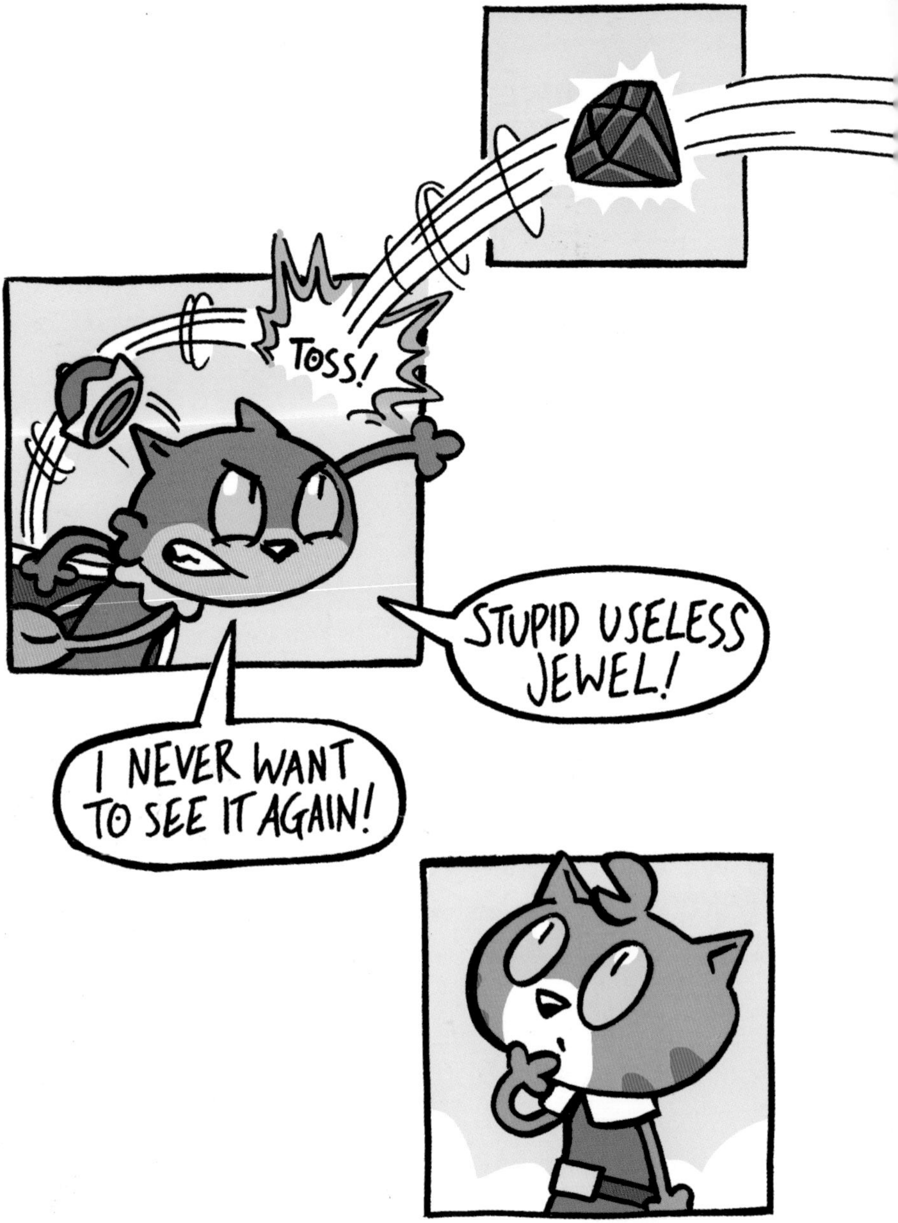
TOSS!
STUPID USELESS JEWEL!
I NEVER WANT TO SEE IT AGAIN!

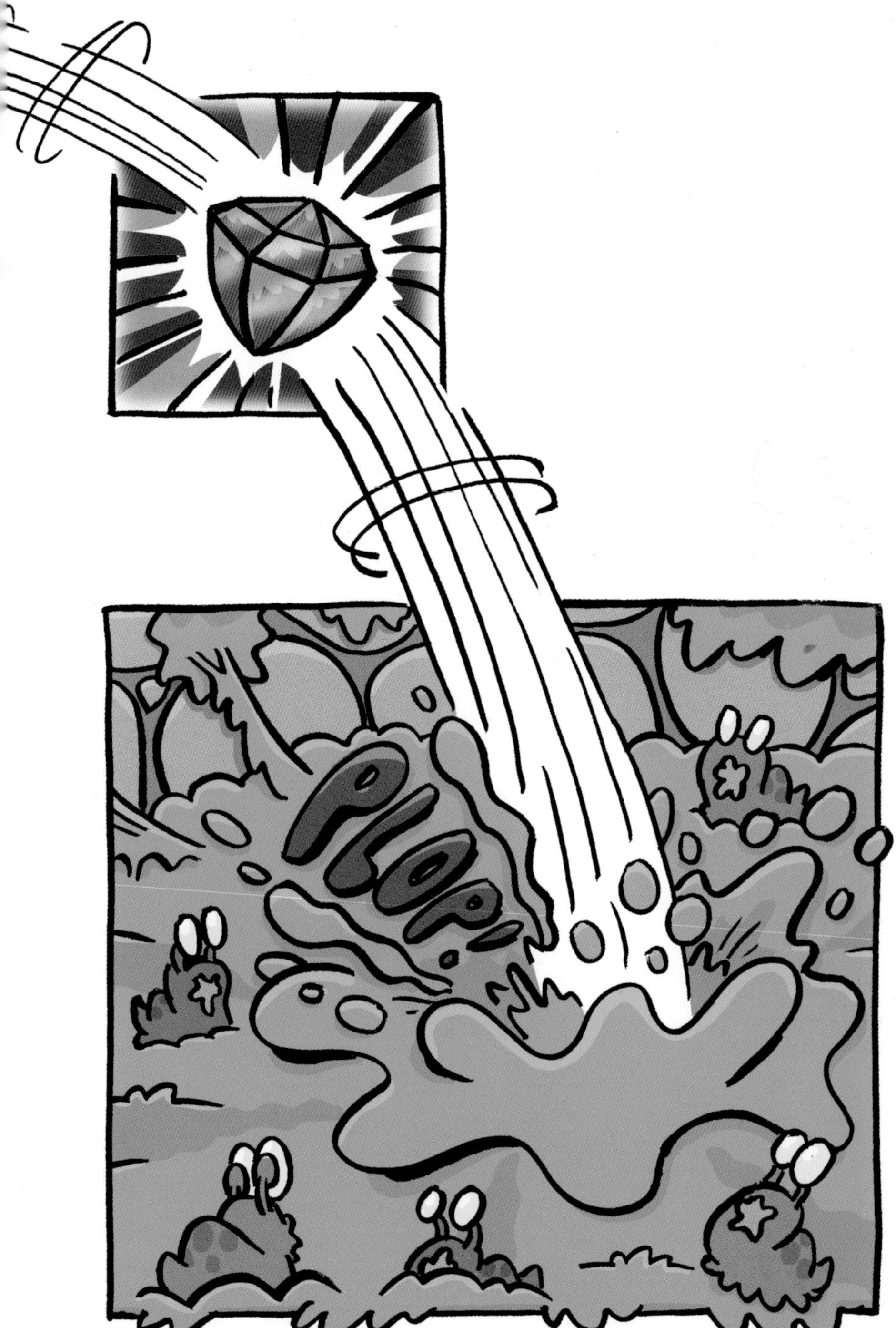
PLOP!

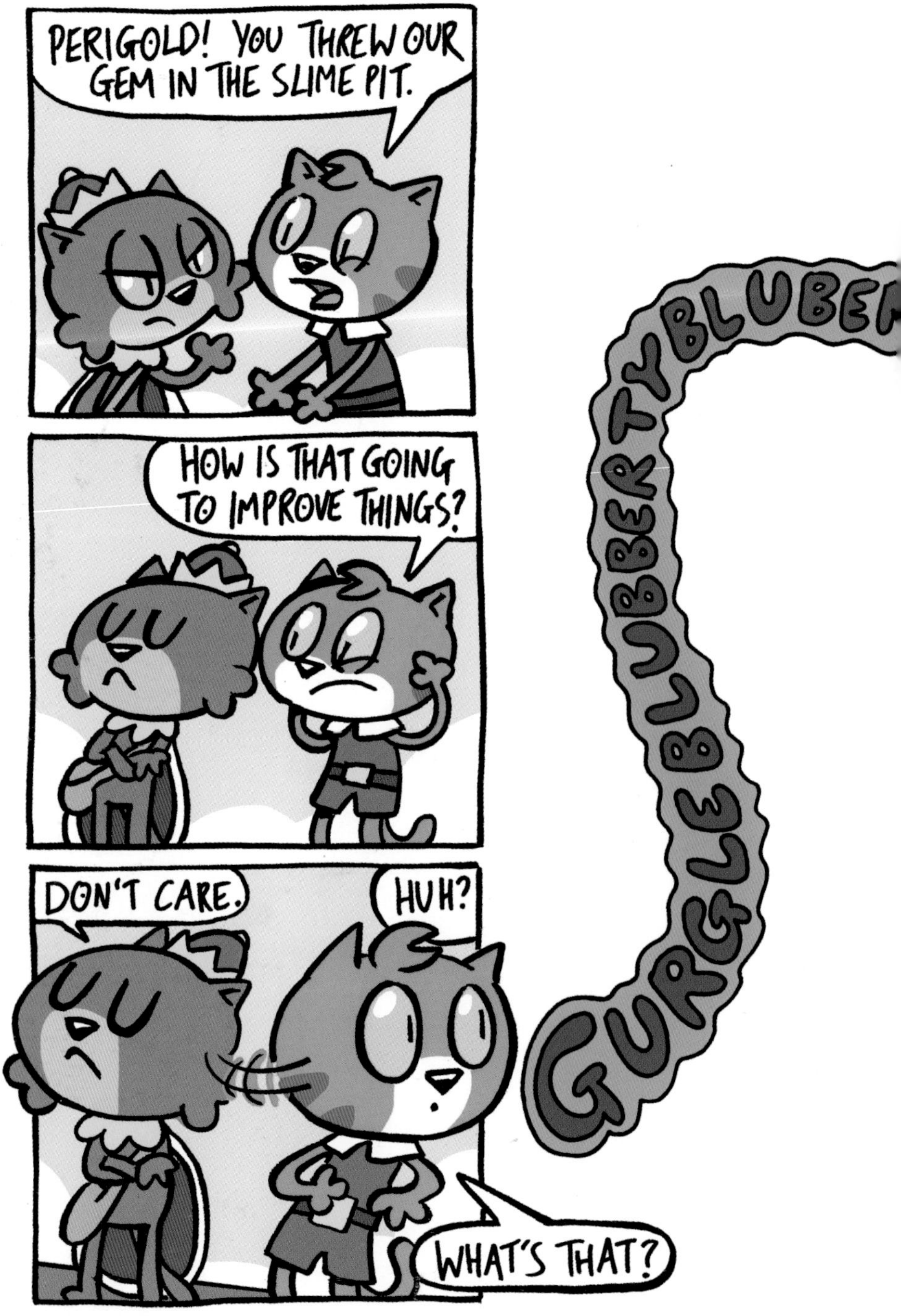
PERIGOLD! YOU THREW OUR GEM IN THE SLIME PIT.
HOW IS THAT GOING TO IMPROVE THINGS?
DON'T CARE.
HUH?
WHAT'S THAT?
GURGLEBLUBBERTYBLUBE

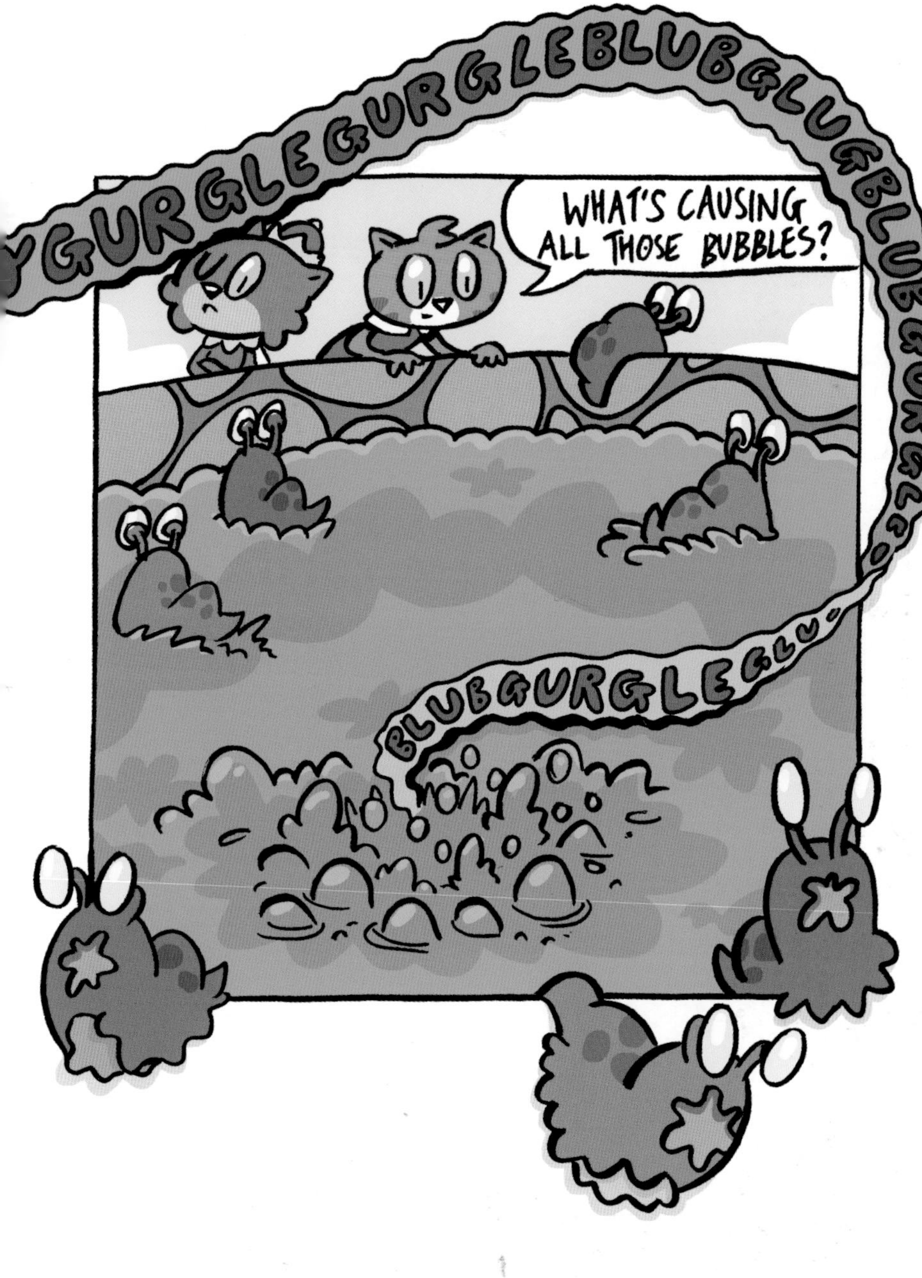

YGURGLEGURGLEBLUBGLUGBLUBGURGL...
WHAT'S CAUSING ALL THOSE BUBBLES?
BLUBGURGLEGLU...

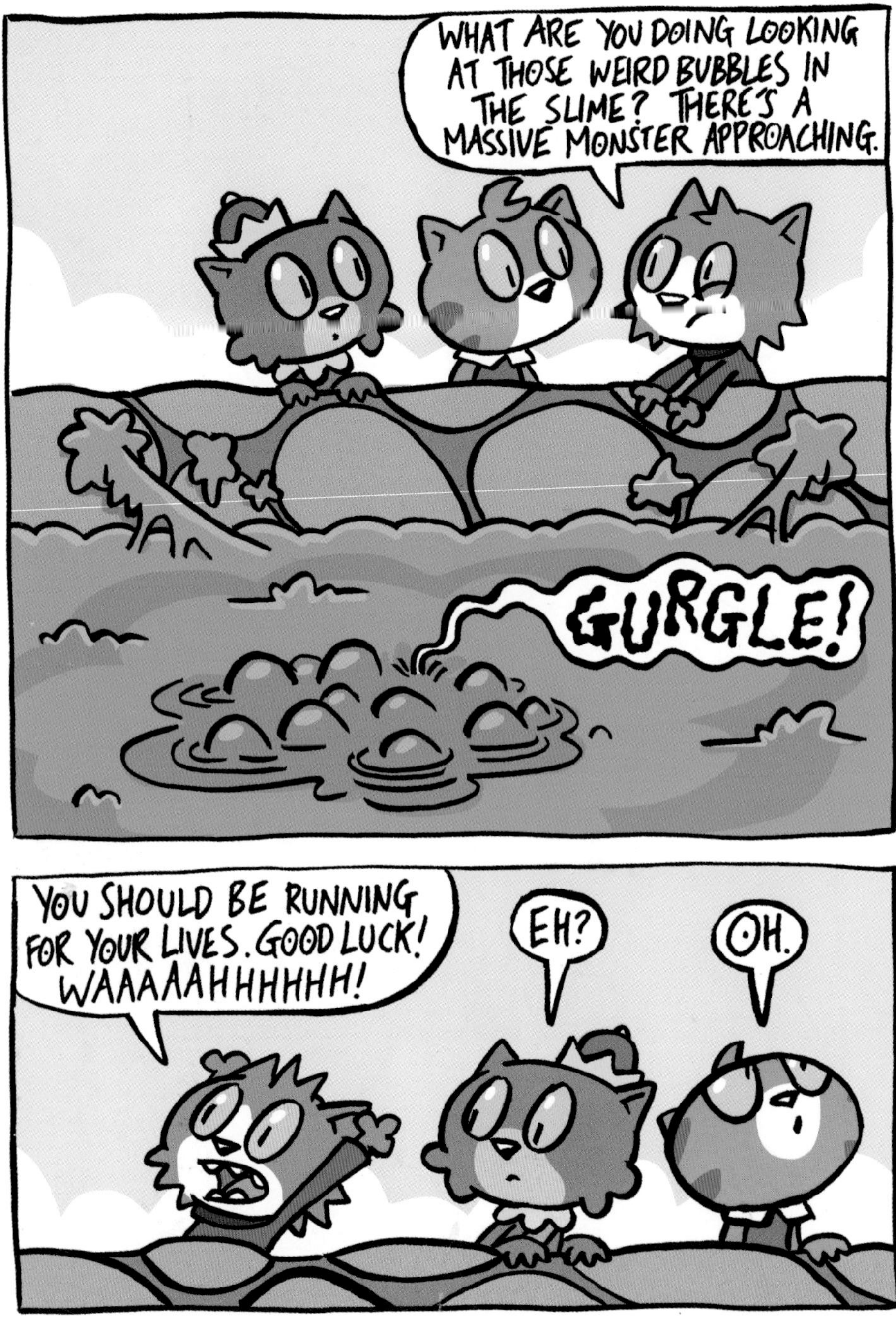
WHAT ARE YOU DOING LOOKING AT THOSE WEIRD BUBBLES IN THE SLIME? THERE'S A MASSIVE MONSTER APPROACHING.
GURGLE!
YOU SHOULD BE RUNNING FOR YOUR LIVES. GOOD LUCK! WAAAAAHHHHHH!
EH?
OH.

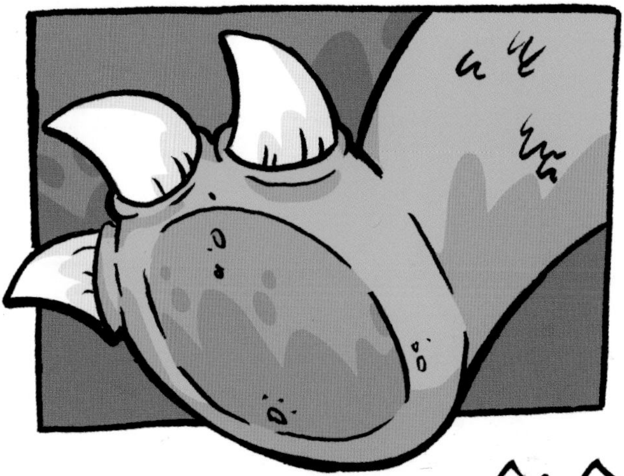

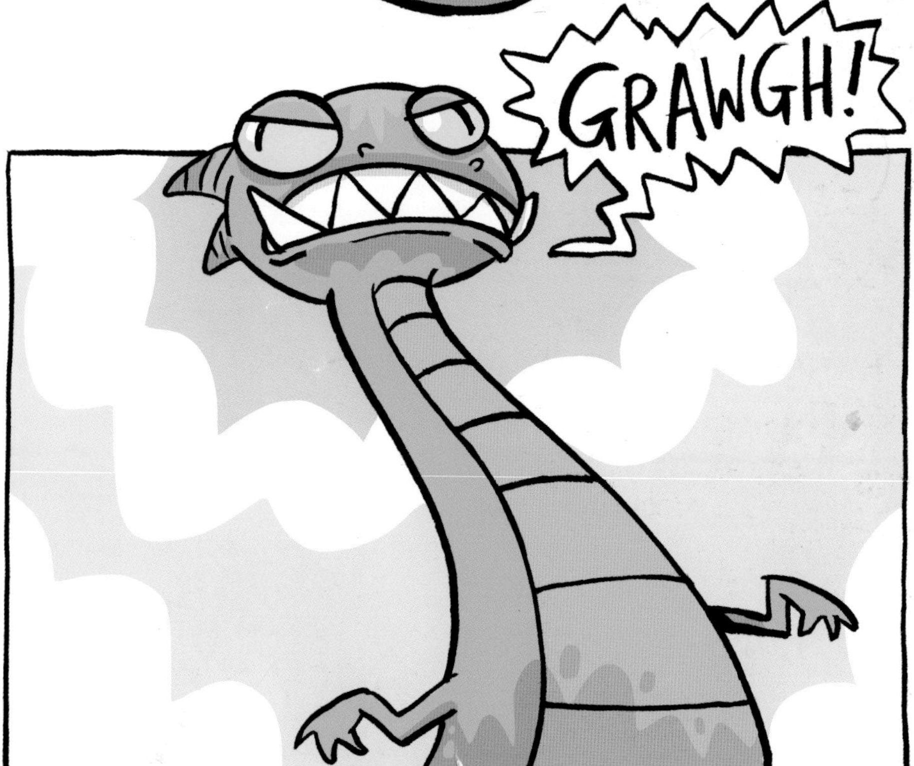
GRAWGH!

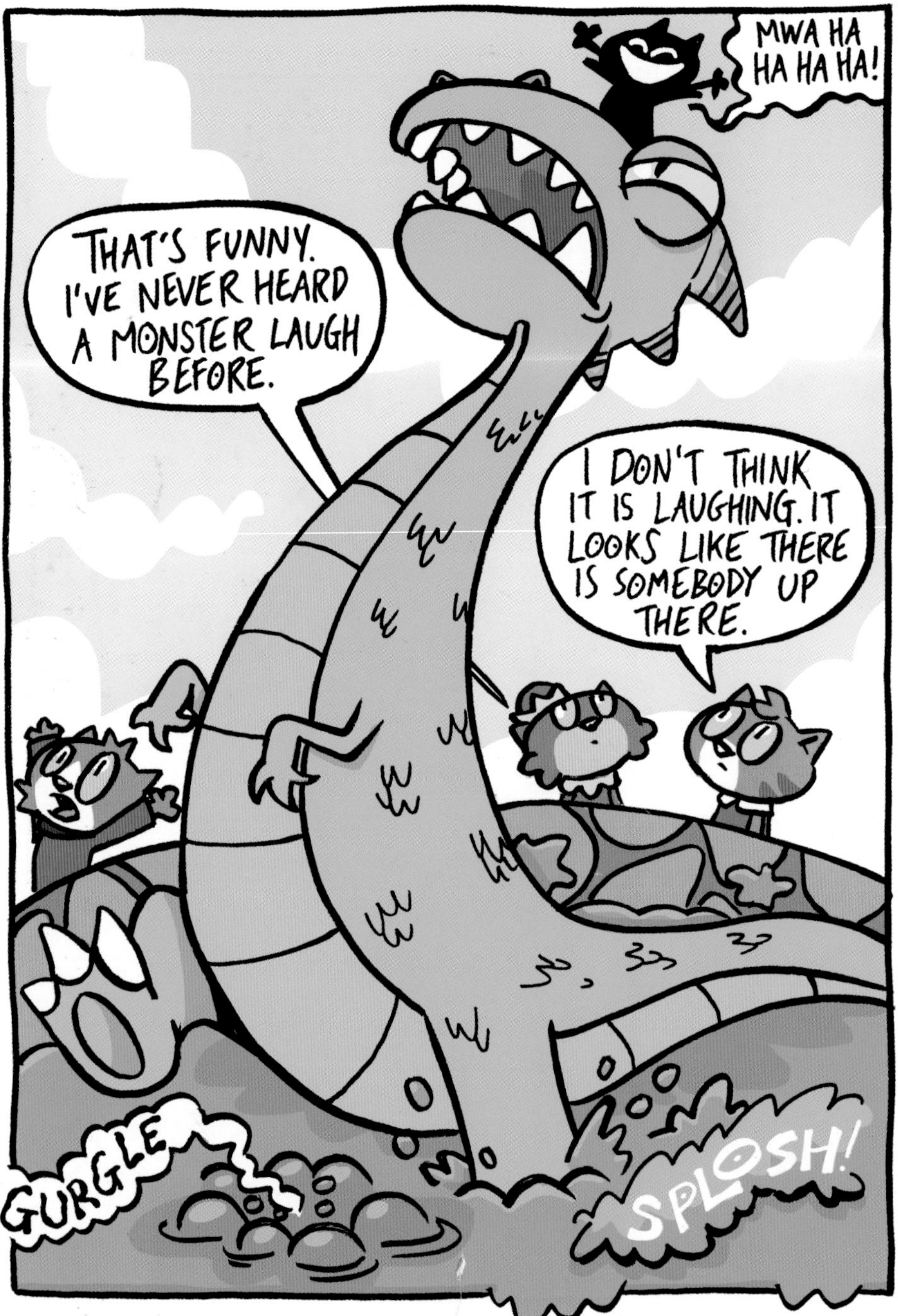
MWA HA HA HA HA!
THAT'S FUNNY. I'VE NEVER HEARD A MONSTER LAUGH BEFORE.
I DON'T THINK IT IS LAUGHING. IT LOOKS LIKE THERE IS SOMEBODY UP THERE.
GURGLE
SPLOSH!

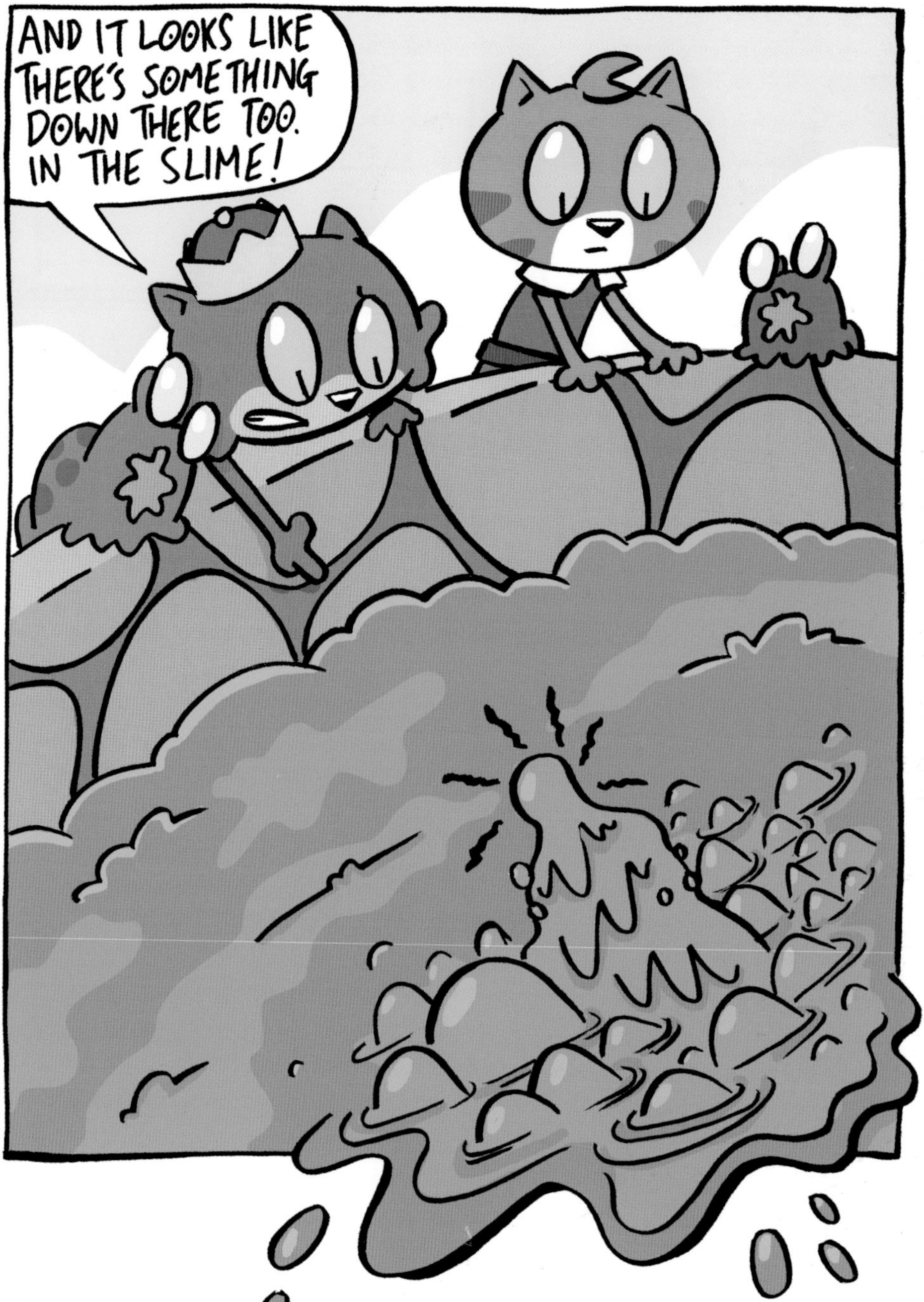
AND IT LOOKS LIKE THERE'S SOMETHING DOWN THERE TOO. IN THE SLIME!

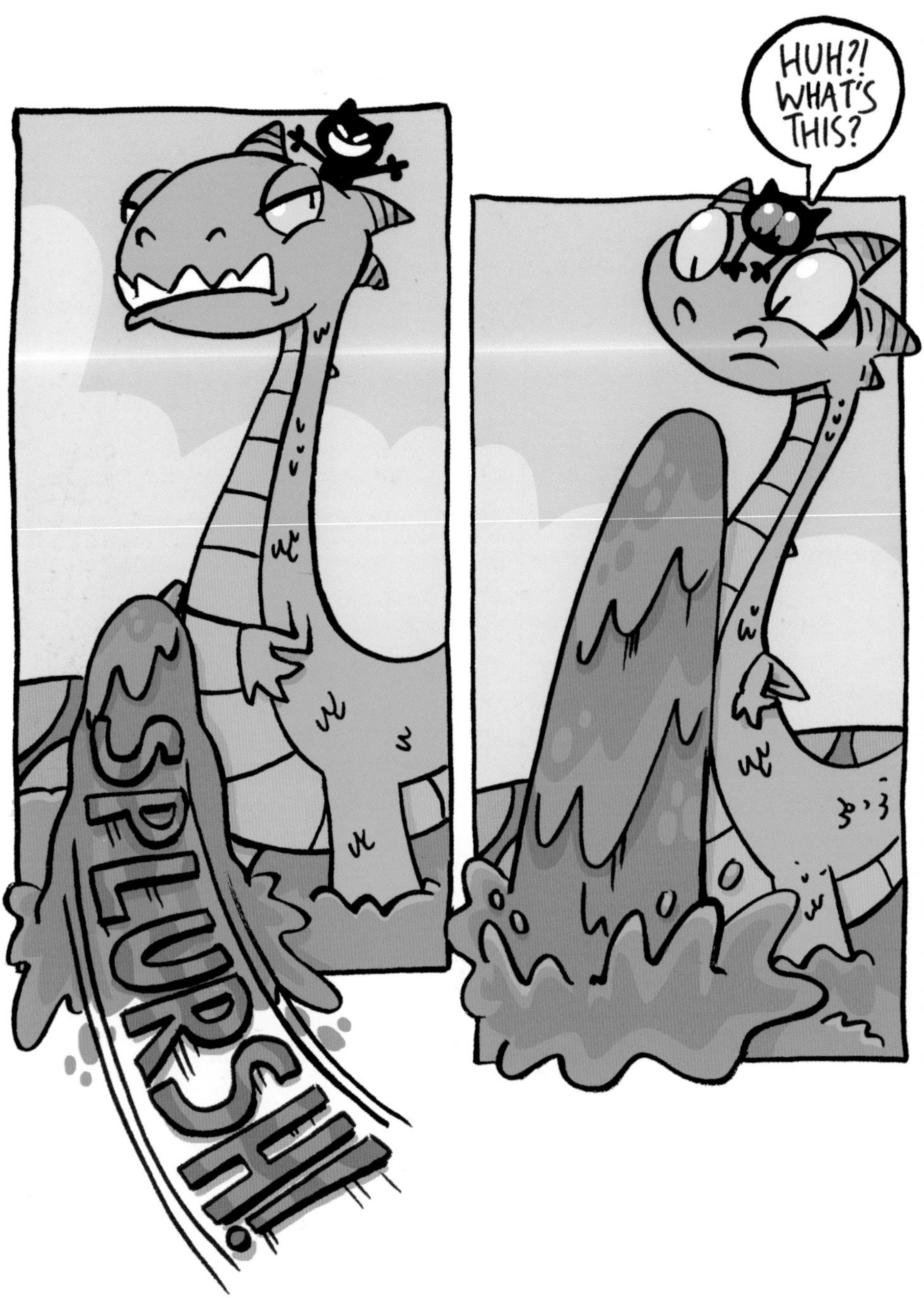
SPLURSH!
HUH?! WHAT'S THIS?

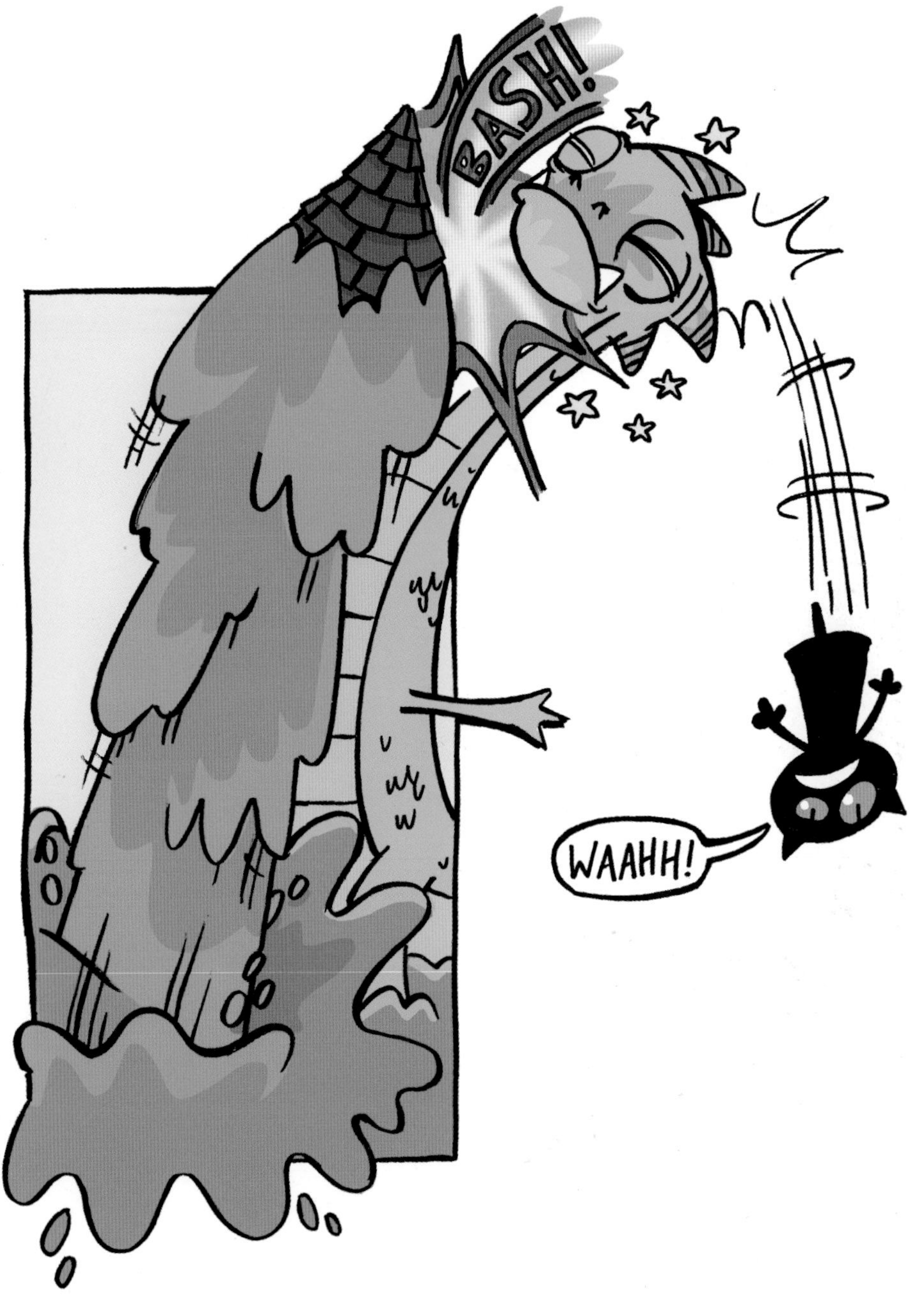
BASH!
WAAHH!

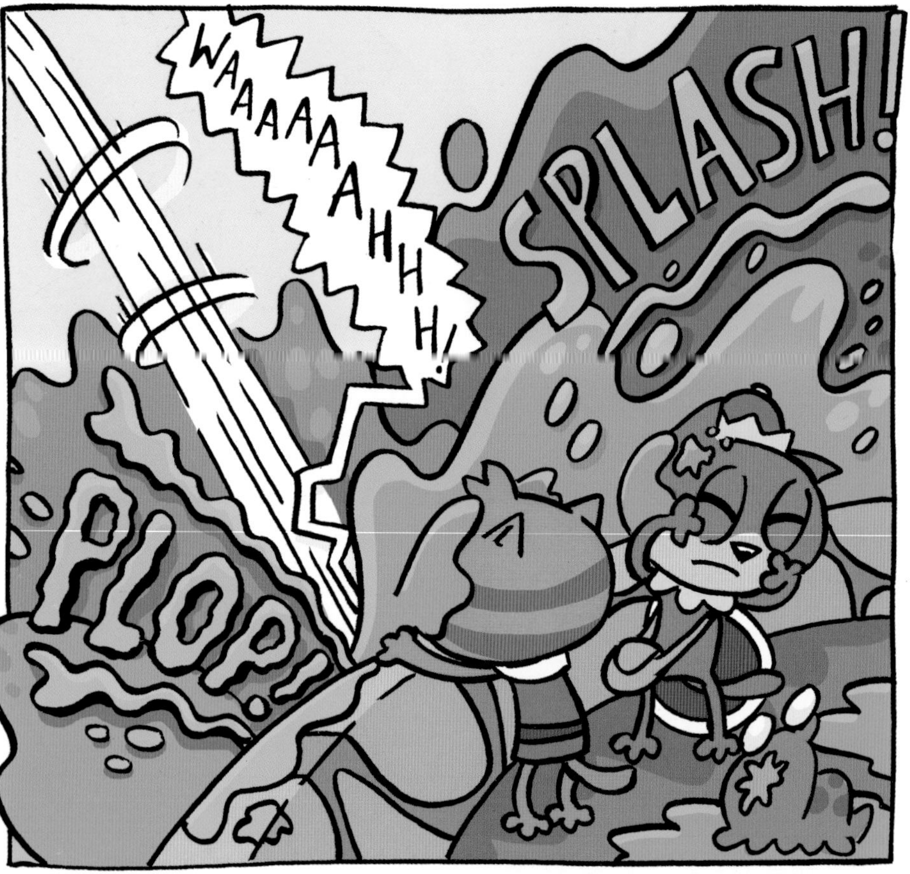
WAAAAAAAHHHH!
SPLASH!
PLOP!

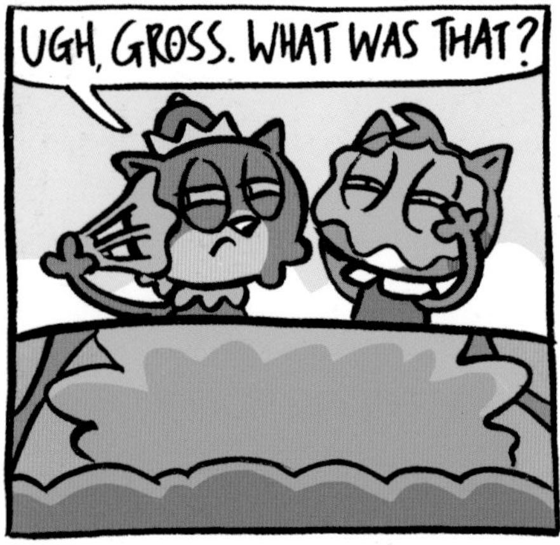
UGH, GROSS. WHAT WAS THAT?

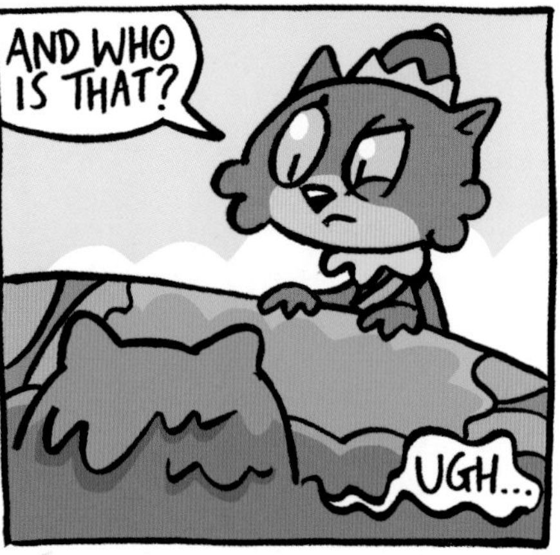
AND WHO IS THAT?
UGH...

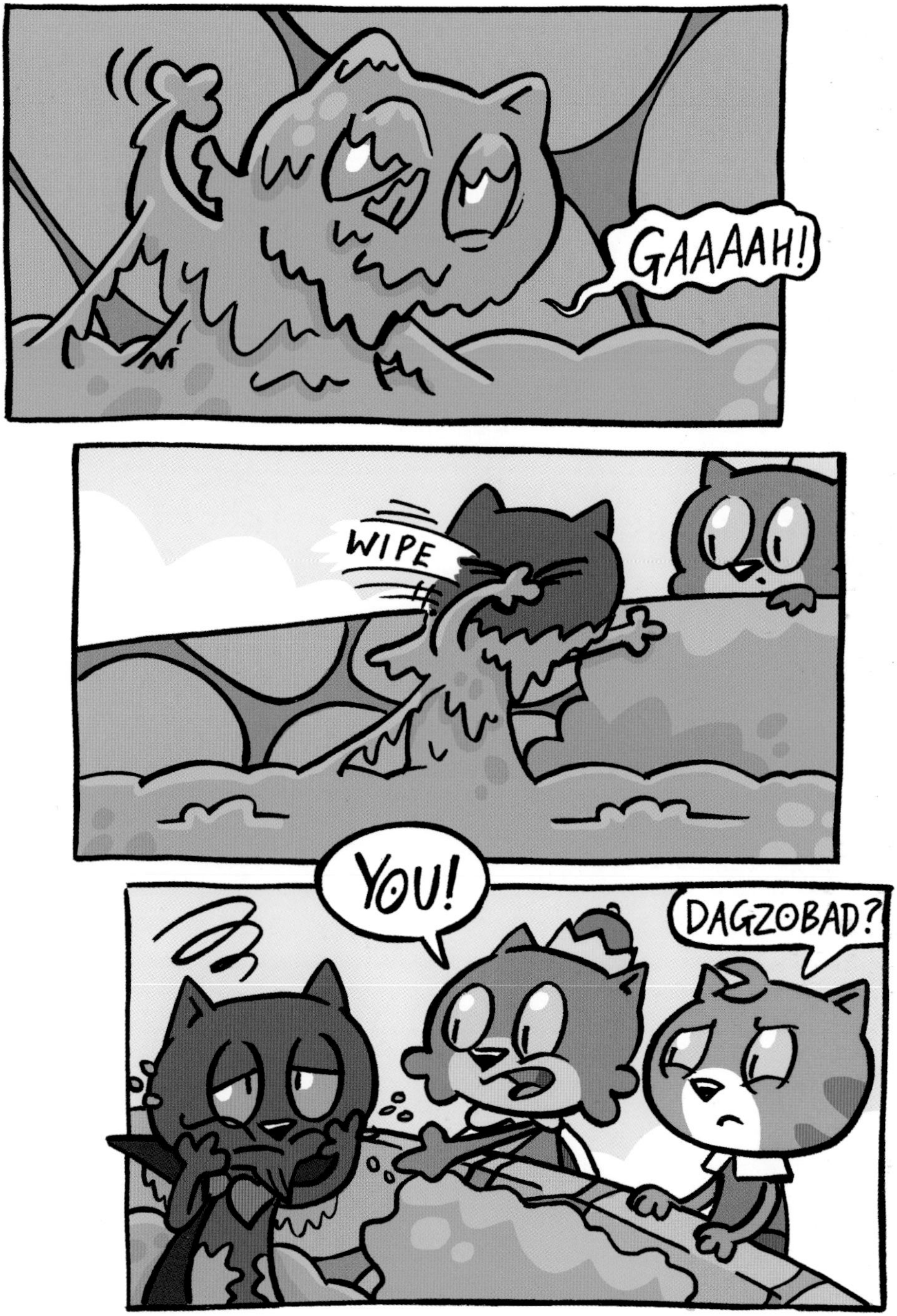
GAAAAH!
WIPE
YOU!
DAGZOBAD?

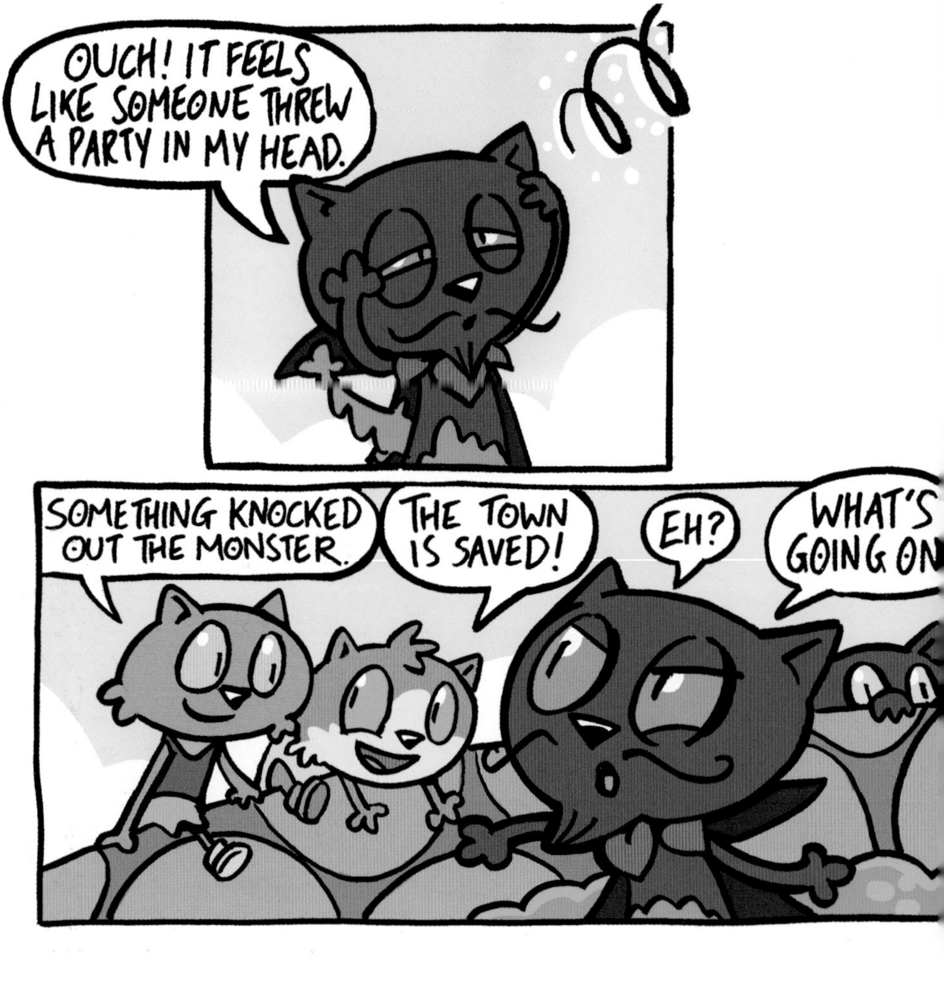
OUCH! IT FEELS LIKE SOMEONE THREW A PARTY IN MY HEAD.
SOMETHING KNOCKED OUT THE MONSTER.
THE TOWN IS SAVED!
EH?
WHAT'S GOING ON

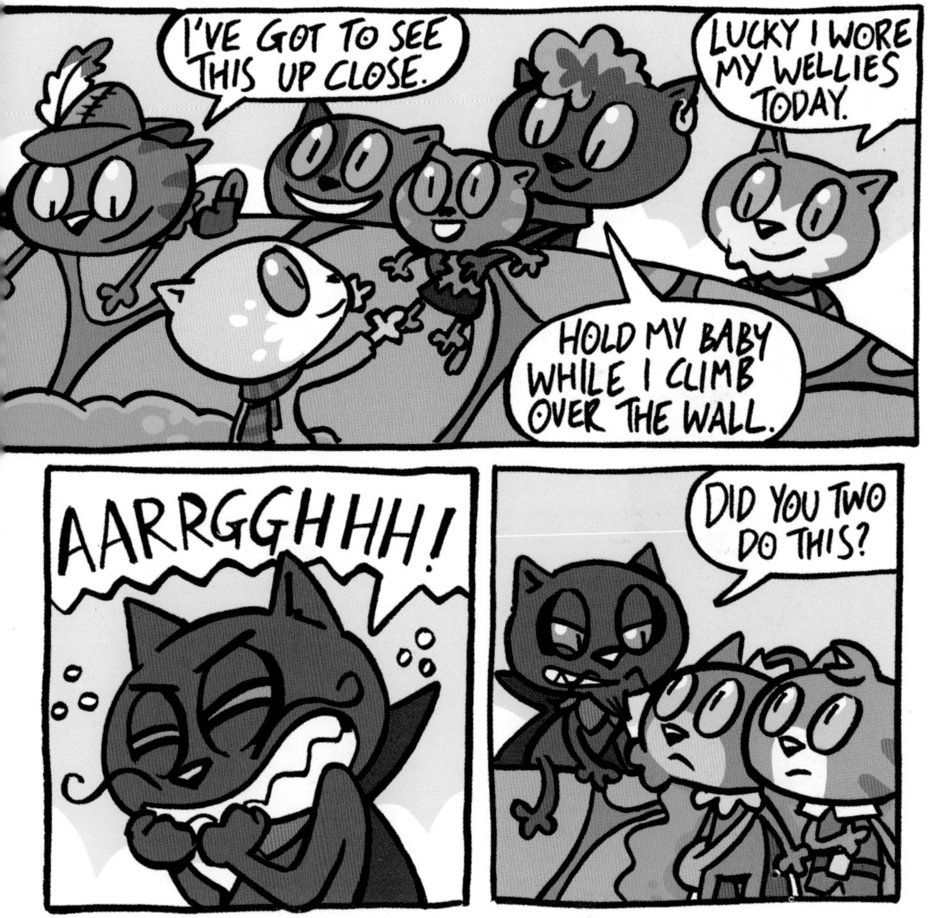
I'VE GOT TO SEE THIS UP CLOSE.
LUCKY I WORE MY WELLIES TODAY.
HOLD MY BABY WHILE I CLIMB OVER THE WALL.
AARRGGHHH!
DID YOU TWO DO THIS?

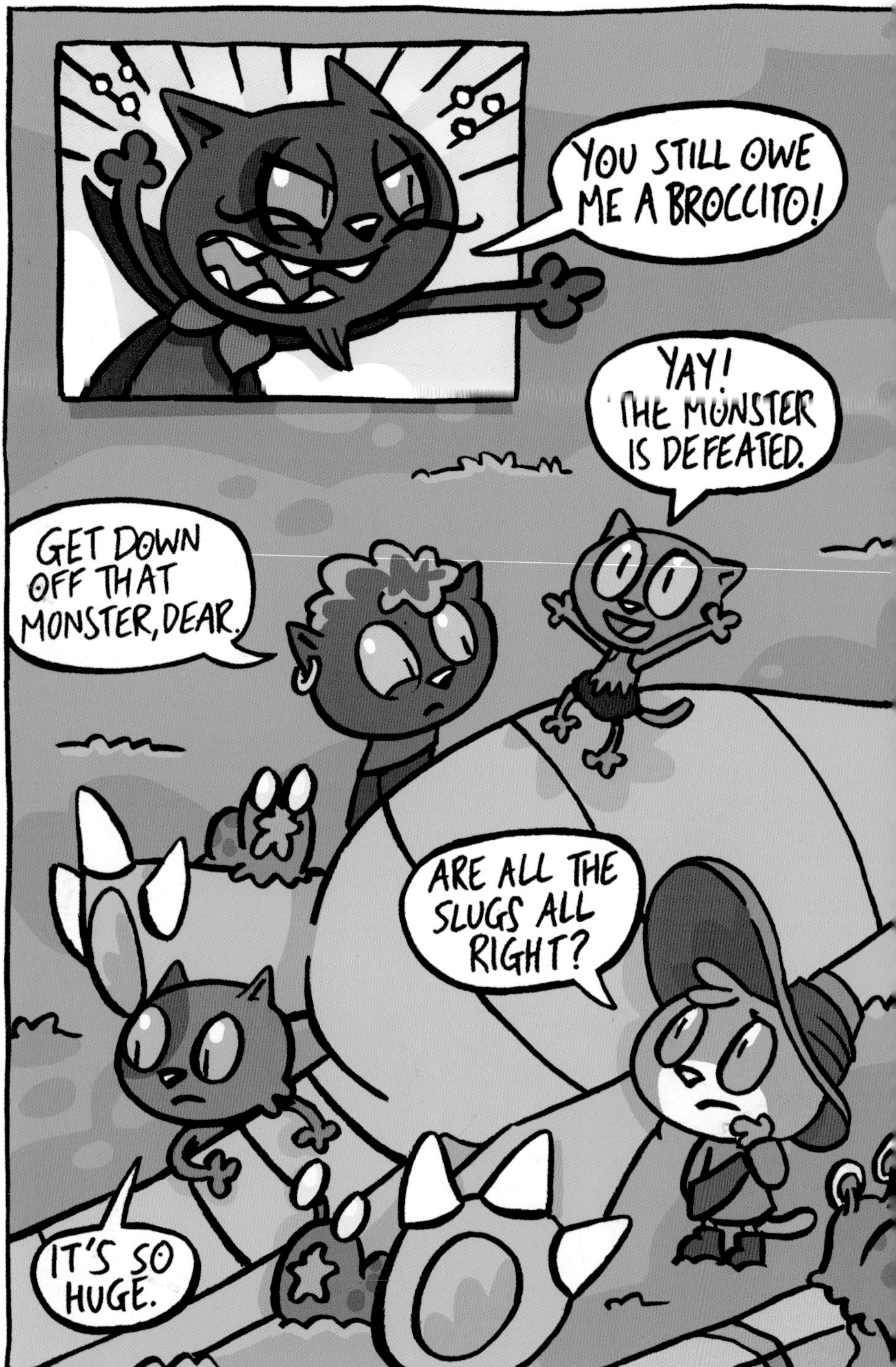
YOU STILL OWE ME A BROCCITO!
YAY! THE MONSTER IS DEFEATED.
GET DOWN OFF THAT MONSTER, DEAR.
ARE ALL THE SLUGS ALL RIGHT?
IT'S SO HUGE.

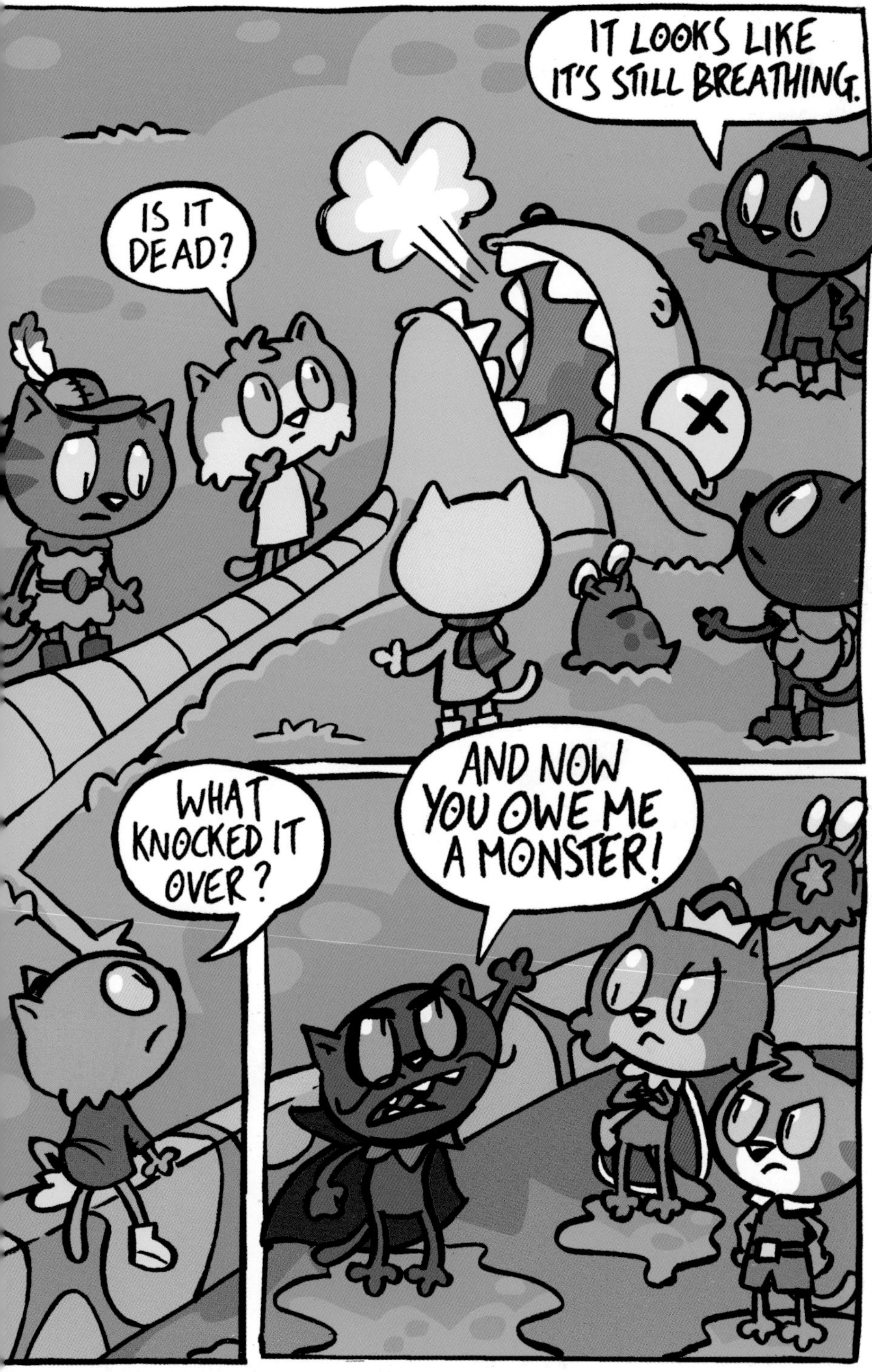
IS IT DEAD?
IT LOOKS LIKE IT'S STILL BREATHING.
WHAT KNOCKED IT OVER?
AND NOW YOU OWE ME A MONSTER!

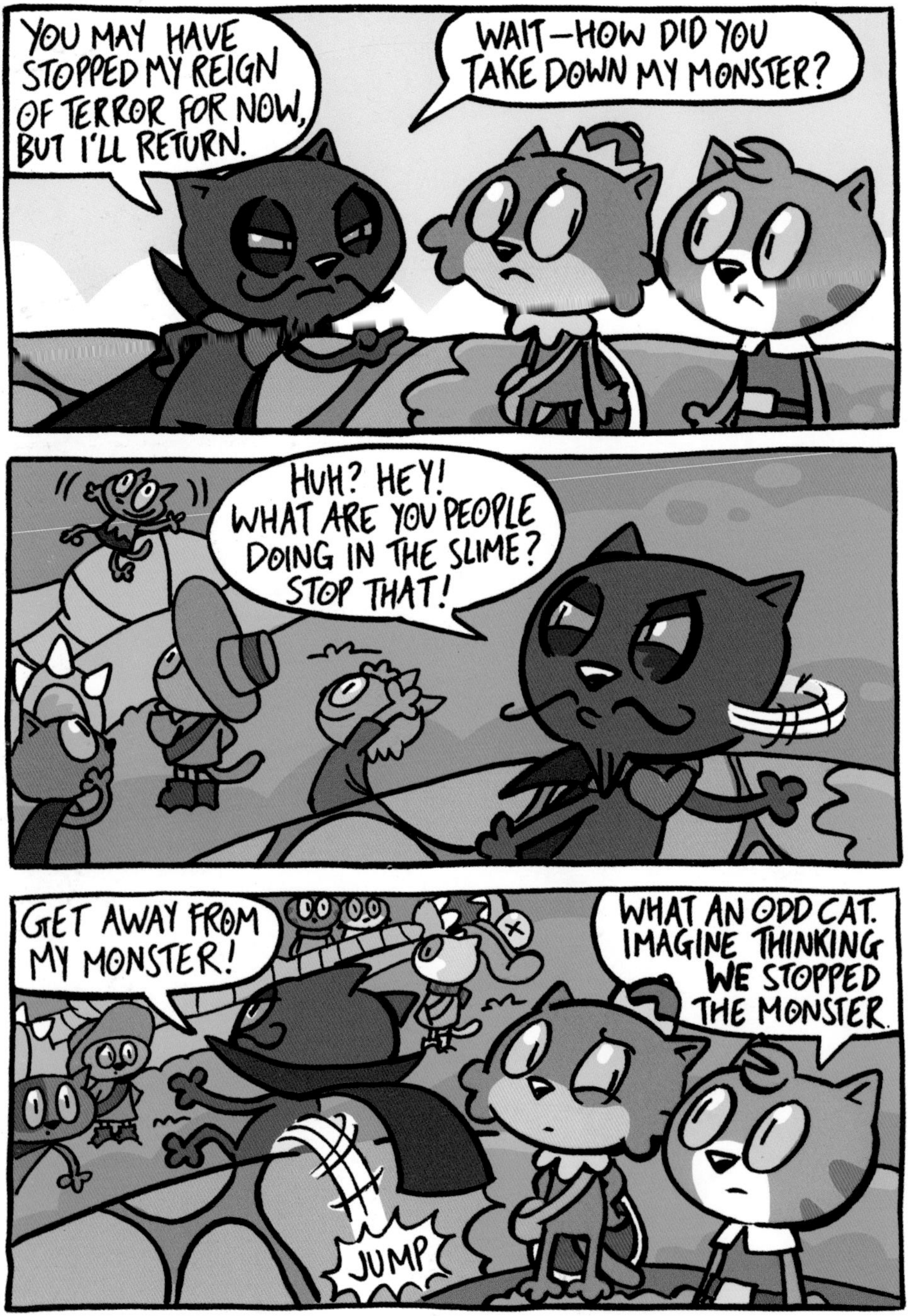
YOU MAY HAVE STOPPED MY REIGN OF TERROR FOR NOW, BUT I'LL RETURN.
WAIT—HOW DID YOU TAKE DOWN MY MONSTER?
HUH? HEY! WHAT ARE YOU PEOPLE DOING IN THE SLIME? STOP THAT!
GET AWAY FROM MY MONSTER!
WHAT AN ODD CAT. IMAGINE THINKING WE STOPPED THE MONSTER.
JUMP

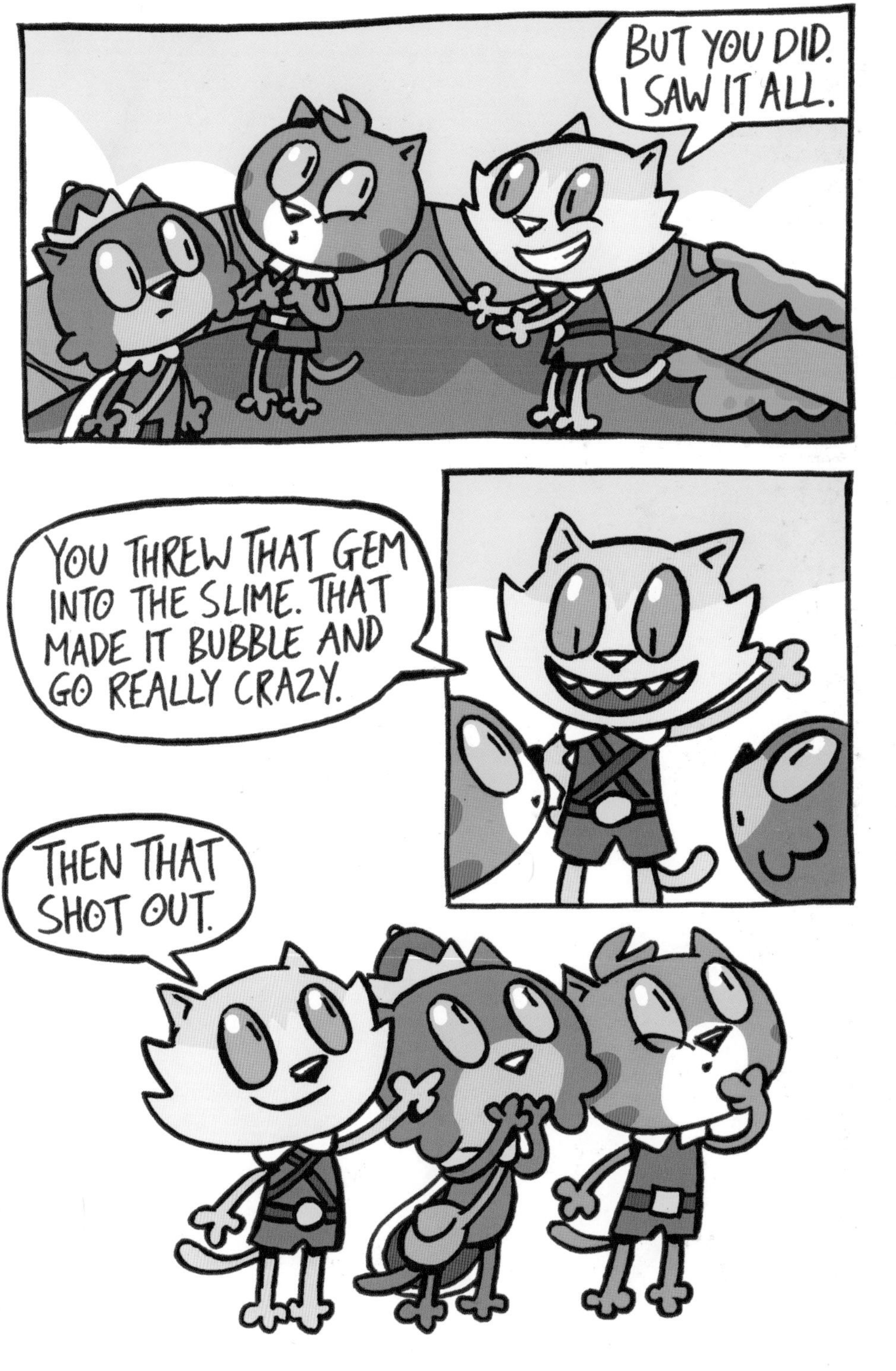
BUT YOU DID. I SAW IT ALL.
YOU THREW THAT GEM INTO THE SLIME. THAT MADE IT BUBBLE AND GO REALLY CRAZY.
THEN THAT SHOT OUT.

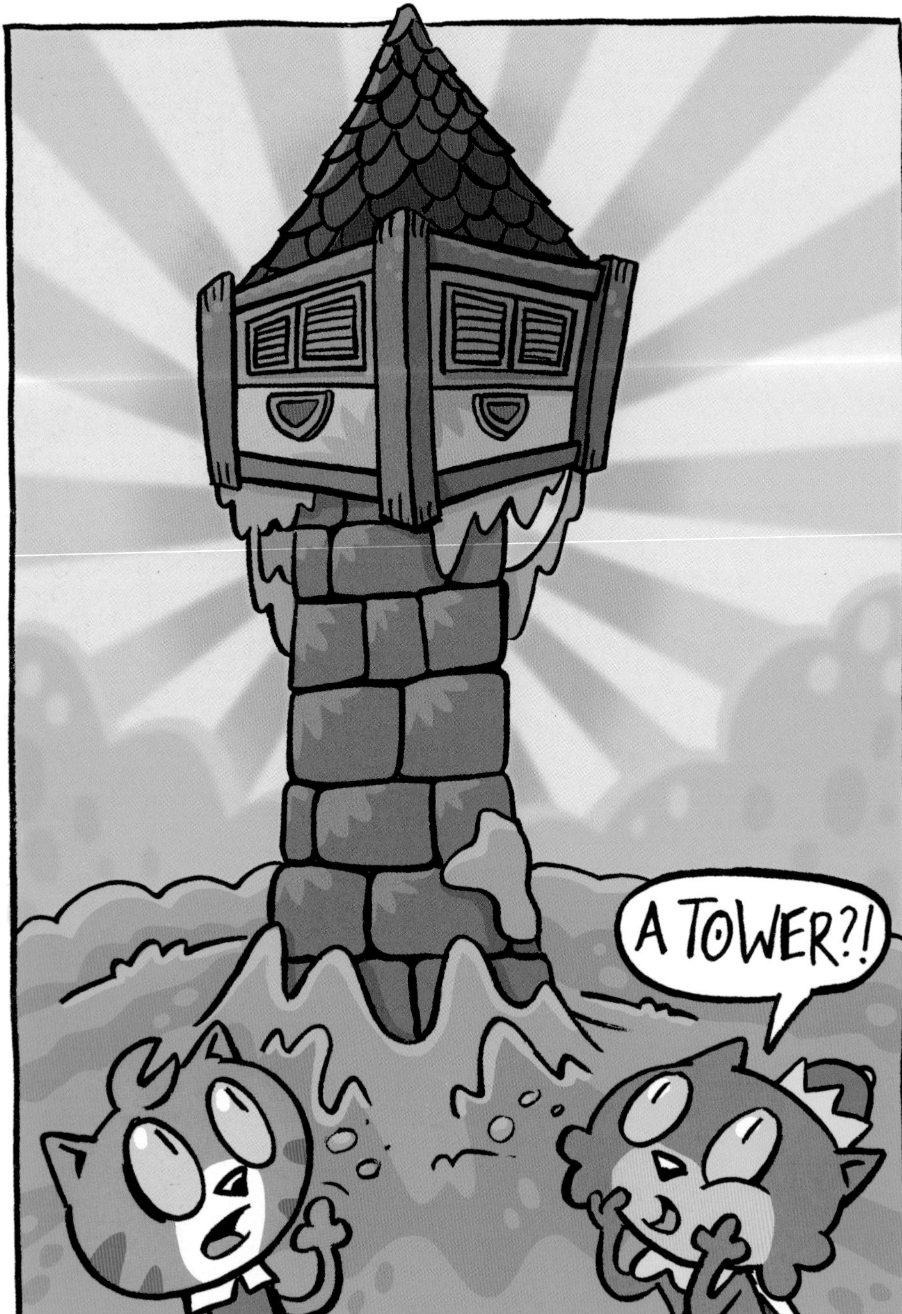
A TOWER?!

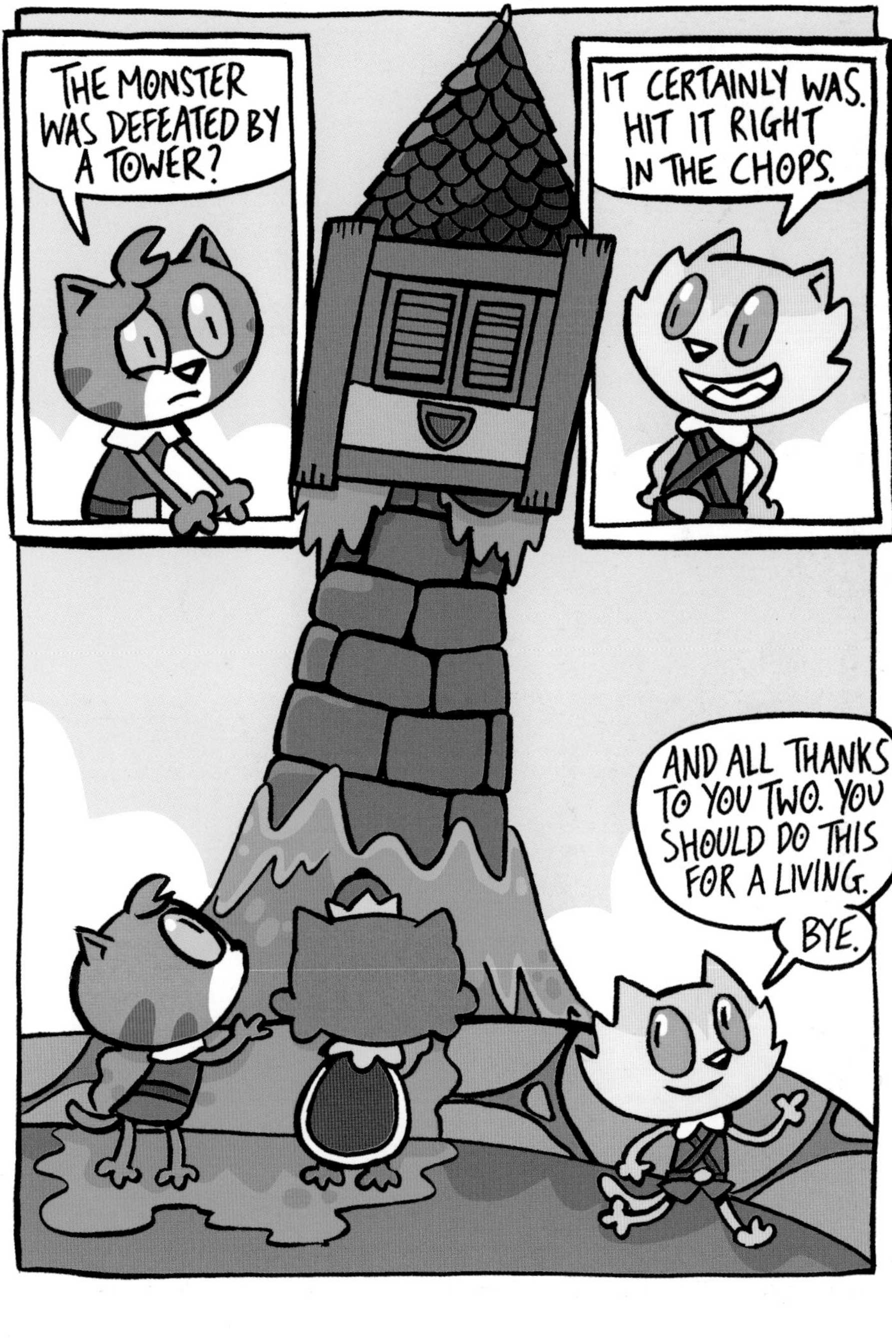
THE MONSTER WAS DEFEATED BY A TOWER?
IT CERTAINLY WAS. HIT IT RIGHT IN THE CHOPS.
AND ALL THANKS TO YOU TWO. YOU SHOULD DO THIS FOR A LIVING.
BYE.

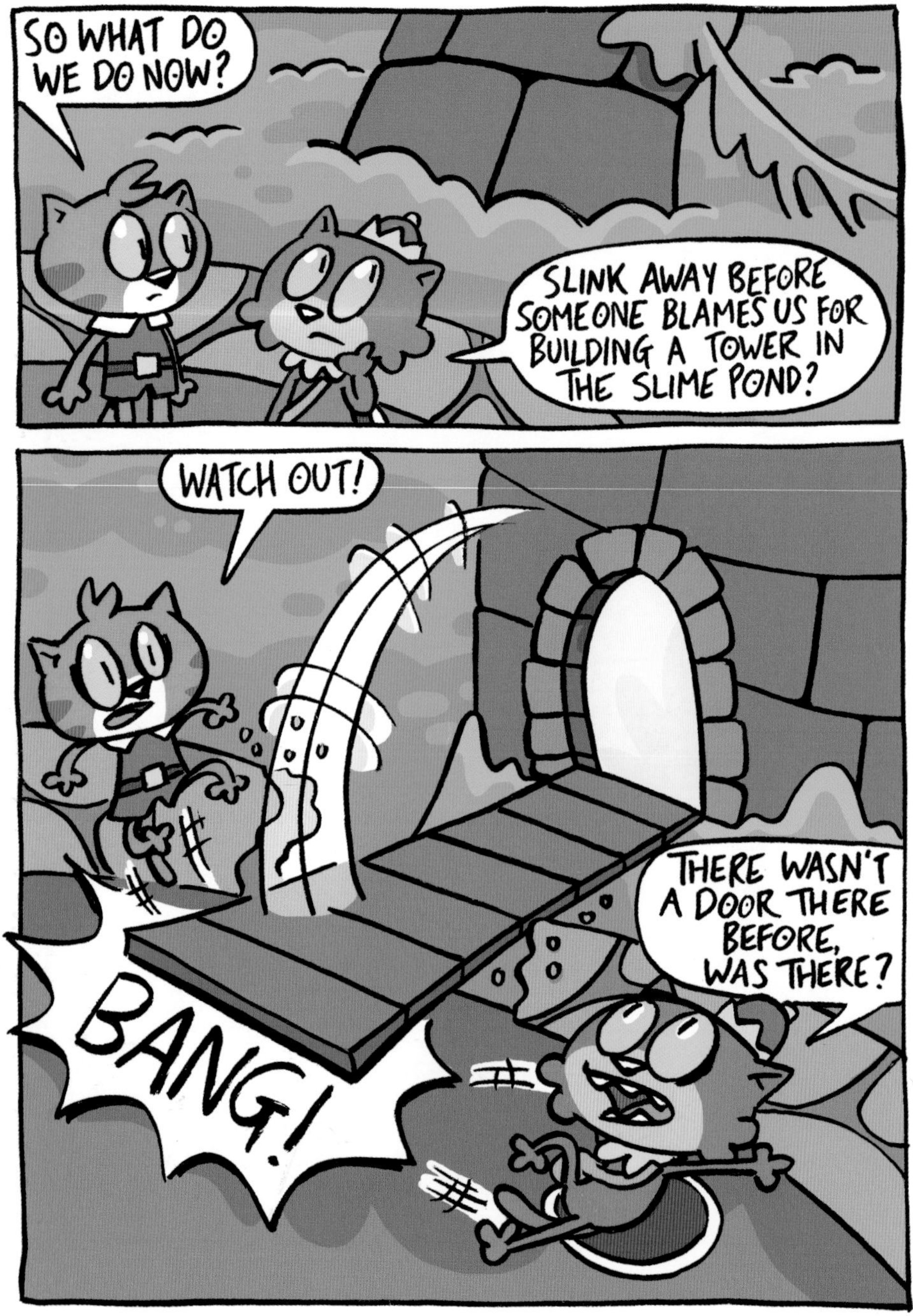
SO WHAT DO WE DO NOW?
SLINK AWAY BEFORE SOMEONE BLAMES US FOR BUILDING A TOWER IN THE SLIME POND?
WATCH OUT!
BANG!
THERE WASN'T A DOOR THERE BEFORE, WAS THERE?

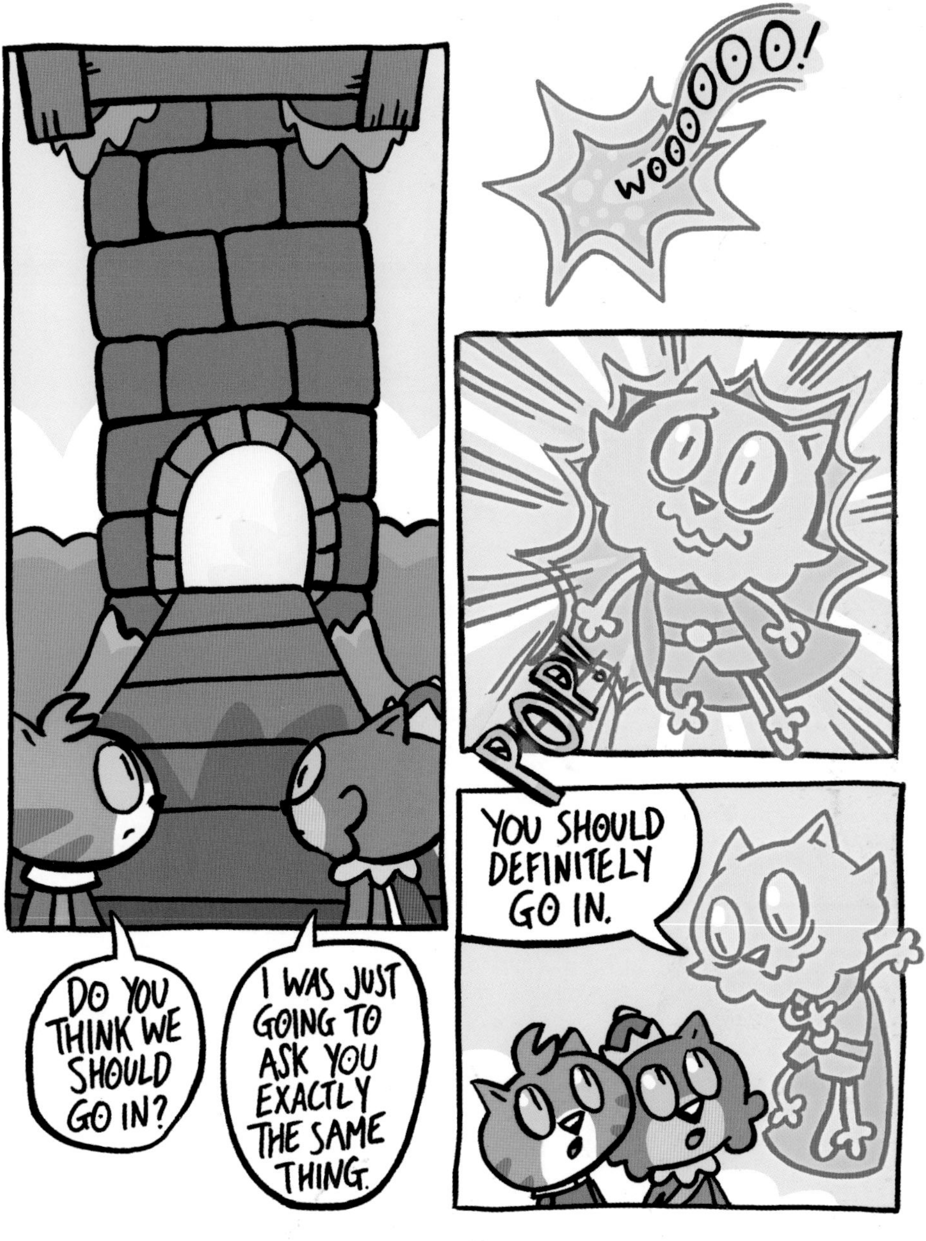
DO YOU THINK WE SHOULD GO IN?
I WAS JUST GOING TO ASK YOU EXACTLY THE SAME THING.
WOOOOOOO!
POP!
YOU SHOULD DEFINITELY GO IN.

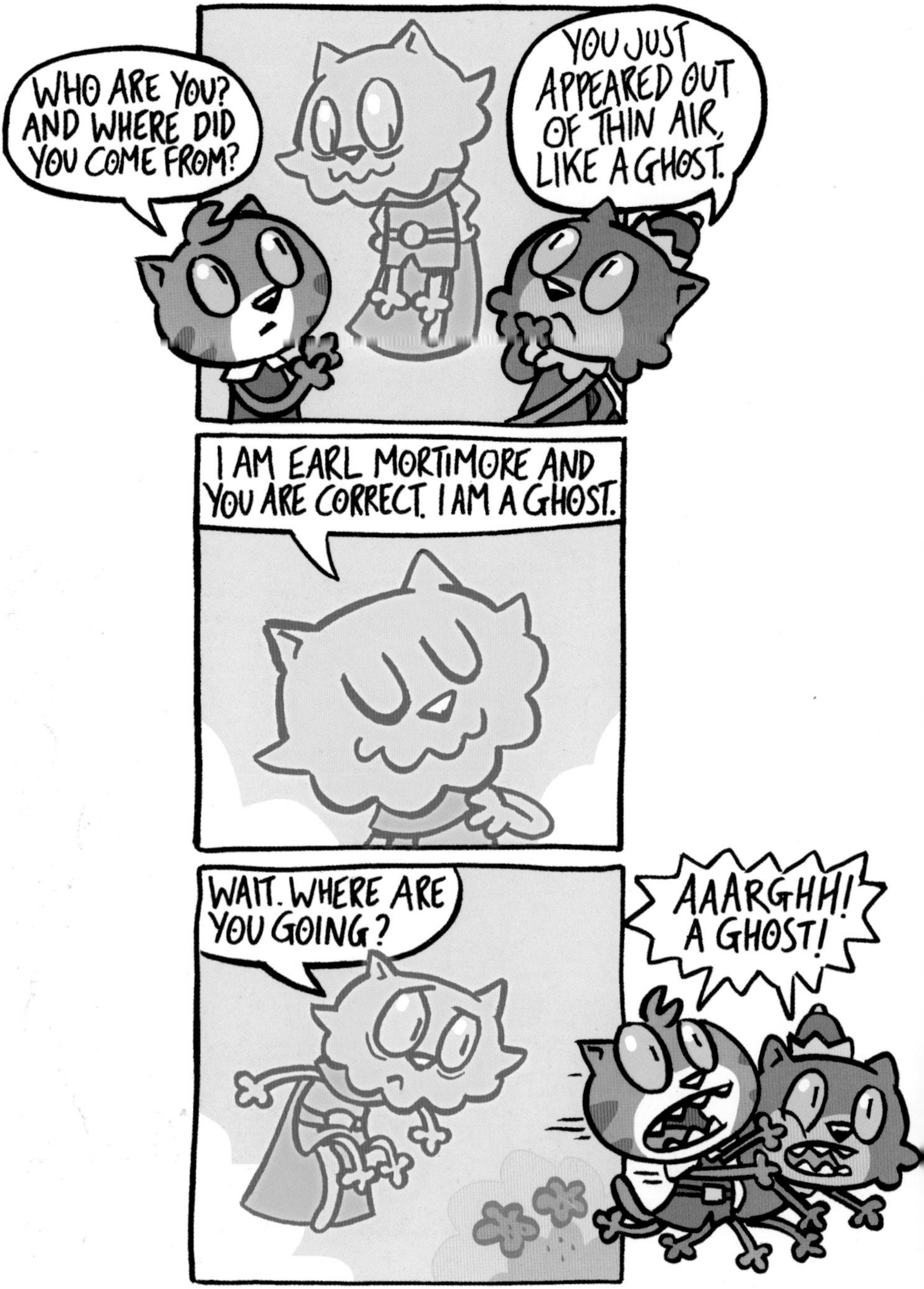
WHO ARE YOU? AND WHERE DID YOU COME FROM?
YOU JUST APPEARED OUT OF THIN AIR, LIKE A GHOST.
I AM EARL MORTIMORE AND YOU ARE CORRECT. I AM A GHOST.
AAARGHH! A GHOST!
WAIT. WHERE ARE YOU GOING?

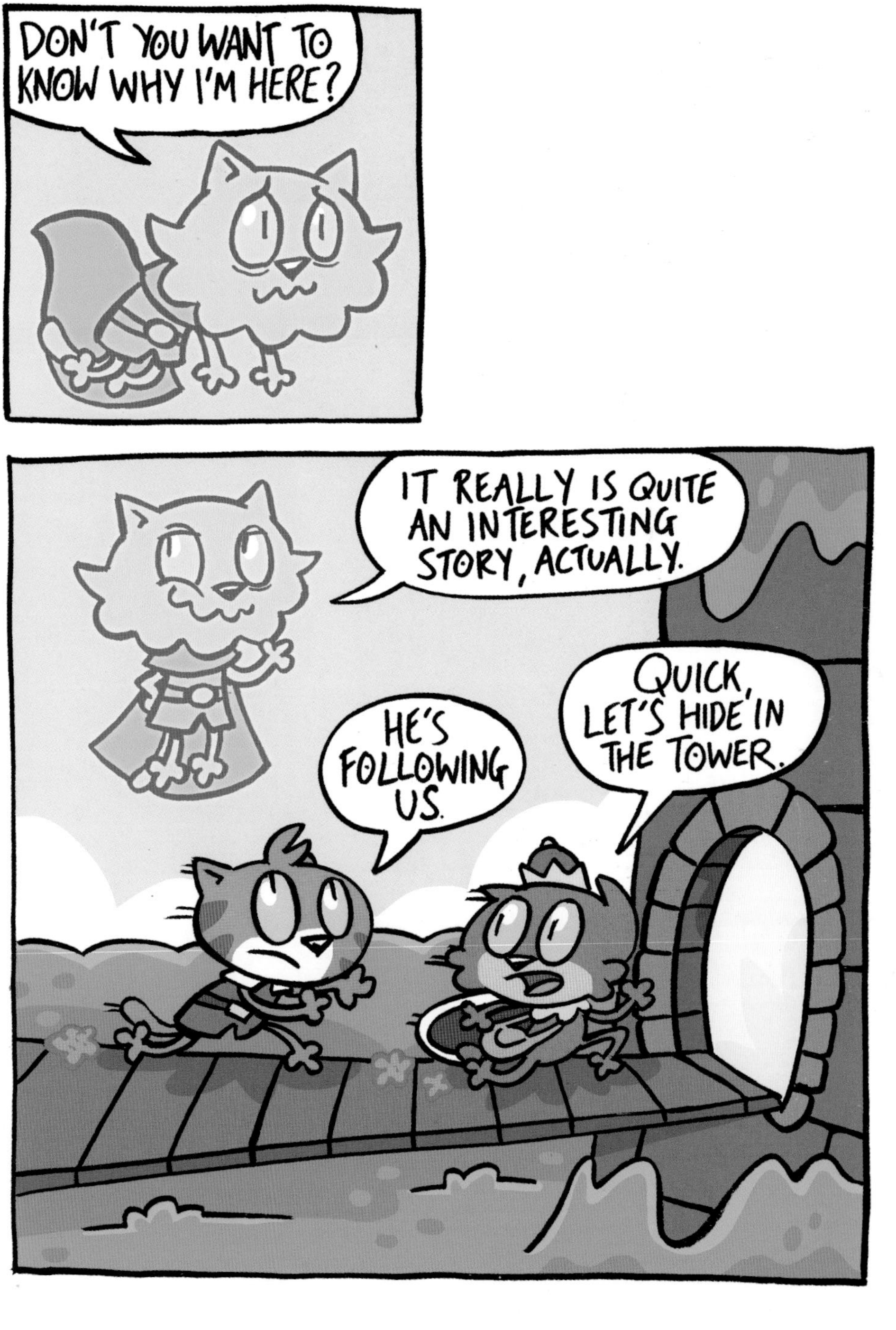
DON'T YOU WANT TO KNOW WHY I'M HERE?
IT REALLY IS QUITE AN INTERESTING STORY, ACTUALLY.
HE'S FOLLOWING US.
QUICK, LET'S HIDE IN THE TOWER.

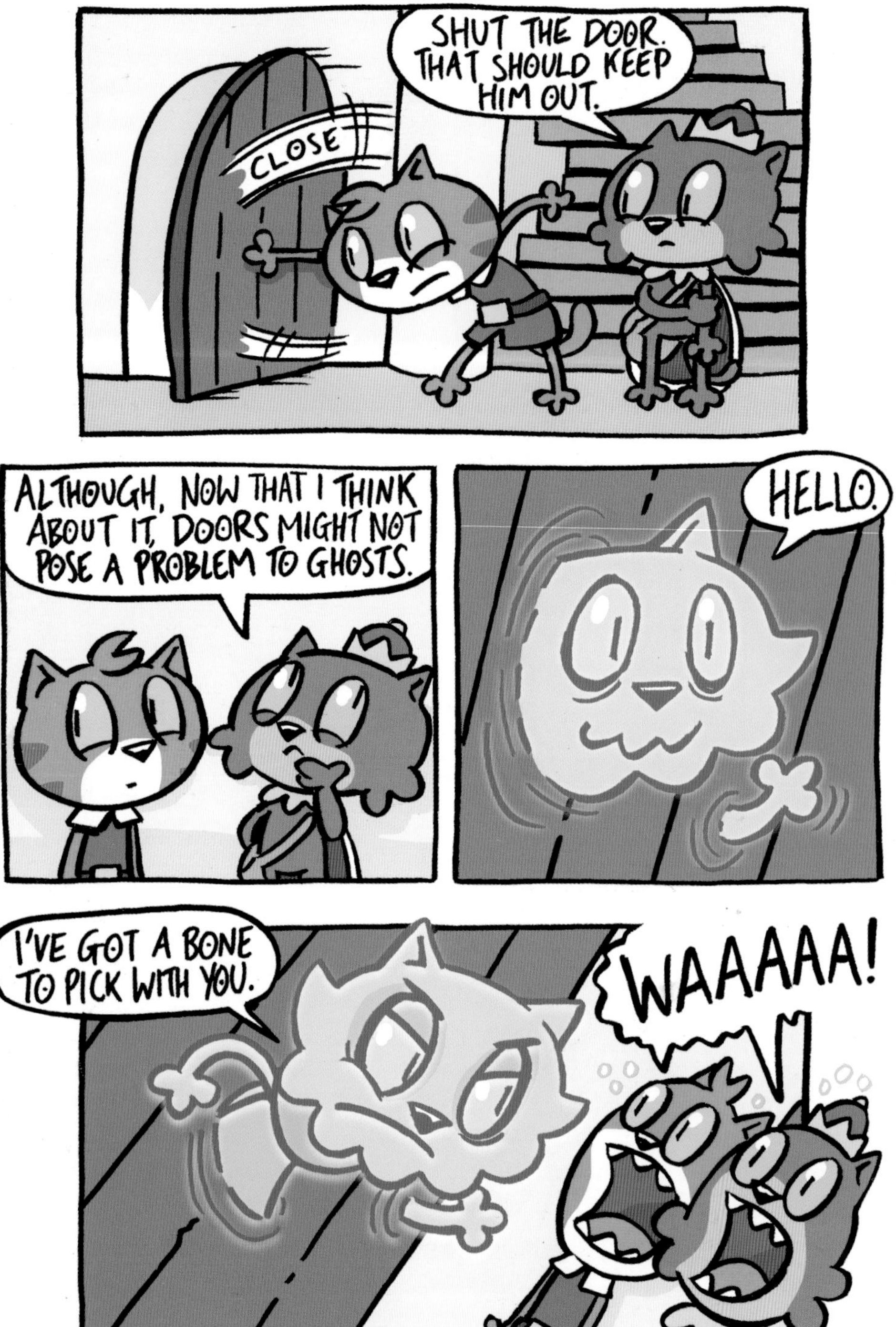
SHUT THE DOOR. THAT SHOULD KEEP HIM OUT.
CLOSE
ALTHOUGH, NOW THAT I THINK ABOUT IT, DOORS MIGHT NOT POSE A PROBLEM TO GHOSTS.
HELLO.
I'VE GOT A BONE TO PICK WITH YOU.
WAAAAA!

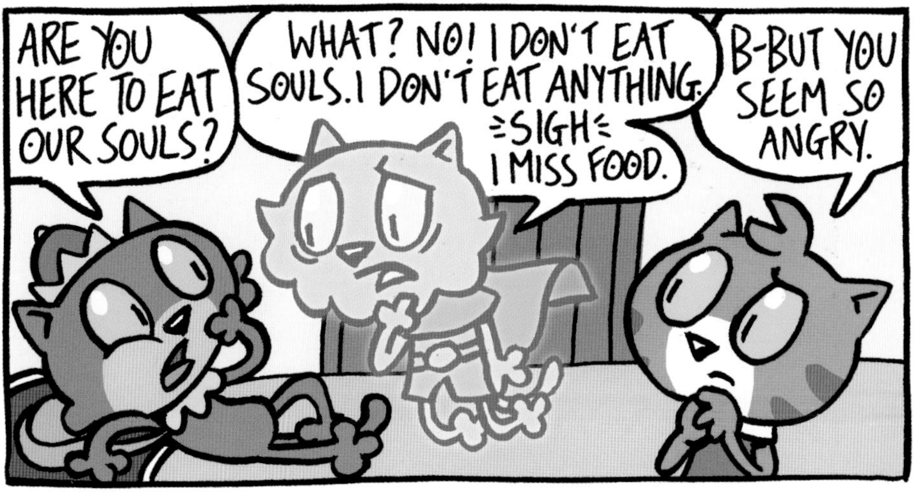
ARE YOU HERE TO EAT OUR SOULS?
WHAT? NO! I DON'T EAT SOULS. I DON'T EAT ANYTHING.
SIGH
I MISS FOOD.
B-BUT YOU SEEM SO ANGRY.

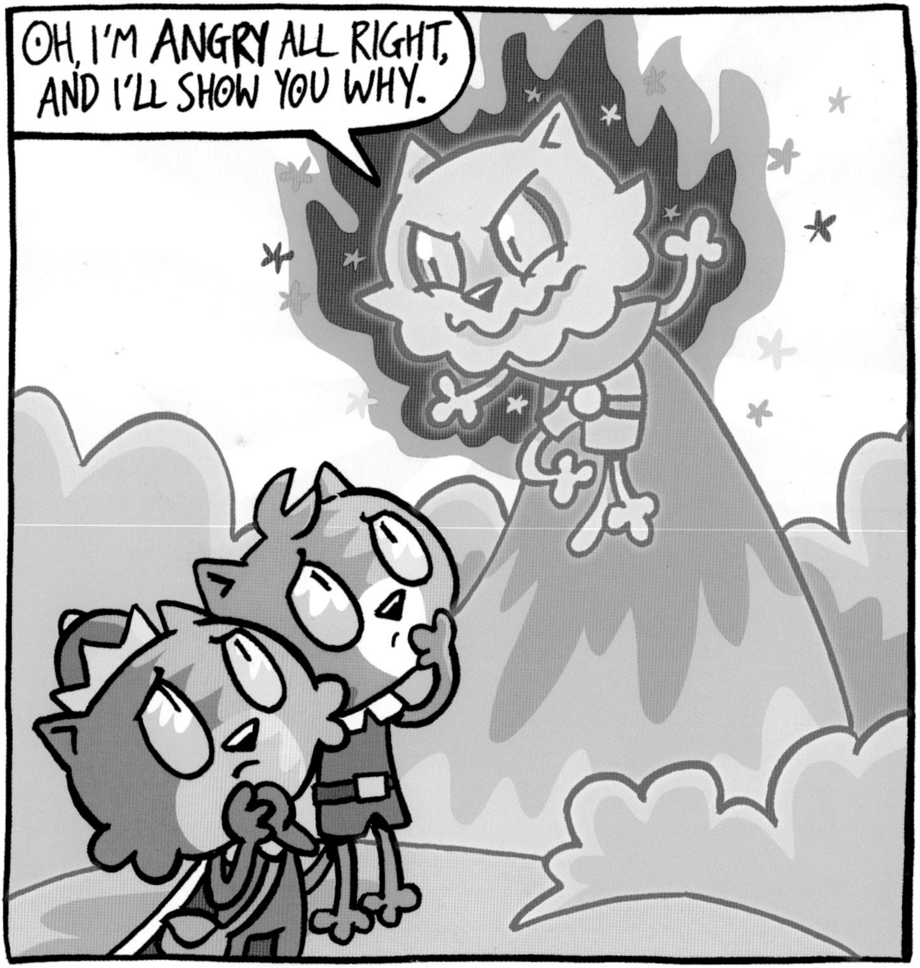
OH, I'M ANGRY ALL RIGHT, AND I'LL SHOW YOU WHY.

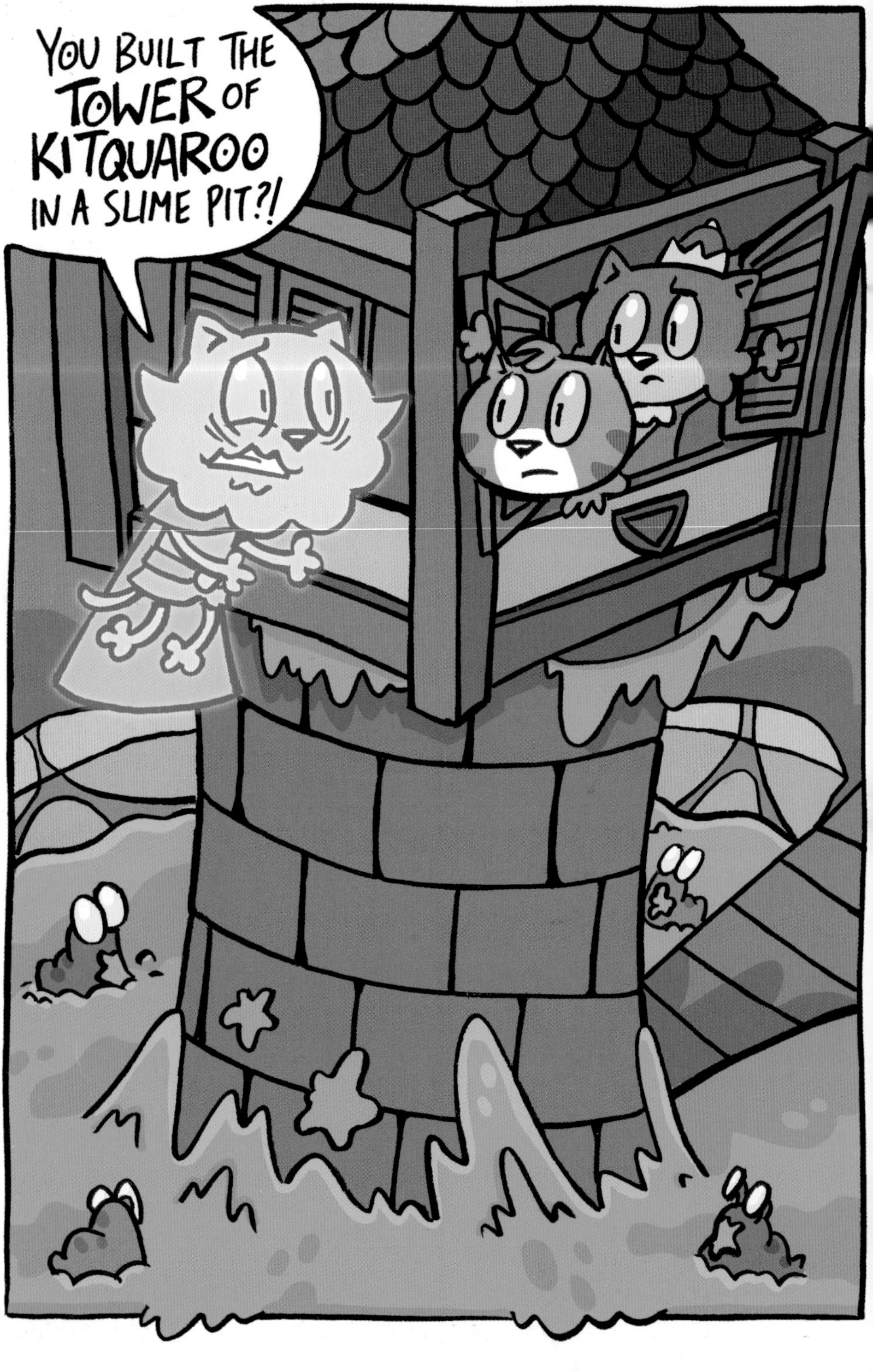
YOU BUILT THE TOWER OF KITQUAROO IN A SLIME PIT?!

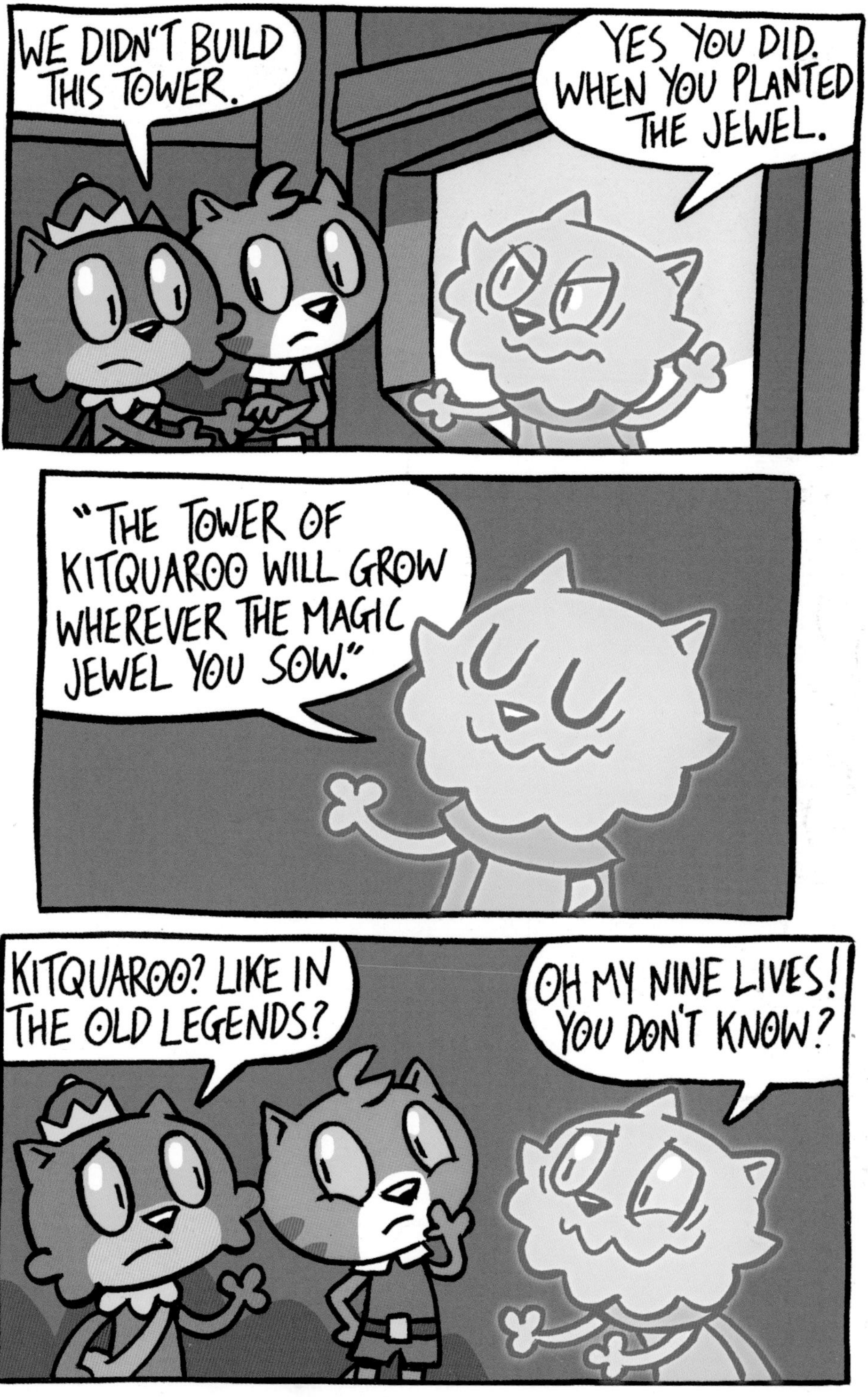
WE DIDN'T BUILD THIS TOWER.
YES YOU DID. WHEN YOU PLANTED THE JEWEL.
"THE TOWER OF KITQUAROO WILL GROW WHEREVER THE MAGIC JEWEL YOU SOW."
KITQUAROO? LIKE IN THE OLD LEGENDS?
OH MY NINE LIVES! YOU DON'T KNOW?

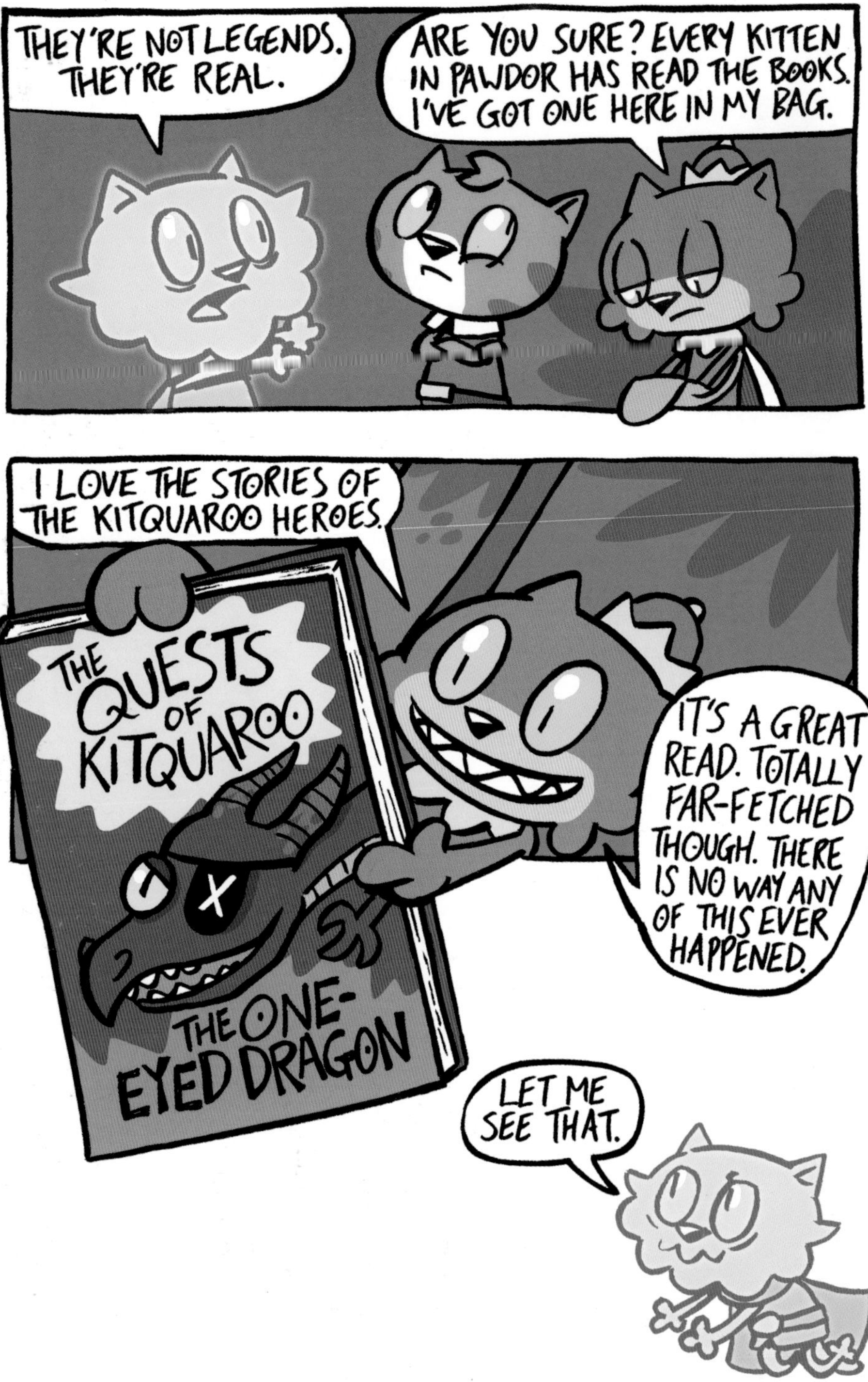
THEY'RE NOT LEGENDS. THEY'RE REAL.
ARE YOU SURE? EVERY KITTEN IN PAWDOR HAS READ THE BOOKS. I'VE GOT ONE HERE IN MY BAG.
I LOVE THE STORIES OF THE KITQUAROO HEROES.
THE QUESTS OF KITQUAROO
THE ONE-EYED DRAGON
IT'S A GREAT READ. TOTALLY FAR-FETCHED THOUGH. THERE IS NO WAY ANY OF THIS EVER HAPPENED.
LET ME SEE THAT.

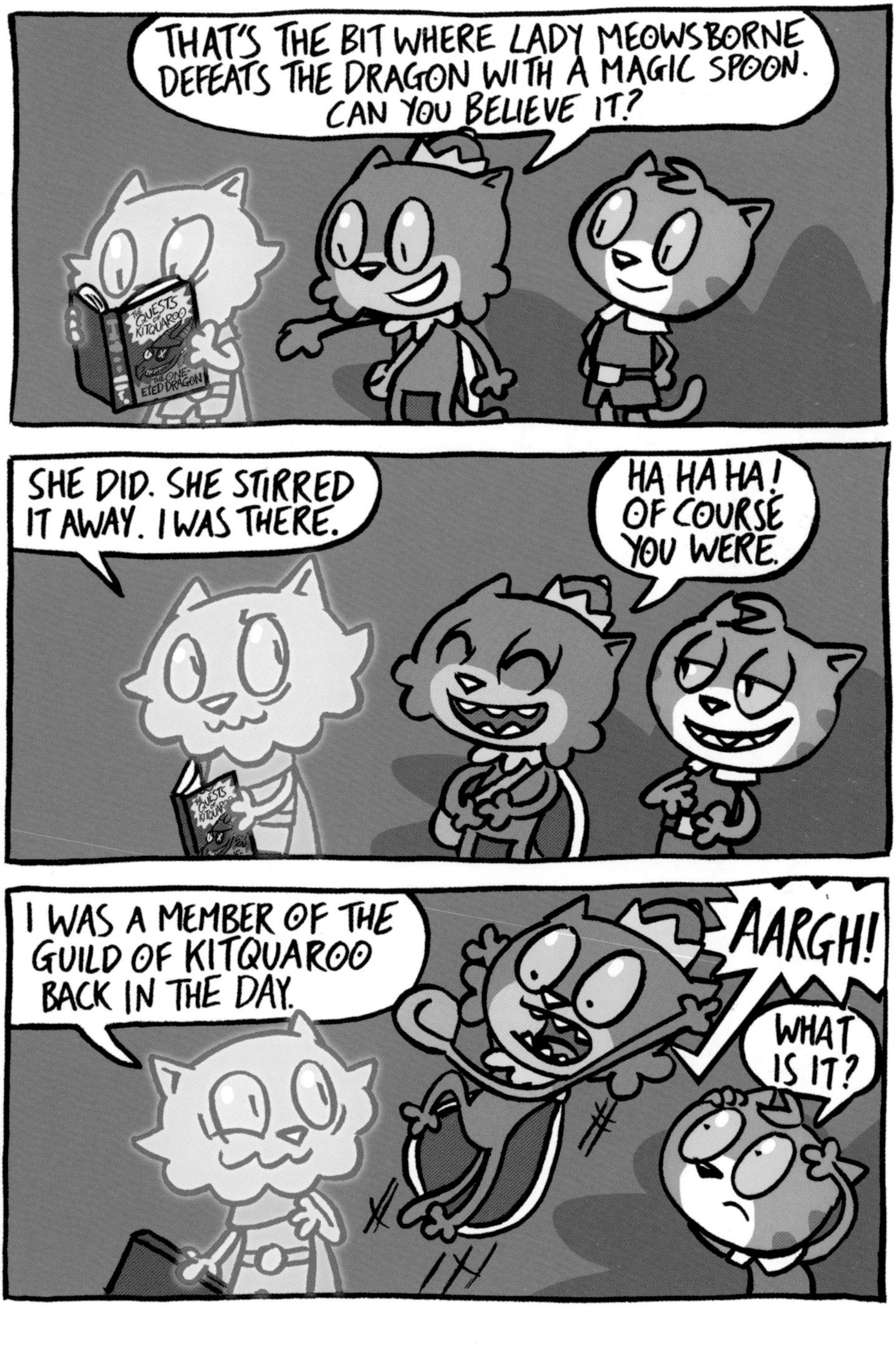
THAT'S THE BIT WHERE LADY MEOWSBORNE DEFEATS THE DRAGON WITH A MAGIC SPOON. CAN YOU BELIEVE IT?
THE QUESTS OF KITQUAROO THE ONE-EYED DRAGON
SHE DID. SHE STIRRED IT AWAY. I WAS THERE.
HA HA HA! OF COURSE YOU WERE.
I WAS A MEMBER OF THE GUILD OF KITQUAROO BACK IN THE DAY.
AARGH!
WHAT IS IT?

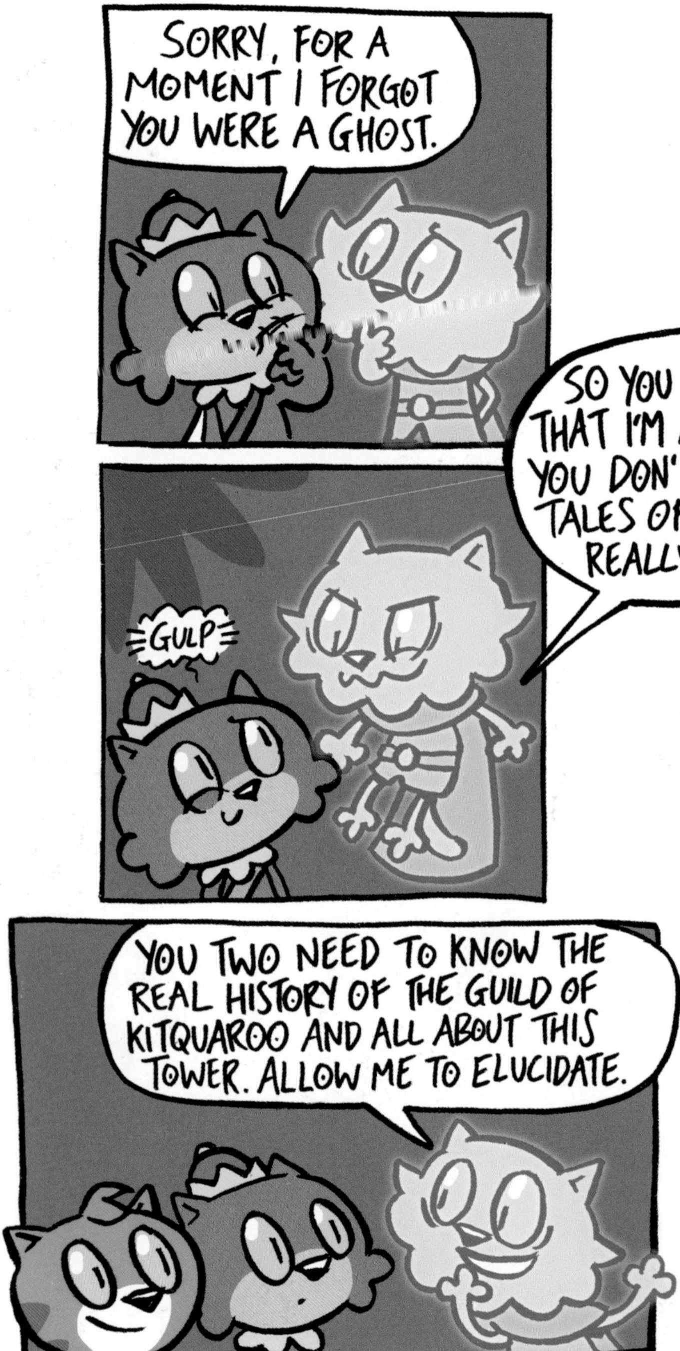

SORRY, FOR A MOMENT I FORGOT YOU WERE A GHOST.
SO YOU CAN ACCEPT THAT I'M A GHOST, BUT YOU DON'T BELIEVE THE TALES OF KITQUAROO REALLY ARE TRUE?
GULP
YOU TWO NEED TO KNOW THE REAL HISTORY OF THE GUILD OF KITQUAROO AND ALL ABOUT THIS TOWER. ALLOW ME TO ELUCIDATE.

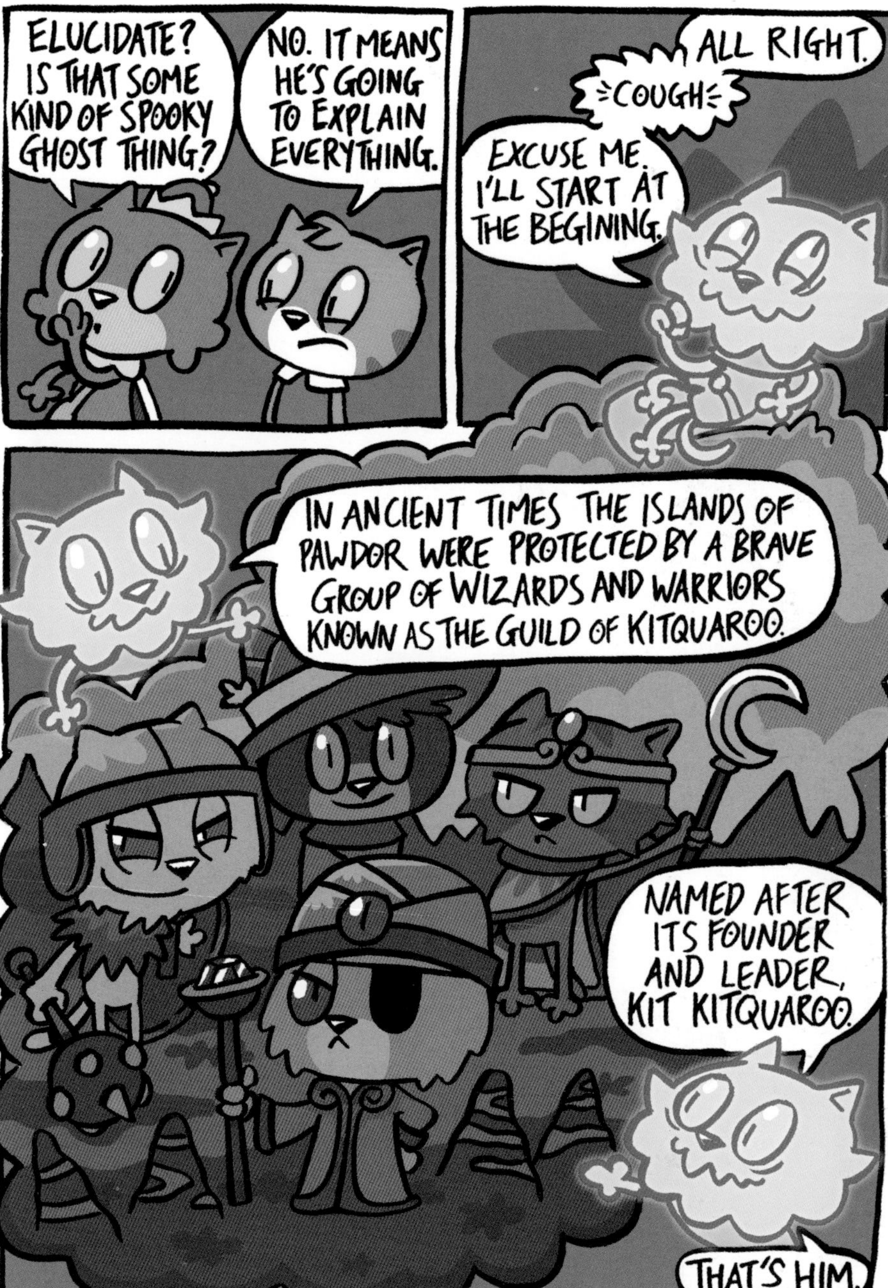
ELUCIDATE? IS THAT SOME KIND OF SPOOKY GHOST THING?
NO. IT MEANS HE'S GOING TO EXPLAIN EVERYTHING.
ALL RIGHT.
COUGH
EXCUSE ME. I'LL START AT THE BEGINING.
IN ANCIENT TIMES THE ISLANDS OF PAWDOR WERE PROTECTED BY A BRAVE GROUP OF WIZARDS AND WARRIORS KNOWN AS THE GUILD OF KITQUAROO.
NAMED AFTER ITS FOUNDER AND LEADER, KIT KITQUAROO.
THAT'S HIM.

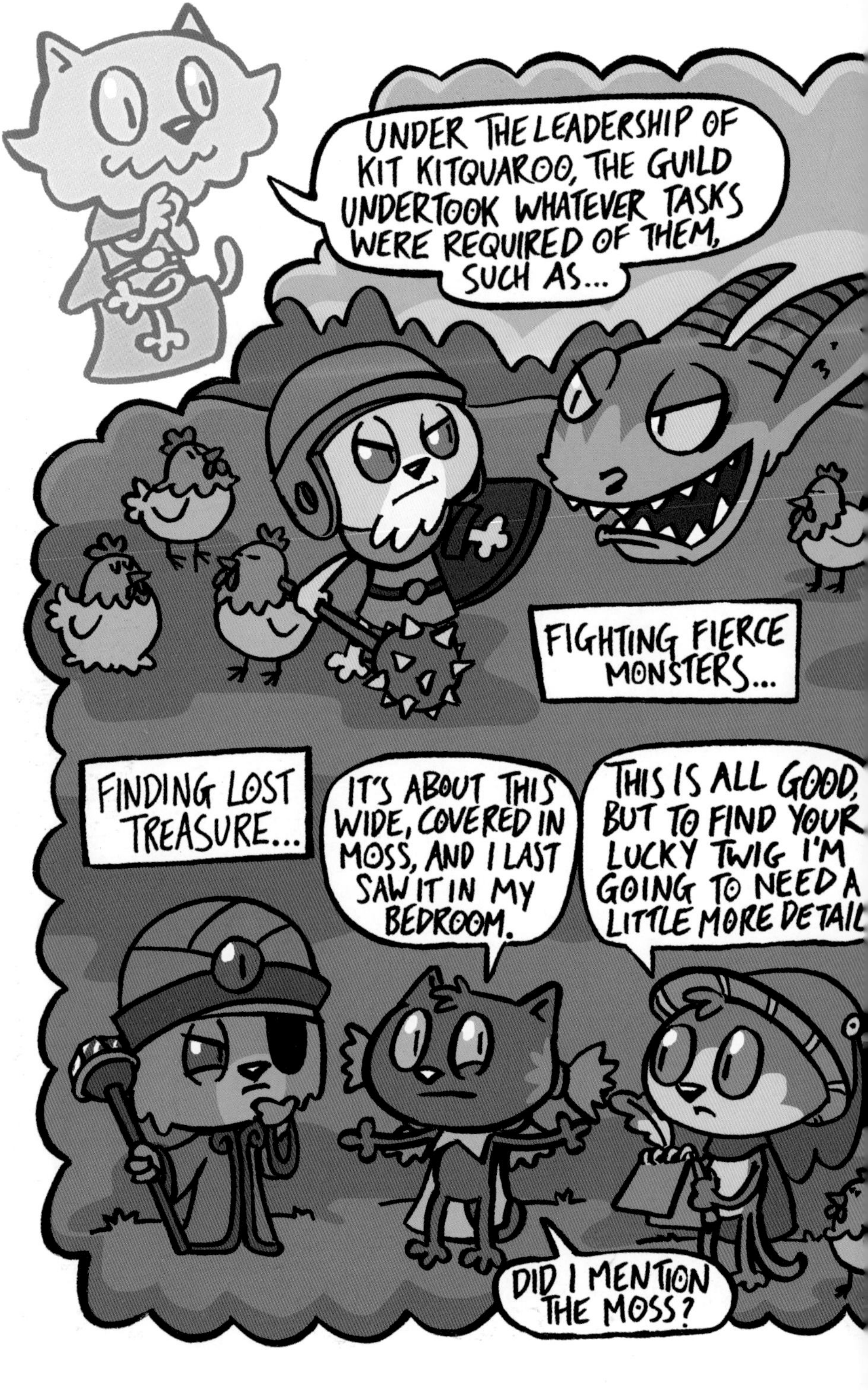
UNDER THE LEADERSHIP OF KIT KITQUAROO, THE GUILD UNDERTOOK WHATEVER TASKS WERE REQUIRED OF THEM, SUCH AS...
FIGHTING FIERCE MONSTERS...
FINDING LOST TREASURE...
IT'S ABOUT THIS WIDE, COVERED IN MOSS, AND I LAST SAW IT IN MY BEDROOM.
THIS IS ALL GOOD, BUT TO FIND YOUR LUCKY TWIG I'M GOING TO NEED A LITTLE MORE DETAIL
DID I MENTION THE MOSS?

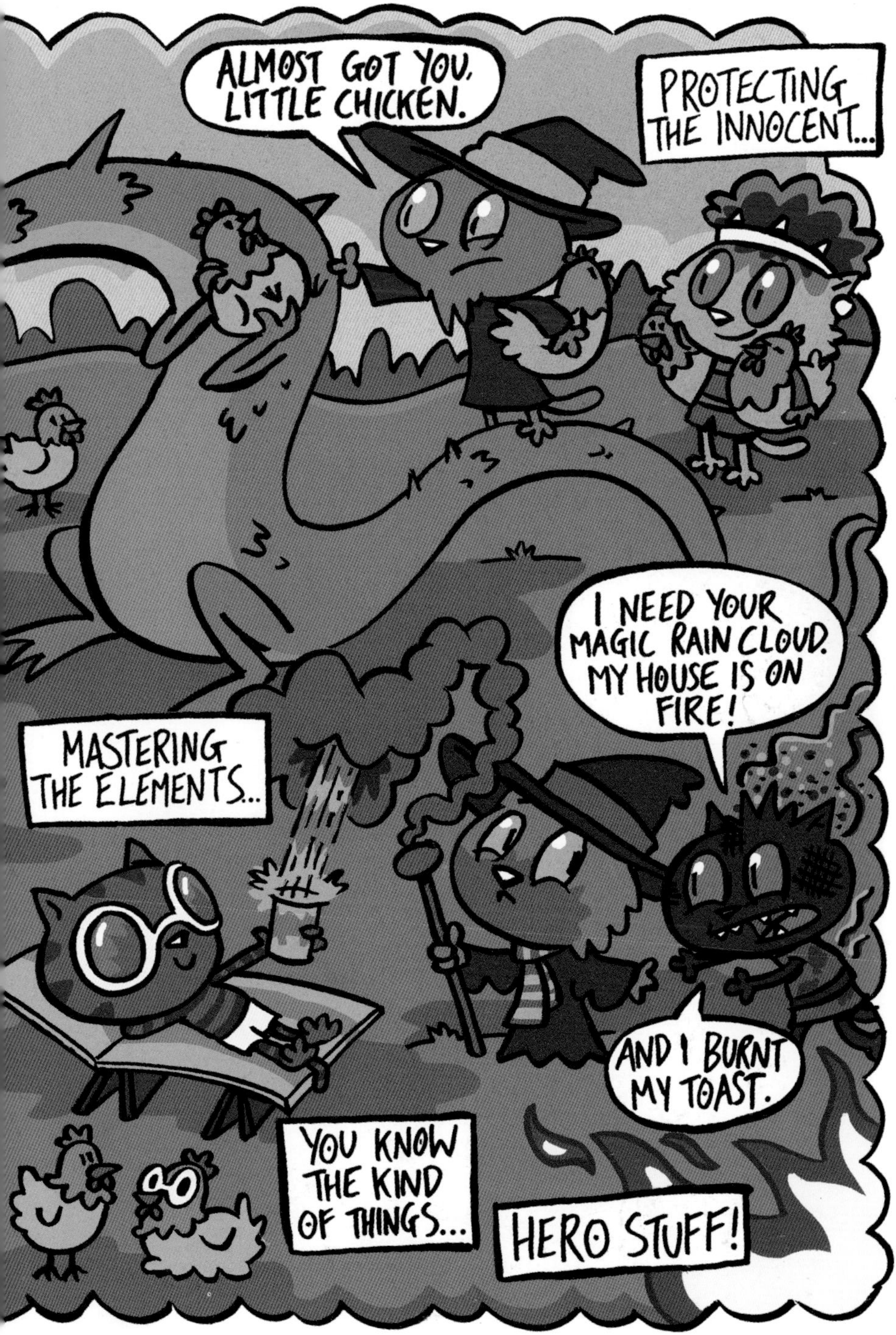
ALMOST GOT YOU, LITTLE CHICKEN.
PROTECTING THE INNOCENT...
I NEED YOUR MAGIC RAIN CLOUD. MY HOUSE IS ON FIRE!
MASTERING THE ELEMENTS...
AND I BURNT MY TOAST.
YOU KNOW THE KIND OF THINGS...
HERO STUFF!

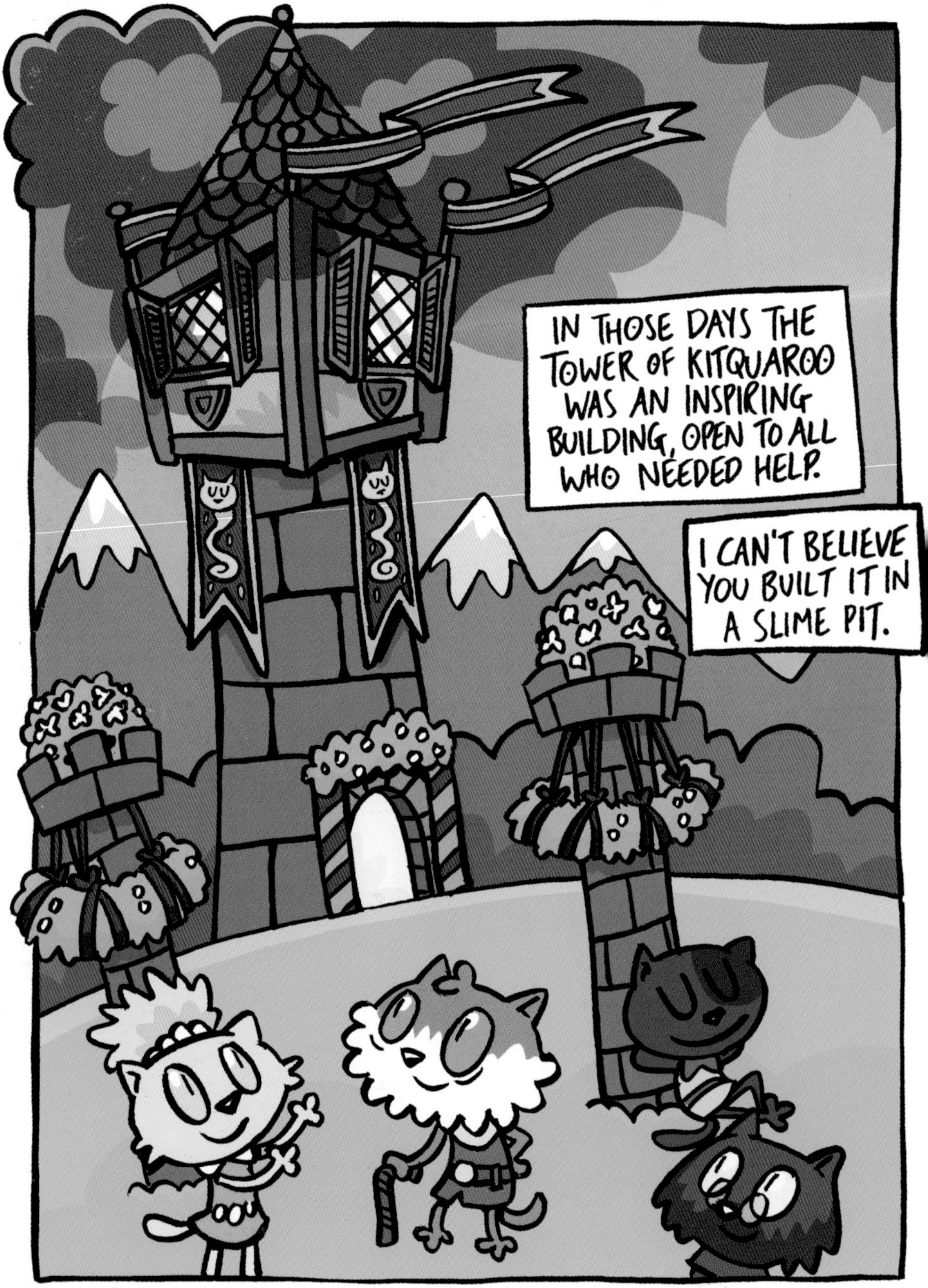
IN THOSE DAYS THE TOWER OF KITQUAROO WAS AN INSPIRING BUILDING, OPEN TO ALL WHO NEEDED HELP.
I CAN'T BELIEVE YOU BUILT IT IN A SLIME PIT.

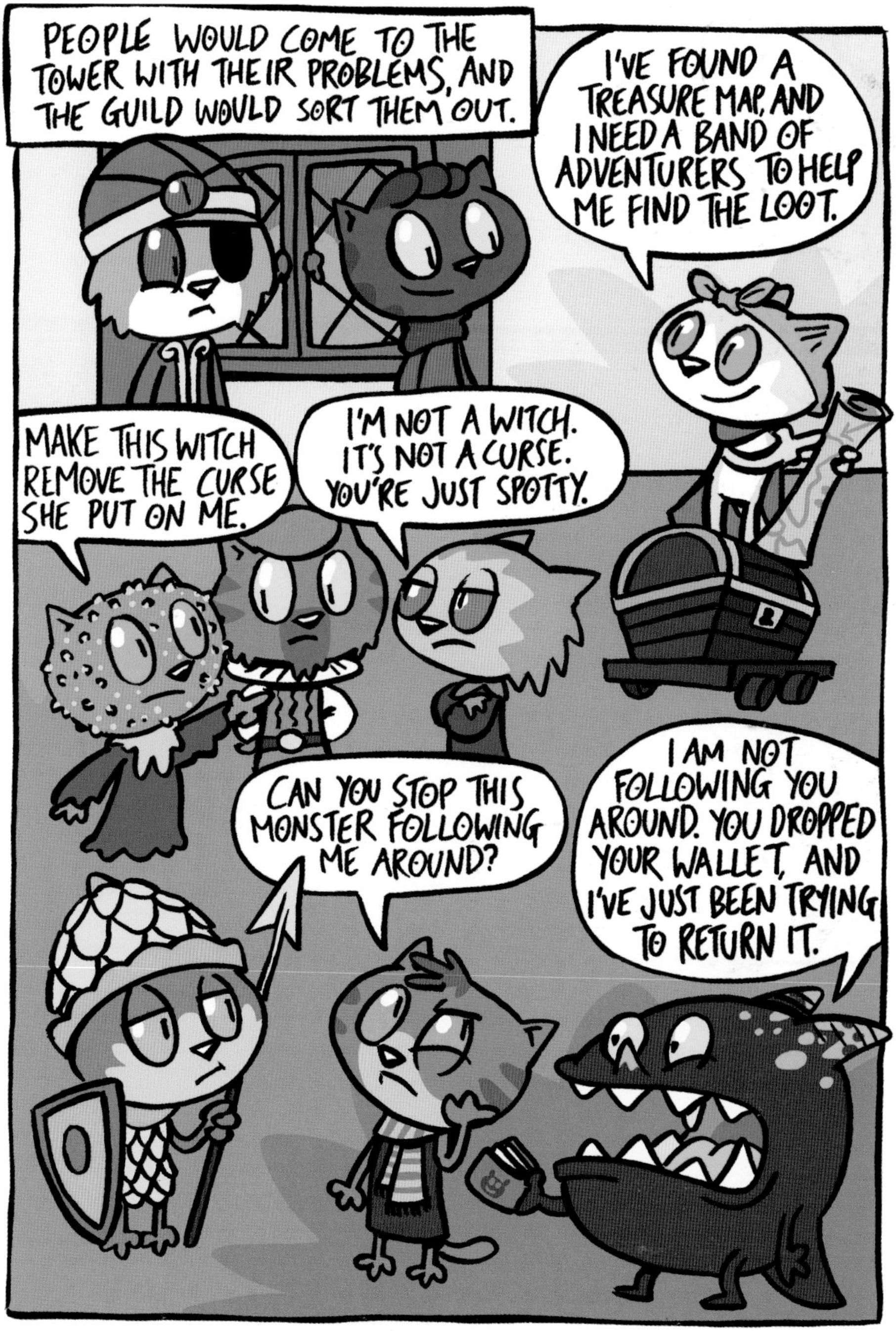
PEOPLE WOULD COME TO THE TOWER WITH THEIR PROBLEMS, AND THE GUILD WOULD SORT THEM OUT.
I'VE FOUND A TREASURE MAP, AND I NEED A BAND OF ADVENTURERS TO HELP ME FIND THE LOOT.
MAKE THIS WITCH REMOVE THE CURSE SHE PUT ON ME.
I'M NOT A WITCH. IT'S NOT A CURSE. YOU'RE JUST SPOTTY.
CAN YOU STOP THIS MONSTER FOLLOWING ME AROUND?
I AM NOT FOLLOWING YOU AROUND. YOU DROPPED YOUR WALLET, AND I'VE JUST BEEN TRYING TO RETURN IT.

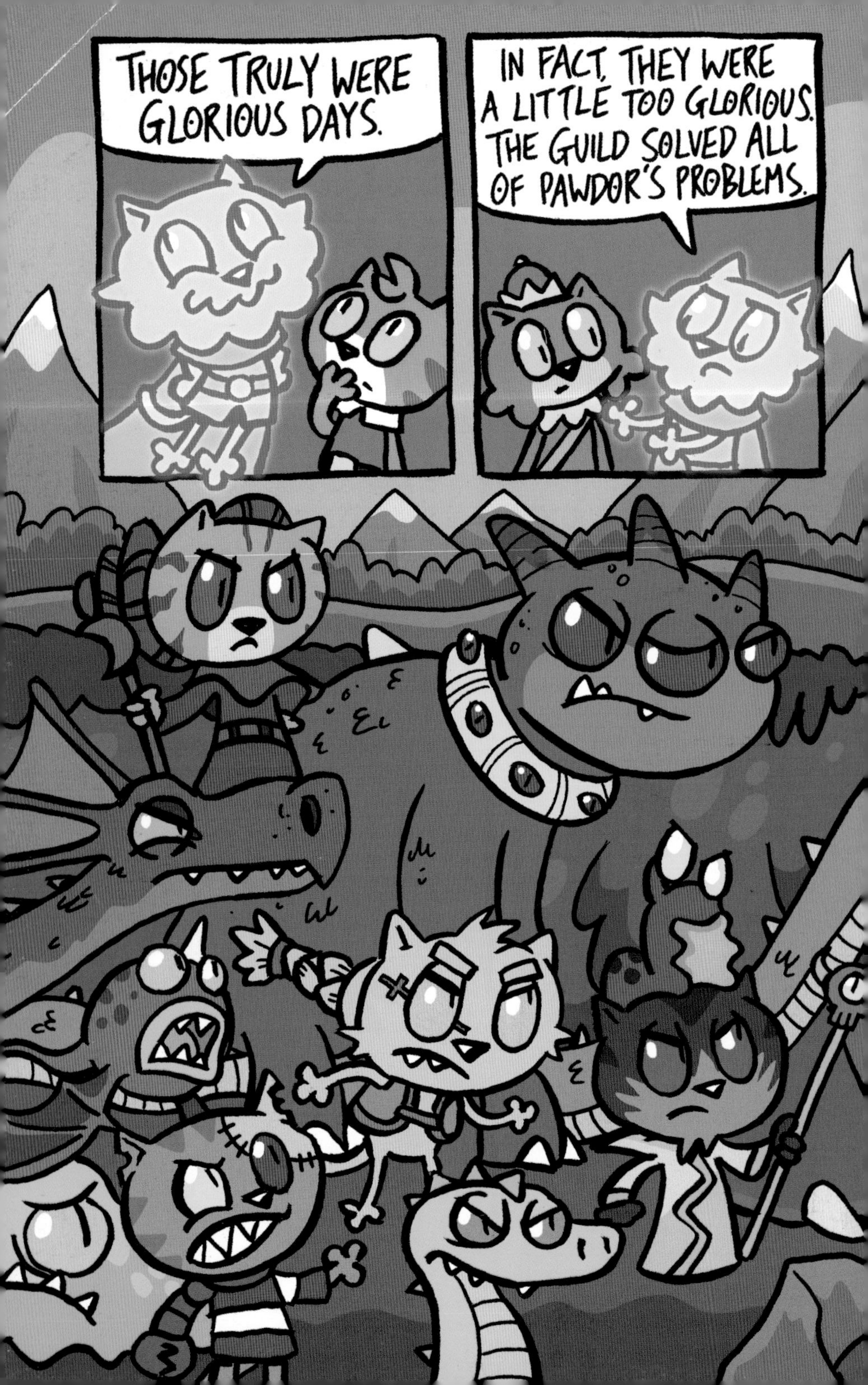
THOSE TRULY WERE GLORIOUS DAYS.
IN FACT, THEY WERE A LITTLE TOO GLORIOUS. THE GUILD SOLVED ALL OF PAWDOR'S PROBLEMS.

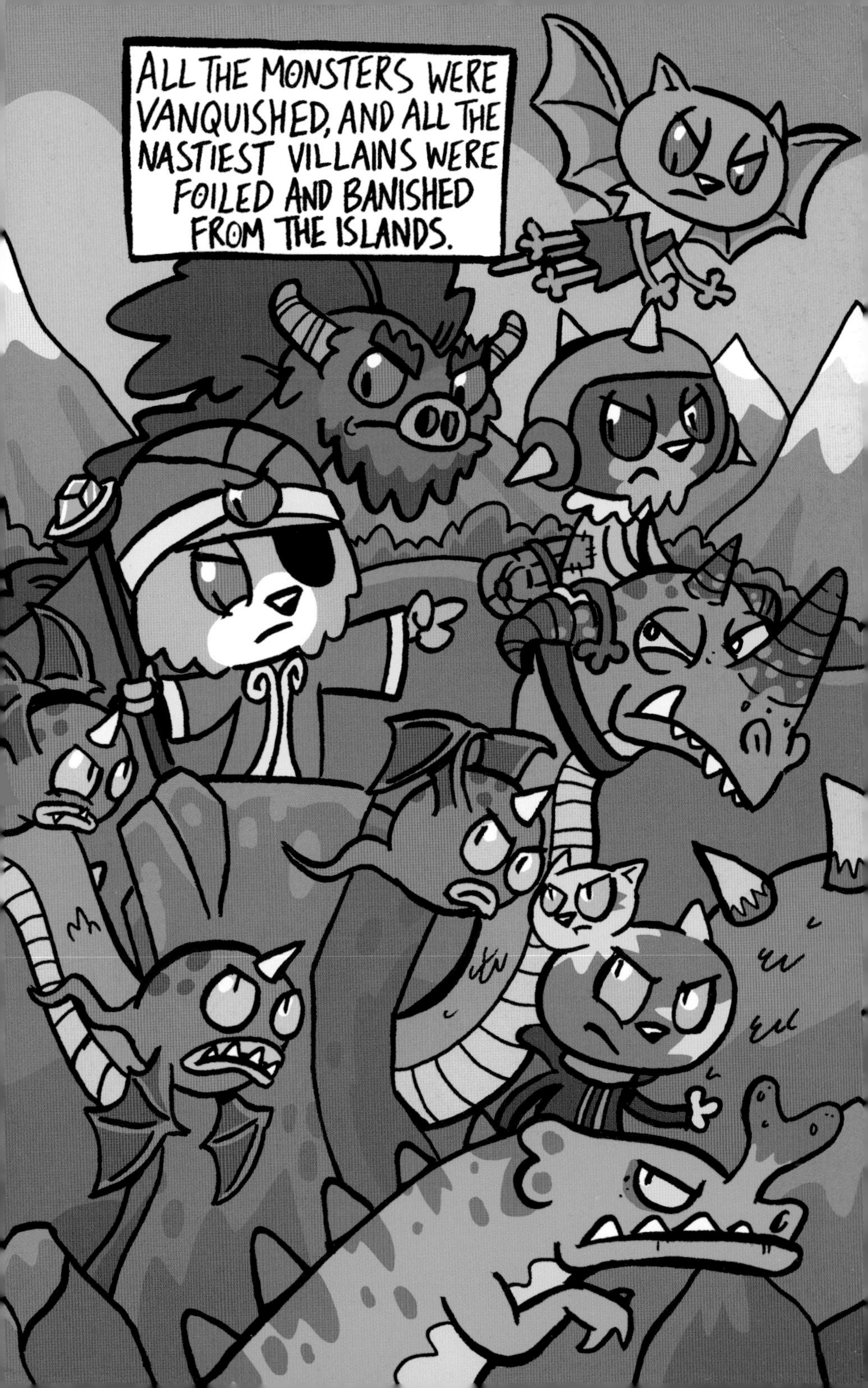
ALL THE MONSTERS WERE VANQUISHED, AND ALL THE NASTIEST VILLAINS WERE FOILED AND BANISHED FROM THE ISLANDS.

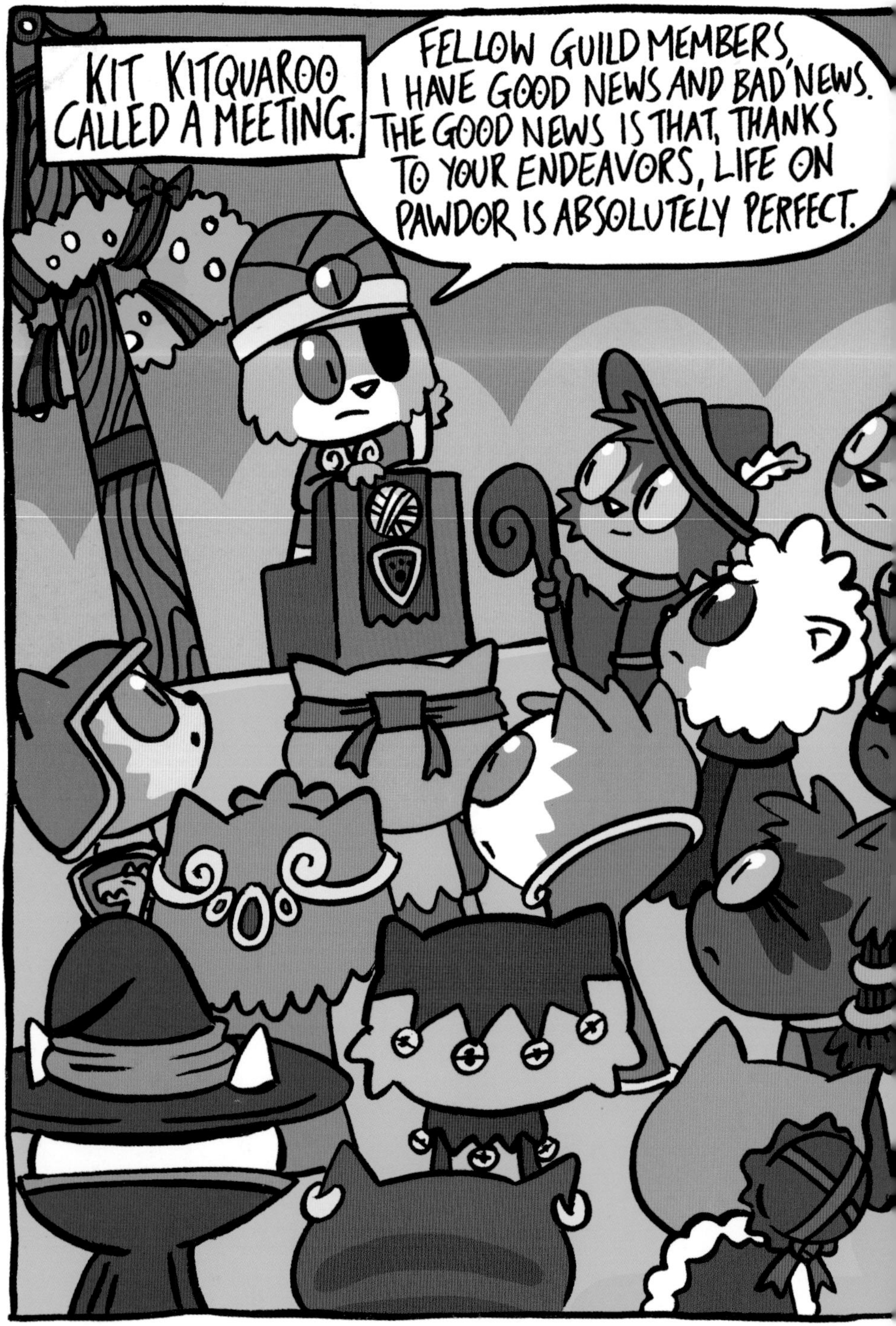
KIT KITQUAROO CALLED A MEETING.
FELLOW GUILD MEMBERS, I HAVE GOOD NEWS AND BAD NEWS. THE GOOD NEWS IS THAT, THANKS TO YOUR ENDEAVORS, LIFE ON PAWDOR IS ABSOLUTELY PERFECT.

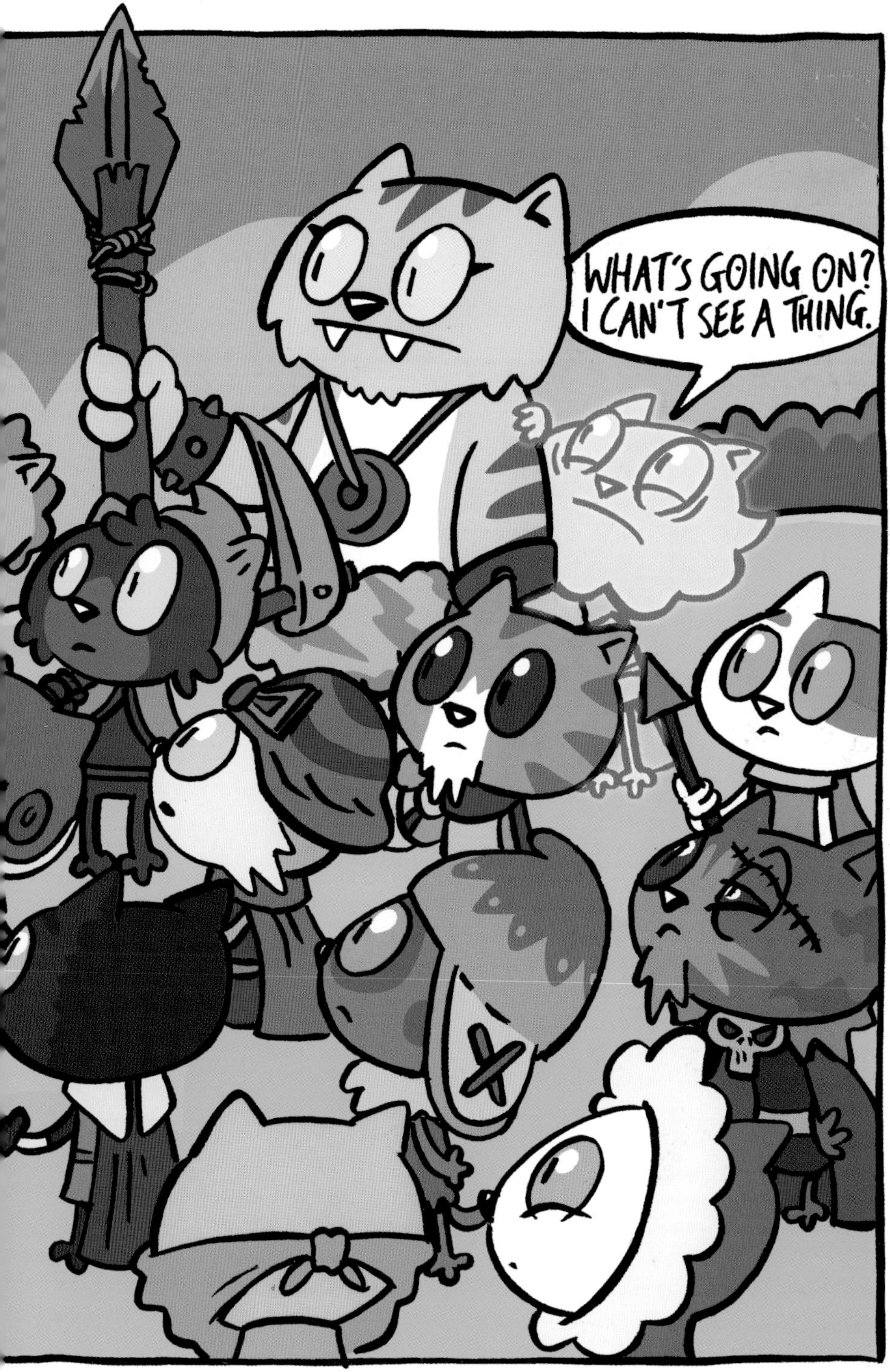
WHAT'S GOING ON? I CAN'T SEE A THING.

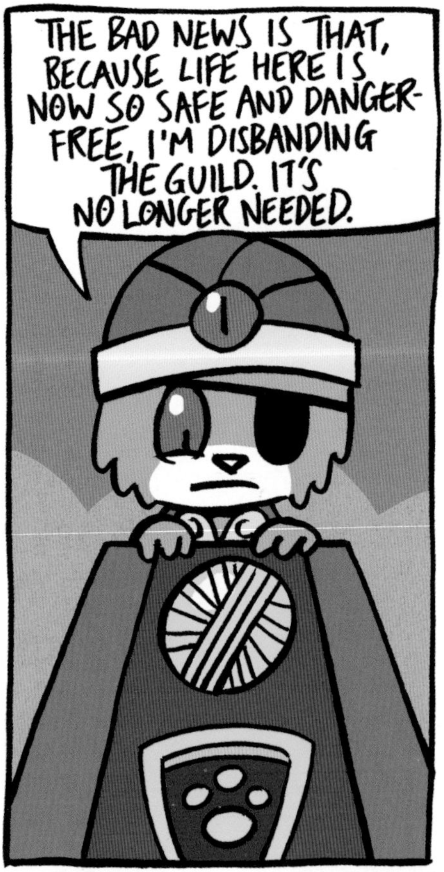
THE BAD NEWS IS THAT, BECAUSE LIFE HERE IS NOW SO SAFE AND DANGER-FREE, I'M DISBANDING THE GUILD. IT'S NO LONGER NEEDED.

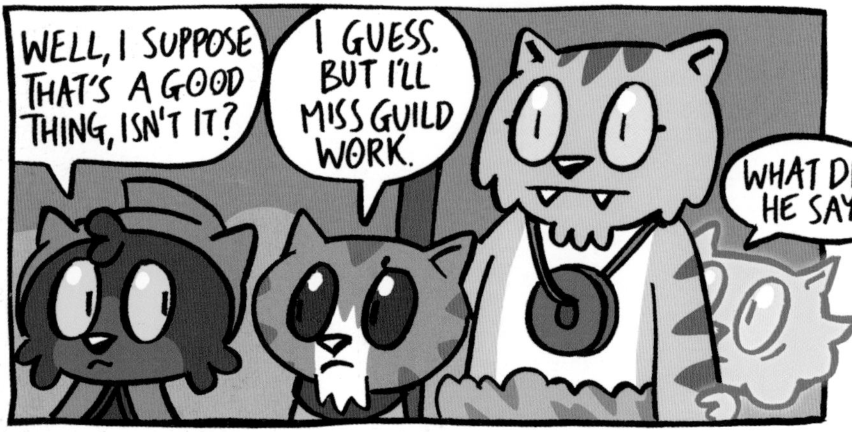
WELL, I SUPPOSE THAT'S A GOOD THING, ISN'T IT?
I GUESS. BUT I'LL MISS GUILD WORK.
WHAT DID HE SAY?

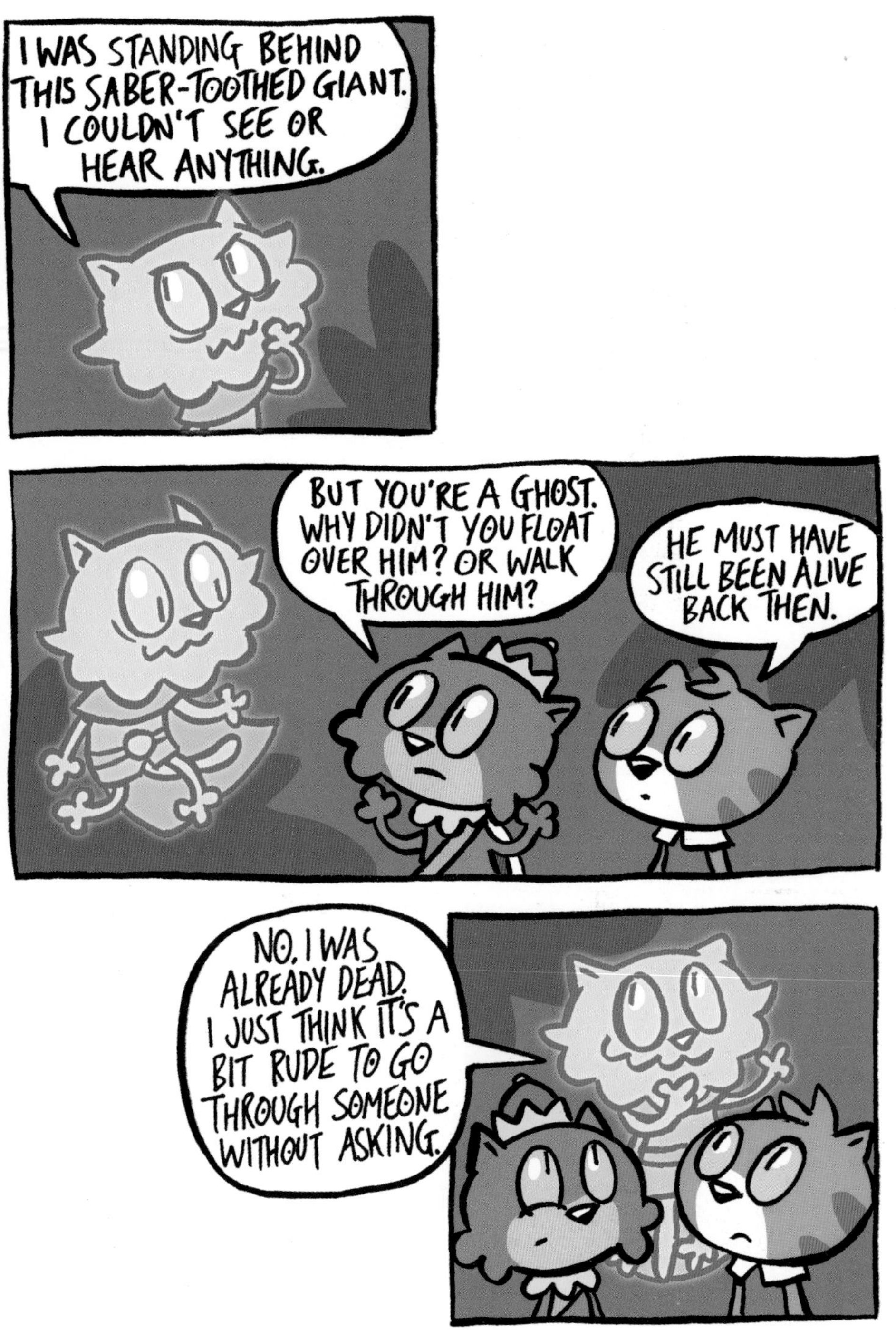
I WAS STANDING BEHIND THIS SABER-TOOTHED GIANT. I COULDN'T SEE OR HEAR ANYTHING.
BUT YOU'RE A GHOST. WHY DIDN'T YOU FLOAT OVER HIM? OR WALK THROUGH HIM?
HE MUST HAVE STILL BEEN ALIVE BACK THEN.
NO. I WAS ALREADY DEAD. I JUST THINK IT'S A BIT RUDE TO GO THROUGH SOMEONE WITHOUT ASKING.

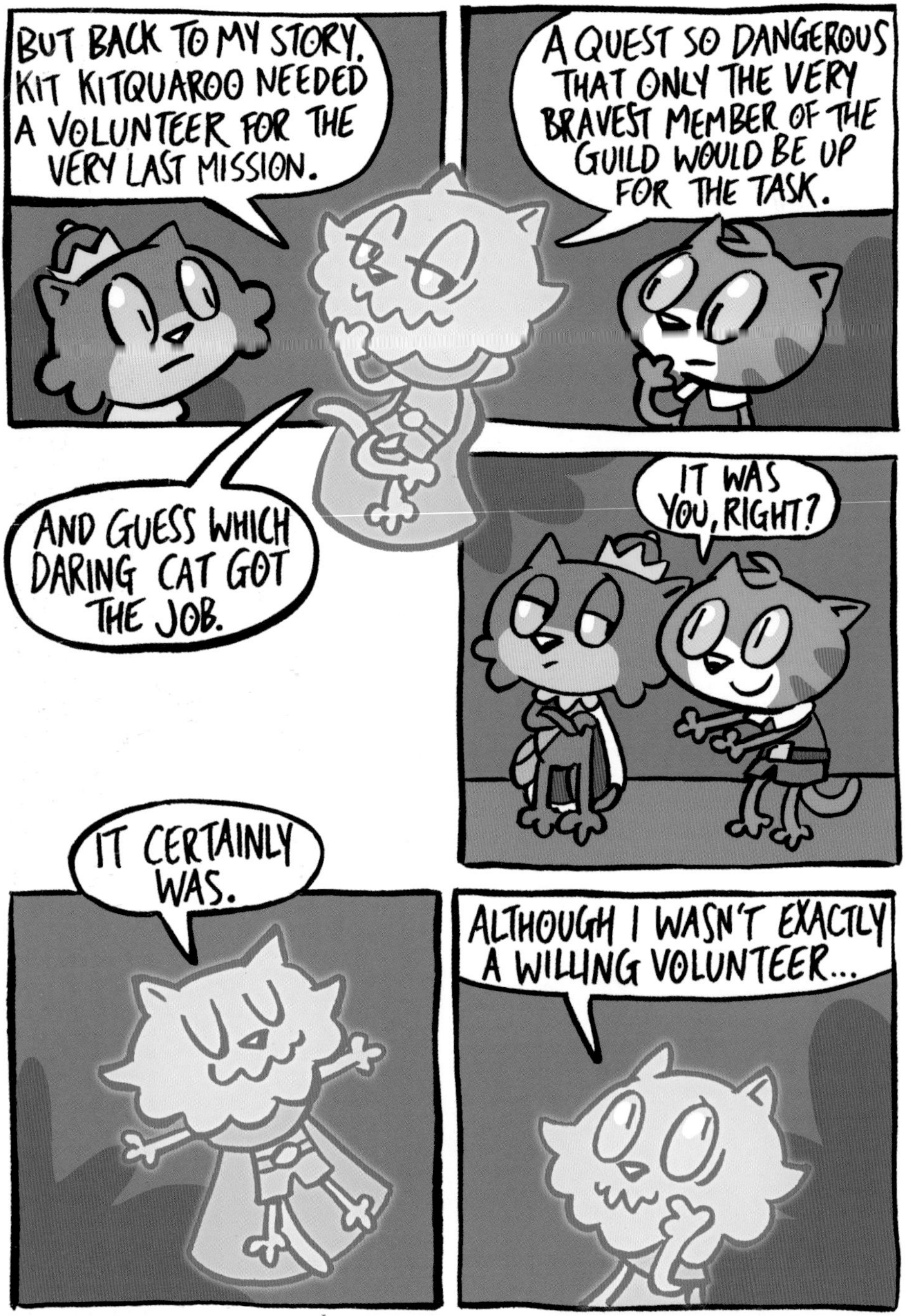

BUT BACK TO MY STORY. KIT KITQUAROO NEEDED A VOLUNTEER FOR THE VERY LAST MISSION.
A QUEST SO DANGEROUS THAT ONLY THE VERY BRAVEST MEMBER OF THE GUILD WOULD BE UP FOR THE TASK.
AND GUESS WHICH DARING CAT GOT THE JOB.
IT WAS YOU, RIGHT?
IT CERTAINLY WAS.
ALTHOUGH I WASN'T EXACTLY A WILLING VOLUNTEER...

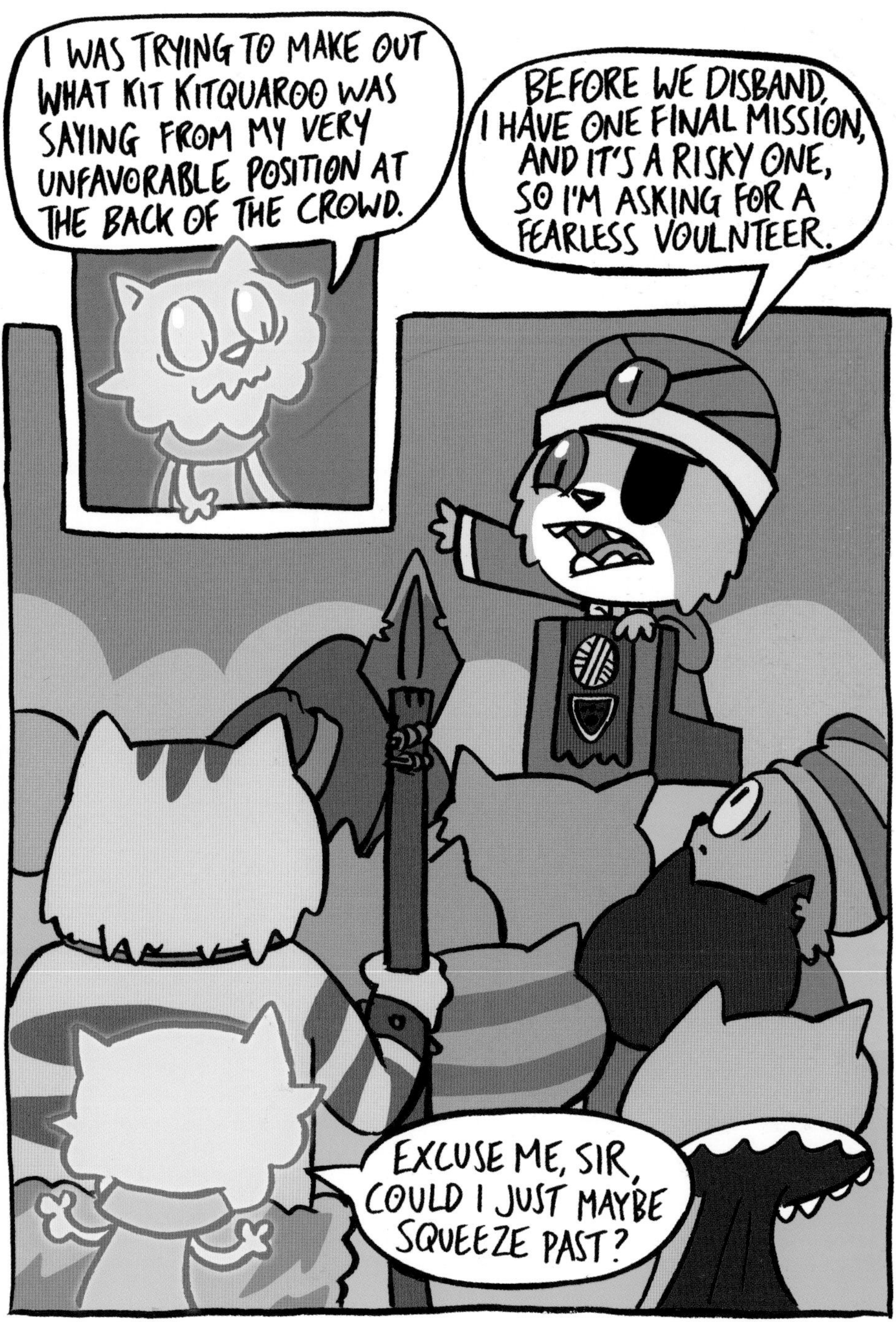
I WAS TRYING TO MAKE OUT WHAT KIT KITQUAROO WAS SAYING FROM MY VERY UNFAVORABLE POSITION AT THE BACK OF THE CROWD.
BEFORE WE DISBAND, I HAVE ONE FINAL MISSION, AND IT'S A RISKY ONE, SO I'M ASKING FOR A FEARLESS VOULNTEER.
EXCUSE ME, SIR, COULD I JUST MAYBE SQUEEZE PAST?

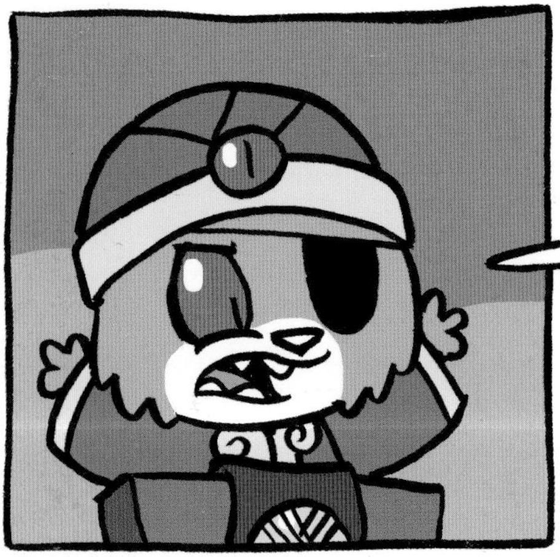
IS THERE ANYONE AMONG YOU WILLING TO TAKE THIS ULTIMATE TEST OF BRAVERY?

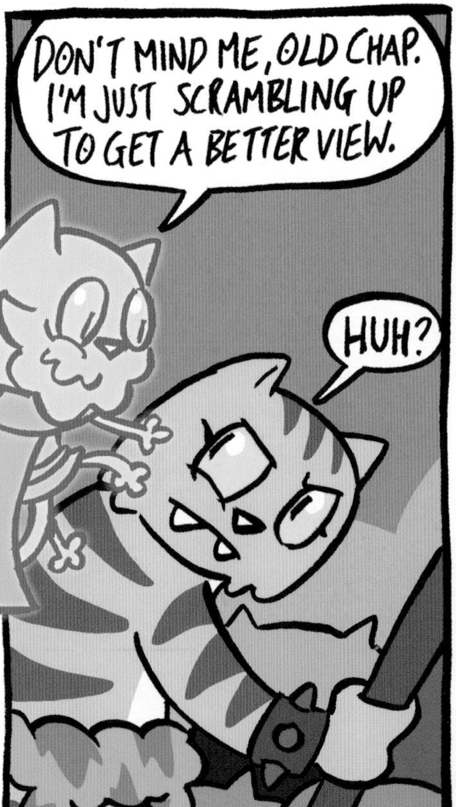
DON'T MIND ME, OLD CHAP. I'M JUST SCRAMBLING UP TO GET A BETTER VIEW.
HUH?

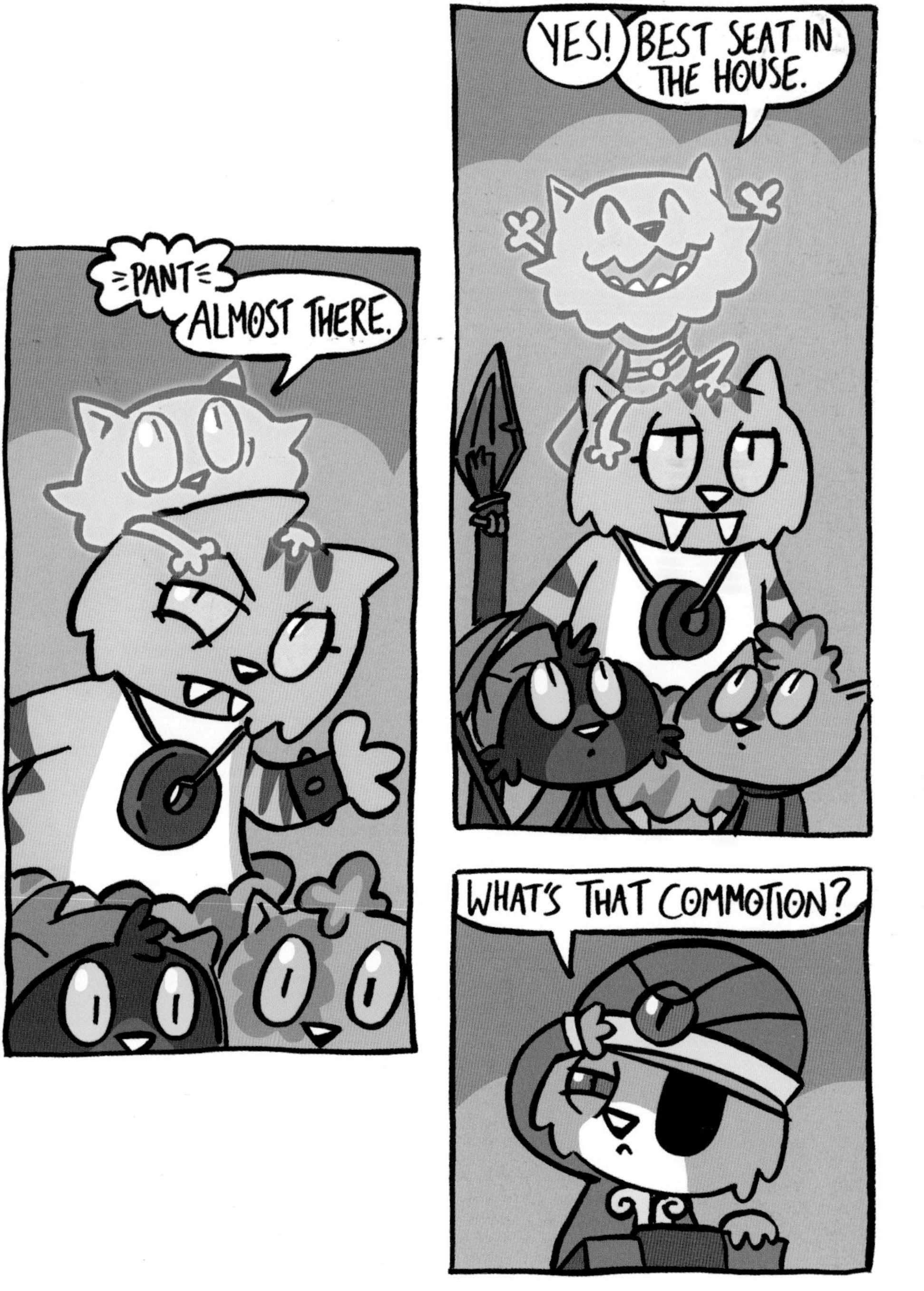
PANT
ALMOST THERE.
YES!
BEST SEAT IN THE HOUSE.
WHAT'S THAT COMMOTION?

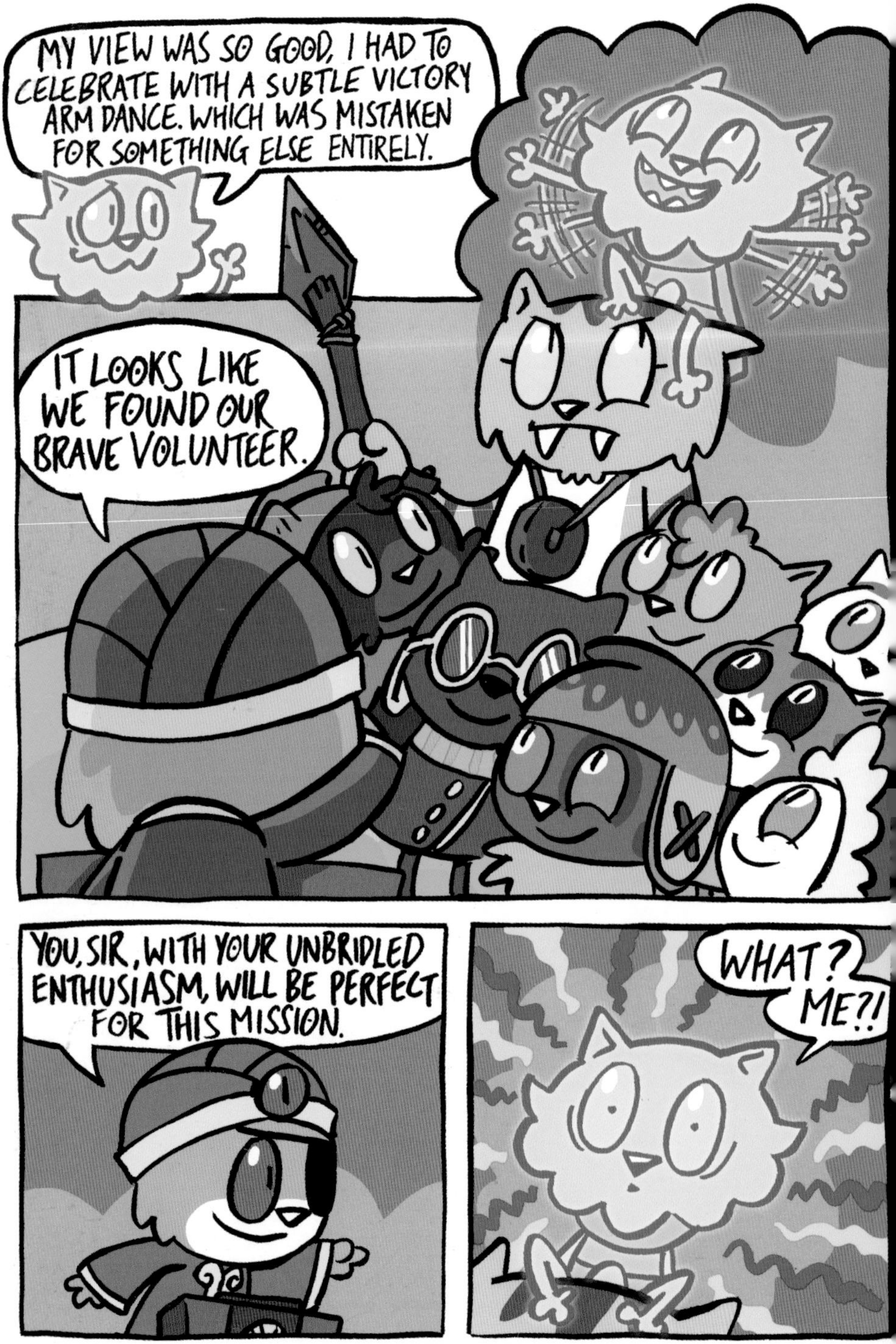
MY VIEW WAS SO GOOD, I HAD TO CELEBRATE WITH A SUBTLE VICTORY ARM DANCE. WHICH WAS MISTAKEN FOR SOMETHING ELSE ENTIRELY.
IT LOOKS LIKE WE FOUND OUR BRAVE VOLUNTEER.
YOU, SIR, WITH YOUR UNBRIDLED ENTHUSIASM, WILL BE PERFECT FOR THIS MISSION.
WHAT? ME?!

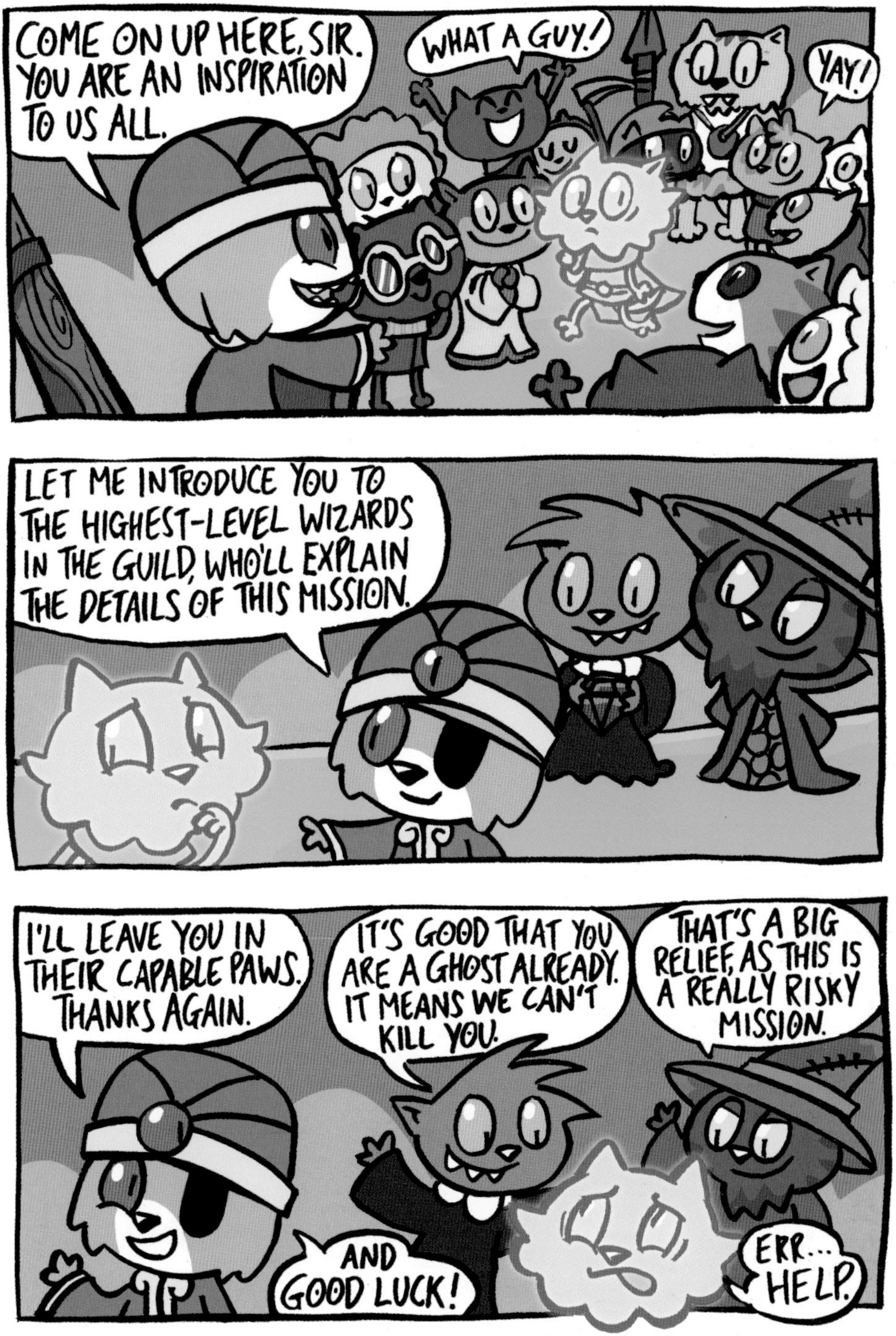
COME ON UP HERE, SIR. YOU ARE AN INSPIRATION TO US ALL.
WHAT A GUY!
YAY!
LET ME INTRODUCE YOU TO THE HIGHEST-LEVEL WIZARDS IN THE GUILD, WHO'LL EXPLAIN THE DETAILS OF THIS MISSION.
I'LL LEAVE YOU IN THEIR CAPABLE PAWS. THANKS AGAIN.
IT'S GOOD THAT YOU ARE A GHOST ALREADY. IT MEANS WE CAN'T KILL YOU.
THAT'S A BIG RELIEF, AS THIS IS A REALLY RISKY MISSION.
AND GOOD LUCK!
ERR... HELP.

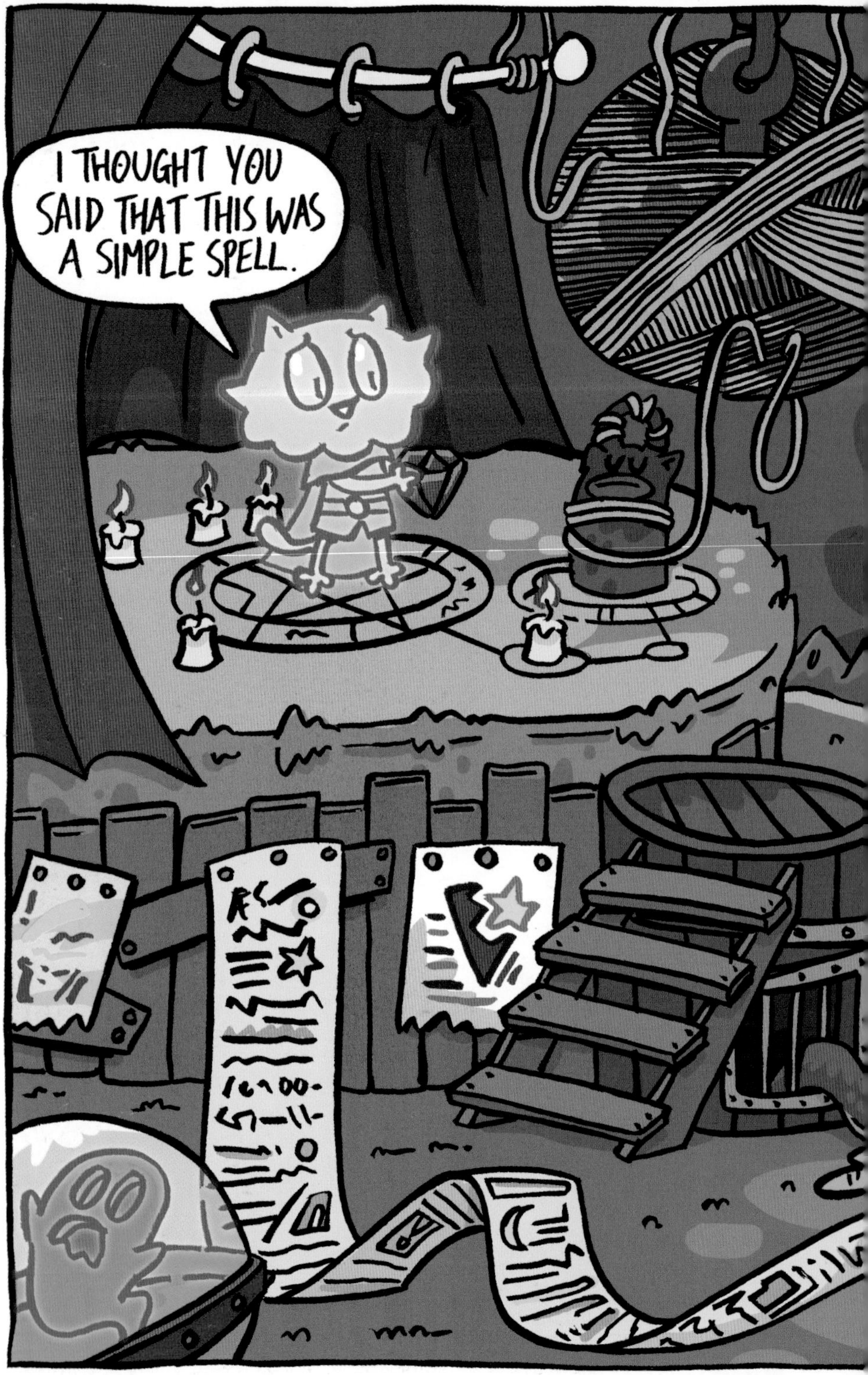
I THOUGHT YOU SAID THAT THIS WAS A SIMPLE SPELL.

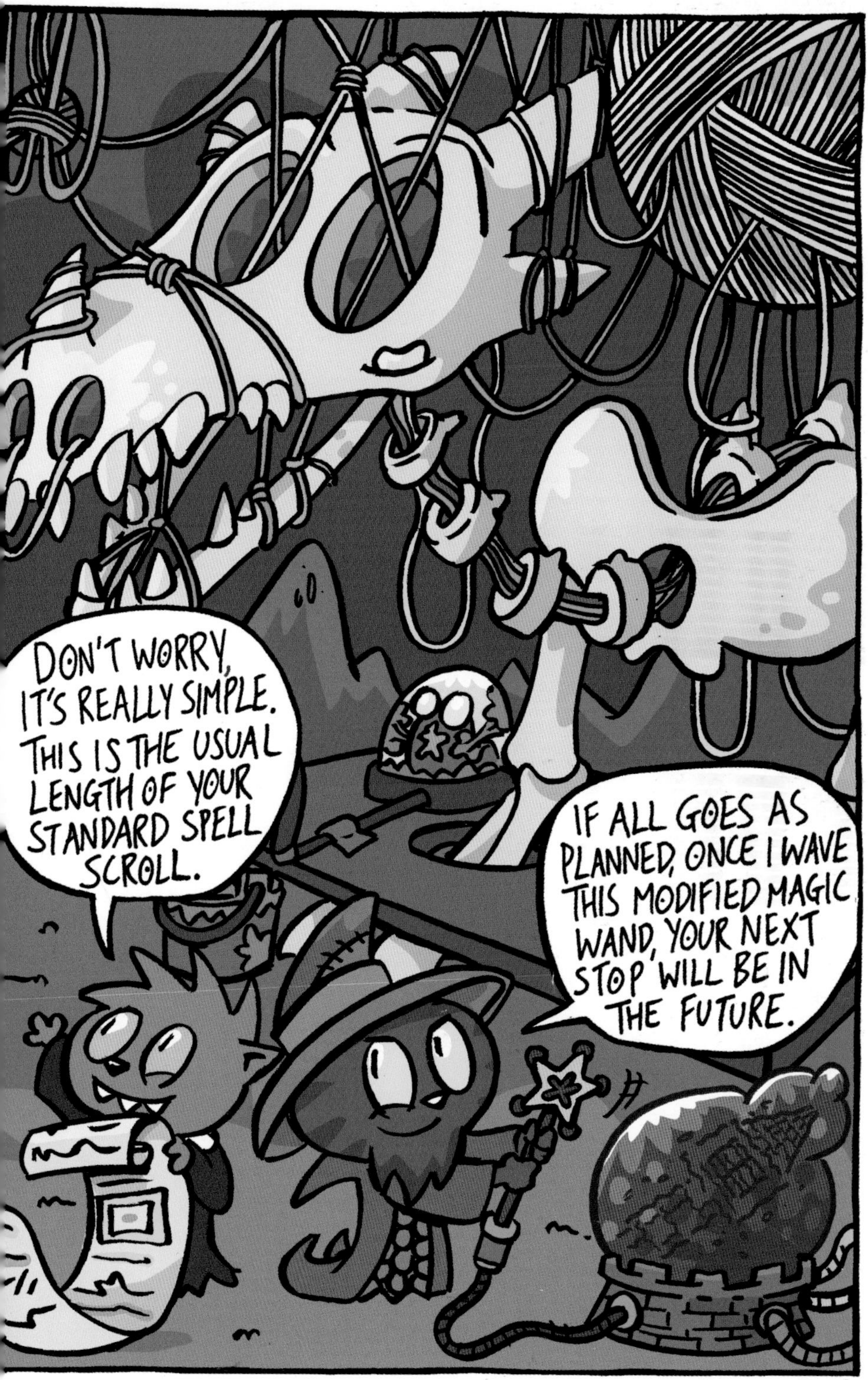
DON'T WORRY, IT'S REALLY SIMPLE. THIS IS THE USUAL LENGTH OF YOUR STANDARD SPELL SCROLL.
IF ALL GOES AS PLANNED, ONCE I WAVE THIS MODIFIED MAGIC WAND, YOUR NEXT STOP WILL BE IN THE FUTURE.

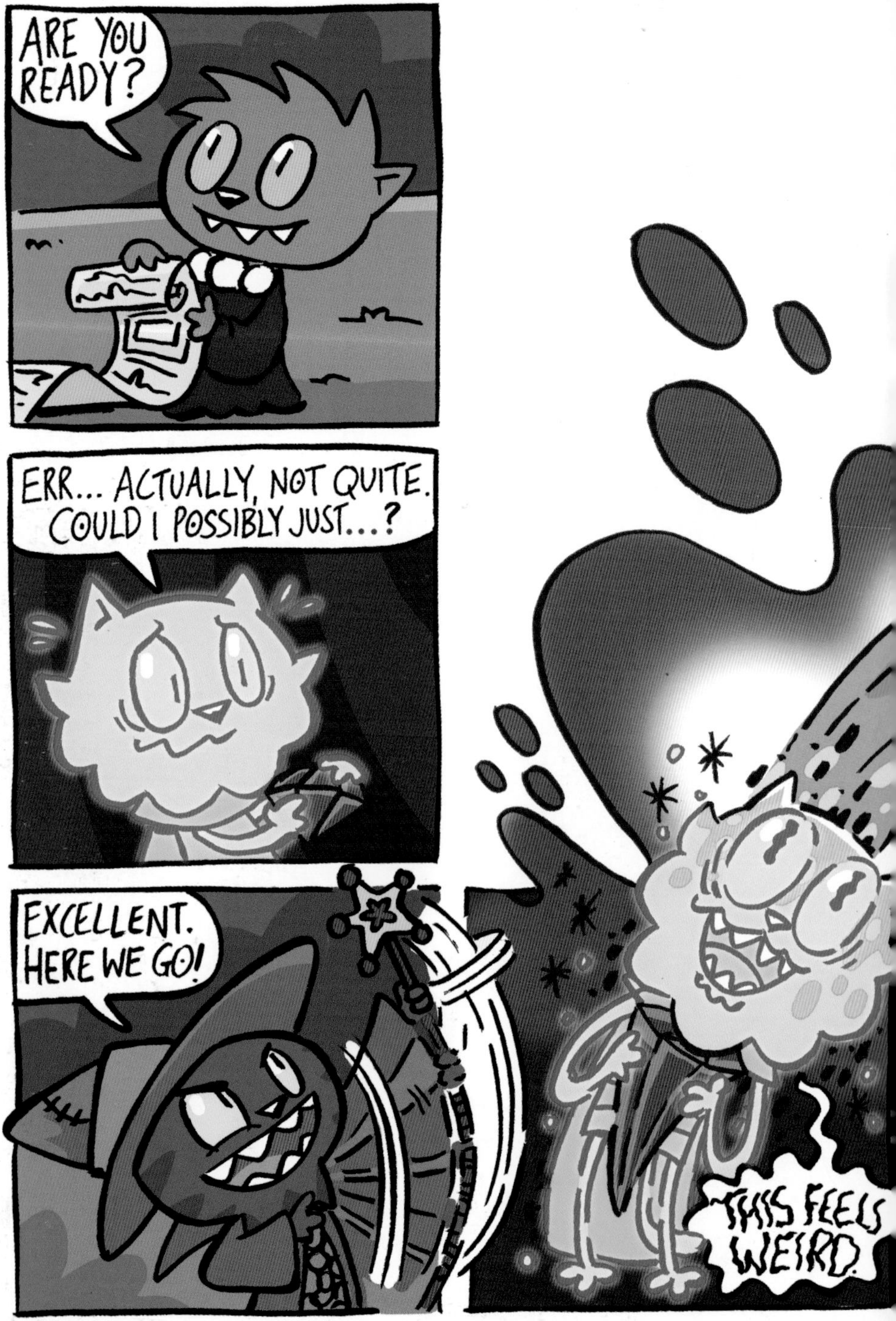
ARE YOU READY?
ERR... ACTUALLY, NOT QUITE. COULD I POSSIBLY JUST...?
EXCELLENT. HERE WE GO!
THIS FEELS WEIRD.

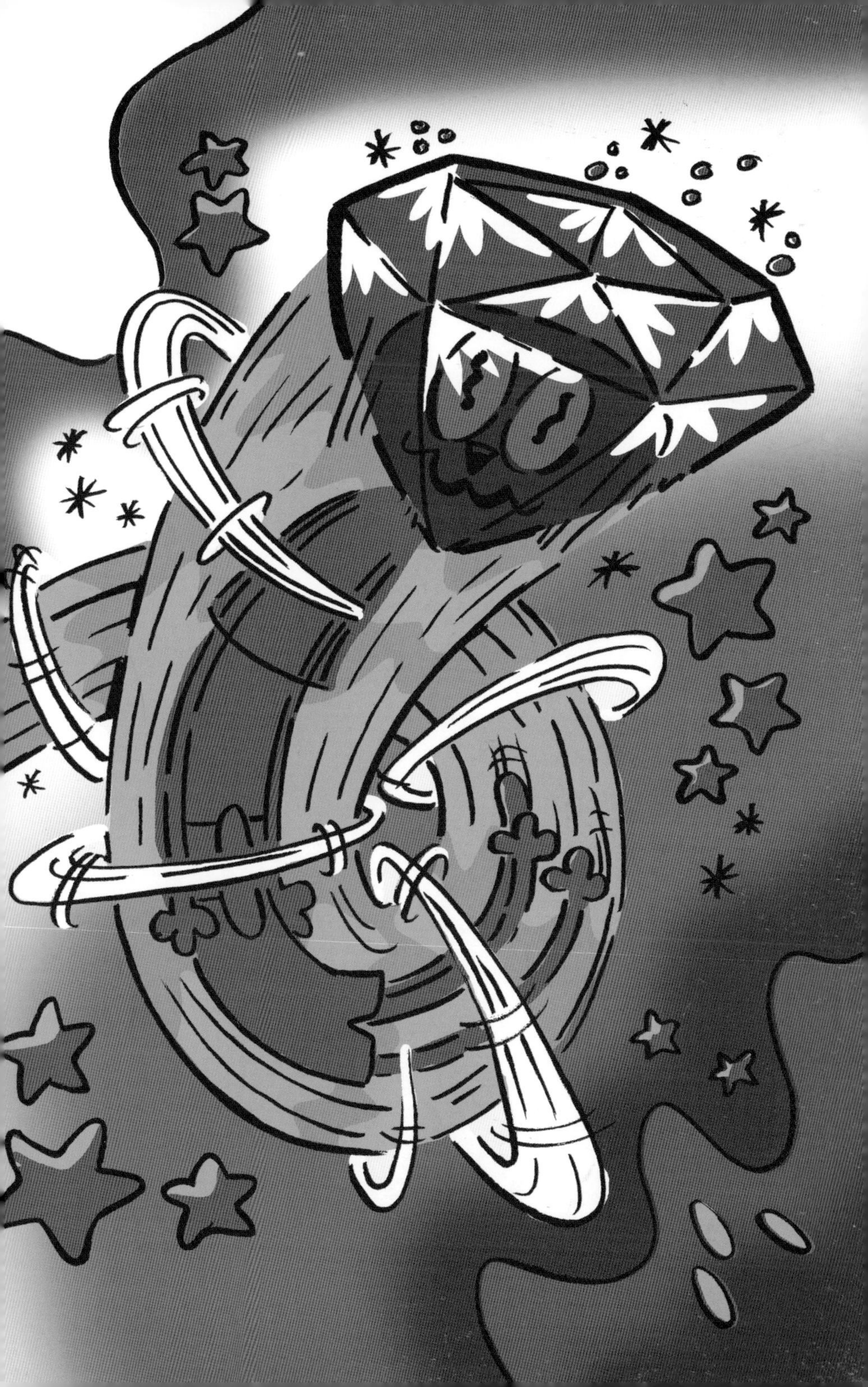

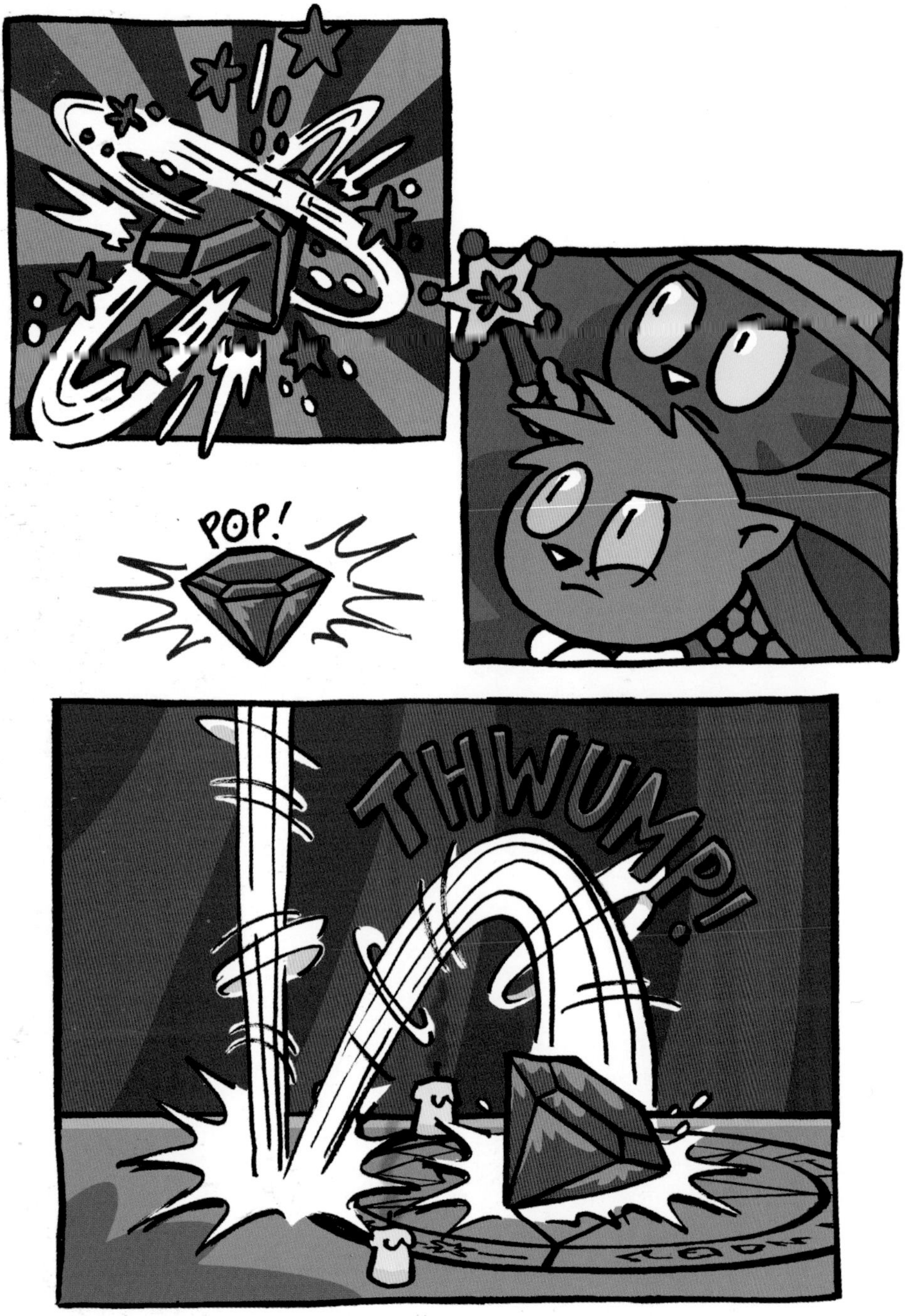
POP!
THWUMP!

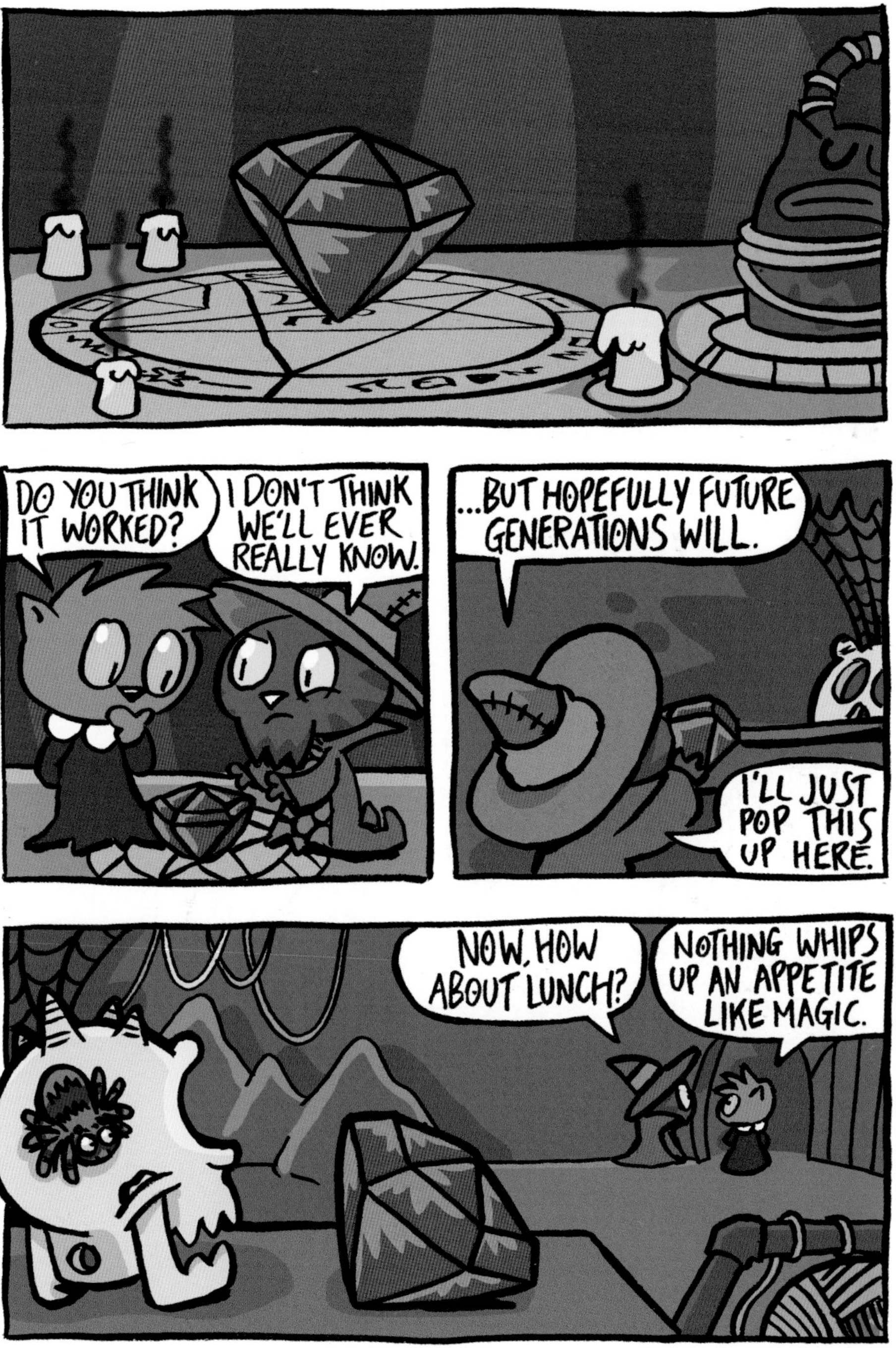
DO YOU THINK IT WORKED?
I DON'T THINK WE'LL EVER REALLY KNOW.
...BUT HOPEFULLY FUTURE GENERATIONS WILL.
I'LL JUST POP THIS UP HERE.
NOW, HOW ABOUT LUNCH?
NOTHING WHIPS UP AN APPETITE LIKE MAGIC.

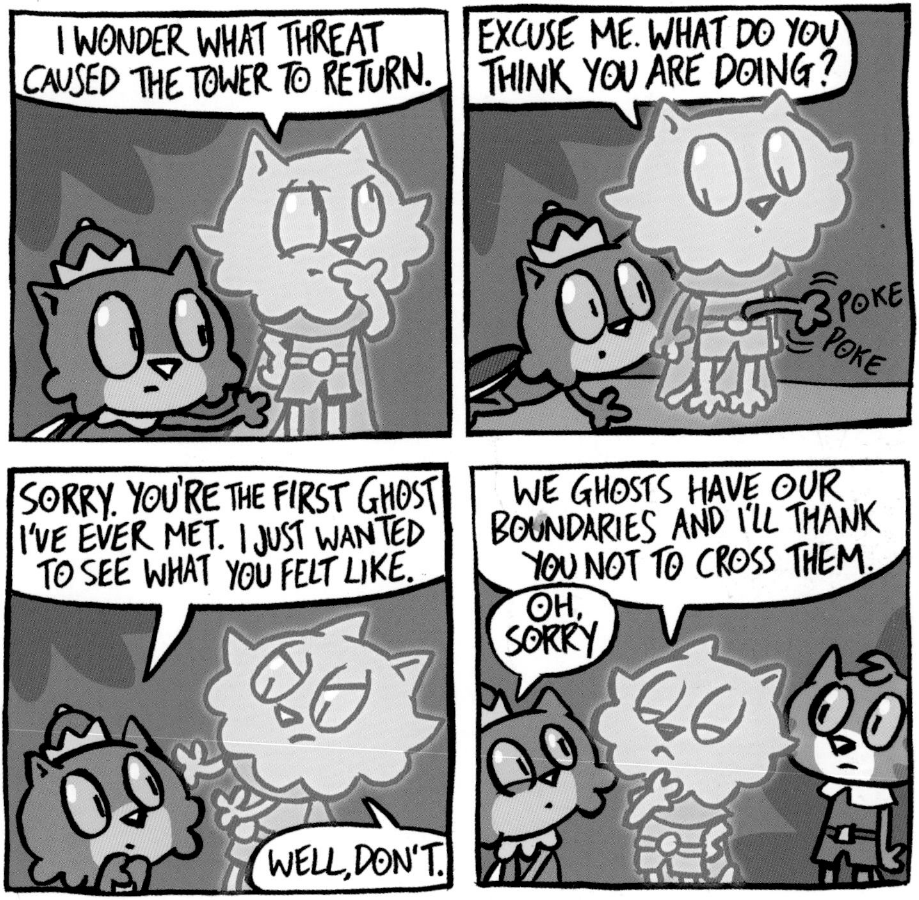
I WONDER WHAT THREAT CAUSED THE TOWER TO RETURN.
EXCUSE ME. WHAT DO YOU THINK YOU ARE DOING?
POKE
POKE
SORRY. YOU'RE THE FIRST GHOST I'VE EVER MET. I JUST WANTED TO SEE WHAT YOU FELT LIKE.
WELL, DON'T.
WE GHOSTS HAVE OUR BOUNDARIES AND I'LL THANK YOU NOT TO CROSS THEM.
OH, SORRY

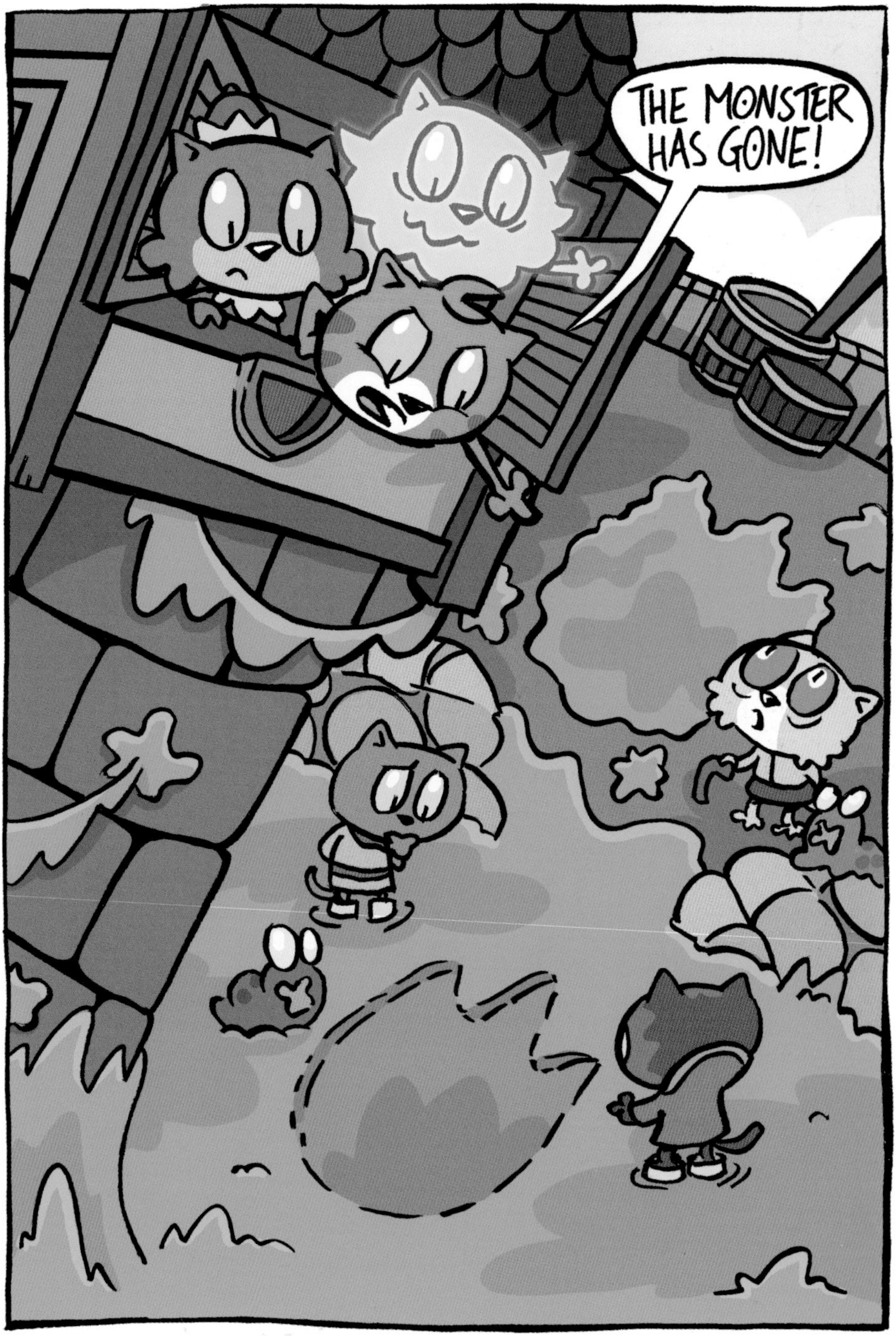
THE MONSTER HAS GONE!

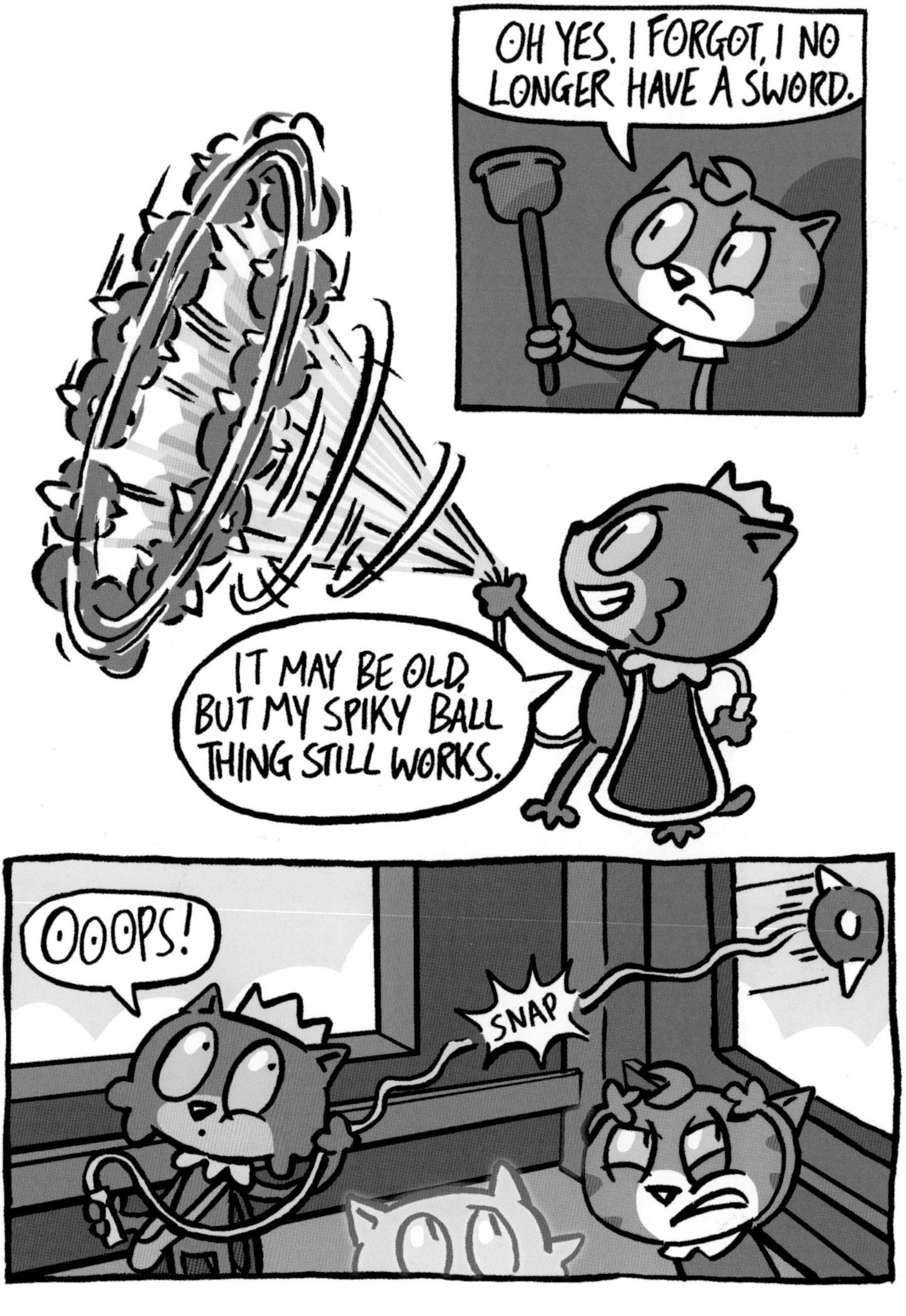
OH YES. I FORGOT, I NO LONGER HAVE A SWORD.
IT MAY BE OLD, BUT MY SPIKY BALL THING STILL WORKS.
OOOPS!
SNAP

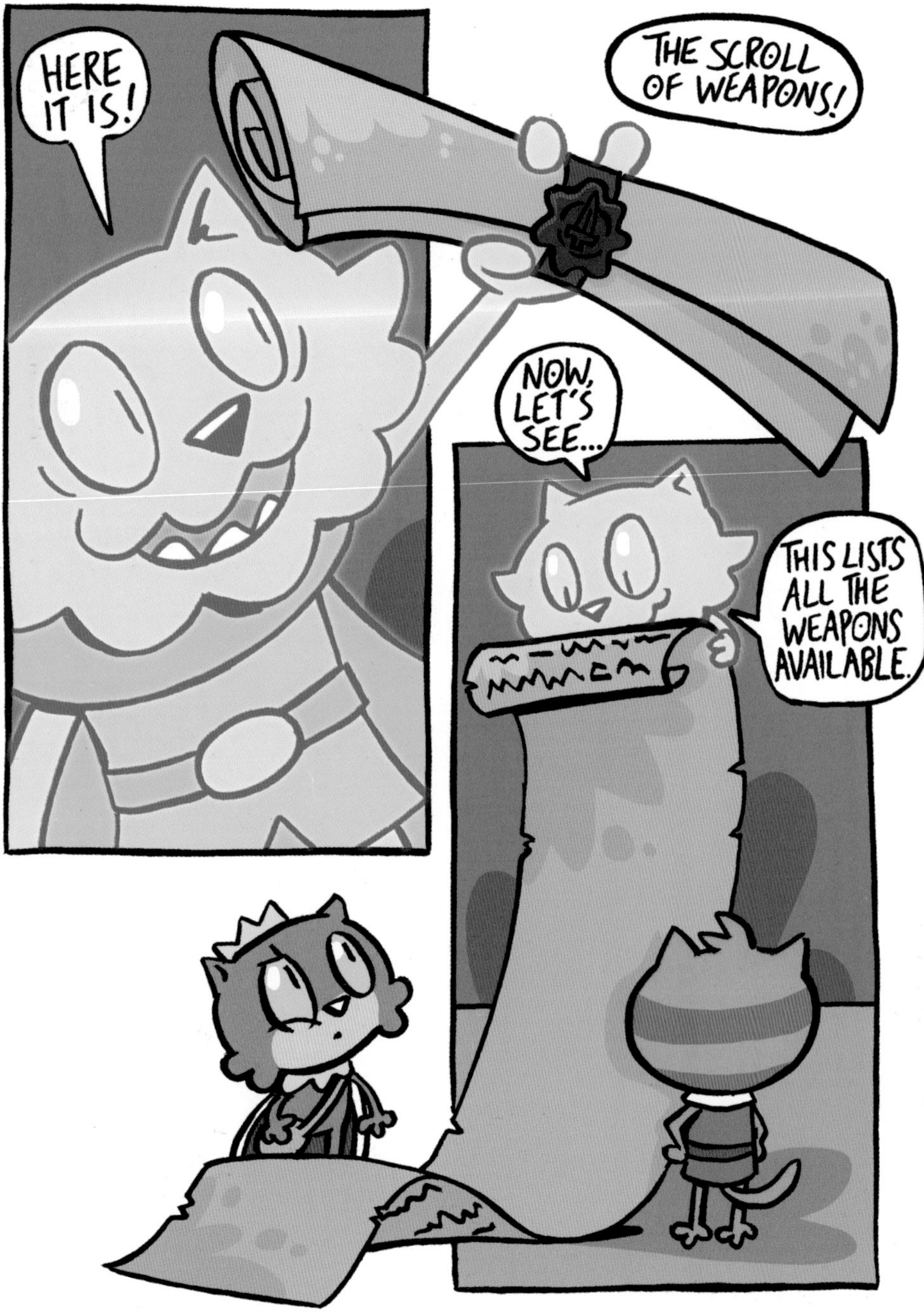
HERE IT IS!
THE SCROLL OF WEAPONS!
NOW, LET'S SEE...
THIS LISTS ALL THE WEAPONS AVAILABLE.

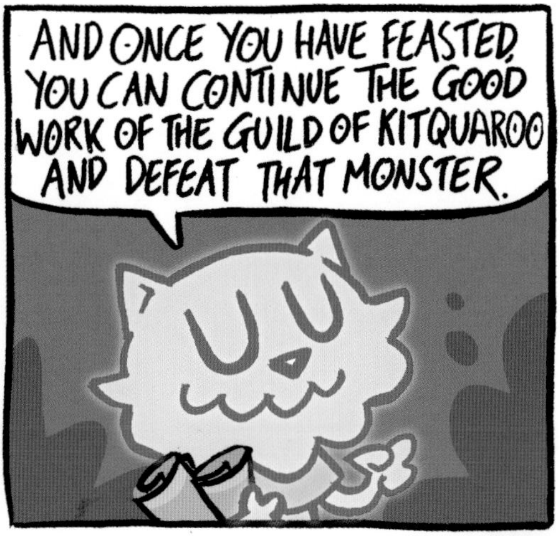
AND ONCE YOU HAVE FEASTED, YOU CAN CONTINUE THE GOOD WORK OF THE GUILD OF KITQUAROO AND DEFEAT THAT MONSTER.

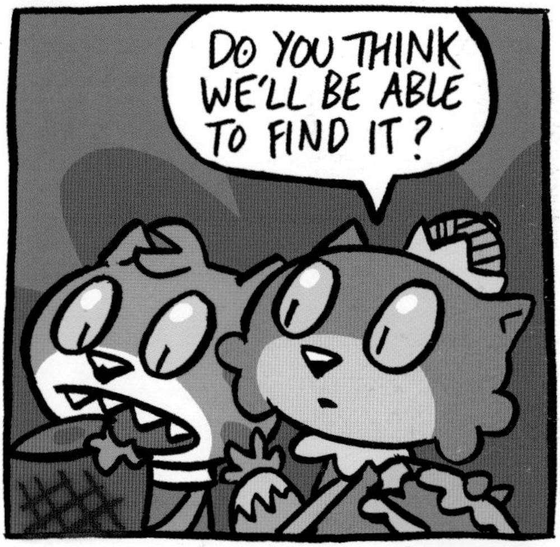
DO YOU THINK WE'LL BE ABLE TO FIND IT?

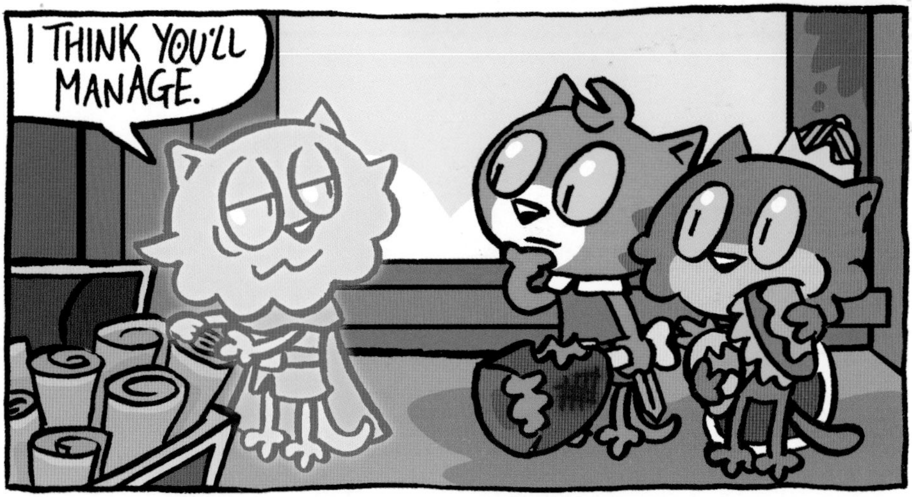
I THINK YOU'LL MANAGE.

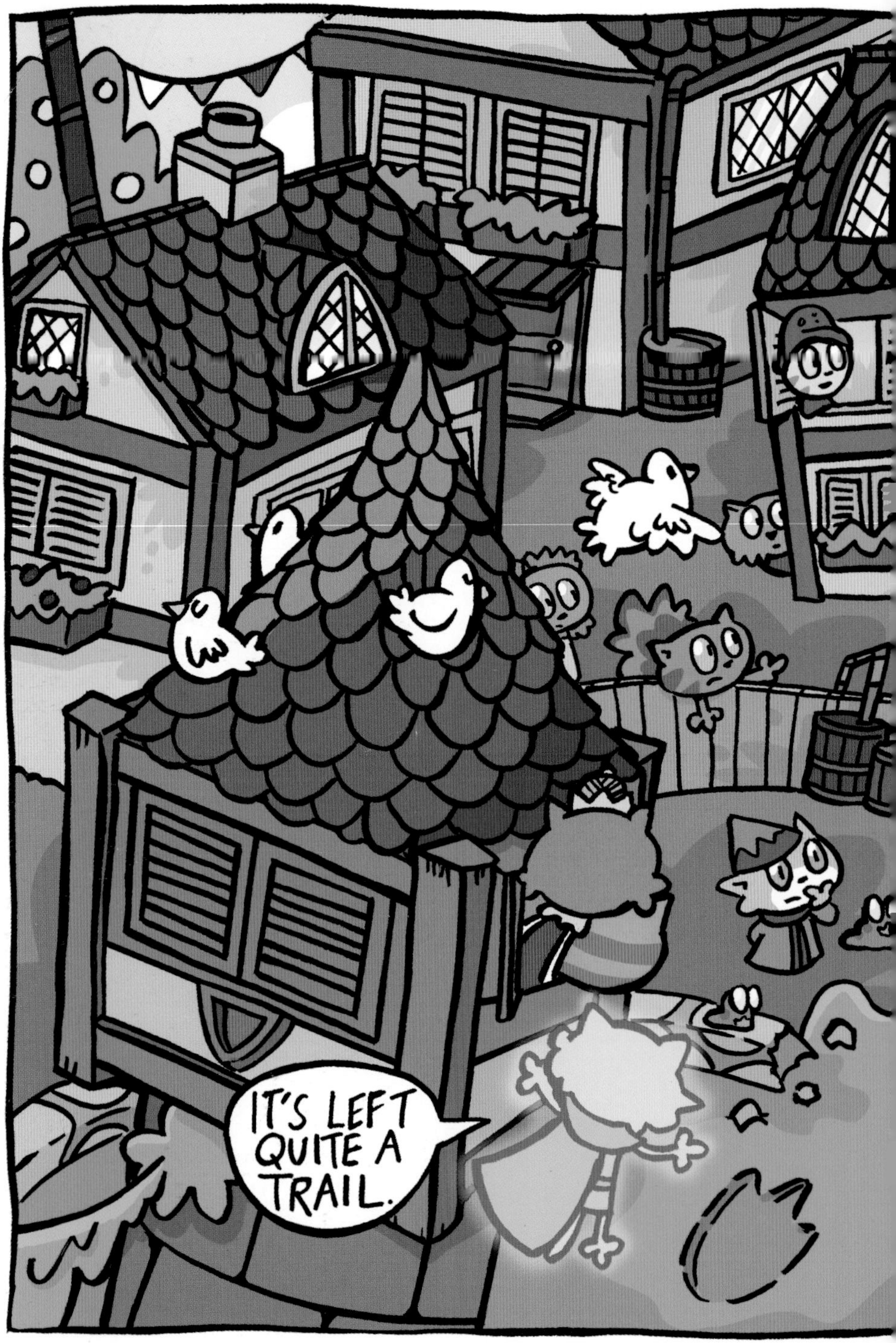
IT'S LEFT QUITE A TRAIL.

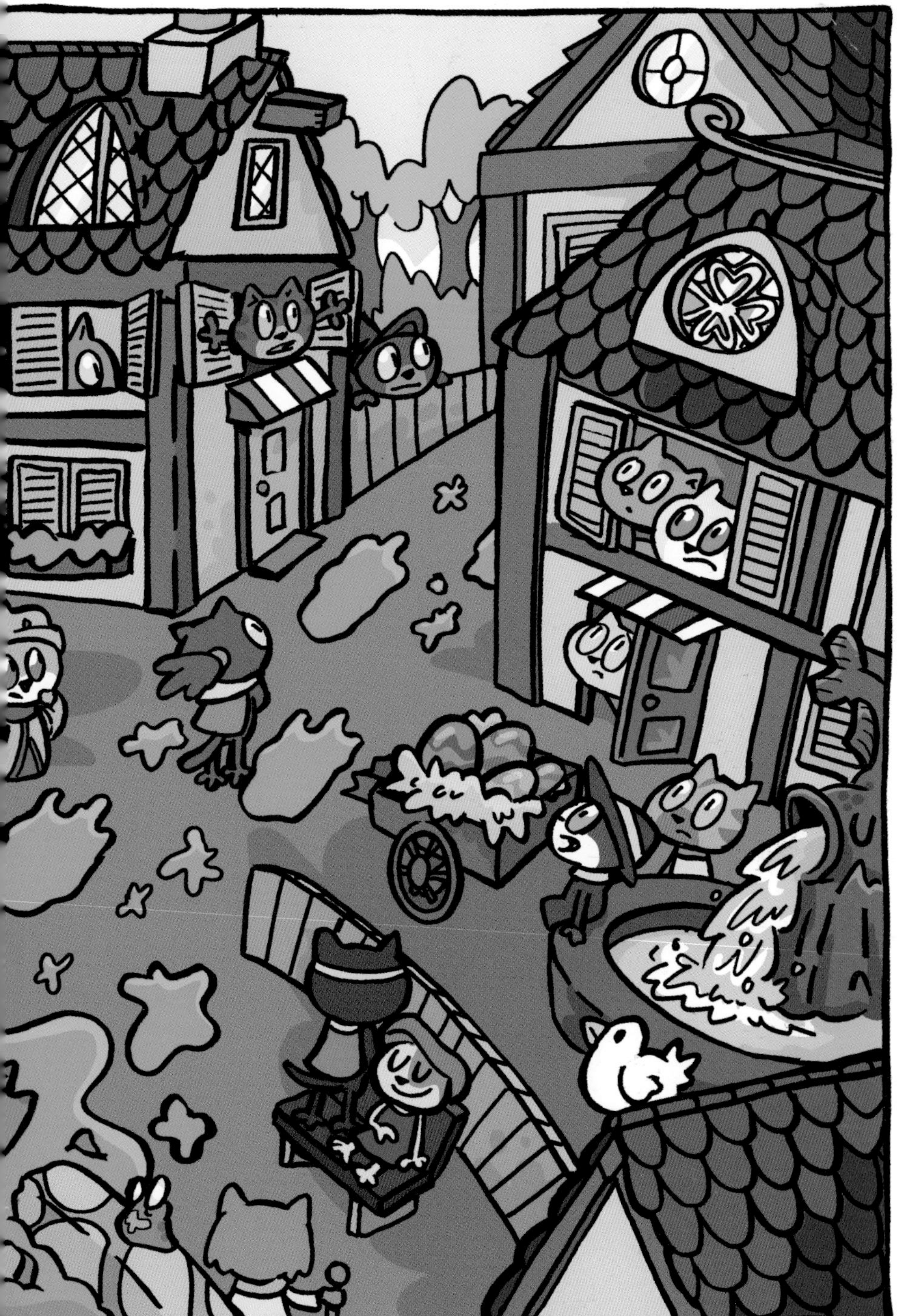

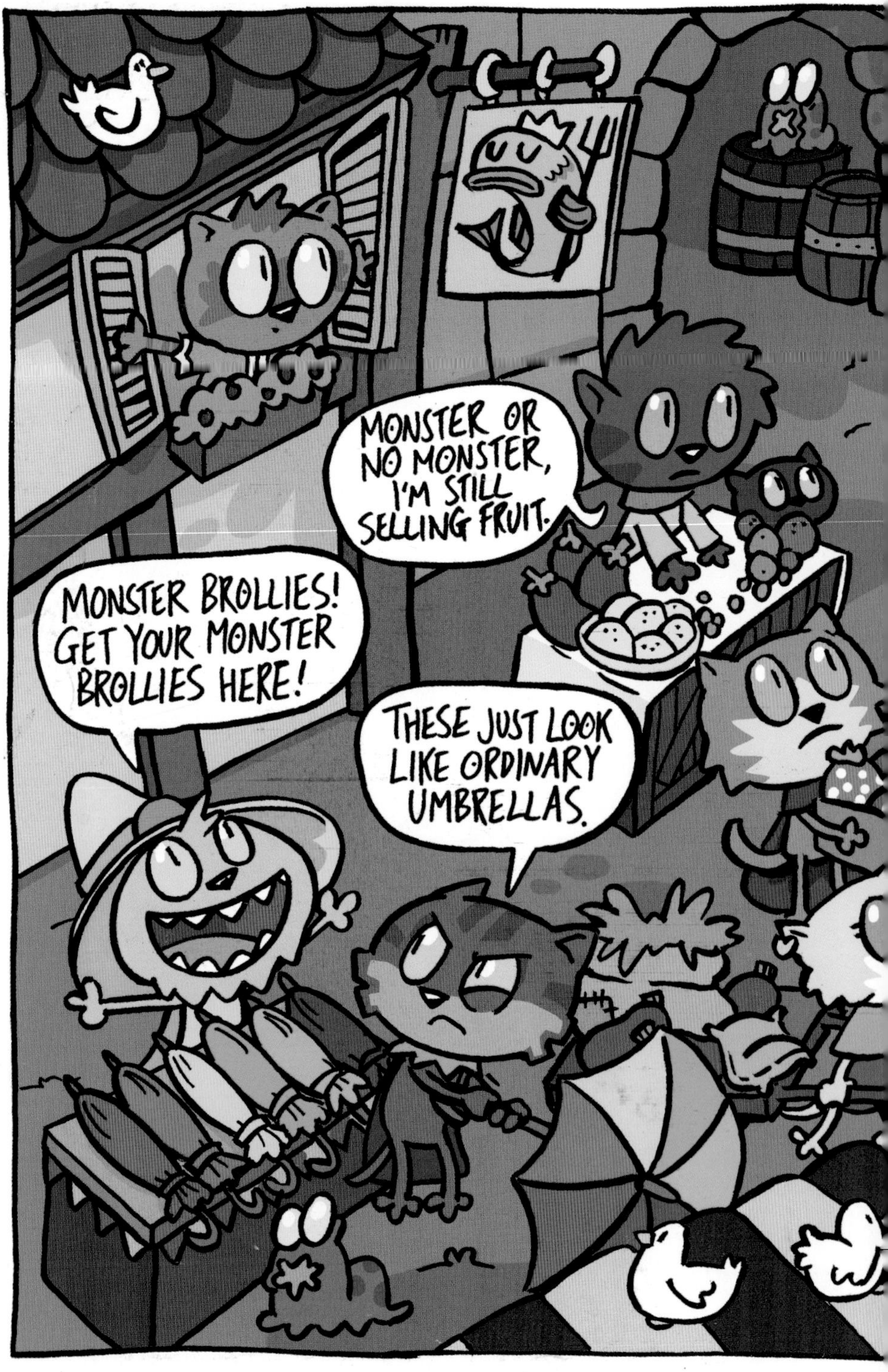
MONSTER OR NO MONSTER, I'M STILL SELLING FRUIT.
MONSTER BROLLIES! GET YOUR MONSTER BROLLIES HERE!
THESE JUST LOOK LIKE ORDINARY UMBRELLAS.

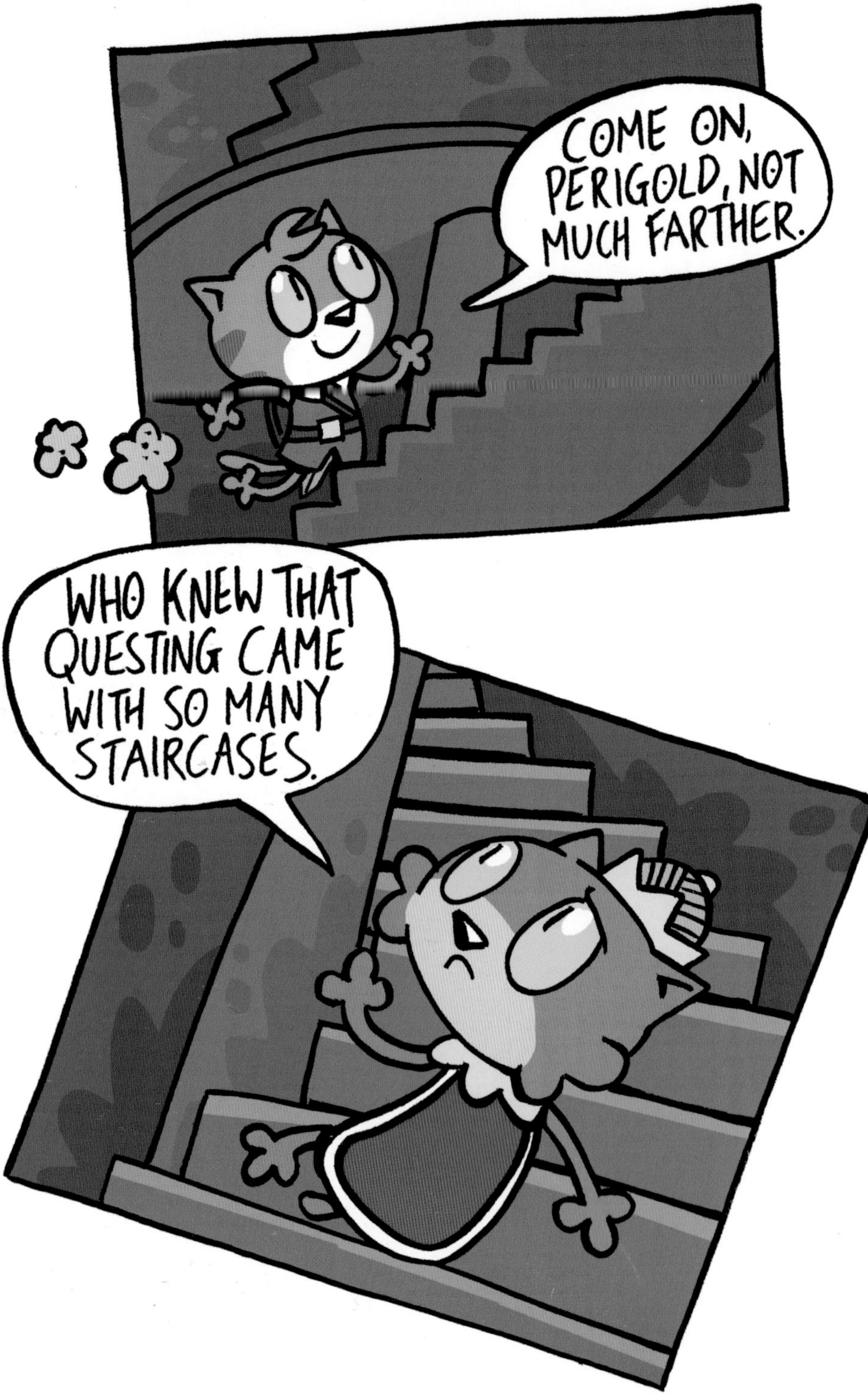
COME ON, PERIGOLD, NOT MUCH FARTHER.
WHO KNEW THAT QUESTING CAME WITH SO MANY STAIRCASES.

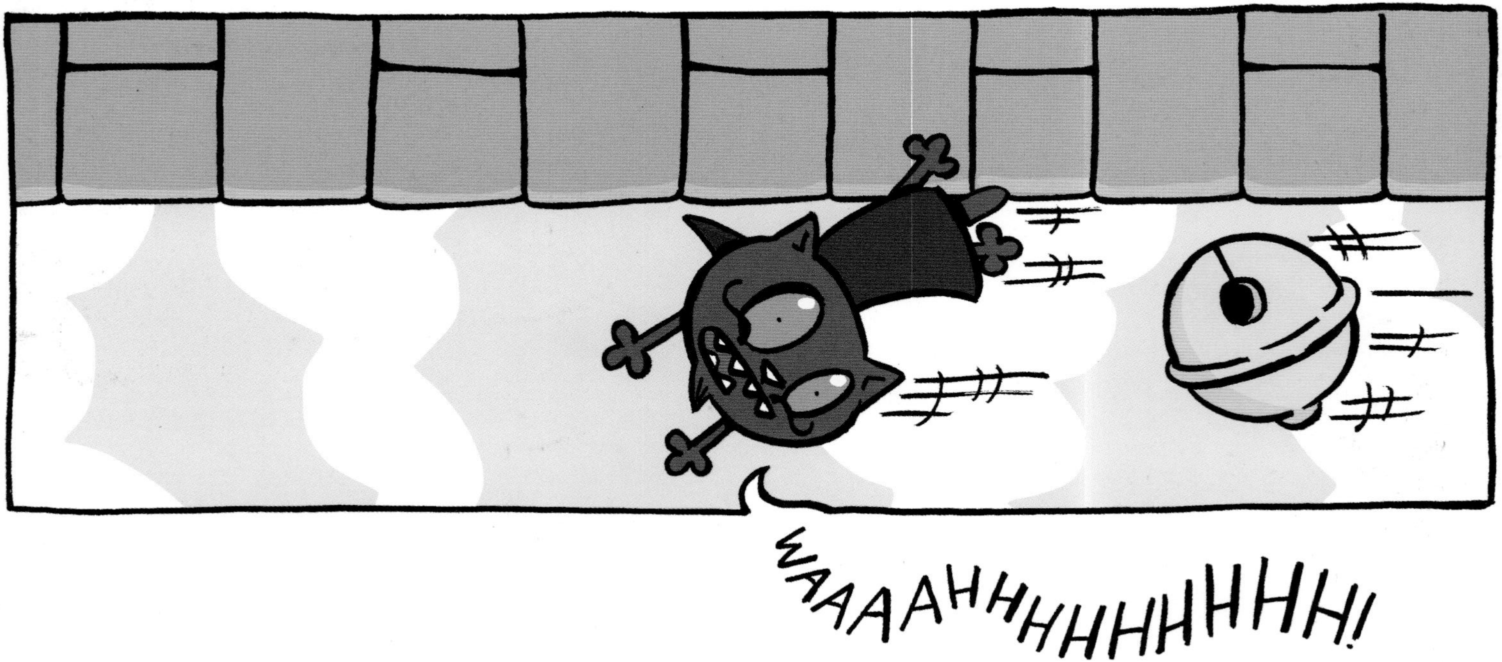
WAAAAHHHHHHHHH!

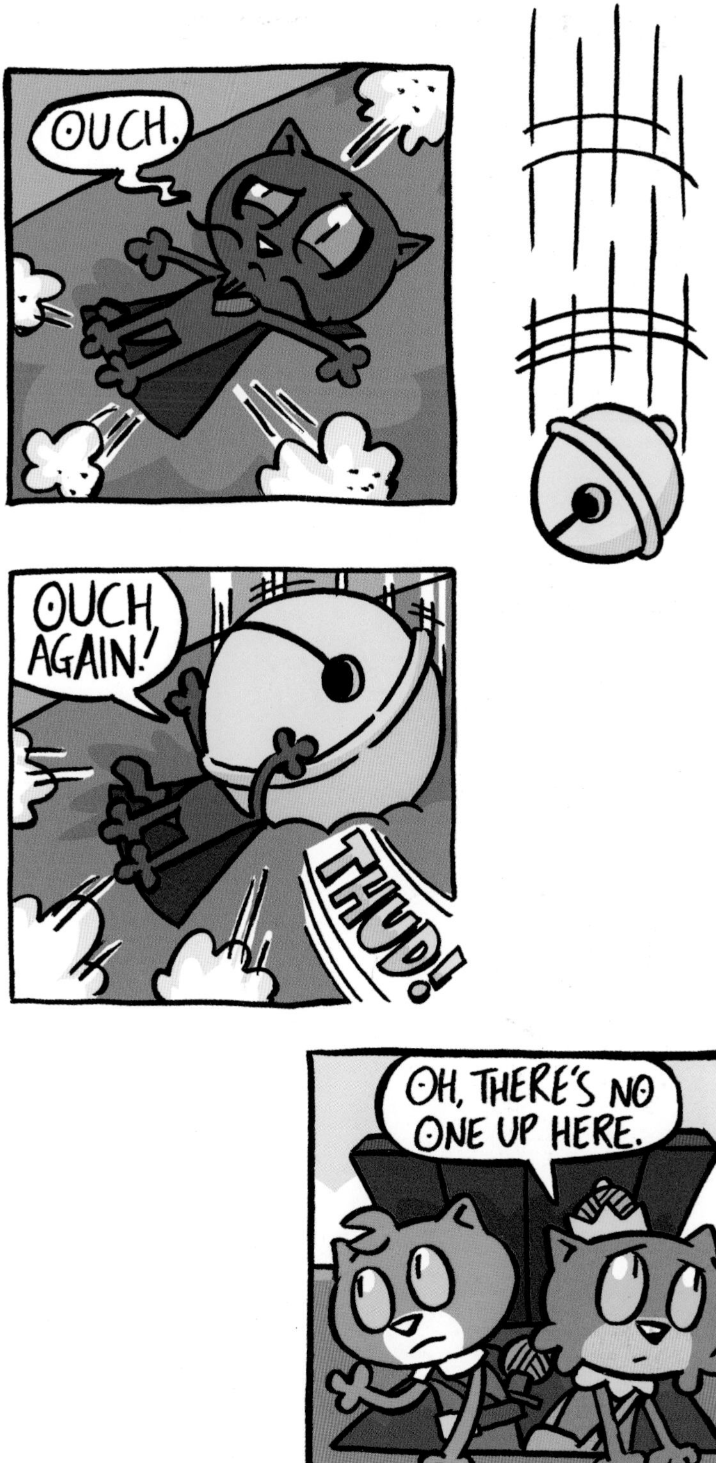
OUCH.
OUCH, AGAIN!
THUD!
OH, THERE'S NO ONE UP HERE.

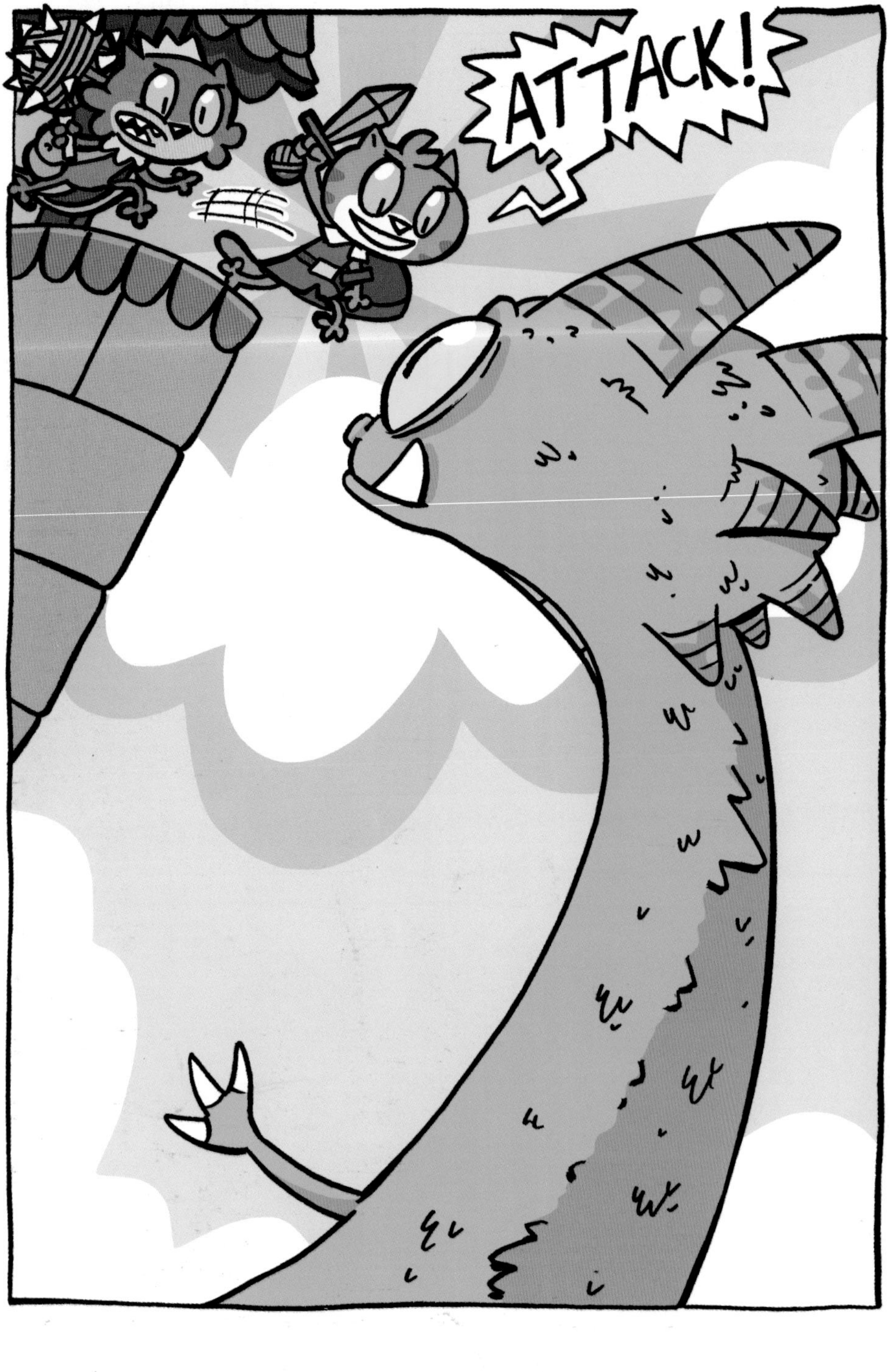
ATTACK!

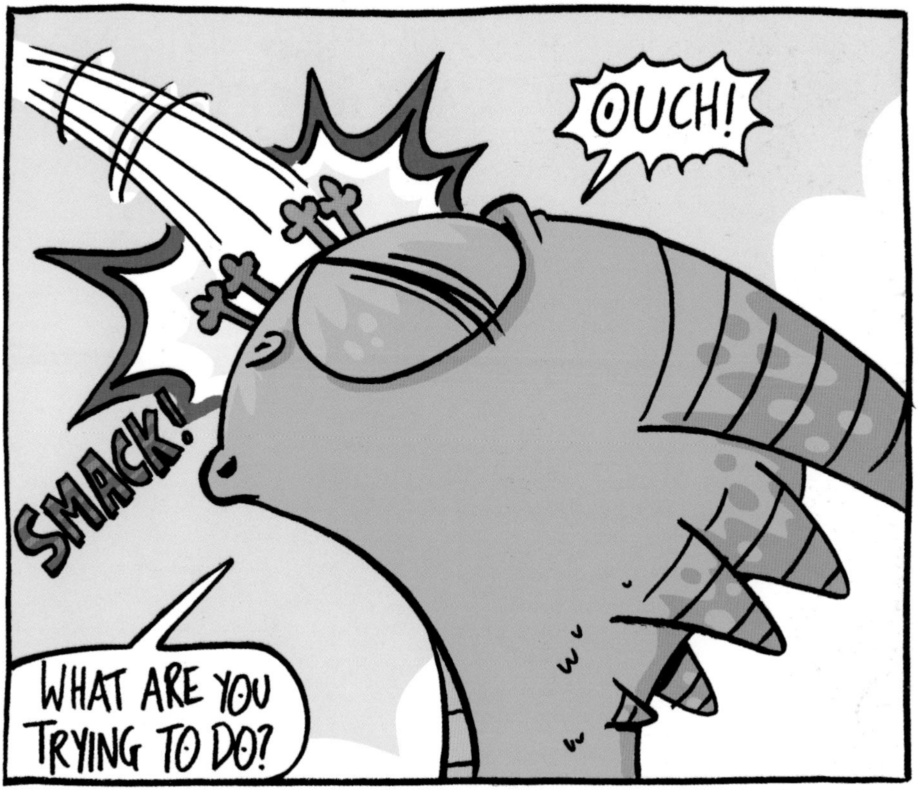
SMACK!
OUCH!
WHAT ARE YOU TRYING TO DO?

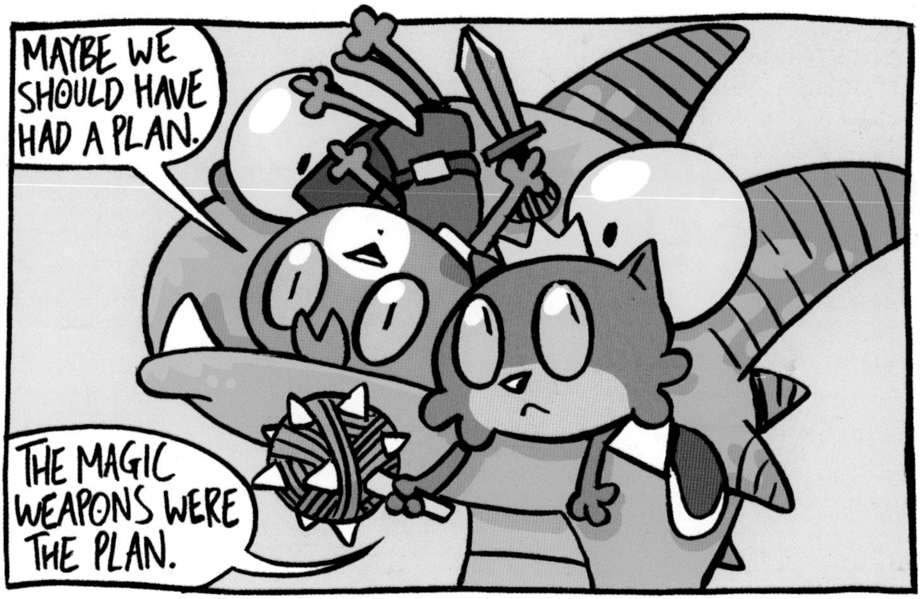
MAYBE WE SHOULD HAVE HAD A PLAN.
THE MAGIC WEAPONS WERE THE PLAN.

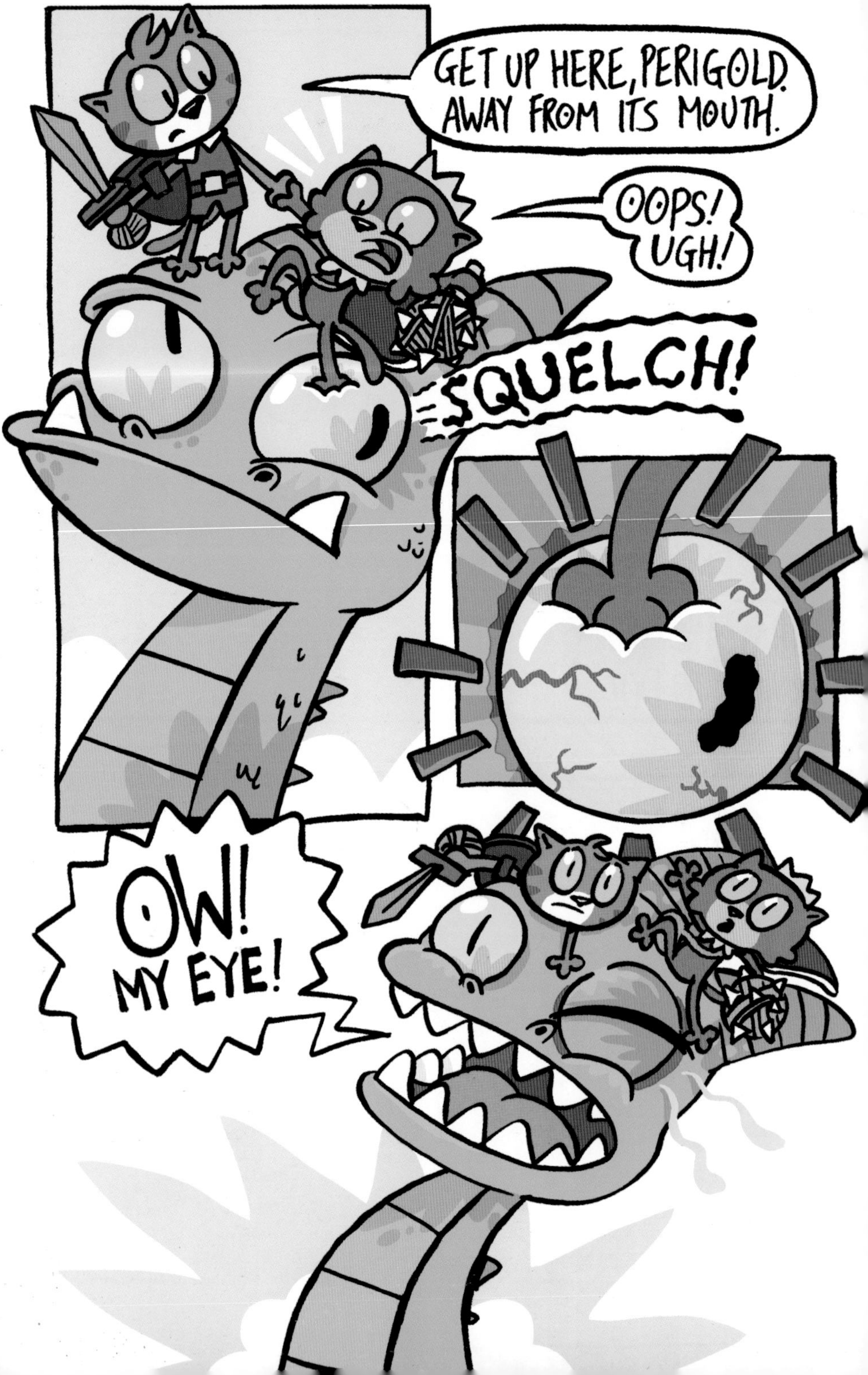
GET UP HERE, PERIGOLD. AWAY FROM ITS MOUTH.
OOPS! UGH!
SQUELCH!
OW! MY EYE!

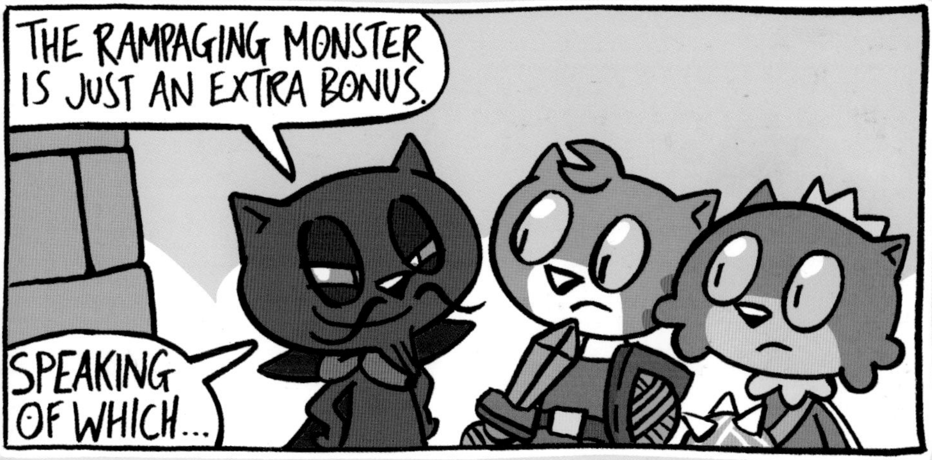
THE RAMPAGING MONSTER IS JUST AN EXTRA BONUS.
SPEAKING OF WHICH...

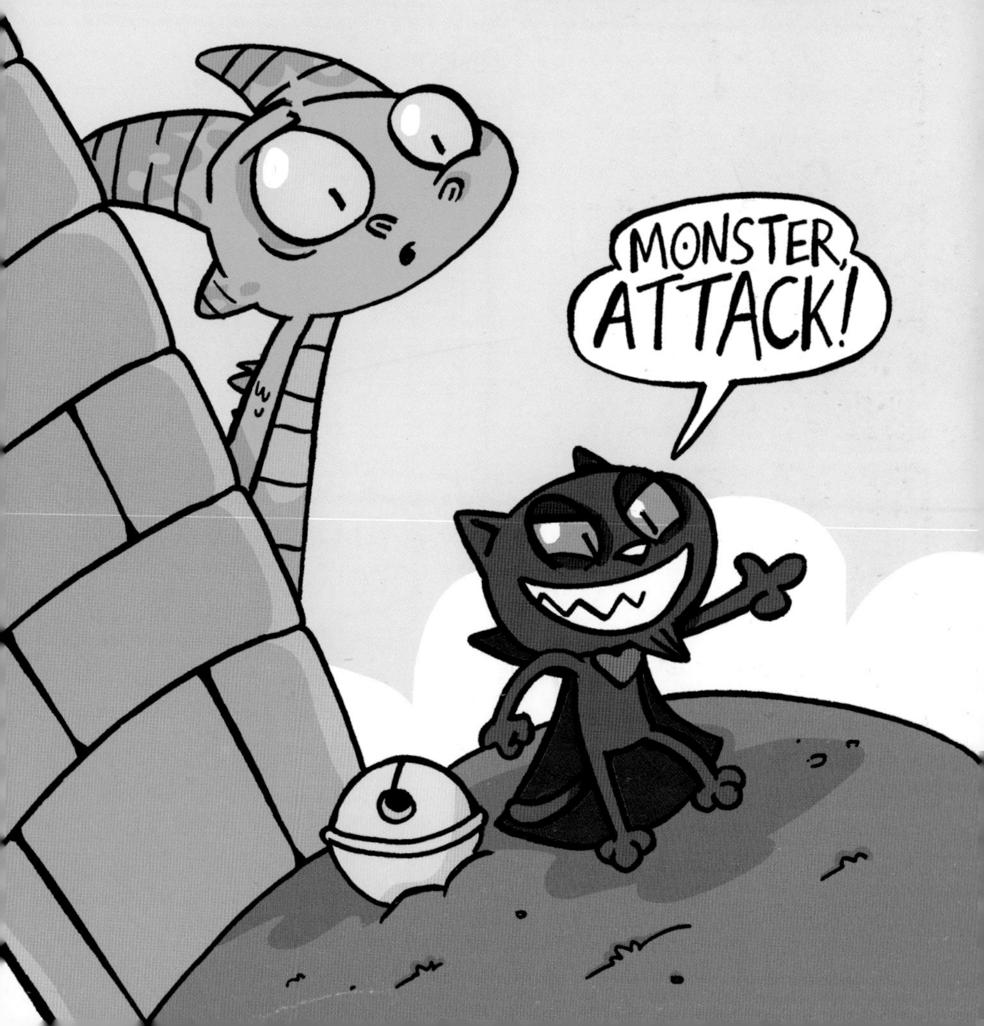
MONSTER, ATTACK!

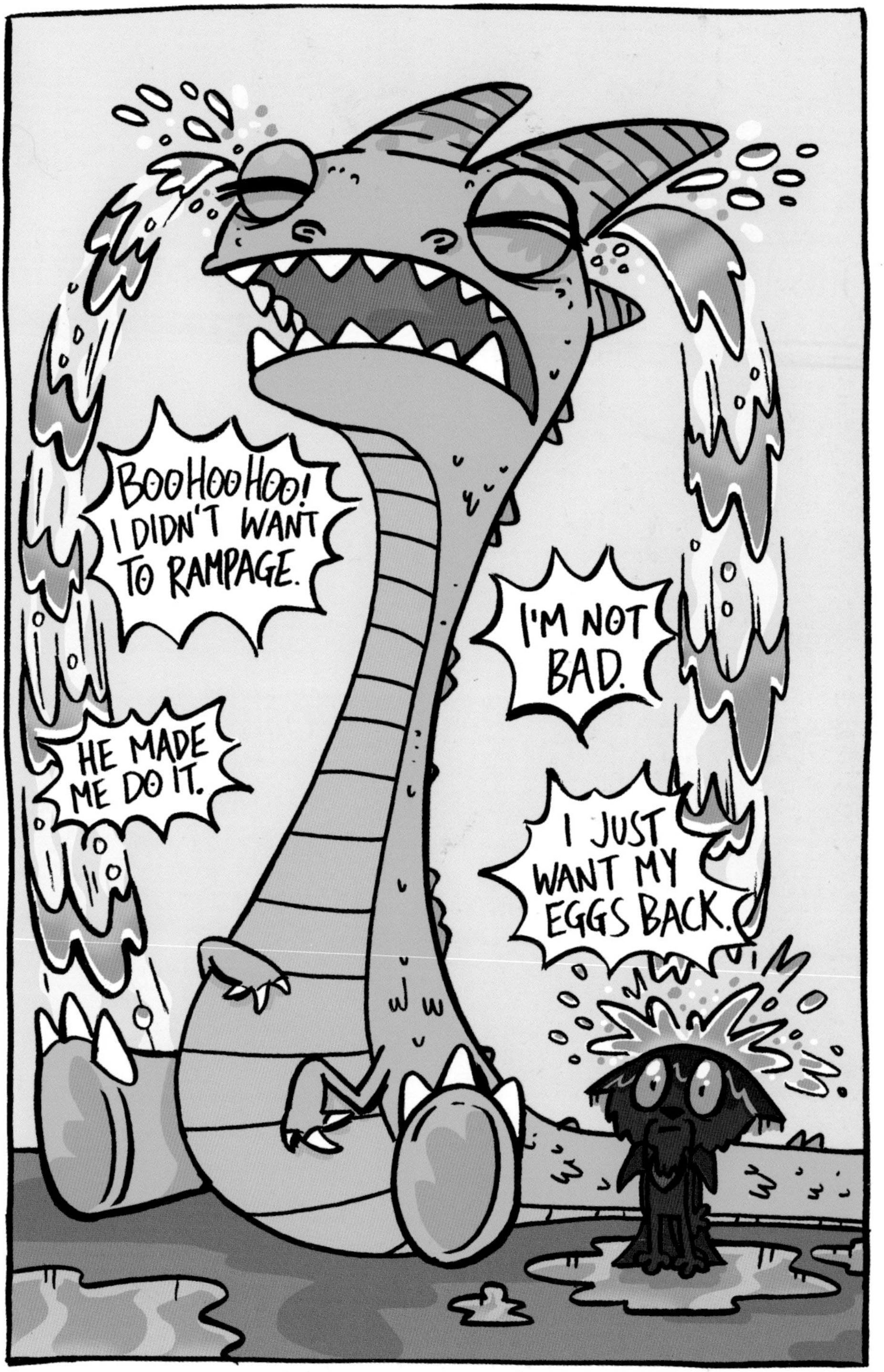
BOO HOO HOO! I DIDN'T WANT TO RAMPAGE.
HE MADE ME DO IT.
I'M NOT BAD.
I JUST WANT MY EGGS BACK.

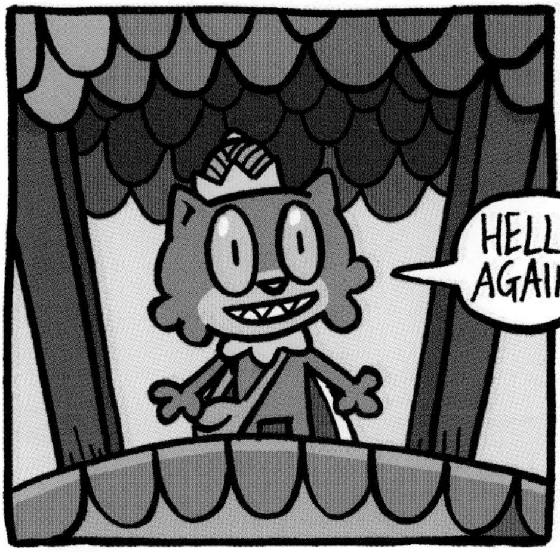
HELLO AGAIN.

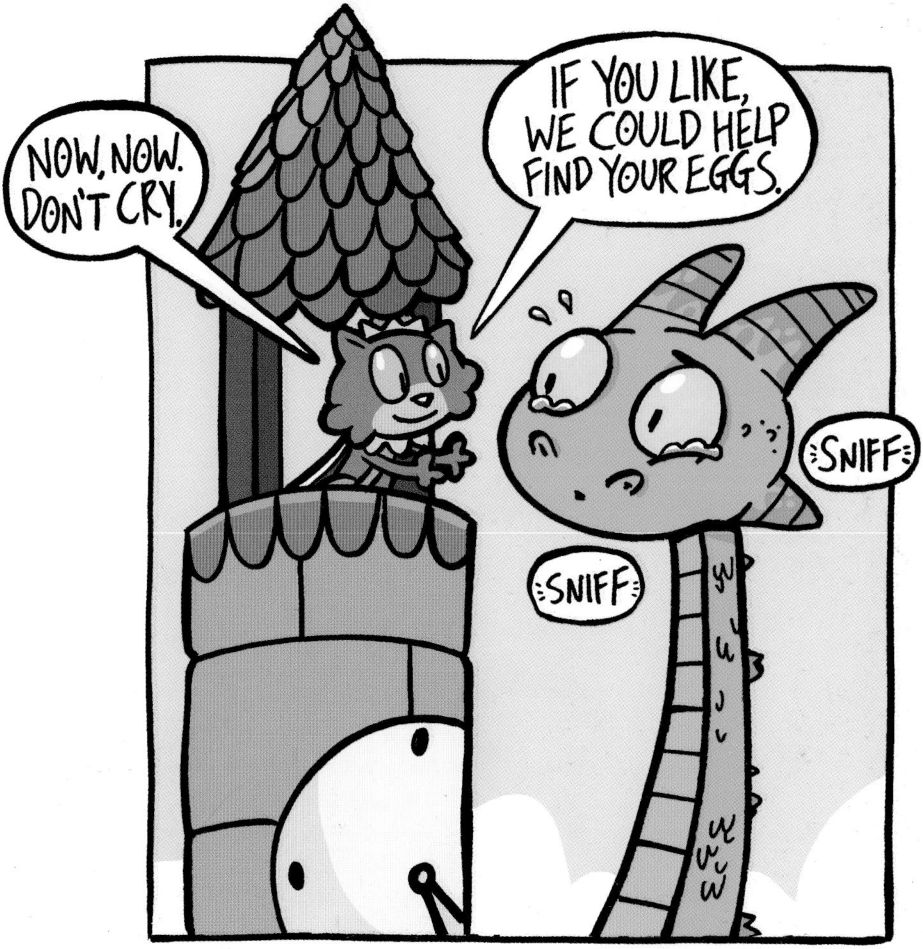
NOW, NOW. DON'T CRY.
IF YOU LIKE, WE COULD HELP FIND YOUR EGGS.
SNIFF
SNIFF

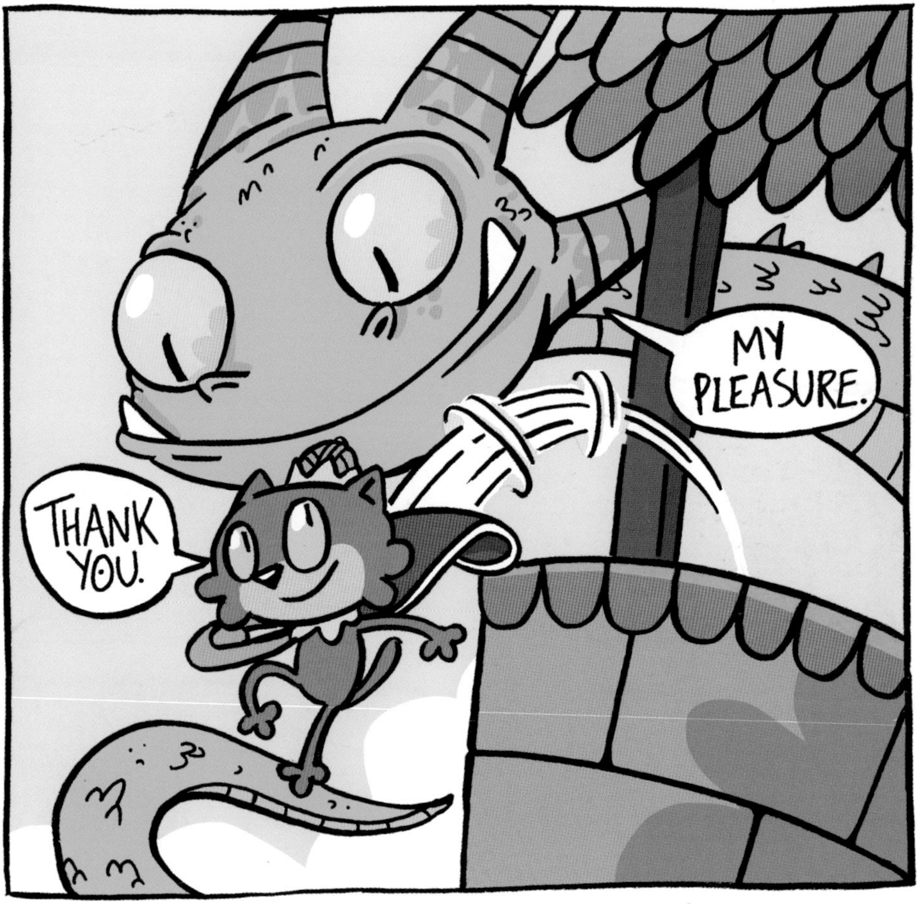
MY PLEASURE.
THANK YOU.

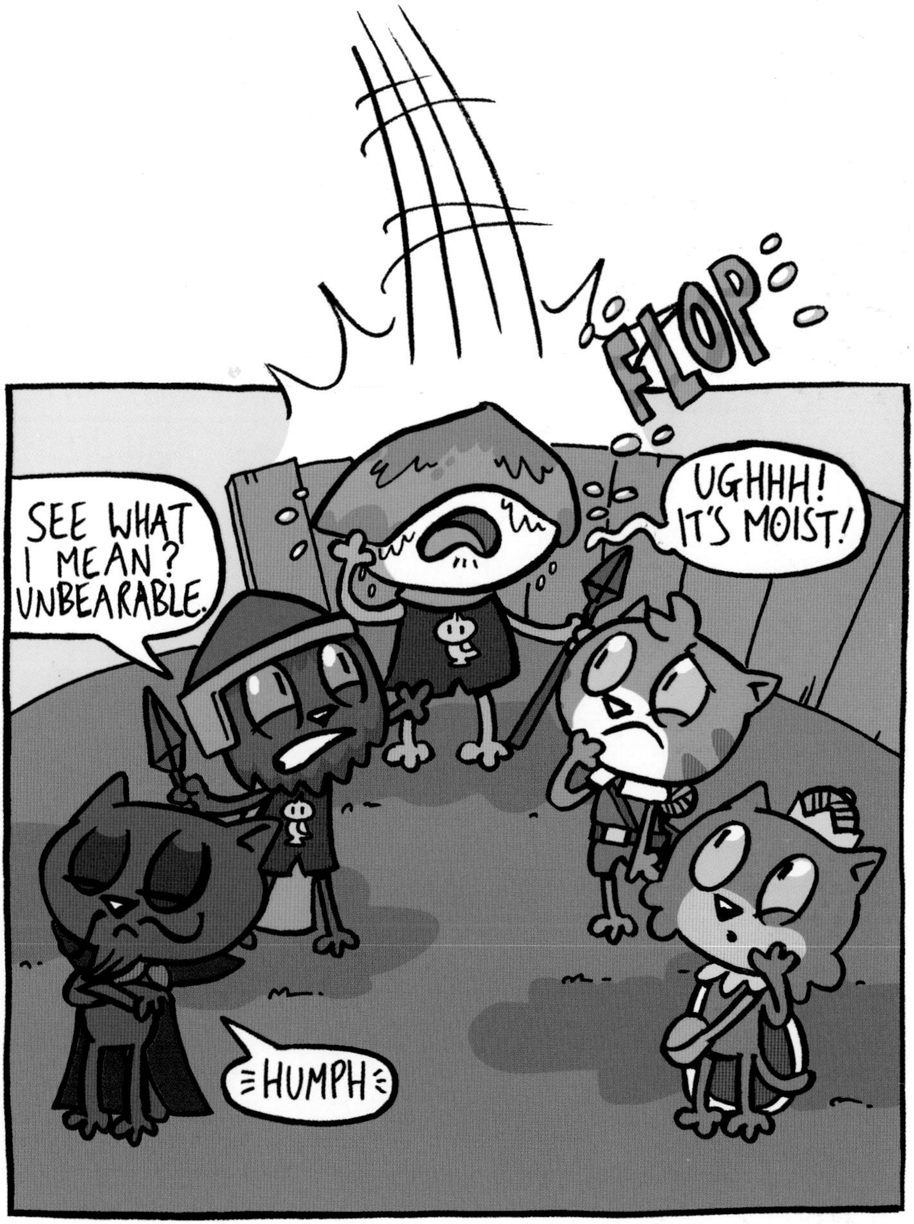
FLOP
SEE WHAT I MEAN? UNBEARABLE.
UGHHH! IT'S MOIST!
HUMPH

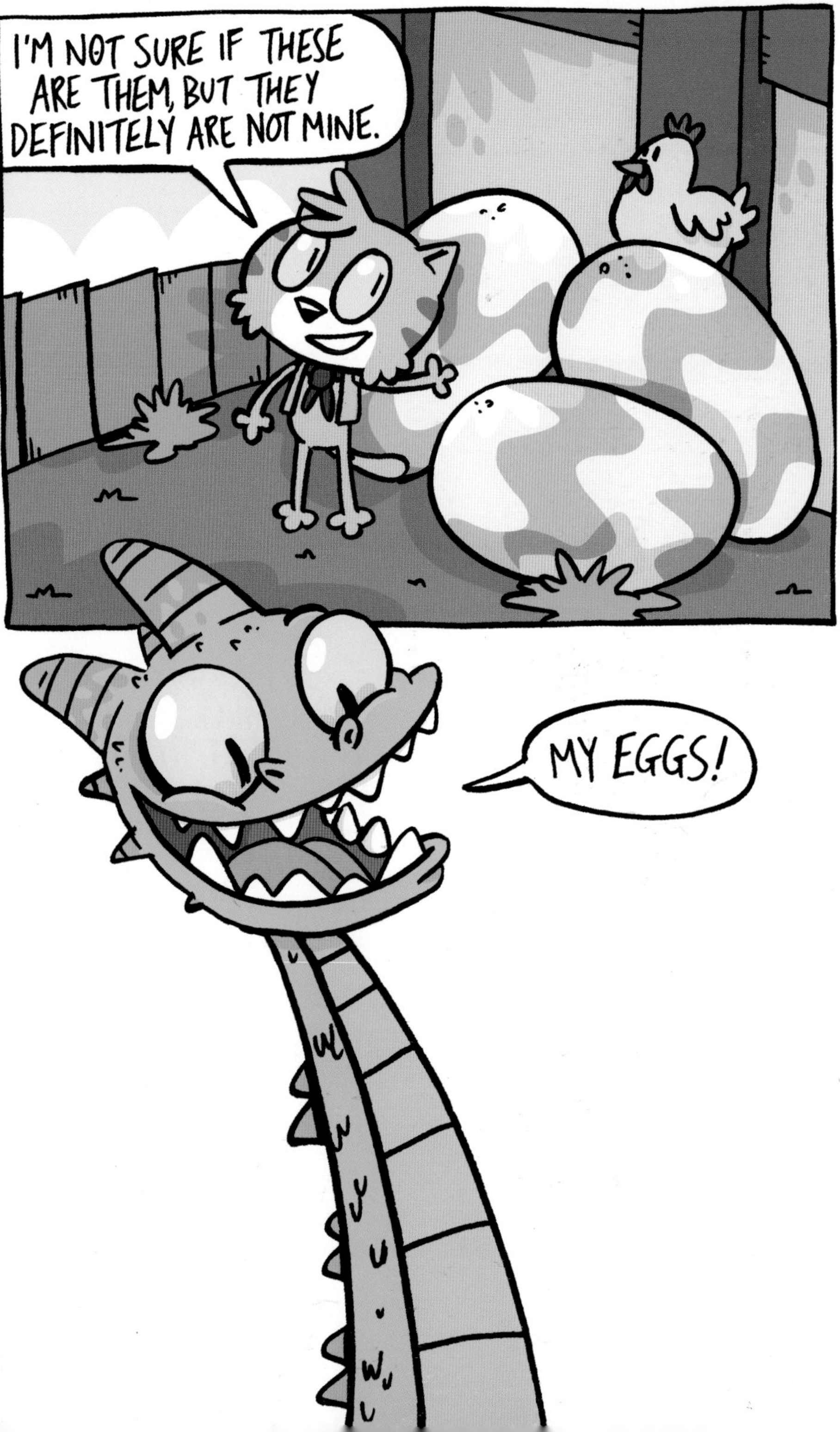
I'M NOT SURE IF THESE ARE THEM, BUT THEY DEFINITELY ARE NOT MINE.
MY EGGS!

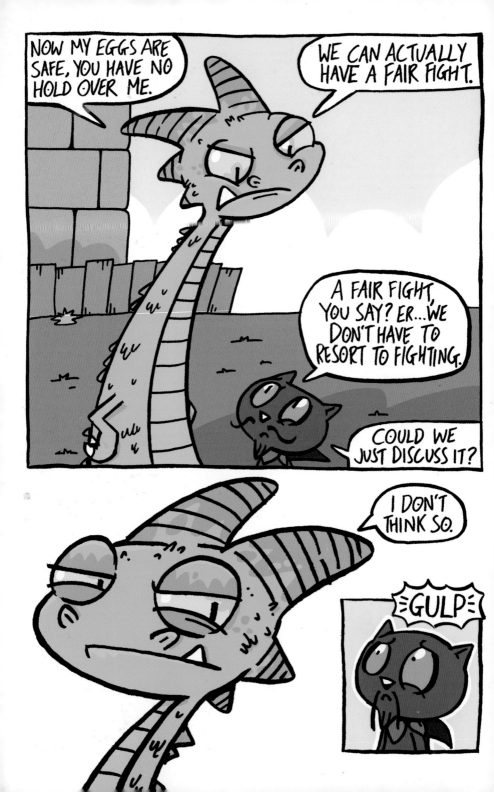

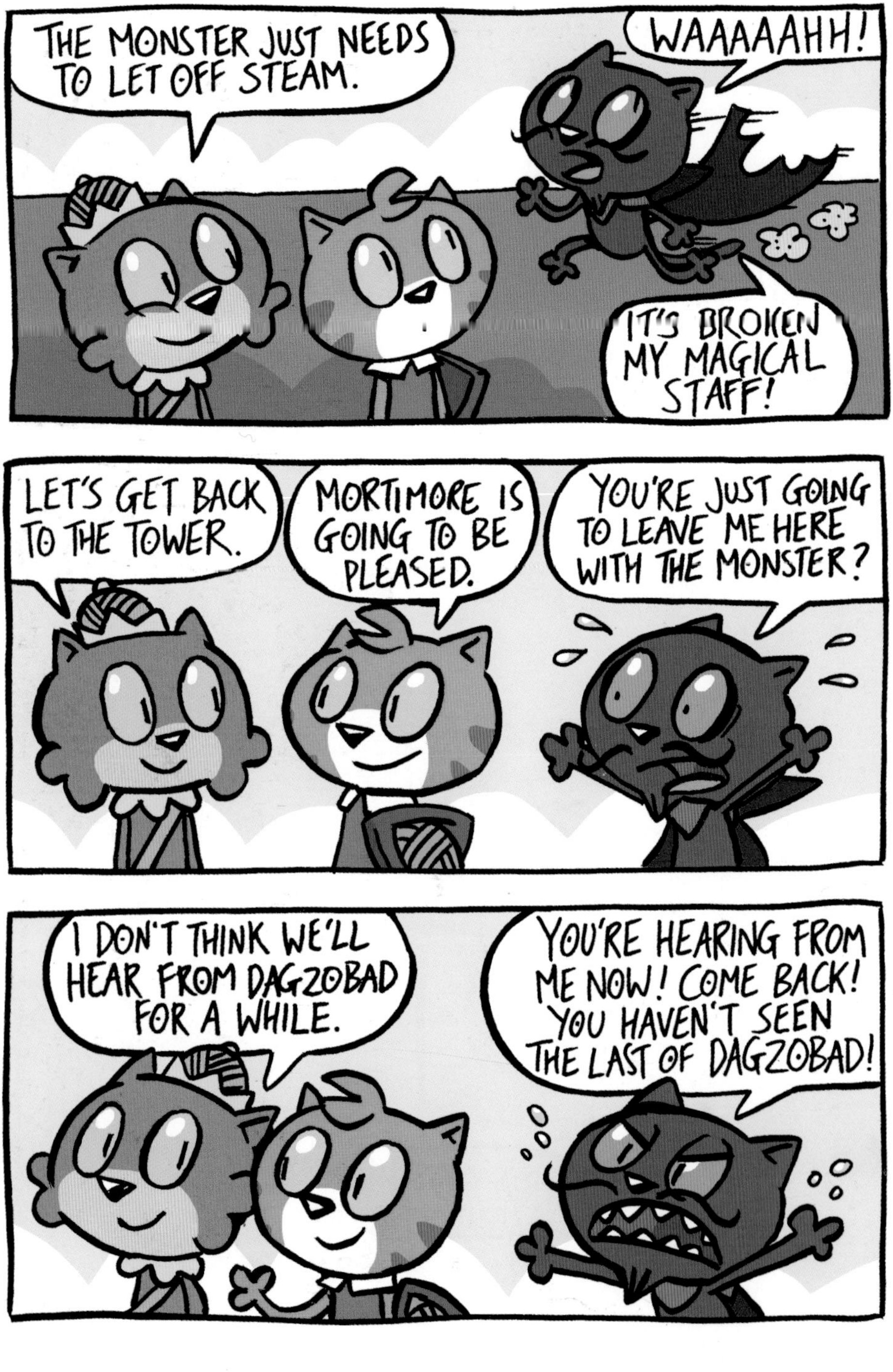
THE MONSTER JUST NEEDS TO LET OFF STEAM.
WAAAAAHH!
IT'S BROKEN MY MAGICAL STAFF!
LET'S GET BACK TO THE TOWER.
MORTIMORE IS GOING TO BE PLEASED.
YOU'RE JUST GOING TO LEAVE ME HERE WITH THE MONSTER?
I DON'T THINK WE'LL HEAR FROM DAGZOBAD FOR A WHILE.
YOU'RE HEARING FROM ME NOW! COME BACK! YOU HAVEN'T SEEN THE LAST OF DAGZOBAD!

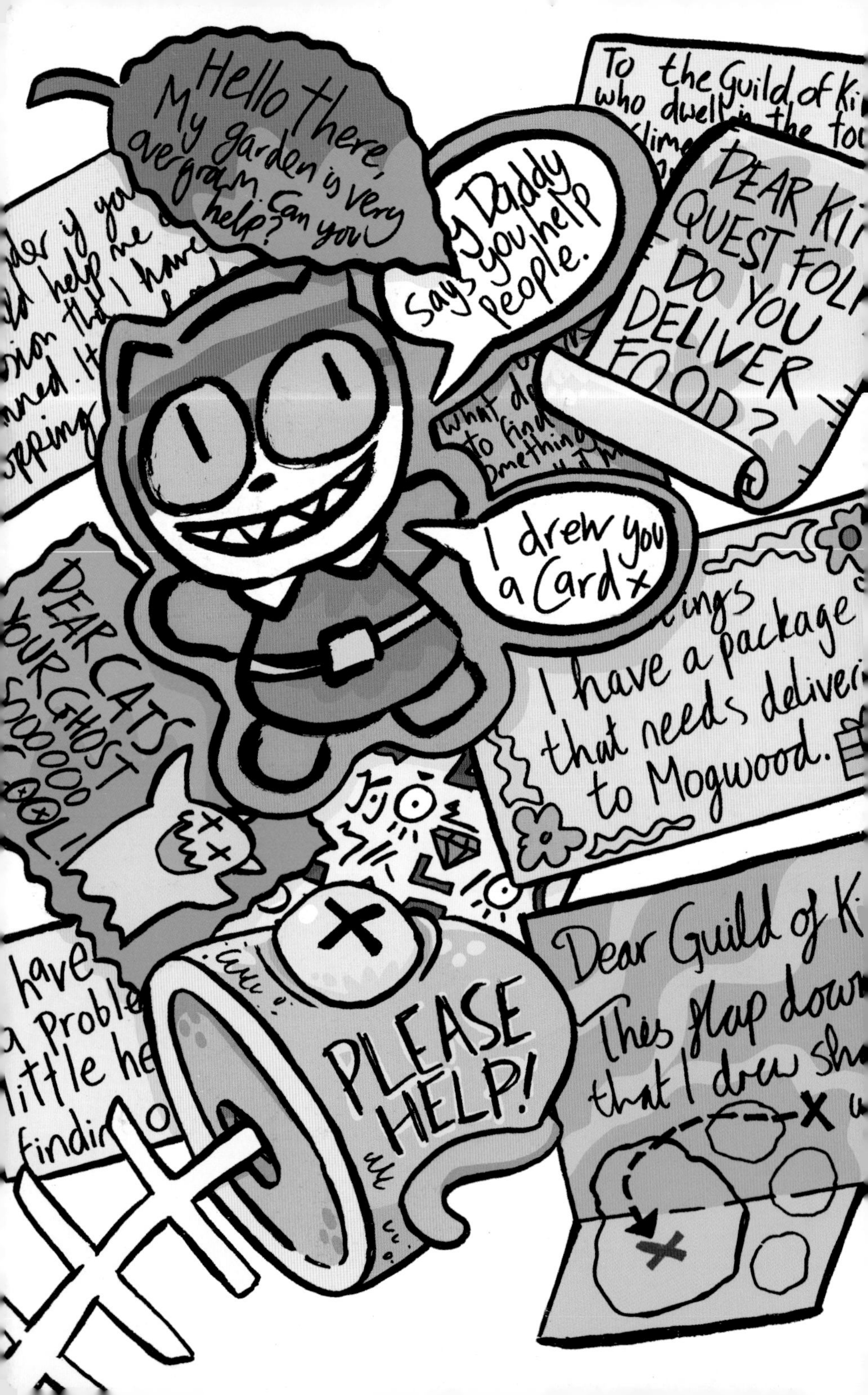

Hello there, My garden is very overgrown. Can you help?
Says Daddy you help people.
I drew you a Card x
To the Guild of Ki
DEAR KI QUEST FOLK DO YOU DELIVER FOOD?
I have a package that needs deliver to Mogwood.
DEAR CATS YOUR GHOST SOOOOO COOL!
PLEASE HELP!
Dear Guild of K
This flap down that I drew sh

For Mum & Dad

RAZORBILL

An imprint of Penguin Random House LLC, New York

First published in the United States of America by Razorbill,
an imprint of Penguin Random House LLC, 2021

Visit us online at penguinrandomhouse.com.

LIBRARY OF CONGRESS CATALOGING-IN-PUBLICATION DATA

Names: Corbett, Phil, author, illustrator.
Title: Kitty quest / Phil Corbett.
Description: New York : Razorbill, an imprint of Penguin Random House LLC, 2021. | Series: Kitty quest ; book 1 | Audience: Ages 8–12. | Summary: Guided by the last, incorporeal member of an ancient guild of protectors, aspiring adventurers Perigold and Woolfrik successfully subdue a rampaging monster and the bumbling wizard controlling it.
Identifiers: LCCN 2020049742 | ISBN 9780593205440 (hardcover) | ISBN 9780593205464 (paperback) | ISBN 9780593205976 (ebook) | ISBN 9780593205983 (ebook) | ISBN 9780593205457 (ebook)
Subjects: LCSH: Graphic novels. | CYAC: Cats—Fiction. | Monsters—Fiction. | Wizards—Fiction. | Adventure and adventurers—Fiction. | Fantasy. | Graphic novels.
Classification: LCC PZ7.7.C6715 Ki 2021 | DDC 741.5/942—dc23
LC record available at https://lccn.loc.gov/2020049742

Manufactured in China

1 3 5 7 9 10 8 6 4 2

Design by Maria Fazio

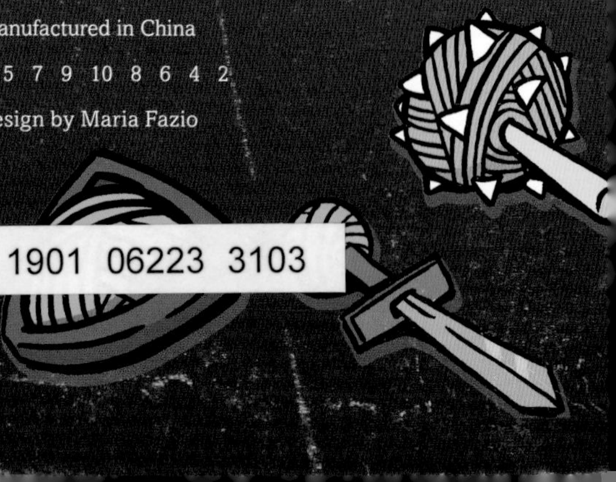